MATTHE___   ___CE

Adam

FEAR

Published in the United Kingdom by:

Red Falcon Publishing, an imprint of
Blue Falcon Publishing Limited
The Mill, Pury Hill Business Park,
Alderton Road, Towcester
Northamptonshire
NN12 7LS
Email: books@redfalconpublishing.co.uk
Web: www.redfalconpublishing.co.uk
Copyright © Matthew Pearce, 2021

This is a work of fiction. Names, characters, businesses, places, events
and incidents are either the products of the author's imagination or used
in a fictitious manner. Any resemblance to actual persons, living or dead,
or actual events is purely coincidental.

A CIP record of this book is available from the British Library.

First printed March 2021
ISBN 9781916321663

For Denise,
Lucas and Reece

FEAR

MATTHEW PEARCE

Prologue

Fear

A parasite with an insatiable hunger. It sinks its razor sharp teeth in and releases its vicious poison. Coursing relentlessly through the victim's veins to its extremities, the poison paralyses its host, speeding up its heart rate and quickening its breath to an uncontrollable momentum. Then, it heads for the mind. Constricting it like a snake, it coils tight, dampening the hosts thoughts and annihilating all reason. Reducing it to an empty shell. Yet... there is hope. The parasite can be starved. If the host is strong it can be controlled, even wielded. Within an instant, something that was so detrimental to the hosts survival can cause it to feel more alive than ever.

He awoke in a sweat with a gigantic pit in his stomach, a dark emptiness that had laid waste to all measure of confidence and swamped his hope in despair. As his father's third son - third of four - his infallible propensity for the hunt meant that he had been chosen over even the siblings that had come before him. It was a great honour to be selected by the tribe to undertake the trial. Yet, honour was far from what he felt as the impending fear of uncertainty settled in. He had reached maturity, and today he would be tested. Either he would pass the trial or this morning's sunrise would be the last he'd ever see.

The trial would consist of courage, skill, determination

and a willingness to survive; a gladiatorial contest of twelve in a last man standing fight to the death. Reaping the spoils, the victor would join the ranks of previous champions of this prestigious event: the Reapers. He knew them in his native tongue as the Avunaye. The significance of such a trial had been drilled into his people throughout the ages. It had been over four centuries since it had last been held in his own lands. If the elder's tales were to be believed, the previous trial on this soil resulted in victors from his own village. A pair of inseparable twins, they had been rewarded for their victory with an eternal existence amongst the Avunaye.

His name was Nahki. A boy of just fifteen years of age, he was already a commended and experienced huntsman within his tribe. His demeanour on the hunt was normally calm and calculated, a steadiness in both mind and body. But today was different and as such, he felt a small quiver in his hands. Today's trial was more important than any challenge he had undertaken before, and so, his innate assuredness had abandoned him. He was not the tallest among his age group, nor was he the most well-built. Yet, his proficiency to wield knife, spear and bow meant that he had mastered his craft and kept his family from starvation. Proud of his ability to provide, he could not help but consider that his skill allowed him to hunt animals. Never before had he considered turning his weapon on a fellow human.

Specks of light fought their way through the darkness that had engulfed him. His moistened, dark skin glistened ever so slightly as the day's sunlight caught on each hair that stood up on his arm. It was time to rise.

'Nahki,' The voice that came from behind was unmistakably that of his mothers. 'It is time, my boy.' she said softly. Her words did not harness a fearful tone. There was no sign of a whimper, nor of any distress, in her voice as she ushered her son to begin what was could be his final journey. Instead, her voice reassured him; there was an underlying confidence to her manner and he knew that she truly believed in his ability to succeed.

'I am... ready.' The slight pause in Nahki's words revealed a sense of doubt in his statement, the same quiver he had noticed in his hands brandishing itself on his words. Yet his mother ignored it and proceeded to kiss him tenderly on his forehead, before explaining to him where it was he needed to go. The location of the trials was known only to the elders and the Avunaye. The information was only to be shared with the families of the chosen competitors; the participant would need to know where to travel to compete, and his loved ones would need to know where to collect his body should he not emerge victorious.

A half days' walk alone in the heat of the sun was a challenge within itself. The elements to one side, being alone meant that Nahki was unable to stop each of the insidious thoughts that were turning over in his head. The trials were to be held within the jungle, a canopied landscape brimming with exotic life, and now ironically hosting a contest which was hinged on death. As the sun was at its highest and most inescapable, he reached his destination. Eleven other contestants would soon be entering the area, each having left their own lives behind them, as Nahki had. He could be the first to arrive, or the last. Nevertheless, Nahki's instincts told him that the fight for survival had already begun. The outer edge of the jungle was relatively clear, as the surrounding tribes would often forage resources from its outer reaches instead of delving into the depths of what lay beneath the canopy. As Nahki ventured further in, the jungle grew more and more dense, its thick plant life and intertwining trees concealing the dangers that this green world possessed.

Nahki stopped. Halted in his tracks, he dropped to one knee. *Something is not right.* He could hear the breeze rustling throughout the leaves of the canopy above, the calming trickle of a nearby stream as it rolled over the rocks within it. The mammoth trees swayed ever so slightly in the wind. He refocussed his mind, considering not what *was* there, but instead on what wasn't. A distinct absence unnerved him. Where were the songs of the birds high above? Where were the chatters of the monkeys in the trees, the chirping and clicking and rustling of creatures both great and small amongst the undergrowth? It was as if the jungle had been vacated, as if life had stepped aside for the death that was soon to ensue. Unsettled but wary that staying in one place for too long would make him far easier prey, he pressed on amongst the overgrowth.

He was down wind, following the rolling stream when he caught the distinct scent of someone that did not belong in the jungle. It wasn't a natural scent, and it stood out amongst the odours of damp exotic shrubbery. Nahki went to climb into the embrace of a nearby tree to gain a better view, however, as he reached out to grasp the trunk of the giant, his fingers touched nothing. *What is this...?* He was confused and swiped at the tree with his other hand, but it was as if the tree was a mere reflection in water, and not actually there. The elder's tales of the trials had included many miraculous things, but in truth, Nahki had always considered them to be embellishments. He stepped toward the huge trunk, and this time, with both hands, he reached out for it, but again touched nothing. Holding his hands within the mirage, he considered the idea of stepping into it, wondering if there was something on the other side. He took a deep breath, once again catching the outlandish scent he had caught before, and stepped into the tree.

As he passed through the veil before him, the light of the sun vanished and darkness took hold. Everywhere he looked, there was nothing, his heart pounded ferociously as he reached out into the black, hoping to touch something solid, something true. He tried to turn back, to re-enter the jungle he had left behind, but there was nothing but darkness in each direction. Fearing what might lie within the shadows, he stood still, attempting to rely on his other senses. *Footsteps*, he thought, recognising the sound of someone running to his left. He turned towards the sound and stepped forwards, there was something there, in front of him. As he touched it, he recognised the roughness and coolness of stone; a wall, or pillar perhaps. Suddenly there was a light that appeared to his right; it was tiny at first, but as it grew closer, it grew larger and brighter. Another light seemed to appear behind it, moving just as quickly through the dark, until they both halted. The lights, of which Nahki presumed were torches, danced in the darkness, with the occasional ringing, the clashing of steel sounding out. He wearily moved towards the pair of lights and as he drew closer, he could make out the figures of two people fighting.

Two boys, seemingly equal in size and ability, set upon each other in a frantic and blood thirsty entanglement. Nahki had never laid eyes on such savagery as he watched each deal blows to the other. The first boy brandished his blade and thrust it into the second boy's abdomen. As the boy's blood and torch dropped to the ground beneath him, his body vanished, as if dragged off by the shadow that surrounded them all. Nahki's breath hastened as he began to panic. The victor of the fight wasted no time, running towards Nahki, torch in hand. Nahki would have been invisible to the boy, but as he grew closer, the light would reveal him. Unsure where to run, Nahki stood motionless, fear possessing him, grounding him to the spot. But as the light approached, the boy stumbled and fell to the floor. An arrow protruded from his back, a blow that would prove fatal given time, yet, before the life had left his eyes, the shadow reached out for him. Nahki could swear he saw a huge hand grab the boy and effortlessly whisk him away, and more unnerving, a pair of red-glowing eyes, hovering in the pitch black.

Seeing another of his competition fall gave Nahki some

hope. There were less of them now, he wasn't sure how many, but it meant that his chance of success was greater than it once was. He was yet to spill any blood, but after the savagery he had just witnessed, he felt ready: ready to fight, ready to kill, ready to survive. He contemplated picking up the torch that lay on the ground ahead of him, but the light would only aid his attackers. In the distance he heard screams, a female, a girl. *Perhaps it was her scent I had followed.*

Possessing the stealth of a jungle cat, Nahki slipped through the darkness, using his sharp ear to warn himself of any danger. After hours of nothing, he caught a glimpse of light belonging to an unsuspecting opponent hiding beside an earthen structure. He considered his opponent's fate for a moment. Nahki knew that if they were to swap positions, his life would never be spared. Making a decision that was much quicker than he was comfortable with, he was quick to use the structure to his advantage, scaling it and leaping from its crown with the absence of any sound. Crashing his weight on to the back of his adversary, Nahki sank his blade into the boys back, just above his right hip, giving it a slight twist as he had done so many times before to animals on the hunt. The pair writhed on the ground, momentum carrying them across the floor. The opposing boy, much larger in build, managed to roll free of Nahki's grasp, scrambling across the floor only to fall at the hands of a third opponent. Within a heartbeat the head of a spear had plunged downwards through the injured boy's neck, instantly severing the spinal cord and leaving him face down, lifeless. This newcomer did not hesitate to withdraw his spear and turn on Nahki with a look of hunger in his eyes as the body of the boy he had just killed, was dragged off like the others. He lunged toward Nahki, who was scrambling to his feet. Splitting the flesh and flicking blood through the air, the spearhead ran flush with Nahki's right arm and caused his grip to loosen on his blade. He could see the hatred in this stranger's eyes. The stranger was taller than Nahki and more muscular. Most likely, he was a labourer from a village akin to his own, perhaps a stone carrier or a builder. The trials would not discriminate against participants of any heritage. Children from a multitude of backgrounds would be forced to fight to the death, the only epithet required being a thirst for blood. This boy's build was enabling him to throw more power into his thrusts and swings, but what was clearly noticeable was his steadfast stance, moving only slightly, with each new attack leaving him vulnerable if Nahki could be quick enough.

Stepping to his right and ducking quickly below a swing of the spear, Nahki passed his blade nimbly to his other hand. Using what little strength he could muster, he sprung towards his attacker. Flying forward, Nahki thrust his blade into his attacker's thigh, shredding through skin, muscle and grinding against bone, causing his opponent to fall to one knee. Grounded and with only a spear to hand, he would have to rely only on his brute strength to succeed against Nahki. He grabbed at Nahki, applying pressure to his wounded arm and forcing him to the floor, using every ounce of his superior upper body strength to pin his worthy adversary into submission.

Nahki found his arms trapped, weighed down by his attacker. He laid eyes on the blood pumping from his wound. *I will lose my life if I do not react now.* Thrusting his body despite his immobilised arms, he attempted to coil into such a shape that he could retrieve his weapon from the thigh of his opponent, but to no avail. His attacker now moved so that one of his giant hands clutched around Nahki's neck, crushing his windpipe, squeezing the air from his lungs and the life from his eyes. Bearing down onto him with all of his weight, the stranger's dark skin glistened from sweat as it caught the torchlight. His eyes were filled with rage, his teeth bared as he applied all his strength into his attempt to survive. Using his left hand, Nahki swiped at the arm that the boy was using for balance, causing him to fall on top of Nahki and loosen the grip on his neck. In an unconsidered move, Nahki sank his teeth into the unguarded throat of the attacker, biting down as hard as he could, striving to bite harder as an unmistakeable metallic taste filled his mouth. This did not deter him, but rather assured him that his own time to die had not yet come. The stranger grasped at Nahki's hair, punching and clawing at his head, desperately trying to get him to relinquish his bite. But Nahki did not withdraw his hold until the body of his attacker lay lifeless atop him, leaving him soaked in blood. He lay there, exhausted, unable to muster any energy to roll the deceased warrior off him. Praying to God to give him strength, but yielding to the possibility that his fight for life was finally over, Nahki let the darkness take hold as he closed his eyes to the world.

'He was the only one left,' a voice brought Nahki around. Barely conscious and heavily confused, he was unsure as to his condition. *Am I still alive?* The sudden realisation of pain told him that he was. His eyes heavy, the boy could just about open them enough to make out the surroundings that he lay in. It was an unfamiliar place, a temple of sorts with scattered flames on pedestals providing light and giving an idea of its enormity. The room contained many sandstone pillars rising from the ground, seemingly endless as they disappeared into the darkness above him. He was aware of himself laying face up on the ground. The floor was deathly cold. It was a sensation that Nahki was unaccustomed to, having grown up under the unforgiving heat of the constant sun where a wind chill had been a welcome reprieve. After taking in his surroundings, Nahki laid eyes on the figure from whom the voice had come. The man that stood before him was swathed in a dark robe and he had short, untidy, hair that spiked in a widow's peak above his brow. His eyes appeared aged, catching the firelight and glistening with a dark red tint. A scar ran down his face, from his right temple to his broad chin; it also appeared to glow as if a molten lava ran beneath the surface.

'Stand,' said the man. His voice was coarse, a demanding tone which showed no sympathy for Nahki's present condition. 'Stand before the Father. Arise and claim your victory.'

Nahki rolled over onto his less painful side and managed to use one hand to bring himself up onto his knees, all the while cradling his injured arm. Still disorientated, he glanced around the room in which he now knelt. Darkness hid each corner in an unsettling vail, disguising the rooms features and providing an unrelenting sense that something was lurking just out of view, cloaked by the lack of light. Using his legs as leverage, he pushed himself up and steadied himself on his feet. The pain from his arm persisted. The bleeding had ceased, but what blood had not yet dried still dripped down his arm and off his fingers. Nhaki could tell that the wound was deep as he clutched at his arm below the elbow in an effort to ease the pain. Once again, he now directed his eyes to the man who stood before him. This man was at least a foot taller than himself and broader in build; he seemed to take displeasure in seeing Nahki acknowledge the pain in his arm. It was a weakness that was not permissible.

'Soon that won't bother you, boy. Soon you will be one of us, if you're lucky,' the man said with a wry smile. 'What's your name, boy?'

The giant before him had averted his gaze and did not even look at Nahki as he addressed him. Nahki felt as if he didn't warrant any acknowledgment, he was beneath the man, both in size and in rank.

'Nahki,' he choked in a broken tone. He knew he needed to be strong for whatever was to come, but the pain had set in deeper now and he was uncharacteristically scared. Something was unnerving him; not knowing who this man was, where he was or what was about to happen to him, he decided to masque his unease. He cleared his throat and attempted sound more assured, 'My name is Nahki, of the Bantu. Who are you? Where am I?'

'You would ask a question to Brandt of the Avunaye?' A voice hissed through the darkness in a cold and unnatural tone. Another man emerged from the shadows from which the voice had come, again dressed in a dark robe. He matched Nahki in height but was much more slender. He had long black hair that glinted with touches of purple and shades of grey, a few flyaway strands hanging limp over his pale face. His eyes and lips both possessed a blue-grey tint that resembled those belonging to a corpse.

'The Avunaye?' Nahki questioned. It was a word of his culture, but these people were most certainly not, with their dark robes and pale skin. The word as he knew it could be translated to mean harvester of crops, or in other cultures could be loosely translated to describe a person or thing that brought death. Nahki's mind wondered over the etymology as he came to the realisation that the latter translation was much like the *avunaye mbaya*, or grim reaper. The cloaked people were nothing of the image he had been raised to imagine. *Are these truly the people for which I have fought to prove myself?*

'We have been given many names by many cultures.' Yet another voice echoed about the room, a deep and commanding voice that bellowed out and bounced off the dark-cloaked walls. Nahki had lost count now of how many different voices had come at him through the darkness. 'This, boy, was the name given to us by your people.'

It was at this moment that sconces lining the outer walls of the room took alight one by one, their luminescence unmasking the rooms hidden features. Beyond the two figures that had already revealed themselves to him, Nahki could see a colossus of a man from which the most recent voice must have originated. He sat upon an intricately crafted throne, a masterpiece detailed with patterns and etchings. He was the largest person Nahki had ever seen, his size contending with that of the elephants that roamed the grass lands of his home. On his head was a mop of brown hair, his skin a golden bronze; he was not wearing anything to conceal his torso, displaying an impressive and somewhat intimidating array of muscles. A golden armlet sat above each of his biceps, both of which would make a fine belt for the average sized man. He rested one hand on the arm of his throne and the other sat atop the hilt of an incredible sword which rivalled the throne in its intricacy. The sword stood as tall as Nahki himself, the metal reflecting a kaleidoscope of colour as the light from the wall sconces danced upon it. He sat rigid, staring at Nahki as though he were waiting for him to make a move.

'You have been chosen, Nahki,' announced the giant. 'Through bloodshed and battle, you have emerged victorious. You are chosen to be the twelfth Avunaye.' His huge brown eyes engulfed Nahki's entire being. Without warning, he raised his right hand from its resting position and pointed towards the edge of the room, where there was a corner that seemed to curl round to the right. 'Begin!'

In an instant, Brandt had turned to Nahki. Reaching out, he wrapped his left hand around the entirety of Nahki's upper arm and began to pull him to the corner. Distracted from it until now, the pain set in again; Nahki flinched as he felt the pressure from Brandt's grip crushing down on his wound. Brandt's face lit up in a smile as the red glow in his eyes brightened. Nahki could feel the heat. An intense heat, as if a hot iron had been pressed against his skin; Brandt's touch was burning at his wound, cauterising it. The pain from his grasp was overwhelming and intense, but Nahki had barely time to register it before he realised what lay before him.

Ten – no, twelve – people appeared before him, each with their arms chained above their heads to the sandstone wall. Furthest to the left was an elderly man. Nahki had to double take as he recognised the man from his village. Next to him was a woman. Nahki looked on in further disbelief; he knew her as a teacher. She had once taught him how to fish. The third, fourth and fifth people were a family Nahki had once known as a child. They had once cared for him when he had gotten lost during one of his first hunts.

Nahki choked on an intake of breath. Beyond this family, his eyes settled on two faces that he knew all too well. Chained to the wall were his friends Kobe and Mosi. The three of them had been inseparable as children; in recent years they had grown apart, as Nahki had taken more to hunting and both Kobe and Mosi had grown to be farmers. Nahki could see the terror in their eyes, fear possessing them as they hung, unable to move for the tight grip of the chains around their wrists.

Nahki's world began to seem smaller and smaller as he continued to take in the rest of the prisoners. The eighth and ninth were his brothers, Hodari and Jamba. Both were older than Nahki. Hodari's normally rebellious expression had been replaced by a look of terror that was so uncharacteristic for him that it made Nahki's toes curl. Jamba's faced seemed expressionless as he watched Nahki process him and the rest of those hung next to him. Nahki had always looked up to Jamba, following him around like a shadow. He was calm and collected and mature. He was everything Nahki had wanted to be growing up.

The tenth hostage was the beautiful Imara. The daughter of a local widow, Nahki had always taken a liking to her. He had often helped her to carry things that were too heavy, and he would bring her anything spare if he got especially lucky on a hunt. In return, Imara had fixed Nahki's spears on a number of occasions, intricately securing the vine that held the spearhead to the wooden handle. Secretly, Nahki had always harboured a desire that one day she might become his wife. Now, he looked on in despair as tears ran down Imara's cheeks.

The final two for Nahki to see were the very people who

had given Nahki to the trial. His father appeared glass like and strong. Attempting to show strength for his family beside him and his young son in front of him, his face remained expressionless and provided no sense of fear. He offered no form of emotion towards Nahki. Instead, his eyes seemed to look right through him as though he wasn't there. Nahki's mother was shaking ever so slightly, looking down at the ground rather than towards her son.

'Through blood and through battle, Father rewards us,' exclaimed Brandt as he released his grasp on Nahki's arm. Brandt walked towards the prisoners, coming to a stop just a few feet in front of them. Some looked terrified, while others refused to allow any emotion to show whatsoever. Turning to Nahki, Brandt raised his hands upwards. 'The blood ritual grants us a new life, and you have been chosen.' Nahki was becoming increasingly panicked by the second. His mind raced with frantic thoughts of what could possibly be going to happen – although he knew that prisoners chained to a wall couldn't mean anything good. Brandt now pointed towards the giant sat atop his throne and bellowed, 'Father gives us strength.'

The scar on Brandt's face began to glow with a deep, unnatural red. His eyes shone bright and his hands turned a blood scarlet. Nahki, whose breath had sped up to become frantic and panicked, looked to his wound. Where Brandt had held him, a mark now replaced his touch. A handprint branded his upper arm.

Before he could say or do anything, more robed strangers emerged from the rooms' hidden depths. They began to advance toward Nahki, Brandt and the pale man standing before the twelve chained captives. *These must be the rest of the Avunaye.* To this point, the whole ordeal had overwhelmed Nahki's senses. His breathing had been fast and ruptured, the pain in his arm had burned hot and unforgiving. And yet now, with his loved ones chained in front of him, he began to feel an emptiness. It was as if all emotion was stripping away with each step taken by the group as they advanced toward him – he could physically feel it leaving him. Nahki looked upon his family and friends, trying to feel what he had felt just moments earlier. But now, he looked upon them without an ounce of fear or sorrow, knowing this wasn't right; a change was occurring within him. The ritual had begun.

The first of the Avunaye to step forward was a woman. She had subtly tanned skin and long pale golden hair. As she glanced at Nahki, her green eyes piercing through his defences, he couldn't help but consider that she was quite beautiful - unlike any woman he had seen before. Even with Imara secured in front of him, Nahki couldn't draw his eyes away from this beautiful being. Within the blink of an eye she had moved again, stopping in front of the elderly villager. With one hand, she reached out, wrapping her delicate fingers around the man's wrinkled neck. Clutching his throat with a strength that juxtaposed her nimble frame, she effortlessly broke his neck.

As the light in the man's eyes diminished, and the screams and cries for help began to sound, Nahki felt something extinguish inside himself. His heart felt heavy, but he could not bring himself to feel sympathy for the old man; he simply felt nothing.

One by one, the rest of the Avunaye proceeded to kill the chained prisoners. Some died as quickly as the elderly man had. Some fell victim to the more sadistic hands of the Avunaye. Nahki could feel the void within him expanding with each and every death he witnessed. His emotions, everything that tethered him to his humanity, was inch by inch being stripped away. The next two to be slain were his brothers, Jamba and Hodari. Stepping forward to carry out the executions, were who Nahki believed to be, the twins from the elder's stories. The male walked up to Jamba and laid his hand on the stone wall. The skin of his hand and his arm appeared change colour and Nahki found his gaze shifting from the terror within Jamba's eyes for a moment as he looked on in disbelief. The twin's flesh was transforming, hardening to match that of the temple's foundation. He then wasted no time, bludgeoning Jamba across the head with his new, rock formed hand. Nahki found himself wincing at the sight the of his kin's demise, and Hodari's scream penetrated his core. He could feel himself wanting to urge them to stop, to respond to their pleas for help, but as Jamba's heart ceased to beat, the cry of his other brother, seemed to quieten. The female twin gave Hodari further cause to cry out to Nahki for aid as she took to all fours and transformed. Her mass expanded, fur replacing skin, as she turned into a huge bear. She gave out an almighty roar, drowning out the whimper of her soon to be victim, before she proceeded to tear through the flesh of Hodari's neck with her razor-sharp teeth, splashing his life's blood all over the ground. The splatter reached Nahki, landing on his cheek. His hand shook uncontrollably as he wiped it away, but in the time it took for the woman to transform back and for his brother to cease to be, the shaking had stopped.

The next of the Avunaye was different to the others. He stood robed, with a hood pulled up over his head covering his face from view. He stood still, seemingly looking down at the ground and whereas each of the others had proceeded to kill their chosen victim in turn, he hesitated. Nahki could swear that he himself could feel the reason for his hesitance. It was as if he could feel this man's remorse, his guilt; it was so confusing. Nahki looked about, looking to those he would soon call his brethren for aid. Brandt did not look impressed with the inaction of the robed reaper, and he looked toward Father for guidance. This was clearly unprecedented.

'Each of us takes a life, Adam, this is the way. The ritual will not be stopped! IT CANNOT BE STOPPED!' The bellow from Father shook the room, dust and sand fell from the ceiling as the ground quaked.

The sound silenced the whining Imara, who had been distraught since the ritual had started. Even some of the killers that stood beside Nahki were taken back. *Do they fear this Father?* Nahki was confused by what he felt. This Adam clearly did not wish to kill the girl that had, at the very least, once held a place within Nahki's heart, yet all the boy could muster was a sense of disgust towards him. *What is happening to me?* Nahki thought, *why... how...* He could not work out what it was that he felt, the emptiness that had manifested within him was prominent, but there were also so many other emotions swirling around inside, he couldn't tell if they were his own feelings or not. He looked down at his hands and could feel a welling of strength within them, a sense of power like nothing he had ever felt before. *Is this my reward?*

Brandt had grown tired of Adam's insolence and took it upon himself to rectify the situation. He grabbed Adam by the arm and dragged him forward, throwing him to his knees in front of the young girl. Adam continued to stare down at the ground showing no interest in the ritual, nor any willingness to comply with his expected part in it. Brandt tore open Adams robes from behind to reveal a back riddled with scars; he had clearly been through many battles or maybe this was not his first defiance. He placed his right hand on to Adam's right shoulder, the hand instantly changing colour with a flush of fiery red. The cracking of Adam's skin beneath Brandt's palm could easily be heard and the smell of burning flesh began to fill the air. Droplet after droplet of sweat began to run down Adams spine over the existing scars, and as the heat increased, Adam finally began to show signs of discomfort, clenching his fists. Dragging his knuckles across the stone flooring he lashed out in pain, punching the ground, each strike leaving a crack or breaking away some of the solid rock.

'Get on with it already!' Nahki yelled. The words slipped out as if someone else had said them. The boy was taken aback by his own exclamation as if he was possessed and it was not him saying the words that had left his lips. Brandt turned to the boy and smiled a wicked smile; he knew exactly what was happening within him and was clearly pleased to see this reaction. Slowly releasing his grip on Adam's shoulder and lifting his hand, strips of bloodied flesh peeled away with it. Brandt placed this hand upon the forehead of the prisoner to his right, Nahki's father. With his arms bound to the wall above, he was helpless to do anything other than shriek in agony. You could see the heat rising from the balding man's head, sweat running down both sides of his face and as blood began to swell within his eyes, his screaming stopped. Brandt then turned towards Nahki. Reaching within his robes he unsheathed a blade and offered it to him.

'Now you,' he said looking Nahki straight in the eyes, still with that wicked smirk across his face.

Nahki took the blade in hand; it was ornate with a fine mixture of carvings and scripture born into its hilt, yet the weapon was strange. Seemingly fashioned from a combination of bone and wood rather than metal, the blade was incredibly sharp. Nahki knew what it was that he had to do now. His mother had given him life and now she was to be the one to release him from this mortal coil. He took a step toward her, no feelings of regret or sadness stirred within as he stepped towards ending his own mother's life. As he took another step, the blonde woman that had started the ritual moved to Adam's side; she whispered something to him and with that Adam rose from the floor and stood wearily before Imara. Nahki stepped forward once more, and as he raised the blade, so too did Adam raise his hand toward the girl chained before him. It was just a momentary pause, but as Nahki looked to the Imara, he could swear that he could literally feel his heart begin to break into pieces, with each slither falling away, being swallowed up by the inhuman vortex that now resided inside of him. As Nahki looked at his mother, bound to the wall, helpless, showing no signs of struggle or fear, he could feel the last tear that would ever grace his skin cascade down his cheek. She slowly raised her head, her hair falling away from her face and she looked at him with her ever loving brown eyes.

'My boy,' she whimpered, smiling ever so slightly, 'know that... a mother's love is eternal.'

1

Krysta Rose-Anderson

As she lay face down, her hand outstretched, she could feel the coolness of the sheet beside her. She had not noticed him leave during the night, but the sensation of emptiness beside her on the bed was all too familiar. The morning sunlight was breaking through the gap in the blind, soft rays of light hugging the wooden floor. With what felt like an overwhelming amount of effort, she cracked one eye open to look towards the alarm clock beside her. 06:23. *Seven minutes before my alarm. Typical.*

A sudden drop in her stomach told her that the night before was one of regret. As she sat and swung her legs over the edge of the bed, she tried to cut through the fog that had cast itself over her mind. The lacey black dress she had worn lay in a crumpled heap on the floor. Her shoes were entangled in a mess of tights, a hole snagged in one of the legs where a heel had ripped it. She got to her feet and made her way across the room, collecting her underwear and the dress, depositing them in the laundry basket in the corner of the room. Slipping into her cotton dressing gown, she opened her bedroom door.

It was a decent sized apartment with plenty of room for a couple, ample space for one person. The décor was simple; the inner walls were painted ivory and a flat screen television stood upon a walnut TV stand which sat flush against a brick wall between two floor-to-ceiling length windows that outlooked the street. On the opposite side of the room sat a large bookcase filled with hardbacks and next to this stood a small table with an empty plant pot on it. In the centre of the room sat two sofas facing each other and a coffee table nestled between them.

Tidying the cushions on the sofas and collecting the used glasses from the coffee table, she turned the television on and walked over to the kitchen. The kitchen was set upon raised wooden flooring, a step up from the rest of the flat, with a marble counter that stood as a definitive separation between it and the other living quarters. Above the counter were several light bulbs hanging bare from the high ceiling via long thin cables, and pushed in below it sat four stools, none of which she could ever recall being used. She placed the dirty glasses by the sink then reached up to the cupboard above and took out a clean one. As she walked over to the fridge to pour herself a juice, she could hear a tapping coming from the window to the right of the TV.

'Just a second!', she quickly put the juice carton back and scurried around the counter toward the window, her feet clapping on the wooden floor. A smile lit up her face as she hurriedly wound the blind up. 'Good morning to you, too', she said as her eyes clapped the cat outside that stood on its hind legs, tapping on the glass with one of its paws. Its soft, short hair was white, with grey markings resembling that of a tiger. It had a tiny black nose and majestically deep green eyes that sparkled as the light caught them. The feline had recently become a frequent visitor in the mornings, showing up as the sun rose, just in time for breakfast. Sitting upon the sill, she unlatched the window and slid it up gently to greet her morning companion. 'Hey there gorgeous,' she said softly, stroking the top of the cat's head with the backs of her fingers and gently caressing the back of its neck, 'still no collar I see'. She cradled the underside of the cat's chin and felt the purring in its neck, 'we're going to have to think of a name for you one day, little one'.

Beep! Beep! Beep! Her alarm sounded from the bedroom, the shrill ring startling the cat, making it pull away from her hand and jump from the windowsill onto the fire escape below. 'Damn it,' she uttered, getting up from her perch. She left the window open as she hurried to the bedroom, the sound of the alarm reverberating around her already fragile head. After switching it off, she picked up her phone from the bedside cabinet, seeing that there was an unread message from her superior. *Early start I'm afraid kid*, it read, *will pick you up at 7 – S.*

She threw the handset onto the bed and began to undress. Then, she walked over to her walk-in wardrobe and slid open the door. It was impeccably organised - mainly due to the lack of its contents. Work blouses, jackets and pants filled most of the hanging space, with three zip-up garment bags on the end containing evening wear for the odd black tie occasion. Next to the workwear hung four t-shirts, two pairs of jeans and a pair of tracksuit bottoms. Below the clothes was a shelf for footwear, mostly sensible flats and then two pairs of black military-style boots from her academy days. There were also a couple of pairs of sandals, some worn trainers and two pairs of heels - the third pair she owned lay on the floor by the door. Hurriedly putting on underwear, suit pants and a white blouse, she headed towards the bathroom whilst buttoning up.

As she stood in the bathroom, she took the face cloth from its resting place on the sink and ran it under the warm water. Once saturated, she swept it across her face, feeling the grubbiness of sleep wipe away. Next, she ran her hands through her shoulder length blonde hair. She had curled it the evening before and didn't have time to sort it now, so a brisk brush with her fingers would have to do. She tipped her head upside down, grouping it all together at the back of her head and tying it in bun, out of the way. She grabbed her toothbrush and ran it under the tap, then topped it with toothpaste. Toothbrush in hand, she headed back through to the bedroom, opened her bedside drawer and revealed her Glock 22 pistol within its holster. She proceeded to attach it onto her belt, holding the toothbrush in her mouth, before putting on her suit jacket. Slipping on a pair of shoes, she headed over to the kitchen sink while brushing her teeth, turning off the TV and closing the window on her way. There was a knock on the door as she leaned over the sink to spit out the foam. 'Come in!', she called out in a gurgled tone. The door opened and in walked her superior and friend, Solomon Grey. He was a tall man, well-built and dressed smartly in a black suit with a white buttoned shirt and a black tie. He always held a very strong posture, one that reflected his previous career in the military. A balding man with a tidily shaved goatee, groomed to a meticulous degree, he stood in the doorway with a perturbed look on his face.

'I assume that has been unlocked all night?' he said sternly whilst closing the door behind him. 'You really need to take more care Krysta, the guy on the front door downstairs let me in without so much as a question.' Solomon took a further step into the apartment and glanced about, noting her shoes scattered by the bedroom door and her unmade bed. 'Good night, was it?' he probed in a father-like tone.

'Nothing to shout about,' she shrugged, wiping the toothpaste foam from the corners of her mouth with a dish towel. 'I won't be bringing this one home to meet you,' she smirked to imply that she did not need looking after. 'Anyway, enough about locks. What I really need is some breakfast. Stop at the café on Broadway on the way in?'

Solomon looked at her, tight lipped and with a frown. 'Not eaten already? There's a surprise. No doubt been fussing over that stray again,' he said, pointing with his head toward the window. Grabbing her keys and her badge off the counter, Krysta smiled at him, choosing to ignore the comment as she head towards the door.

Krysta's apartment was situated in Lower Manhattan, New York, ideally located so that her commute to work was short, only ever really lengthened by traffic. Having graduated from the academy in Quantico, Virginia, she worked as a special agent within the Federal Bureau of Investigation. Krysta had graduated from Stanford University with two bachelors degrees after moving back to America from England, where she lived as a child with her father until he passed away. She had met Solomon at Quantico a few weeks before graduating when he, several other agents and the deputy chief of staff had visited to scout for promising recruits. They had been partnered together now for a couple years. Krysta had grown to see Solomon as both a role model and a guardian of sorts, just as he had seemed to have grown quite fond of her.

Traffic was light this morning, so the drive was brief. They stopped off at the café on the way so that Krysta could grab a coffee and a croissant for breakfast, greeting the owners who by now knew them both by name. Solomon explained the reason for the early start to Krysta during the drive. Not that she minded – she loved her job and living alone with nobody to talk to was boring as hell. *The earlier the better*, she thought as Solomon explained that the FBI had received a tip off regarding a case they had been working for the past year. It was a case that had infuriated them for months and had almost been closed due to a lack of evidence.

'63rd called it in last night,' Solomon explained, glancing over to Krysta. 'One of Markovic's warehouses out in Flatlands is to be seized this morning.'

'Brooklyn?' Krysta questioned. 'We had those checked, rechecked even. "Squeaky clean" I believe were chief's words.' Krysta air quoted the statement, exhibiting a combination of sarcasm and frustration while gripping onto her coffee.

'Well... that was before a caretaker walked in during his

shift and found a dozen dead bodies strung up on one of the walls,' Solomon continued, causing Krysta to violently swallow the mouthful of coffee she had just taken. 'I have to check in with Davenport before I give you and the rest of the team full details, but looks like we'll be heading straight over there to check it out.'

Krysta could feel the calm in Solomon's voice despite the morbid topic. She marvelled at how he kept nonchalant under any circumstances, able to mask his emotion under a plain exterior. Now, she could feel him looking out of the corner of his eye at her, no doubt wondering if she was still listening to him, which of course she was. Solomon had two children of his own, both teenagers. Yet, a lot of the time Krysta felt as if she was the third. He kept a close eye on her and she paid him the same respect as she had shown her father. She appreciated his guidance and support, and had often found it a comfort, what with no close family of her own anywhere around. Not to mention the shit they had to put up with on a daily basis – it was nice to have him by her side for that.

As they arrived at the office, Solomon pulled over to let Krysta out of the car. She climbed out of the vehicle and headed over to the main entrance, Solomon pulling away to park in the underground parking lot. After scanning her ID card, she walked over to take the stairs.

'Still not using the elevator?' an unmistakably teasing and yet recognisable voice asked as Krysta entered the office floor from the stairwell. 'Bout time you got over that, isn't it?'

The voice belonged to Kyle Johnston, although everyone called him Kit. He was an ASAC: Assistant Special Agent in Charge. Kit was of average height, slim build and toned physique thanks to regular morning workouts at the gym before work. He had short, mousey blonde hair that always looked unkempt. Often unshaven, clearly aiming for a 'ruggedly handsome' look, Kit was a charmer with a very cosy upbringing thanks to his parents' money. His mother was some sort of well-known psychology writer that had made millions from her books, and so Kit had grown up wanting for nothing. Unfortunately, this had taught him very little respect either. Regrettably, Krysta had been at the receiving end of his lack of maturity during their two-year-long relationship when she had walked in on him screwing his sister's best friend. Now, she paid him little attention as she walked to her desk.

'We can't expect her to get over her fears just as quickly as she got over you, can we now, pretty boy?' Special Agent Luciana Rodriguez stated in a matter of fact tone, raising her eyebrows at Kit by way of telling him to shut up. Rodriguez had little patience for most men, let alone cheating bastards like Kit. About the same height as Krysta with, dark, spikey hair, she had a caramel complexion, huge eyes and was a little ruffled around the edges. As quite the tom boy, she was always more interested in kicking ass than kicking back. She had once told Krysta that her father was a military man and she had spent her childhood moving from base to base. The experience had hardened her, and she soon learned to look after herself. She gave Krysta a nod to signify that she had her back. Then, she lowered her feet from where they had been resting on her desk and stood up, walking toward Krysta. To say that Lucy's bark was worse than her bite would be naïve, as she was one of the top hand-to-hand combatants within the F.B.I; she had put Kit on his ass a couple of times in training, much to his ego's dismay. Kit knew better than to get into a war of words with her and so simply scoffed at her remarks and moved on.

'Thanks, Luce,' Krysta smirked, 'think you may have dented that big old ego of his.'

'Don't let him get to you, sweetie. He aint worth it,' Lucy said, comforting Krysta. She could see she was still hurting over the whole ordeal, despite however much she tried to cover it. Lucy playfully punched Krysta on the arm. 'Anyway, I saw you slip off last night with the "stallion" from Texas... what was his name again?'

'The "stallion", as you called him, bolted" Krysta replied. 'Gone when I woke up." She pushed a strand of hair from her face and looked towards the floor. 'I'm never letting you talk me into going out again'.

'Fuck him. Who needs guys anyway, right?' said Lucy quickly. 'How 'bout we go put some douchebag mobsters behind bars?' she suggested with a grin.

The team had just about all gathered in the briefing room around a central interactive table when Krysta and Lucy entered. Solomon, Krysta noticed with a quick scan around the room, was the only one noticeably missing. The team, including Solomon as its leader, was comprised of seven members. All of them special agents looking to work their way up through the bureau, possibly leading teams or divisions of their own someday. Stood talking on the opposite side of the table were agents Michael Ward and Claire Davenport.

Mike, as he was commonly known, was a stocky man in his early thirties with a huge pair of arms. He was 'the muscle' of the team, as Krysta and the others liked to call him. Standing just shy of six feet tall, he had scruffy brown hair and a short beard. Although she knew he must trim it, Krysta often considered that the real reason he kept his beard was because he simply couldn't be bothered to shave it off. A physical man, Mike had played a lot of football in his youth, graduating from high school and seizing a scholarship with his abilities as a quarter-back. He was able to overpower most perps without any backup, something that Krysta enjoyed watching even to this day.

Claire was the brains of the team; she had been snapped up by the F.B.I immediately after graduating from high school. As part-time hacker, she had been involved in some controversial activities in her teenage years which had caught the bureau's attention; instead of prosecution, it had been decided that her abilities would be harnessed for use by the F.B.I and as a result she had joined the institution at the young age of twenty. She used her skills to help the team prevent several terror attacks over the years, but her real talent was being able to find people that did not want to be found. She was petite in size and a brunette. She wore her hair up in a pony and often wore contacts, but today her horn-rimmed glasses sat atop the bridge of her nose. She was consistently smartly dressed and displayed a quick wit, a quality that the team found endearing. Krysta had come to see her as 'the little sister' of the team.

Entering the room just before Krysta and Lucy was special agent Paul Hale. Quiet and reserved, Hale had been with the team the shortest amount of time; he had joined the F.B.I. from the military where he had been of captain grade within his unit. He was roughly six feet tall with black hair, blue eyes and well-groomed facial hair. He stood with a noticeably rigid stance, ready and awaiting his orders as though he were still in the military. His dedication and attention to detail towards his work had quickly earned him respect from everyone within the team. It was often a game among the other members of the team to try and guess what Hales' background was, as he was never forthcoming with any information. Riddled with tattoos, his past was something of intrigue to the rest of them.

Solomon now finally entered the room accompanied by Kit, who seemed to look very smug as he looked over at Krysta and Lucy.

'Claire, if you would...' Solomon gestured as he walked over to table, Kit following two steps behind him like a sheep. Claire activated the tabletop screen and began to open various files, all of which seemed to be related to the investigation into Vladimir Markovic. 'I realise some of you have been working on other cases, but as of now you will all be working on the Markovic case. Any other cases will be reassigned,' Solomon continued. 'You all know Mr. Johnston, assistant Special Agent in Charge. He will be liaising with us on this one.' The reaction of the room told Krysta that this news was unwelcome to several members of the team. But Solomon had spoken, and they all knew better than to argue. 'Claire, if you would bring everyone up to speed.'

Claire began to open image files on the tabletop for the team to view. Markovic was well known within the F.B.I. Born in Serbia, he had moved to the United States in his teens and quickly made a name for himself by integrating into the world of drug and arms trafficking. He was suspected of being involved with many other illegal activities, including human trafficking, slavery and aiding terrorist sleeper cells gain entrance to the country. Without a doubt, Markovic was on top of the F.B.I.'s most wanted list. However, a lack of solid evidence was preventing him from being thrown behind bars. Countless properties belonging to Markovic and his gang had been seized over the last year. He had even been arrested and taken to court, only for the trial to be dismissed as a result of missing or inadmissible evidence, and of course the disappearance of multiple key witnesses. Whether bullied into keeping their mouth shut or literally disappearing, at least five witnesses had escaped the F.B.I until this point. The case was not one that any of the team wanted to be lumbered with. Hundreds of man hours had already been spent on it, without reward.

'We all recognise our friend Vladimir Markovic,' Claire began. 'Any of you who have touched on this case in the past will also recognise his closest associates. Kryln Cardoza, big in arms dealing, he spends a lot of time in Central America. However, he does like to grace us with an appearance right here in town from time to time.' Kryln Cardoza was a mammoth of a man born and raised in Nicaragua. He was wanted by authorities in many countries for countless murder charges and gun trafficking. 'Next up is –'

'Benjamin Brascus. Son of Richard Brascus, the owner of multi-billion-dollar Brascus Oil Industries.' Kit interrupted Claire, receiving several disgruntled looks from the team.

'Yes, Brascus,' Claire continued, once Kit was done giving his two cents worth. 'He's originally from England and, if you believe what the papers tell you, he is quite the playboy. He is also suspected of funding some of Markovic's human trafficking exploits, dealing in the kidnapping and the auctioning of young girls in Eastern Europe.' As the list went on, Krysta began to grow restless. She herself had spent a lot of time putting together this information, and going over it all again now only fuelled her desire to push on with the investigation. Then, her eyes caught sight of a face she didn't recognise.

'Who's this?' She quizzed, pointing to one of the pictures.

'That is –'

'It's Alexei Kuznetsov,' Kit spoke above Claire whilst raising his hand, signalling to her that he was taking over the briefing. 'More affectionately known as Alexei 'Jack o' Diamonds' Kuznetsov. Supposedly ex Bratva. That's Russian organised crime syndicate, or mafia, for any of you unfamiliar with the name,' he flashed a smirk toward Krysta and Lucy before continuing. 'This mean son of a bitch is wanted in pretty much every country other than his homeland... sick bastards over there seem to see him as some kind of "hero of the people". We're unaware as to whether he has cut ties with the Bratva, but he has been seen in the States on several occasions, usually turning up just before the shit hits the fan. As I'm sure you all recall, other teams have been investigating the bombings in Ohio and Washington last year. We have now been lead to believe that those bombings were thanks to this guy.' Kit continued to display a lot of knowledge on the subject, showing off with a flamboyancy and confidence that only he could exude. But truth be told, he was losing the attention of the team; he was an unwanted partner in this case and his constant interruptions were beginning to annoy everyone, including Solomon. Krysta looked up at her superior in dismay, her eyes pleading with him to shut the bastard up. He caught her eye and cleared his throat.

'This guy is new,' Solomon interrupted, stamping his authority on the meeting. He pointed to a figure in one of the most recent images they had of Markovic, another individual Krysta didn't recognise. Sure, the man had his back to the camera, but even Solomon seemed surprised by the inclusion of an individual he didn't recognise in such a complex and intricate case. Claire looked to Solomon for permission to continue, to which he gave her a nod.

'He is new, yes sir.' Claire confirmed. 'Despite mine and my team's efforts, we are still trying to figure him out. I'm afraid this is the best image we have of him, we're still waiting on image enhancement. Not much to go off I know but as you can see, he's a big guy.' The stranger had dark, shoulder length hair and easily stood a foot taller than Markovic. The picture depicted some sort of rendezvous between Markovic and the unknown man outside of a storage unit - clearly an old one by the quality of the CCTV footage. Something about it unsettled Krysta, and clearly the other team members too.

'Sir?' Agent Hale spoke up, seeking permission to speak. The look returned by Solomon was one of frustration. He had told Hale countless times before that this was not the army and such formalities were unnecessary. 'If I might comment, sir. It looks to me like this man is calling the shots in this photograph, sir. Markovic doesn't look like he's just given orders. He looks like he's just received some, sir," he suggested, pointing to the image. Krysta could see what he meant. The man was taller than Markovic, and the expression on Markovic's face was almost compliant. Soloman nodded at Hale.

'Claire, keep looking into this guy and see what you can find on him,' he instructed. 'If this new guy is intimidating enough to make Markovic quake in his boots, then I want to know everything about him.' Solomon leaned over, placed both of his hands on the table and looked around the table at his team. Krysta had seen the look in his eyes before; his orders were coming. 'Okay. Krysta, Lucy and Mike. You'll be leaving with Special Agent Johnston and myself in five minutes. We're heading over to Flatlands. We're told that Markovic has a warehouse over there with a dozen dead bodies hanging from one of its walls.' Solomon, much like in the car, did not flinch in the slightest as he divulged the information. He went on to describe the reported disfigured and mutilated corpses that reportedly hung a foot off the floor, suspended from the rafters and hands bound above their heads by barbed wire. 'Hale, you will be assisting Claire in her intel search. I'm assuming we will be using some of your military contacts to make some head way. Wait for orders from above.' Hale responded with a simple nod. 'Right then. Suit up and let's move out.'

2

Seamus McCarthy

As the sun rose and the burnt orange light that bathed the earth turned to a sun-kissed yellow, the city began to wake. Quiet streets began to grow busier with life, cars passing by, bicycles speeding along. The coolness and quiet that had aided him on his run swiftly slipped away and was replaced by a basking warmth. A cool bead of sweat ran down his temple as he turned the final corner and continued on towards home. It was the middle of spring; the basswood and elm trees that lined the streets formed a green canopy, fingers of light reaching down from the heavens to caress his skin. They pierced Mother Nature's green blockade and created a warm, gentle glow around him as he ran his final distance toward completion. A sense of accomplishment washed over him as he slowed to a halt and bent over, palms to thigh. Befriended by a familiar lack of breath and a satisfying ache throughout his legs, this had become a morning routine that helped prepare him for the day ahead. His breath steadying, he stretched his legs, purging the lactic acid from his muscles. Then he ascended the few steps to his front door, receiving a friendly nod by way of greeting from his neighbour. Before turning the door handle, he took a deep breath, igniting his lungs with the air of the city he had come to love. Breathing out slowly, he allowed a slight smile to invade his face as he made his way into the house.

His home was alive with bodies that were hurriedly moving from one room to the next in the usual morning panic. The entrance hall, tidy before he'd left, was now strewn with coats and various shoes. His daughter Alannah bolted past him towards the bathroom. She backed up on herself as she realised he was home.

'Morning dad, good run?' she smiled. He didn't have a chance to respond before she'd taken off again, closely followed her brother. Like a red-blue whirlwind as his worn-out backpack flashed past, he didn't even take the time to acknowledge his father before almost knocking him off his feet.

The tantalizing aroma of freshly made coffee caught his attention while he discarded his running shoes. Following it, he headed through to the kitchen to find his wife Moira with a slice of toast held between her teeth, frantically rummaging through her handbag.

'Hey, hon,' he said, giving her a kiss on the cheek.

'Mm,' she responded, freeing one of her hands to remove the toast from her mouth and attempting to swallow her food before smiling. 'Your shirt's hung up on the door. Kids should be leaving in a minute, as should I or else we are ALL going to be late!' She raised her voice and shouted toward the bathroom, hoping they would take note. When no response came, she rolled her eyes and turned her attention back to the contents of her handbag. Mornings were always chaos in the McCarthy residence. Both Declan and Alannah attended New York University, which both Moira and himself had been immensely proud of. It was just unfortunate that Seamus' own traits of organisation and time keeping had most certainly not been passed on to them. He poured himself a glass of milk and downed the entire contents in one, before he turned and subtly slipped his arms around his wife's waist. Noticing her frantic demeanour, he kissed her softly on the neck.

'Relax. If you're looking for your keys, you left them on

the side next to the toaster,' Seamus whispered softly into her ear. The search for keys or phones had become a common occurrence, one that he had been inclined to learn to manage or else chaos ensued. She turned to face him, standing on her tiptoes and wrapping her arms around his neck as she kissed him passionately on the lips.

'Thankyou,' she smiled softly as she slipped herself out of his grasp and reached for her keys. 'Now I really need to go. Declan, Alannah! Hurry up!' She gave Seamus one last peck before grabbing her jacket and heading out of the kitchen. Her exit was accompanied by the sound of the two kids bounding through the house rushing to follow her out. Moira was studying to be a nurse. Until recently, she had always worked in a shop bagging groceries and stocking shelves. She had always had the desire to help others, yet the arrival of two children and the commitments that came with them delayed her decision to return to college and follow her ambitions. Seamus remembered how they had discussed it so many times, and how she had finally felt confident enough to take the plunge back into education. Now, he placed his glass in the sink and smiled as he heard the car pull out of the drive.

Following a quick shower, Seamus donned his uniform in front of the full-length mirror in the bedroom. In meticulously polished black shoes, pressed and ironed black pants and a crisp shirt, he stood proudly tidying his short dark hair, combing it over to one side in the style he preferred. He picked up his badge, the shield that he bore 'to protect and serve' and pinned it to his chest before placing on his peaked hat. Then he took the pistol and holster from his bedside table drawer and placed it in his bag.

Seamus had joined the New York Police Department straight out of high school, eager to live up to the legacy set by his father. He had been an Assistant Chief within the department, well respected by all his colleagues back then, but also known to all the present officers as his portrait was hung pride of place on the current chief's office wall. Seamus' father had always shown a desire for his son to join the ranks of the NYPD. Seamus' first memories were of his father letting him sit on his lap in the squad car when he and his mother would visit him at work, and eating sandwiches in the police department cafeteria if he had a day off school. His dad had been his hero. He had been decorated with the medal of Exceptional Merit, and was awarded the Purple Shield after giving his own life to the job when he was gunned down during an armed robbery. Seamus' mother on the other hand had never wished for her son to follow in her husband's footsteps. She feared that he would suffer the same sad fate as his father, and couldn't bare to lose them both. But Seamus felt the compelling need to protect and serve and applied the moment he could. The day he passed out from training was the best day of his life. He felt so close to his father as he swore oath to protect the people of his country, almost as though he was bringing him back to the NYPD in some way. As it happened, it also turned out to be the day that he would meet Moira.

His arrival at the station was greeted by the light-hearted chuckle of Sergeant Joseph McCabe, who briefly looked up from behind his thick wad of paperwork. Joe McCabe was a well-rounded guy that enjoyed the little things in life. He loved to laugh and joke, but knew that everything had a time and place. He wore a badge which displayed an eagle perched atop a shield, which sat pinned to his breast with pride. Seamus had a lot of respect for the man.

'On time as always, eh McCarthy?' he noted without even glancing at his watch, 'I can but continue to hope that one day you'll sink to the standards of us mere humans.'

Seamus merely laughed at the comment. It was a running joke that he slept somewhere within the station every night to ensure that he wasn't tardy. At this point, he simply went along with it. 'What can I say sarge? The city loves me and I love it.' Manhattans' chaotic nature made for interesting morning commutes. Seamus had a knack for being bang on time, a knack that eluded most of his colleagues' comprehension entirely, and so he had become known for it. He entered the changing room to find his colleagues getting changed, which was odd as usually nobody was in here at this time.

'Here he is, man of the hour,' announced a comedic a voice as Seamus entered. In front of the lockers stood two half naked men who were frantically changing into their uniforms like a pair of eager children. The voice belonged to officer Malik Seif, and the half-naked associate stood beside him was officer Axel Reeves. The pair of them had joined the force at the same time as Seamus and the three of them had grown very close over the years. However, Seamus had a lot more patience for the calm and collected nature of Axel than Malik's overzealous personality. Malik stood buttoning up his shirt with a Cheshire cat-like grin across his face; his jet-black hair was slicked back into a tidy side parting, catching in the light as a result of the copious amount of hair product he liked to use. His mischievous eyes rested on Seamus, unblinking, waiting for a response.

'Okay, I'll bite,' pronounced Seamus. 'Why am I the man of the hour?' Seamus found that Malik's sense of humour was more of an annoyance at best, but it was better to take the bait and get it over as quickly as possible.

'F.B.I duty. Got a call asking for a couple of fine officers from the NYPD to help secure a crime scene.' Malik divulged the information as he finished readying himself. Axel remained silent, continuing to comb his mousy brown hair. It was always a sign of mischief on the horizon if Axel was quiet. His lack of input was never a good sign. 'I figure it's some sort of test see, cause we put in for the sergeant opening,' Malik continued to ramble, which came out more as thoughts that he seemed to be speaking aloud .

Seamus had applied for a sergeants' position before but was unsuccessful. Even though he had passed a lot of the tests, he hadn't been believed to be ready. This time round Malik had also applied, adding to the pressure as there was only one slot available. Seamus was intrigued and despite knowing that there was probably a catch or a twist to this tale - as there so often was with Malik. The opportunity to show his worth was all too alluring.

'So do we report now or-' but before Seamus could finish his sentence, Malik chuckled. There it was, the inevitable catch. Despite expecting it, Seamus' heart still sank a little at its presence.

'Oh!' Malik exclaimed, 'Sorry, bro. I meant me and Axel had been summoned for the big league, see.' His face bore a fake apologetic expression, his eyes smiling a wicked grin. 'Think chief wants you babysitting the new guy or summin', buddy.'

Exhibiting a dejected half smile, Seamus stepped to one side to allow for his colleagues hasty exit as they grabbed what they needed and headed out, Malik giving Seamus a quick pat on the back as he passed. *What's that for? You can be such a dick sometimes, Seif.* Seamus attempted to lift his spirits as he turned to make his way to see if there was any truth to Malik's suggestion of him training a cadet. But as he exited the room, he punched the end locker in a burst of uncharacteristic rage, causing an unsuspecting officer to flinch as he entered. The officer expressed a concerned frown towards him, but Seamus merely stormed through the door, letting it bang shut behind him. *Why am I not good enough for F.B.I duty? Maybe I could argue my case to the sarge, or maybe to the chief? Maybe I could insist that after all the hard work I've put in over the years, I should be one of the officers chosen, maybe...* Seamus' thoughts were in a tangle as he made his way back toward the main office. It wasn't that he didn't want to 'babysit' the new kid, he quite enjoyed training, imparting his knowledge on the unexperienced. He just wished that they'd see his potential. He knew deep down inside, with every fibre of his being, that he was meant to do more, meant to be more.

'McCarthy!' McCabe yelled from behind his desk as Seamus stood despondently inside the doorway. 'You got a 10-53 up on Columbia and then chief wants you to take out Lorenzo, show him the ropes,' he relayed the order in a hasty fashion and then returned to the pile of paperwork before him.

Taking a deep breath in, Seamus acknowledged the order, straightened up his attire and headed for the exit. As he stepped out into the concrete jungle of the city outside, the warm air soothed his anxiety. *The city knows my worth.*

3

Serena

As the morning drew closer and the coolness of night vanished, the heat of the day thrust itself upon the world. She enjoyed the heat, the gentle caress of the sun on her skin and the still air. Although she had grown to appreciate the city and what it had to offer, she would usually only stay for the warmer seasons of the year and escape to warmer climates when the cold returned. Throughout the years, she had manoeuvred herself into a position of wealth; with wealth came a considerable amount of power, which in her opinion was a prerequisite to anything. Her natural adaptability enabled her to settle anywhere, yet she favoured the lavish lifestyle to which she had grown so accustomed. Despite her wealth and the extravagance it brought, she was plagued with questions, questions that had for so long gone unanswered despite her attempts to find out the truth. She had travelled the world but found no solace. This morning held hope.

The vehicle slowed to a halt and her driver, confirming that they had reached their destination, exited the car. Before carrying out his duty of opening her door, he stopped for a moment to take a breath. He lifted his hat, mopped his sweat ridden brow and straightened his tie; the heat within the car had been unbearable, almost enough for him to pass out. But he knew that she would not accept his unkempt appearance. It was perilous to invoke her displeasure.

As the driver opened the door, the instant injection of sunlight hit her skin and she sat for a moment, eyes closed, basking in its pleasant warmth. She felt it from her head all the way down to her toes. She wore glamorous open-toed red heels that laced around her leg just above the ankle, with a mid-length black skirt that rippled as she moved. A short-sleeved scarlet coloured blouse buttoned up over her chest just enough to allow her to boast her womanly assets, for she was beautiful, a resemblance of Helen of Troy. She had golden skin and a head of fiery red hair that fell to below her shoulders. Ordinarily she did not wear glasses, but for her visit today she had decided that they would be an appropriate accessory to manipulate her hosts perception.

The driver had stopped the vehicle alongside Washington Square Park. She wanted to walk through the park before the meeting. She craved the exposure to the sun's warmth and, quite honestly, the thought of being confined in an office with an old man disgusted her somewhat, so the walk would conveniently delay the impending torturous task. Optimistic that today would be a success, the usual tension she felt before a meeting was lessened. The pressure was on for her to retrieve the information she needed, sure, but a confidence washed over her now as this would be, at the very least, a step towards her goals.

'Wait here,' she commanded. The driver simply gave a nod in reply. He was newly appointed into his role, but she could tell that he was a quick study. Already he knew that she had little time for his words - she valued action and thus, he saved his breath. She entered the park, following the stone path which would lead her to the central fountain, a place seemingly brimming with life as crowds of students congregated here before the start of their day. She chose to avoid the masses, remaining on a narrower path that veered off next to a line of trees. As she continued her walk, she was almost knocked off her feet by a young man and woman, both in a hurry to get to wherever they were headed, not at all aware of what or whom they were running into.

'Sorry!' the girl exclaimed as she continued to bound past. The boy, on the other hand, halted in his tracks to deliver his apology.

'Sorry,' the young man panted, trying to spit out his words without giving away that he was completely out of breath. "We're running a bit late. I'm so sorry!' His sweet and sincere appearance did not fool her of course. She could tell exactly what the hormonal young man was thinking as his eyes fixated on her. She was strikingly beautiful and she knew it. She humoured him, however, as she could use this fact to her own advantage.

'It's alright,' she replied, pressing a crease from her skirt, 'Actually... I'm on my way to the Linguistics Department at the university. You wouldn't happen to know where it is?' *And to save me the bother of finding it myself, you are going to lead me there,* she thought to herself.

'Well, I'm heading in that direction as well,' he lied, eyes transfixed on her magnificence as he pointed in a random direction. 'I'll take you, if you'd like.' He was growing more confident with each second that she did not dismiss him.

'Sure,' she smiled coyly, 'Thank you.' She gestured for the young man to lead the way, knowing that he would ensure that she reached her destination. With such a glorious trophy on his arm, he would not want to disappoint.

The park was in full bloom. The pillared trees stood rigid in the breezeless sunshine, flaunting an array of colour. The nuances of red, orange and green dominated the recreational paradise, while the pinks and snowy whites of the cherry and magnolia trees provided a wild contrast that she found quite charming. As they began to exit the park, she turned to take in its natural beauty once more. On the boundary of the park, hidden behind a row of trees, stood the charmingly classic linguistics building. The stone was draped in purple and violet pennants and the grounds were brimming with eager young minds, grasping at their chance to make a mark on the world through the workings of their glorious minds. She scoffed at the thought that any of these insignificant little people could ever hope of making a mark on history, such as she would undoubtedly do. The pennants each displayed the department's Latin motto. She paused and read each of the words letting them sink into her mind. *Perstare et Praestare*: To Persevere and To Excel. It was something she intended to do exactly.

The inside of the building was just as grand as the outside. The walls were simple stone brick and there was a marbled floor that reflected the light of the chandelier above them while echoing each of the footsteps taken by the pair. They were the only two in the foyer as they came to a standstill next to a large clock.

'Miss Serena?' A strong, masculine voice from behind said her name. 'Miss Serena, I am Professor Timothy Rosenbourg,' said the voice, which she had now turned to see had come from a beige suited man stood in a doorway to the right of main doors.

'Ah,' said the boy. 'You're here to see Professor Rosenbourg!' There was a hint of jealousy in his tone. The professor, a gentleman perhaps in his forties, looked quite young for his true age. He was handsome, with greying hair and slight wrinkles protruding from the corners of his eyes.

'Yes,' she responded, releasing her grip on the boy's arm and stepping toward the professor. The boy had served his purpose and was of no interest to her now. Realising this, he grasped the straps of his worn-out red and blue backpack, nodded his head at the two and swiftly exited the room through the main entrance.

It seemed that Serena and Professor Rosenbourg were each slightly taken aback by the others' appearance. She had expected an old codger, someone that should have probably retired a long time ago. Someone whose only meaningful contact with other people came from teaching, and thus he clung to his work, an old fool. Instead, this roughly fortyish, ruggedly handsome man stood before her, staring at her much like the adolescent had done moments before.

'I must say Professor, I am surprised,' she confessed as he turned and beckoned her into his office. 'I'm surprised at how a man so few in years has managed to gain such a reputation as you have.' Her statement was sincere, and yet her tone was laced in a sense of doubt. *Will this be a waste of time?* She couldn't help but wonder.

He smiled knowingly at the comment as he walked to stand behind a large, mahogany desk. 'I merely had a head start, continuing the work of my father,' He grinned. 'But, I will admit that my work has become quite the obsession.' As he said this, he stepped to the side and twirled around, arms outstretched. The walls were plagued with masses of artwork, artefacts and pieces of scripture. She froze, taken aback; the room was filled with it all. Bookcases brimmed with texts, gilded titles about lore and myths. Other relics included tribal masks from around the world, ancient weapons and totems laid within glassed cases. She had walked into a museum.

'Very impressive,' she said, flashing a fake smile. 'Now, shall we get down to business?' She had no time to waste enlarging this man's ego by listening to him drone on about his array of relics, most of which she had seen the likes of many times before. She was here for information that would be far more valuable to her than old trinkets. She removed her glasses, sat down on one of the chairs situated before the mahogany desk and crossed her legs ostentatiously.

'Right yes. Down to business,' he agreed, dropping his outstretched arms and hurrying around his desk to take his seat. 'You mentioned on the phone a particular interest into my research on Swahili folklore,' he paused and scratched his stubble. 'Particularly the Avunaye, was it?' he quizzed with a pleased look on his face as he remembered the subject of their prearranged meeting. She, of course, did not share his enthusiasm and sat unmoving, waiting for him to get on with it.

They sat and spoke for quite some time regarding the details of the Avunaye. Professor Rosenbourg sifted through several texts as they conversed, explaining the varying interpretations of the legends and information gained over centuries that had been sourced from numerous cultures. Yet, the more knowledge that the professor exhibited, the more frustrated Serena became.

'Yes, yes,' she said in exasperation after fifteen minutes of rambling. 'But what was it that fuelled these rituals, the initiations, how did they work? What was the catalyst?'

'How they worked?' Professor Rosenbourg said, surprised. He was seemingly confused by her frustration that the information he was giving her wasn't adequate. 'I'm sorry Miss Serena, but I don't think I understand what you mean. This is all just legend and myth. You don't believe such a thing existed, surely?'

The bewildered expression on the professor's face began to infuriate her as he continually struggled to comprehend what it was she was asking for. It was at this moment that the realisation dawned on her. The answers she sought did not reside here. She stood up from her seat, pat the creases from her skirt and slowly walked around the professor's desk, seductively running her fingertips along its bevelled edge.

'Is everything quite alright, Miss Serena?' he croaked. She continued to encircle him, running her fingertips along the arm of his chair, slowly dragging them up his bicep and across his shoulder. He shuddered at her touch, yet he did not contest her advance. His self-control and lack of resistance to her touch disappointed her somewhat. She had always felt a great pleasure from her effortless dominance over men, her ability cause them to lose their inhibitions. It seemed Professor Rosenbourg, however, had no inhibitions to lose. Now she stood behind him, running her fingers through his short hair, caressing his scalp.

Exhilarated by what was about to happen, she could feel her body temperature beginning to rise dramatically. Every molecule of her being had entered an excitable state and her skin buzzed with a rapidly increasing heat. She could feel the blood pulsating through her veins, an unignorable warmth rippling outward from her core until it reached the boundaries of her flesh. Like a heavy stone thrown into the depths of a lake, her heart continued to pound with an intensity and ripples of excitement flourished through her body. Beneath her clothes, her body was its own being. Her soft, supple skin, now dampened with a chilled layer of perspiration, tingled with passion. She inadvertently felt her breasts begin to swell, her nipples hardening beneath her blouse. The control aroused her. Professor Rosenbourg remained seated, rigid, unnerved by her forwardness and unable to move. His breathing hastened. His heart was at a gallop with an excitement that had long escaped him throughout his bachelorhood. He did not even seem aware of the bead of sweat now dripping to his brow.

In one swift movement, she spun the chair around, causing Professor Rosenbourg to take a sharp intake of breath. Speechless and exhilarated by her sudden tenacity, he grasped at the arms of his chair with such tension his fingers began to go white at the knuckles. His eyes were transfixed on Serena and his manhood began to throb beneath his suit pants. She stood before him, now running her hands through her fierce red hair as she had done his own just moments ago. She looked down at him squirming in his seat and ran her index finger slowly away from her hair, down her cheek and around to her pouted lips, gesturing the need for silence and secrecy.

'The door,' the professor muttered with a fleeting glance over to the entrance. It had been closed, but not locked. She was a fan of his discomfort. Like a wolf eyeing up a lamb, she smiled mischievously and slowly swung her legs over one after the other as she mounted the chair atop the willing professor. Suddenly unfreezing, Professor Rosenbourg overcame any hesitation he might have had and grabbed Serena at the waist, pulling her in. She rolled her hips, rubbing herself against his erection. With an increased intensity, he grabbed at her blouse, squeezing her breasts, fumbling at the buttons in a desperate attempt to release her from the confines of her clothing. As he struggled to unhook each button, she looked on and realised just how feeble a man he was. The reality displeased her. Continuing to watch him undo her blouse buttons in a hastened yet clumsy fashion, she looked him in the eyes with a dark, malevolent stare. An ember-like glow took to the back of her eyes and she contorted her face into a wry, wicked smile.

Imprisoned in his chair, Professor Rosenbourg paused to wipe his brow. Now, it occurred to him that he had begun to sweat profusely and he couldn't grasp the reason as to why. Held captive between her thighs, he accepted failure with the buttons and began to squirm in his chair. The erotic atmosphere that had taken over the room now shifted almost as quickly as it had arrived. Now, a sense of impending danger and panic took over his body. The heat he felt was becoming intense and he was starting to feel unwell, but she was unwilling to relinquish her hold on him. Grasping at her forearms in an attempt to move her, he let out a yelp and quickly retracted his hands as the touch of her flesh scolded his palms.

'What-what is this?!' he cried as he looked at his raw palms. To this, she could only laugh.

Running her hands back through her hair, arching her back so that her breasts nuzzled against his face, Serena began to laugh. She laughed until suddenly and bizarrely, her blouse took to flame. Fingers of red and orange fire began to lick up and down her skin. Within an instant she was ablaze, engulfed by an inferno, and yet she continued to laugh, unphased. The terrified professor writhed in agony, clawing at the confinements of his chair as the fire she possessed cracked and blackened his skin. The last image captured by his eyes before they burst within their sockets was of a beauty, naked and magnificent, encapsulated in flame, deriving immense pleasure from his pain.

As the fire began to wane, she stood, stepping away from Professor Rosenbourg's blackened and burnt out corpse. She wiped ash from her cheek as the flames died, calmly brushing the flecks of debris from her skin. Nude but for her heels, she grabbed an overcoat from a hanging rail in the corner of the office. She donned it, straightened out her barely ruffled crimson locks and returned her glasses to rest on the bridge of her nose. Turning back to glance at the smouldering remains she had created, a satisfied smile spread across her face. She may not have gotten all the answers she had come here for, but she had enjoyed her brief stay.

4

Krysta Rose-Anderson

A combined feeling of nausea and dread possessed her. It was only a brief journey, but flying was not an experience Krysta had ever been able to grow accustomed to. Her palms were clammy, and she could feel a trickle of sweat running to the small of her back as she sat nervously in the seat, counting down the minutes until she would be back on land. It wasn't even the flying that she disliked the most, but rather the feeling of entrapment within a confined space. The sensation that the walls were closing in on her, leaving her hanging on the edge of a state of panic. As the helicopter began its descent, a mild sense of relief began to envelope her and she let out a controlled sigh. Slowly, she released her tight grip on her thighs as she sat on the edge of her seat, impatiently waiting to disembark the aircraft. Lucy gave her hand a discreet, quick and reassuring squeeze. She knew that Krysta didn't like to fly, but more importantly she knew that Krysta was too proud to let Solomon and the others in on her fears. The chopper settled down; they had returned to land and Krysta could now begin to relax. The helicopter had landed in a clearing a few hundred yards away from the industrial site. The warehouse they were looking for was situated fairly close to a body of water. As the team exited the chopper and made a dash toward the site, Krysta could hear the sound of the water. It became a lot clearer as the din from the helicopter subsided.

The building was one of many large commercial warehouses, their outer walls all thick with painted steel cladding. The direction of the teams intended destination was easily deciphered. In amongst a sea of burnt orange and red structures stood the distinctive charcoal coloured exterior of Markovic's property. The immediate area outside of the building had been cordoned off with police tape and cones by local officers. Two such officers stood awaiting the team's arrival a couple hundred feet from the entrance to the warehouse.

'Agent Grey?' one of the officers called out as the team grew closer. Solomon and Kit were leading the way whilst Lucy, Krysta and Mike fell in behind. 'Agent Grey?' the officer questioned again, waiting for an acknowledgement and receiving a nod of confirmation from Solomon as he came to a halt.

'Special agent in charge Solomon Grey,' Solomon confirmed, flashing his ID. 'This is my team. Agent Johnston here will liaise with you guys and the backup when it arrives. Got to get everything moving.'

'Glad you're here, sir. The name's Officer Jenks,' the officer introduced himself. 'Just to fill you in, we've cordoned off the area, we were just awaiting yourselves and forensics to get here to take over. I've been informed that more of my own officers are on their way to help secure the premises.' Officer Jenks was very polite and was tall, smart and well spoken. His partner looked the opposite, with short, stubby legs and the eyes of an inquisitive child.

'Special agent in charge Kyle Johnston,' Kit interrupted, offering an outstretched hand for Officer Jenks to shake.

'Assistant,' Solomon snapped, stamping down his authority. It was the second time Kyle had butted in this morning. 'Assistant special agent in charge Johnston. Ensure that the area is secure and see to it that forensics find their way to the crime scene, then come find me.' He continued to relay orders. Mike and Lucy were to head up to the offices on the upper floor of the warehouse; there was a fire escape at the front of the building leading up to an entrance. If the office was intact, there may be CCTV or other evidence that they could use piece together events. Although it seemed unlikely for any evidence to have been left behind, Solomon felt somewhat assured by the CCTV cameras on each corner of the outside of the building. Krysta was given orders to accompany Solomon into the building to check out the scene. Solomons' in-depth briefing earlier that morning about what they expected to find deterred her somewhat.

'Me and you, Mikey baby!' Lucy howled as she and Mike headed off to carry out their observations.

'Party time,' Mike smiled ironically and rubbed his hands together, before chasing after Lucy who had marched on ahead.

Whereas Mike and Lucy had accepted their assignments as gospel, Krysta could tell that Kyle had gotten too used to having things his own way. *The dick does not like taking orders.* Despite his discontentment however, Kyle set to his task with the two officers in tow, leaving Krysta and Solomon to head over to the main entrance of the warehouse.

The well-maintained exterior of the building gave no indication to what Krysta and Solomon would walk into. The feeling of dread that had plagued Krysta on the helicopter ride quickly returned as she and Solomon donned protective feet covers and stepped into the building's darkened interior. The cavernous expanse was dimly lit and damp, with the scent of rotting wood initially filling the air. The roof was dripping into stagnant puddles on the floor. The seemingly endless rows of metal racking, brimming with packing crates and barrels, were fathomless. One or two flickering LED lights hung above their heads, suspended in an industrial manner from the high ceiling. Their wires disappeared into the darkness above, and they provided such inadequate light that the two detectives pulled out their flashlights to see the dirt ridden floor laid out before them. Officially, the warehouse was used to store scrap metal: condemned machinery, automotive parts and such like. Unofficially, it was suspected that this building - along with many more like it - was used as a mass store of narcotics, weaponry and maybe even people, waiting to be smuggled in or out of the country. Krysta pictured some of the crates she saw being used for transporting young girls as she continued to move from row to row following Solomon's lead. The thought made her ill. How many girls would survive being boxed up in a place like this long enough to even dream of being sold off into one of Markovic's prostitution rings? *What is that smell?* As they pressed onward, an overwhelming odour overcame the dank smell of rotten wood. It was the pungent, but unmistakable, stench of death.

'We're close now,' Solomon announced the obvious, acknowledging the foul odour that had engulphed the air.

'No shit!' Krysta exclaimed, covering her nose and mouth with her sleeve and trying desperately to breathe in any molecule of fresh air that remained.

'That fucking reeks!' sounded an all-too-familiar voice through the darkness behind them. Krysta turned to see Kyle enter the light. As he approached, he took out a handkerchief from his jacket pocket to cover his nose and mouth to help withstand the sudden effluvium. They were nearing the rear of the building and the closer they got, the more intense the feeling of dread in the pit of Krysta's stomach became. Kyle's sudden lack of colour amused her slightly, but she had to admit that she too was struggling with the stench.

'Solomon?' Lucy's words crackled over their earpieces. 'It's a bust up here boss. Computers are trashed, everywhere is a mess. Looks like punk kids have been fucking about up here, graffiti everywhere.'

'Okay, Luce,' Solomon replied, massaging his temples. 'Grab a couple evidence bags and get as much as you can. Maybe Davenport can work her magic on the drives – oh, use gloves.'

'Copy that boss. Hey, looks like the rest of the cavalry has arrived as well. C.S.I and a few more squad cars just pulled up,' Lucy informed them. Krysta watched Kyle's lip quiver, knowing that he wanted to add his ten cents at that point. Evidently, he thought better of it, as he and Solomon caught each other's eyes. Krysta could imagine that the un-voiced conversation they had within that one glance had put Kit right in his place. He returned to quivering with his handkerchief. The three of them continued to the end of the aisle, none of them even remotely prepared for the scene that their eyes would soon rest upon.

Fear. A desperate, crippling sense of horror. The despair that there was even someone in this world capable of such an act possessed Krysta like a demon. She tried to take it all in. The scene, the smell, the sounds; all were incongruous to anything she had ever laid eyes upon before. It was her job to investigate and process the crime scene. She had been trained to cope with death, to analyse the scene of a homicide, to imagine and map out how the atrocity occurred, putting herself into the shoes of the perp. But this - this was different. Her immediate instincts were conflicted between fight or flight. On one hand, she felt the overwhelming urge to vomit. Her other instinct was to flee - to hold nothing back and to run as far away as fast as she possibly could. She had never laid eyes on anything so horrific, and her mind seemed to be rejecting the images, preventing her training from kicking in.

Twelve, she counted. At least it must have been to begin with. Twelve lengths of barbed wire hung down from the steel rafters above, each wrapping around a pair of wrists and dangling the bodies belonging to them roughly eight feet off the ground. Some of the victims had been mauled to such a degree that it was hard to tell whether they were male or female. Krysta guessed that there was a mixture of both here. The twelfth in the row was definitely a woman. Stripped of any clothing, her naked corpse hung, dried blood clinging to every inch of her skin. Her head had been removed, torn asunder, and now laid on ground beneath her own feet. Between her eyes, there was some sort of bone or other sharp object protruding from her skull. Taking a more in-depth look, Krysta thought that it could be a shaft of wood. Unable to look at this individual for any longer, she stifled a gag as she continued down the line. She caught a glimpse of one poor soul three places from the end. With his bloodied hands strung up over his head, the wire securing them appeared to have cut into his skin, sliced through flesh and run flush with bone. Blood had dried on his arms and shoulders where it had run freely from his wrists. His head drooped slightly, but Krysta could see the pain in his face. His right eye was frozen open and his left was nothing but an empty socket. His upper chest had been burned. The cracked, blackened skin almost formed the shape of handprints. Krysta was beginning to examine the marking, but her attention was suddenly taken by something else. His abdomen had been slashed open, leaving his bowels overhanging his mid-rift. Thick, almost black, coagulated blood gathered on the ends of his intestines, hovering above a pool of blood and bile on the ground.

That was enough. She could take no more for now. Turning away in disgust, she looked towards Solomon for some sort of comfort, but she could barely get her words out.

'What... the... fuck...?' she breathed, stumbling slightly in the poor lighting and having to reach out for support. Solomon quickly caught her.

'Let's get out of here. We need to get some fresh air and brief the C.S.I,' Solomon insisted. Krysta happily obeyed. She turned to ask Kyle if he was coming with them. However, it seemed the scene had most definitely been too much for his weak stomach. He had already left the two of them behind.

Condensation dripped from the bottle as she took another sip. Krysta sat perched on the edge of an open boot of one of the NYPD's S.U.V.'s, trying to regain her focus and calm herself. Her palms were clammy and her brow was caped in a cool sweat. She had opened her mind to a place darker than she could have ever imagined and she was struggling to let the light back in. Solomon had stayed with her momentarily before leaving her to recuperate. He was now giving out his instruction to the newly arrived officers on site. It was his investigation after all. He had re-entered the building with the crime scene investigation team, leading them to the centre of this hell so that they could carry out their work before he would continue to investigate the remainder of the building with some of the other officers. Stood outside with Krysta were a couple of NYPD officers. One, a smarmy looking character whose badge gave his name as Seif, had slicked black hair that he was constantly touching to check that it hadn't fallen out of place. He would look over to Krysta every now and again with a Cheshire-cat grin on his face. She took little notice however, still trying to calm her nerves to get back to the job in hand. The second officer stood next to the first, still and unflinching. His badge read REEVES and Krysta's first impressions told her that he took the job more seriously than his creepy counterpart. Starting to feel more like herself, Krysta screwed the lid back onto the bottle of water she had been cradling. Seeing the first officer's dissident behaviour at such a fragile crime scene, she considered putting him in his place but thought better of it. As she stood, the shrill ring of a cell phone cut through the air.

'Malik,' the officer stated, answering the call. Straightening herself out, she headed toward the two officers. Upon seeing her walking towards him, Officer Seif turned and began to walk away, continuing his conversation.

Krysta had every intention of questioning them on their business and telling the smug one to have some respect, but before she could say a word her own phone vibrated. Taking it out of her pocket, she opened and read the message that had come through from an unknown contact. It simply read *Solomon*. Unnerved, she forgot altogether about pulling Seif and Reeves up for their insolence and attempted to get hold of Solomon on the radio.

'Hey, Solomon. Everything alright in there?' Krysta received nothing but static by way of reply. Trying again, she took a few steps towards the warehouse. This time she could hear a whistling in amongst the static, something familiar. *What is that? I recognise that tune.* She tried to think of what it was. 'Lucy, Mike? Either of you have eyes on Solomon?'

Before either of her teammates had the chance to answer, the piercing sound of a gunshot vibrated from inside the entrance to the building. The sound snared everyone's attention and the two officers began to run towards the building alongside her. A second shot fired, followed quickly by a third and, as though the shots were merely from a starting pistol at a race, everyone outside darted towards the entrance of the building, whilst a chorus of 'Shots fired!' rang out over the coms.

Crossing the threshold into the building's cavernous interior, Krysta saw Kyle hurriedly relaying instructions to a group of officers; he was sending them to aid the C.S.I team.

'Kyle, where are they?' she panicked.

'Fuck knows, Krys,' He hastily replied. His alarm was evident; he was clearly shaken to the core and was clearly not coping under the pressure. 'Krysta, you two,' he beckoned pointing to officers Seif and Reeves, who had entered the building alongside her. 'With me. Now.'

Ready to throw themselves into the fray, the three obeyed their orders. The four of them swiftly headed into the industrial labyrinth, rushing aimlessly into its depths.

There was little indication of where they needed to go, and the lack of sufficient lighting made the situation worse. It wasn't until the sound of another gunshot resonated throughout the building that they had a heading. Commotion began to fill the air. It was a delicate operation, but it was supposed to be simple: investigate the crime scene and let C.S.I and forensics do their job. It was never meant to turn into a shoot-out. *What the fuck is going on?* Krysta and her newfound team darted in and out of rows of crates and racking, their firearms at the ready as the gunshots continued. As she turned yet another corner in the confounding warren of wood and steel, she noticed that Kyle was no longer running with them.

'Kyle?' she called, wondering where the hell he was. She slowed and looked behind herself to check that he hadn't fallen behind. Confirming that this wasn't the case, she looked back round only to find herself alone, the other officers lost from sight. 'What...?' she questioned as she stopped at the end of an aisle. It didn't make sense. How could she have lost them all? They had all been running together. She stood for a moment, looking up and down the darkened rows of box laden racking. A strange sensation washed over her; she could swear that the lights were dimming further, the darkness closing in on her. A silence fell upon the warehouse as the distant sound of footsteps faded away. She would have sworn she had lost her hearing, if not for the sound of her own rapid breathing piercing the void.

'Kyle?' Krysta shouted again, louder and more desperate this time. 'Solomon?' She received no replies. As she stood, stumped, unsure of which direction she should be heading in, she heard the whistling again. It was the same tune as before, the one she had recognised. It emanated through the darkness. It was behind – no - in front of her. The sound moved quicker than Krysta's legs could respond. She power-walked, lost in the black. Now, she looked down the path to her right and her heart sunk with a devastating weight. An unfamiliar, darkened figure stood part way down the aisle, a chilling phantasm. The figure's eyes glowed a wicked red, two fiery doorways to damnation, taking Krysta's breath away. She quickly fumbled for her flashlight, her hands trembling madly. She managed to click it on, shining the ray of light down the aisle to see who it was. But the figure had vanished from sight.

Panicking, she shined her light a full three hundred and sixty degrees around her. Suddenly, she heard a crash up ahead. As she moved towards the noise, she was relieved to see Kyle and the two officers dart out of an adjoining area, all heading in the same direction. They all reached the end of the row and halted in their tracks. Debris was scattered all over the floor, from obliterated pallet boxes to unidentifiable objects. A path of destruction lay before them. Krysta could hear the calls of familiar voices at its end, but the lingering debris in the air meant she couldn't see who it was or where they were. Quickly moving on, she began scrambling over and around the shattered obstacles that filled her path, followed by the others. Krysta, Kyle and the two officers stopped dead at the sound of a voice.

'Enforcers of the law! You do entertain me. You bend and break as easily as vermin.'

The voice was that of a man. It was deep and overflowing with malice. There wasn't an ounce of fear in his words, simply hatred. *We need to get closer.* Signalling to the others, she pushed on. The voice had sounded from just beyond the end of the aisle. They were close. Just as they reached the precipice, however, she heard the familiar voice of Solomon.

'Put him down!' he cried. A fear plagued his voice, the words trembling as the desperate command left his lips.

Krysta knew it was Solomon, but she had never heard him sound so afraid. *I'm coming Solomon.* She moved onwards. Ten feet to the end. Five, three. The sickening sound of a snap echoed through the warehouse. A scream left Krysta's mouth as the lifeless body of a police officer came hurtling across the end of the aisle, flying right across Krysta's path and smashing against the steel pillar of the racking to her right. Terrified and in awe of the human projectile soaring in front of her, Krysta stopped. She closed her eyes for a split second and took in a deep breath. Giving the signal to move in, she navigated the corner and laid eyes on their attacker.

It's gotta be him. Krysta recognised the mammoth of a man that stood before them from the briefing earlier that morning. Her command of 'Freeze!' backed up by her comrade's shouts of 'Police! Get down on the ground!' meant nothing to him. The man turned to look Krysta in the eye and laughed. He stood taller than any person she had ever seen. He wore huge black boots and dark coloured pants. A black tank top accentuated his broadened arms, but her attention was drawn to his face. Jet black hair, spiked up in a quiff, sat upon his head and a deep scar ran from his hair line down to his chin. His beady eyes unnerved her as they held a dark, fiery tint that appeared to glow in the dimly lit room.

'Solomon,' Kyle gasped from beside Krysta as he spotted his superior, beaten, sitting helplessly on the floor, slumped against a box.

Krysta instinctively pulled out her firearm at the sorry sight of Solomon, aimed it at the gargantuan stranger and pulled the trigger. Solomon was alive, but she could see from where she stood that he was wounded and in need of desperate medical attention. Her bullet flew true and hit the scarred stranger in the chest, piercing his flesh. Beside her, Kyle also fired, his bullet hitting the attacker in the shoulder. Neither hit seeming to bother him, the man simply stood staring at the pair of them as though he were measuring them up. The red tint in his eyes seemed to flash and glow brighter. His scar too seemed to begin to glow, as if his veins were full of hot lava and he was about to erupt.

Krysta felt as though the earth had stopped spinning. Mere seconds passed, yet the stranger moved so quickly there was nothing she could have done. A look of pure rage flashed across his face as he turned to grasp one of the large wooden crates that stood behind him. He moved with such unnatural speed that the following shots by Krysta, Kyle and the NYPD officers seemed to either miss completely or simply get absorbed by his sheer enormity. He clutched the crate, swung round and launched it with some ease towards Krysta. Frozen, there was nothing she could do but wait for the impact. Within a couple of seconds, the wood would smash against her, knocking her backward and causing her head to smash against the concrete flooring. She would bleed and the life behind her eyes would dim. She would not get to take part in the ending of this episode, rather, her light would fade from the world.

Having accepted her fate, Krysta felt a sudden force throw her backwards, out of the projectiles path. Krysta was thrown to the floor. She heard the impact of the crate as she flew backwards through the air, the wood shattering into splinters against her saviour. Hitting the ground with an almighty thud and bashing her head on the dirt ridden concrete, a pain instantly began shooting up and down her body. She mustered the strength to open her eyes. A man stood where she had just moments ago; he had appeared just as quickly as her attacker had managed to grab and throw the box, throwing himself into the fray and launching Krysta out of harm's way.

As the light grew dimmer and she struggled to remain conscious, Krysta allowed the heaviness to consume her eyelids but could still hear the commotion. Using all her might to focus on the sounds, she heard more gunshots fire. The voice of the attacker was the last thing she heard before losing consciousness completely; it was the mightiest of roars.

'Adam!'

5

Seamus McCarthy

He couldn't wait to get out of the station and answer a call. Seamus was so eager that he took the first call that came in before even waiting to hear what it was. Much to his own surprise as everyone else's, he even insisted on taking the cadet with him. The call regarded a straightforward domestic disturbance, but it would serve as good practice for Lorenzo, the young rookie. Short and stocky, Samuel Lorenzo carried an ever-present confidence with him, an inherent cocky nature that resulted in a mixture of first impressions amongst his colleagues. Seamus knew the boy's personality had clashed with some of the more experienced officers, however, he saw a strong and determined individual. His assumed front was clearly nothing more than a mechanism to attempt to fit in. He seemed like a young man full of character, with the will to do right and the self-assurance to remain steadfast in his principles. He would be an officer of the law who hopefully, with a little guidance, wouldn't be seduced by the city's dark and corruptive depths. Most importantly to Seamus, the cadet was a New Yorker, born and bred. The lad had a softly bronzed complexion and an honest rounded face. Hardened by his upbringing in the urban jungle, he could hold his own. However, he was still to master the poker face. His expression foretold his thoughts and so he could never hold a bluff.

'How come we took the first call, sir?' Lorenzo enquired. 'Wasn't there nothing more important for us top dogs to be taking on?'

'Every call is important, Sam. We're in a big city - and she never sleeps.' He hoped that this response would quell Sam's hunger for heroics. Thankfully it seemed to do the trick. The last few days had been chaotic to say the least, and he wasn't up for any kiddie stuff today. The whole department was on high alert as a manhunt for an individual that his fellow officers referred to as 'The Beast', and his suspected accomplice 'Adam', was still ongoing. Two of his colleagues had died that day. Officers Jenks and Chen. Two upstanding keepers of the peace, their lives had been snuffed out in an instant by some sort of gargantuan abomination - a behemoth with inhuman traits, if Malik's words were to be taken seriously. Seamus had spent the past few days torn by his emotions. He felt angry that there was someone like that loose in his city, and was plagued with guilt for not being one of the officers on the scene. If there had been more, could they have been a force of intimidation for The Beast? To add insult to injury, the day had also brought death into his kids' lives. A fire had broken out at their university, claiming the life of a professor. The combination of both incidents had forced Seamus' hand in taking the first call out available. The city was going mad.

'Just around this corner boss,' Sam stated as they approached their destination on the outskirts of the city.

Run down and derelict buildings made up the street. Even the few inhabited buildings looked in dire need of an injection of funding for repair and refurbishment. The pavements were littered with rubbish and deserted possessions. An elderly couple, sat out on deck chairs, watched the two officers, unblinking, as they drove slowly along the road and pulled up outside the address of the disturbance. The building looked to be uninhabited at first glance. Nevertheless, on the front steps sat a group of young boys, seemingly minding their own business.

'Ah shit! It's the pigs!' barked a dishevelled woman from across the street. 'Best not be botherin' them kids. They aint done shit yet here you are again!' she spat as she stood, scratching at her crotch through her night gown like a dog with fleas.

'Just responding to a call about a disturbance ma'am,' Sam nodded at the woman as he exited the vehicle, attempting to mask his disgust at her appearance but failing miserably. *Rookie mistake. She aint gonna like being called ma'am.* Seamus climbed out of the squad car. Of course, Seamus was right, but the cadet had to learn. The woman spat some more foul language at Lorenzo, who had now lost all colour in his face. *At least he knows better than to argue back.* Seamus chuckled at the cadets' dumbfounded expression.

'C'mon, Lorenzo,' Seamus beckoned, saving the young officer from any further verbal abuse. Their appointment did in fact appear to be with the gang of kids, as Seamus let his eyes rest on a familiar face. 'Smithy. What the hell are you doing here?' Seamus recognized at least one of the four boys. The others sat with their heads down, or with their caps preventing him from making out their faces. The teen, Carl Smith, known more as 'Smithy', was notably the runt of the pack. Smithy had had previous run-ins with the law, allowing Seamus to have developed a rapport of sorts with the boy. As the son to an abusive drunk and an ever-absent mother, Smithy had practically grown up on the streets, rarely attending school and getting into a number of difficult altercations. Seamus felt sorry for the kid for having such a rough start to life. Still, the law was the law.

''Sup, 'Carthy,' Smithy said, stepping toward the officers with a swagger. He stood as bold as brass before Seamus and Lorenzo in his worn-out pumps, track suit bottoms and a discoloured vest that looked as though it had been attacked by moths. 'Who's the chump?' he asked, nodding towards Lorenzo before glancing back at his comrades with a smirk.

'Officer Sam Lorenzo,' Seamus announced, 'meet Carl Smith. Smithy,' Seamus gestured towards the boy. 'And who else is here, Smithy?' He glanced about the pack again, but still couldn't recognise any of the others, who continued to shield their faces from view.

'Oh, the crew,' Smithy straightened up. 'T-Bird - I mean Man – I mean, uhh, Bird Man and T-Dog. Shit!' Smithy slipped up on his introductions and instantly had the attention of the hyenas behind him. Suddenly, all the confidence he initially exuded drained from his face.

'Smithy sit the fuck down,' one of the lads reacted to Smithy's blunder, keeping his cap pulled tort over his face. He clearly felt the need to take charge, or at least stem the flow of information from Smithy's flapping tongue. He wore a black New York baseball cap, a clean white top, a new looking leather jacket and plenty of visible jewellery on his hands and around his neck. He was wearing expensive jeans and a brand-new pair of top-of-the-range sneakers. Seamus now recognised the boy and instantly felt disturbed, as this was not someone that Carl should be hanging around with.

'Dante,' he said, crossing his arms in disappointment and stamping down his authority on the situation before there was any chance of the kid contesting.

'Look, pig,' Dante said with a hint of sarcasm. 'We aint done shit before you start with all that. In fact, it was us called you, 'n here you come runnin' along like good little pigs.' He stood up, getting as close to Seamus and Sam as possible without literally stepping on their toes. The other two continued to sit on the steps at the entrance of the building, seemingly uncaring of whatever else was happening around them.

'Wasting police time is a serious offence, Dante.' Seamus ignored the attempt at intimidation. It was an empty threat, he knew that. This kid was way too streetwise to be intimidated by such a remark. Seamus had said it more for the trailing pack than anything else.

'Whoa pig, easy!' Dante responded. 'Shit went down here 'other day 'n we figured you'd like to know,' he pointed up at the apartment building. 'Some fighting or summit', all hell by sounds of it and now...' he paused and smiled. Tapping his nose with his index finger as if to indicate he would say no more, he stood waiting with a smug look on his face.

'And now... what?' Sam was growing impatient. Seamus could see that biting his tongue was taking its toll on the young officer.

'This is solid intel, bruh.' Dante grinned. 'Shit's expensive.'

'We could just take you and your buddies downtown. How's that sound?' Seamus retorted, this time smiling sarcastically towards Dante. The kid conceded defeat and rolled his eyes. He began to explain that they'd seen a body inside the building, beaten, bloodied and burnt. Seamus groaned inwardly at the revelation. After handing over the information and acknowledging that he was not going to get anything out of this exchange, Dante and his followers rapidly made an exit, clearly not interested in hanging around to answer any more questions. As they took off up the street with Smithy straggling behind, Seamus and Lorenzo were left to investigate.

The main door was wedged partially open, probably just enough for the kids to have squeezed through. Seamus gave it a push but there was a surprising resistance. Pushing again, harder this time, the door opened a couple of inches more. A mass of dust and debris fell from the ceiling, filling the entrance with a dusty cloud. *What the hell?* He'd seen some run-down housing in his time, but this was as if a demolition crew had started work and abandoned the job. Decisively, he gave the door one last push to create a gap big enough for the two of them to easily get through. As they entered, Seamus realised why the door had been so difficult to open. Broken chunks of plaster and obliterated furniture were piled up behind it.

'Place is a mess, sir,' Lorenzo pointed out, 'Maybe we should call in a works crew or something?'

Seamus raised his hand dismissively as he stepped further into the hallway. He was transfixed by the state of the building and captivated by the level of destruction. He was amazed it was even still standing. Huge, gaping holes had been knocked out of the dry wall, there was a gap in the ceiling allowing him to see straight up into one of the apartments above. The water pipes looked to have been torn out of the floor and were leaking stale water all over the place. What little working lights remained flickered eerily.

'Kids said first floor hallway, yeah?' Seamus checked, continuing to step cautiously further down the hallway towards the staircase at the end.

'Er, yeah...' Lorenzo replied, distracted as he stepped over a pile of unidentifiable debris scattered in what looked like rat droppings. Aware his reluctance was pointless, he gave in and joined his partner at the foot of the stairs. The pair of them began to ascend cautiously.

'So, what's up with the Dante kid? Bad news?' he asked.

'Bad as they come at that age,' Seamus replied. 'Caught running drugs, guns... you name it. Got away with only a slap on the wrist by snitching on his boss...' Seamus trailed off. As they reached the top of the stairs, he halted. His heart felt as if it had skipped a beat or two. He noticed a sudden cold chill flash down his spine as he laid eyes on the body.

'Holy shit, dude!' Sam exclaimed upon seeing the body for himself. 'D'you think he's alive?'

Seamus didn't answer the question. Instead, he rushed over to the body as quickly as he could while watching where he was stepping. The man, as Seamus confirmed once he was up close, looked to have been beaten to death. Lifeless and half naked, he lay in a foetal position. His arm, face and torso appeared burnt. *Looks to have been in a fire, but no signs of one happening here.* Seamus was perplexed. More surprising than the burns was where the victim lay. He was positioned on his side, partially inside one of the walls as if he had been forced into it. Splinters of wood and bits of spackle surrounded him. Seamus was about to give Lorenzo the order to call in a homicide when he noticed a small degree of movement beneath the man's charred exterior. Watching closer, Seamus observed as his chest rose and fell, indicating life.

'Call it in Sam!' Seamus exclaimed. 'We need an ambulance – and back-up!'

For the extent of the journey to the hospital, Lorenzo asked incessant questions about the man they had found - unbelievably - alive.

'How'd he get there? What had happened to him?' he quizzed as Seamus drove. Seamus, however, had a different question on his mind. It was one that he couldn't shake, despite the din from his garrulous partner. *Another fire... could he be connected to the one at NYU?* Despite little evidence linking the two events other than the involvement of fire, the thought lingered in the back of Seamus' mind until they pulled up in the hospital parking lot. He had a feeling – and not a good one.

He knew that it would only be a fleeting encounter. She would no doubt have her hands full and he too had little time to spare whilst the victim was undergoing initial examination in the Emergency Room. Regardless, he had to see her. Seamus knew she'd be somewhere on the emergency ward. She had worked through the night on a double shift and would soon be heading home, but hopefully he would catch her. Attempting to keep out of the way of the chaotic doctor-patient traffic, he spotted Moira across the blue and white tiled floor, sat next to a desk on the far side of one of the ward. Despite the weary expression on her face, she still radiated beauty just as much as she had on the day he first laid eyes on her. She had tied her dark, curly hair up out of the way, but a few unruly strands had broken free and lay by the side of her face. Stood in her sky-blue nurses' scrubs, she was reading through some notes with a doctor beside her. Seamus swiftly made his way across the room towards her. As he approached, she looked up from the paperwork and spotted him. A gleaming smile spread across her face, brightening her exhausted countenance.

'Hey!' she said, wrapping her arms around him, expressing a worn-out sigh as she held him tightly. The world fell away for an instant as she kissed him, before it came rushing back as chaotic as ever. 'Not that I'm not glad to see you, but why are you here? Is everything alright?' she asked, curious as to the reason for Seamus' presence.

'Found a body - a guy,' he answered. He had to keep reminding himself that the victim was alive. It just seemed so unbelievable. 'He was in a bad way – tons of burns.'

That's when he saw it. Moira would always get this glint in her eyes when she knew something that had perhaps escaped him.

'What?' he asked. 'What do you know?'

'Not much, hon,' she replied with a shrug. 'I think Doctor Carson is seeing to the burn victim. You'd be best talking to him once he's finished his initial examination.'

'Thanks, hon,' Seamus replied. 'I'll go see if I can find him. See you at home.' He kissed her softly on the forehead before leaving to find Lorenzo and the doctor.

Hunting down Doctor Carson was a task in and of itself. He had evidently finished his preliminary examination by the time Seamus had found Lorenzo and the victim. Seamus enquired with a young nurse at the reception desk, who informed him that the doctor had moved onto another patient. It took Seamus some time to track him down.

'Doctor Carson!' Seamus exclaimed, spotting a man that looked akin to the description the ward receptionist had kindly given him. He was moving briskly down a corridor as Seamus continued to call his name. Seamus had to almost sprint to catch up to him before he disappeared around a corner. Thankfully, the doctor stopped and turned to see whom it was calling his name repeatedly.

'Can I help you?' the doctor asked as Seamus caught up to him.

'Doctor Carson,' Seamus affirmed. 'I'm officer McCarthy. I'm one of the officers that found your John Doe, the burn victim that's just arrived on the ER,' he explained. 'I wanted to speak with you to see if your preliminary examination had revealed anything that will help us explain what happened to him, or who he might be?'

The doctor proceeded to explain his initial findings. Unfortunately, they did not quell the unrelenting desire for confirmation of the man's involvement in the university fire that Seamus had hoped for. Instead, his discoveries presented more questions. The subject had suffered severe injuries, including broken bones and deep lacerations to his torso and arms. He had suffered third and fourth degree burns to his back, arms and face.

'His burns aren't consistent with those of being caught in a blaze,' the doctor went on. 'They're more consistent with pressure burns, the likes of which you'd get if you'd had an iron pressed against your skin. If I had to make a presumption, I would say that you're certainly looking for a perpetrator in this case – that is, someone else has caused these burns. The question would be the tool used to implement the burns. They cover roughly a quarter of his exterior. Whatever it was, it would have had to have been excruciatingly hot to cause trauma such as this.' Doctor Carson's diagnosis continued. The man was wearing only a pair of torn pants and he carried no form of identification. 'He does have a tattoo,' he revealed. 'Sadly, at present it is indistinguishable due to the damage he has sustained. I hope I've been of some assistance officer, but I'm afraid I really have got to get on now,' the doctor confessed as he began to back away from Seamus. 'What I will say, is that he is quite something, your John Doe,' Seamus wasn't quite sure what the doctor was suggesting. His expression must have given away his thought process. 'I'm amazed he's still alive,' were Doctor Carson's final words as he walked away to continue his rounds.

Well by the sounds of things this guy isn't going anywhere for a few days. He's certainly not going to be answering any questions. It was time for Seamus and Lorenzo to head back to the station, leaving two officers to guard the poor bastard as he was moved from the Emergency Room to a private one. Seamus briefed the medical staff and hospital security that nobody else should be allowed access to him, and that they were to report any changes regarding his condition to the station.

The journey back to the station was swift. Lorenzo had very little to say, which was unusual considering the morning that they'd just had. Seamus had half expected to have his ear chewed off. In fact, unlike the journey to the hospital, he had sort of hoped for it this time; it would have been a welcome distraction from his own thoughts. The doctor's examination had not given him piece of mind with regards to any connection to the fire at NYU. Chillingly, his son had been the second-to-last person to see the professor on the day of the fire. The professor had had a meeting with an unknown woman that morning, according to his son. He was found burned alive in his office, with no identifiable incendiaries about his person. The fire department even suggested that spontaneous combustion due to some sort of technological device in his pocket was a possibility. Now, they had been given another burn victim. Found in similar circumstances, there was little to suggest that the two weren't linked in some way. The whole ordeal simply unnerved Seamus.

Sam Lorenzo soon perked up once they arrived back at the station. He couldn't wait to offload to Sergeant McCabe, Officer Reeves and Officer Seif about the morning's activities. After being told to show some respect to the victim, Lorenzo continued to relay the events with a little less excitement. Seamus was just glad that the burned man was a new topic for them all to discuss, finally shutting Malik up about the warehouse.

'Sounds like you had a hell of a morning,' Malik said, following Seamus to a desk, standing over him as he began to write out the report for the incident. 'Been a crazy week,' he admitted, with a sort of half-laugh. Seamus tried to concentrate on what he was writing so that he didn't forget any details, but Malik appeared to be deeply intrigued by the John Doe.

'He's at Lower Manhattan Hospital,' Seamus said, reluctantly answering one of Malik's endless reel of questions. 'We're just gonna have to wait and see if he wakes up,' he continued.

'Yeah...' Malik seemed to at least half accept Seamus' response, turning an apple in his hand as though he were physically mulling it all over. 'Curious this turning up same week as those warehouse guys though, don't you think?'

The thought had crossed my mind. Seamus didn't respond, continuing to bury himself in the paperwork before him.

6

Adam

'Half a pound of tuppenny rice, half a pound of treacle.'

That whistling. He had heard it before so many times – yet, at this moment, the tune resonated in his mind. It was a tune that his brother enjoyed whistling. That simple fact stoked the burning rage that currently swelled within him. His eye lids were heavy. *How long?* How long had he been in this state? The light that managed to pierce through the cracks blazed against his eyes, an open flame. Everything was bright, white and painful. God, it was so painful.

He could feel the regenerative powers within him taking effect. Like the oceans tide clearing a beach, his body was beginning to wash away the chaos that had encased him. Deep inside, he could sense his cells exploding back into life. Inflammation reducing, fractures fusing together. The soft, newly formed bones ossified and compacted, new cartilage replaced old, pulsating the feeling of strength throughout his being. Myogenesis disseminated outward from his core to every one of his extremities. Muscle fibres overlapped, weaved and inter-twinned, growing stronger by the second. Processes that would naturally take months or years were completed in minutes. It was time to move.

His eyesight had returned. The small room he occupied was intended for one patient, he presumed. The respiratory machine whirred noisily, and the cardiac monitor beeped so loudly he thought his ear drums would burst. The sound of the people outside of the room felt just as deafening as his hearing slowly adjusted, his senses still completely out of whack. He was accustomed to the sensory overload that often accompanied what he had come to call a 'rebirth' - but the uncertainty of how long he had been out for panicked him slightly. Disrobing, tearing the mask from his face and the cannulas from his arms and hands, he sat up on the bed. More noises began to wail as the monitors became aware that he had detached himself. Slightly disorientated, he remained still for a moment to try and gain his bearings.

Someone is coming.

He glanced toward the door. He could see the silhouettes of two police officers through the glass – one on each side. Having pushed himself off the bed, his legs would not hold him and he fell to the floor with an almighty thud. He landed with such force that his knee and hands caused cracks in the flooring, leaving a permanent imprint of where he knelt.

'Oh my god.' A voice sounded behind him. 'Someone page Doctor Carson!' cried the nurse that stood in the now open doorway. He seemed dumbfounded by Adam's current position. Stood in the entrance, he stared at him with a look of utter disbelief on his face. 'How could you - your injuries - you were too...' he stuttered.

'Please...' Adam croaked, barely able to his words out. Everything still felt fragile. 'Please, stay ba-'

'What's your name?' the nurse interrupted, stepping toward Adam hesitantly. 'Do you know where you are?'

Enough with the questions. Adam needed to get out of here. He did not belong here.

'The doctor will be on his way,' the nurse informed, looking unsure as Adam began scrambling his energy together to stand. 'Maybe we should try and get you back onto the bed.'

'Stay where you are,' another voice announced. 'Get him back up on the bed. He shouldn't be up and about.' It was a police officer. Clearly Adam had drawn some attention to himself this time, and it was evident that he was not free to leave They probably had questions for him. *Shit*. They would have endless questions that he would not be able to give them answers to. He rose to his feet, feeling a flourish of strength envelope him. The charred and dead skin that covered a large portion of his body just moments ago began to fall away, revealing new and healthy flesh. Both the onlooking nurse and officer were gobsmacked as Adam shed his skin like a snake.

'Okay... let's get you back onto the bed,' announced the police officer, stepping toward Adam.

'No, please. I said stay- ' but before Adam could finish what he wanted to say, the officer tried to grab him by the arm. It was an automatic reaction, one that filled his heart with sorrow and he couldn't stop it. The instant the officer touched his arm, Adam pushed him away. Still feeling bewildered, unable to control the amount of force exerted onto the officer, Adam's push caused him to launch backward. He felt the man's sternum crack at the touch and then he was gone, propelled against the wall, crashing through and landing lifelessly in the hallway beyond. The nurse fled the room in fear and others rushed to aid the officer. Adam stepped through the newly formed hole in the wall and looked down upon the man he had unintentionally wounded.

'I... I'm sorry,' he voiced in a display of penitence. *I have to go.*

The hallway and surrounding wards were buzzing with people and Adam could not afford any more accidents. He glanced about the signs and lights until he found the stairwell that would lead him to freedom. Very aware of his only clothes being a hospital gown, he began compelling himself, one foot in front of the other, towards the door to the stairwell. As he moved forward, his momentum grew to the point where he did not know if he could stop. Clumsily, he flew into the door of the stairwell, taking it clean off its hinges and sending it smashing against the adjacent wall. As splinters of the door scattered, Adam began his ascent up the stairs towards the roof. He could hear the fear in the voices of hospital staff and patients alike as they called out for help and security. He continued his stumbling attempt to reach the top of the stairs, foundering at regular intervals like a lame horse.

He stopped. A single set of steps now stood between him and the roof. He could hear them below, in the stairwell and on different floors. Enforcers of the law, called to capture and detain – probably the ones from outside his hospital room. Adam hesitated for a fraction of a second. He allowed the guilt of his actions to wash over him. Not just recent ones, but those as far back as he could recall. But he couldn't help thinking that handing himself over to them would do them no good; it would only cause as many - if not more - problems for them. They wouldn't understand. They could not understand. *This is best.* He resumed his stride, taking the remaining steps two at a time, and burst through the fire exit at the top of the building.

It was not quite midday and so the sun hadn't yet reached its peak. The light was blinding for an instant, but the warmth of the suns' rays rejuvenated him as they ran down the length of his body. Blinking repeatedly, he turned his eyes upwards at the bright blue sky above. He reached out at the beams of light and allowed them to dance upon his fingertips before clenching his fist. Feeling his strength swell within him, he proceeded to step toward the boundary of the roof. His step became a march, his march a bound and then his bound a leap. He left the confines of the hospital and as he passed through the air, his eyes sharpened and his skin began to flake. Thin barbs developed along his back and arms, thrusting from follicles and evolving into a golden-brown plume. His outstretched feet expanded and tore, his toes merged and hardened, with claws projecting from their tips concluding in four huge developed talons. As he tumbled through the air the metamorphosis completed and two large yellow eyes snapped open, taking in all the surroundings to the most minute of detail. Then, with unfurled wings, Adam took to the sky.

With a wingspan of more than twice the size of a grown man, his white head and razor-sharp hooked beak pierced the cloud above within moments. Higher and higher he soared, and, as the air grew thinner, the weight on his heart grew lighter. For now, at least, he was at peace. He flew slowly to the north west, leaving the city behind, passing over water and land searching for an escape to the wilderness. Adams' naturally enhanced vision was further improved by his current form. From as high as fifty miles up, he could still make out the lay of the land below and, as he began to pass over more mountainous and wooded terrain, he spotted them.

Rolling over in the air, he tucked his huge wings down by his sides and began to dive back down towards the Earth. He was exhilarated by the immense speed at which he began to fall. His heart raced as the air caressed his feathered body, as it flowed swiftly along him. Unblinking, he was in awe as the world grew larger before him and, passing through ice cold cloud, he playfully let out an almighty screech. As the ground grew closer, he stretched out his wings, slowing down his descent. The sheer size of the wings and the wind beneath them caused him to slow at an impressive rate. Mere meters from the plant-enriched floor, he began the change once again. His entire plume of feathers malted and soft cinnamon and grey fur began to sprout in its place. His beak grew shorter and his head grew larger as he developed an elongated snout. A jet-black nose, short, rounded ears and deep amber coloured eyes finished the transformation of his face. Where there had once been talons, now hung softened fur covered paws, a he had a dark grey tail with a black tip. The soil on the ground shuddered as he landed steadfast on all fours.

Charging through the thicket of trees, leaping over rocks and fallen trunks, he had picked up their scent along with that of their prey. If his nose did not betray him, it was the smell of a white-tailed deer; he could practically taste it in the air. The speed at which he travelled meant he had soon caught up with the hunt. The thrill of the chase possessed him. He was known to the pack and so as he overtook the stragglers bringing up the rear, they each howled a welcoming greeting. He howled back himself, before dropping his head and continuing onwards to catch up to the front runners. Bounding over bushes and rocks alike, he caught up to the alpha female who was mere feet behind her target. After exchanging a glance with her, he lunged forward toward the fleeing deer and clipped its hind leg. The deer lost its footing and began to stumble, sending it tumbling to a momentary halt that gave the alpha female the opportunity to sink her teeth in and snap the life from it. Adam ground to a halt and awaited the rest of the pack to catch up. With their meal successfully caught, she waited dutifully for the alpha male to appear; her silky grey-brown fur coat glistening when the sunshine caught it through the trees. The pups showed up. There were three of them; the older one first, followed by the two younger that had fallen behind in the chase. But there was no sign of the alpha. The female looked at Adam. He could see the fear in her pale blue eyes. She howled, a call out for her partner, her protector, yet no response emulated from the forest. Her children all joined in with the call, the sound reverberating throughout the plants and trees, but not one of them could yield a response. And then, Adam did.

It was less of a response, and more of an indication as

to where the Alpha had gotten to. Adam's enhanced hearing had picked up a frightful sound that did not belong in the wild. Dashing off alone, he frantically tracked the alpha male down. He headed toward the whelping that he had heard, and soon caught wind of the Alpha's scent. Clocking prints in the mud, Adam concluded that he must have been stalking something else. He followed the wolf's tracks.

Minutes after commencing his search, he came across the Alpha. It was an impressive beast, a buff coloured tan, grizzled with grey and black. Large for his breed, he was a truly natural dominant force, yet his dark yellow eyes were filled with an uncharacteristic fear. His large, blocky muzzle was caught in a snare trap that had been pulled taut due to his struggle and was cutting deep into his flesh. The snare was made from a fine wire. The more the wolf writhed in its confines, the more the wire drove itself into his skin and the worse his situation became. Despite the pain, the terror in his eyes was not completely due to his injured snout.

The Alpha recoiled as it heard the whispers that carried on the air from the woods ahead. Adam sensed it too. The Alpha was afraid of a predator more fearsome than he. This predator did not use teeth and claws. It did not run and leap and slash and bite. It did not kill for meat and blood and flesh. It killed for sport. *Two of them.* Adam listened to their voices as they drew closer. *Will they kill him or set him free?* The Alpha was no doubt not their intended prey. However, he was a terrifying animal for a mere human to look upon. He contemplated quickly freeing the wolf himself, but ashamedly, curiosity got the better of him. Moving into some nearby bushes and thick foliage, he waited to see how the situation would play out.

The first to enter the clearing was an older man. He was followed closely by his younger counterpart. Adam watched on, just out of sight, taking note of their every action. The younger of the two raised his rifle at the mere sight of the wolf and the elder slowly followed suit. Adam tensed his body, ready to reveal himself and attack should the men grow any more hostile. He had grown to have little faith in man, but every so often they would surprise him with their sensitive natures. He hoped this would be one of those times, picturing the female and her pups awaiting their alpha.

Dressed in thick plaid jackets, the two men were dressed appropriately for their day in the forest. As Adam watched on, the elder relaxed slightly, lowering his weapon and nearing the wolf to investigate while keeping a safe distance. Adam could see wisdom in the man's eyes. He was an experienced hunter. He wore a cap, which he lifted to scratch at his temple as he contemplated his next action. The younger man, clearly fearful of the animal, continued to aim his gun at the defenceless wolf.

'Dad, we should just put him down. We get any closer and he's gonna have our hands off,' the younger man said, his voice quivering slightly. His father continued to ponder, however, raising his gun ever so slightly then lowering the barrel again. His mind was not yet made up. *Set him free.* Adam was hoping that against the odds, they might choose kindness over fear. But the hunters' Delphian mannerisms unnerved him too much.

Adam stepped out of the dense undergrowth and bushes that had concealed him. The mere sight of his enormous frame drew a look of overwhelming fear which took over both men's faces. Adam stood almost as tall as them. He was gigantic, built more like a giant bear than a wolf - but a wolf he was. He sauntered across their path and stood beside the injured alpha in defence. The Alpha attempted to stand beside his ally, but still ensnared he could not.

'Dad?' the panic-stricken son croaked as he stood unmoving, pointing his rifle at Adam. Adam simply remained rooted, resolute and unafraid. He stared intently at the father, his amber yellow eyes attempting to convey a message of peace between species. The man stared right back at the monstrous beast before him. Adam could smell the fear possessing him. *He is going to shoot.* As the father slowly brought his index finger to the tip of the trigger, it was clear in his eyes that he had made his decision. A deep grumbling resonated within Adam, a roar that was slowly making its way through him, urging to be released. He raised his upper lip and bared his sharp canine teeth. Slaver ran from the side of his mouth. The ferocity that had built up inside him found its escape and the deep, prolonged cry that he emitted silenced the world around him. He had tipped the scale.

The fear that had possessed the hunters and urged them to take aim had now consumed them as they ran faster than their legs could hope to take them. They stumbled and tripped, using the occasional tree for balance as they bolted through the undergrowth. With the hunters now fleeing, Adam turned to the trapped wolf. A look of understanding was shared between the two, with the Alpha's yellow eyes glistening under a layer of tears. Adam inspected the snare. Its complex engineering was something he couldn't hope to free the wolf from in his current body. Taking a step back, he shook off his thick fur coat, each individual hair falling to the ground as if they had simply never been attached. Reverted into his human form, Adam stood nude before the trapped wolf. Taking the wire of the snare into his hand, his brute strength took over and he proceeded to snap the mechanisms of the trap to release the animal. Freed, the Alpha stood and stared at Adam unblinkingly, his eyes thanking him for his help. Then, the wolf turned and dashed into the forest to re-join his pack.

He felt a sense of accomplishment. It was a small deed, but he knew from experience that even the smallest of things can have significant effects. The wilderness had been an enjoyable escape, but he felt drawn back to the city of

New York. Changing form once more, Adam took to the skies yet again and headed back toward the place he would call home. At least, it was home for now. He flew slowly, allowing himself to soar and savouring every moment of the peaceful freedom he felt miles above the hectic world below. Yet, as he glided effortlessly through the evening air with the sun melting away behind him, he wondered how she was. He had tried to distract himself from all thoughts of the event, but now, with the blank slate of the earth laid out in front of him, his mind wondered. The crate would have hit her. He'd had no choice but to intervene and push her out of harm's way – his body could take the impact, hers couldn't. He simply hoped that little damage had been done. Had it not been for Brandt catching up with him, he would have checked on her before now. As he descended upon the city, he knew exactly where to go. He flew straight to the apartment building, where he would await reassurance patiently until morning. He gracefully landed onto the rail of the fire escape, clutching it within his talons. He tucked in his wings and began to once again shed his form. His feet and claws drew inward, transforming into stubby, fur covered paws. His feathers shed, floating down to the busy city street below and leaving room for his body to sprout new hair of subtle grey and snowy white. Looking into her window, his own reflection looked back at him. He saw a small, rounded face with a black button nose and tufty ears. His eyes, catching the light, shone with an emerald-green glow.

7

Luciana Rodriguez

Tepid raindrops pounded her umbrella as she dashed through the spring mist towards the entrance of Krysta's apartment building. It had rained all week, as if the world had adopted her current emotional state in an ironic pathetic fallacy. She had missed her friend and colleague; it had been just over a fortnight since the warehouse. They had spoken over the phone, but the ever-persistent feeling of guilt that harassed her since that day had thus far prevented her from visiting. As she reached the door, she hesitated for a moment before finding the courage to reach for the intercom. Before she could press the button for Krysta's apartment, however, she was greeted by a beautiful bouquet of lilies and tulips. A voice sounded from beyond the array of budding plants.

'God – sorry!' There was no need for apology, Lucy had most certainly had worse things shoved in her face. She laughed in response.

'It's fine,' she replied, 'I've been hit with worse.' Lucy wasn't sure why, but something about this faceless stranger simply charmed her.

'In that case, let me get the door for you.' Fumbling for his keys with his one free hand, he finally managed to unlock the door for them both to be able to seek sanctuary from the rain. In an act of chivalry, he signalled for Lucy to go in first with his free hand, the bouquet still covering his face from view.

'Thank you,' Lucy said as she closed her umbrella, shook off some of the rain and headed into the building's foyer. The gentleman followed her inside and finally lowered the arrangement to reveal his sodden face. He shook his head as if he were a wet dog and then ran his fingers through his hair.

'Much better,' he announced before exhibiting a kind, toothy smile.

Wow. Lucy was about to instinctively blurt out her first thought, but for a change her head was quicker than her mouth. The man in front of her wore laced tan coloured boots, midnight blue denim jeans and a dark brown plaid shirt that was buttoned up except for the very top button and tidily tucked into his pants. His hair was fairly short, a crew cut with a subtle mix of dark brown and blonde. His eyes - try as Lucy might, she could not put a colour to them. It was as if they were a mix of blue, green and light brown yet simultaneously devoid of any colour at all. He had shallow smile lines, but no other visible aging.

'I'm Jake,' he announced, extending a hand and putting a sudden end to Lucy's gawping.

'Of course you are,' she chuckled as she shook his hand, receiving a puzzled look by way of response. 'I'm Lucy'. She gathered herself and indicated she was ready to move on. Jake straightened himself and followed Lucy up the stairwell to the second floor. They both stopped at the entrance to Krysta's apartment. She laughed at his confused expression. 'It's alright, I've heard all about you Jake.' The sound of Lucy's laughter must have reverberated into the walls of the apartment, as before either of them could knock on the door it opened, and in the doorway stood Krysta.

She stood leaning up against the door, her right arm in a sling. She was dressed comfortably, bare footed with sweatpants and a thin, zip-up hooded top. Her golden hair flowed freely in light curls and she looked well rested. She exhibited a huge smile, although Lucy was not sure if it was for her or for the walking bouquet of flowers that stood beside her.

'Hey, hon! Come on in. You too, Jake,' Krysta said, a gleeful smile plastering her face. Lucy didn't need telling twice and eagerly slipped inside, past her friend. She paused and turned back once she had made it past the threshold, expecting the handsome man to follow her in. However, Jake simply stood coyly in front of Krysta. It was an awkward moment as she waited for either of them to make a move. A few seconds seemed to feel like hours, and finally Lucy's patience withered.

'Maybe I should come back later..?' Lucy suggested, half hoping that her interruption would kick the two into some sort of action.

'No, no, I'm sorry,' Jake shook his head. 'I've interrupted. We didn't exactly have plans. I'm gonna...' pointing toward the stairs, he confirmed that he would leave them to it. 'Here,' he said, thrusting the flowers at Krysta. 'I'll see you soon.' Krysta took the bouquet, admiring the arrangement.

'If you're sure...' Krysta said, half-heartedly. 'Thank you for the flowers, they're gorgeous.' Jake then simply smiled, nodded and left.

'What, no kiss goodbye?' Lucy teased as Krysta closed the door. 'I see what you mean though,' Lucy laughed, playfully making a gesture suggesting that she approved of Jake's physique. Krysta merely smirked and nodded in agreement as she placed the flowers by the kitchen sink. Lucy kicked off her shoes and sat on the couch whilst Krysta began to snip the ends off the flowers and arrange the bouquet in a vase. Her sling stood out like a sore thumb and Lucy couldn't help but feel bad seeing it in person.

'How's the arm feeling, girl?' the words almost stuck in Lucy's throat. Leaving the vase on the counter, Krysta headed over to her friend and curled up on the couch beside her.

'It's okay, a little sore but it'll be fine. I can't wait to get this thing off though,' she said, indicating the sling. 'It's annoying the hell out of me. Ugh and I'm so bored. I can't wait to get back to work,' Krysta admitted. Lucy attempted a sympathetic smile, but her guilt niggled at her. Quickly changing the topic of conversation, she began to ask questions about Krysta's other visitor.

'How long has Jake been popping by then? Must be getting serious, what with him bringing flowers an' all,' Lucy winked. The pair giggled like schoolgirls for a moment.

'He's just a gentleman,' Krysta admitted as the giggles subsided. Lucy could practically see her thoughts within her eyes. She was happy. 'He just stopped by the other day to see how I was and if I needed anything.'

'And you said...?' Lucy interrupted with a wicked smile.

'I'll have you know I have been very well behaved,' Krysta stated in an over-the-top, matter of fact manner. 'Begrudgingly,' she smiled mischievously.

'Yeah, but *flowers*?' Lucy quizzed, as if the bouquet was a completely foreign concept to her.

'Like I said. Perfect gentleman.' Krysta inched across the sofa, moving closer to Lucy. 'Besides, they're tulips. It's not like he brought me a bunch of roses or anything.' Krysta half-laughed off the topic and then gave Lucy a puzzled look. 'Anyway, enough about that. Are you okay? You seem distracted. I wouldn't say it's like you to offer to leave for a guy,' Krysta smiled as she questioned Lucy's current demeanour. Lucy simply laughed nervously. Try as she might, she could not think of an excuse to explain her behaviour, but she could not reveal the truth.

Thankfully, the conversation was quickly interrupted by the arrival of Krysta's grey and white feline friend. The cat slipped into the apartment through the partially open window and made itself at home on the sofa, right between the two of them. Lucy was grateful for the sudden distraction as she was instantly able to change the subject.

'This little guy been given a name yet?' Lucy asked, stroking the cat down the back of its neck and then fussing with one of its ears.

'No name yet,' Krysta replied. 'No tag yet either, it would seem.' The pair of them fussed over the cat for a minute or so as it sat purring.

'Why not call it Jake?' Lucy howled at her own suggestion. 'Or Adam? Seems to be the name on everyone's lips at the minute.'

The mention of a work-related topic seemed to capture Krysta's full attention. They spoke for some time about the investigation, about Adam and the progress - or lack of - that the team had made. Their attempts to track down the two characters from the warehouse had thus far come up empty. Despite technically saving Krysta's life, the F.B.I had put a warrant out for Adam, as well as one for the cop killer that everyone seemed to have dubbed 'The Beast'. As they continued to talk, Lucy updated Krysta on how the team were doing, as well as other aspects of the investigation.

'Solomon has been in talks with the director. We've been having problems getting the go ahead to move on some of Markovic's units,' Lucy divulged. They had brought Markovic in for questioning following the incident at his warehouse. He, of course, denied any knowledge of what had happened and seemed to have several airtight alibis for his whereabouts. He had also filed a complaint, suggesting a level of harassment from the bureau. Something that had incensed the entire team.

'That's bullshit!' Krysta exclaimed upon news of the complaint. She rested her forehead in her hands and ran her fingers through her hair, pulling slightly in a sign of frustration.

'Yeah, I know. We're gonna have to arrest someone or get some evidence soon, else shit's gonna hit the fan,' Lucy shrugged. The news was not what Krysta would have wanted to hear. She had already committed so much to the investigation and wouldn't want to give in until it came to a definitive end. Preferably for everyone, it would be an end in which justice had been served and Markovic resided behind bars. The conversation slowly steered away from work and back to Jake, before moving on to general life. Being away from the force for two weeks would have been a blessing for Lucy, but she could tell how much being out of the action was on the way to driving Krysta crazy.

The rain had stopped, and Lucy had all but forgotten the guilt she had felt when she arrived. The time spent with her friend had done them both good. She had been able to relax, and Krysta was no doubt feeling more like a member of the team again. Lucy sat stroking the cat that nestled between them on the sofa. Looking into those tranquil beryl eyes, Lucy felt, just for a second, at peace. But then, Krysta brought up the subject of the warehouse once again and the feeling of self-reproach returned. It was time to go.

Lucy stood up to leave, her sudden movement surprising both Krysta and the cat, each shifting from their nesting places in silent question of Lucy's mannerisms.

'Everything okay, hon?' Krysta questioned.

'All good,' Lucy instantly responded. She was in a hurry to leave but she did not want to give that impression to her partner, or at least she hoped that Krysta would not notice. 'I've just realised the time Krys,' she explained as she put on her shoes. Krysta was baffled, but Lucy had no excuse for her sudden actions. Before her friend could question her, she quickly said her farewells, gave Krysta a kiss on the cheek and made for the exit. The cat followed her towards the door and leapt up onto the table besides the bookcase, marginally avoiding the plant pot. Lucy turned and went to give the majestically snowy companion one last fuss, but the cat quickly jumped back down to the floor and darted for the window. 'I'll see you soon,' Lucy said, opening the door and quickly blowing her friend another kiss. Krysta was still perplexed by what was happening and merely stood speechless as her colleague left the apartment. She was oblivious to the single sapphire coloured velvet rose that stood in the once empty plant pot.

Her mind racing, Lucy couldn't even recall the journey back to her own doorstep once she had reached it. She didn't even notice her front door ajar until she went to place the key into the lock. *What the hell?* She pushed the door open gingerly. Glancing back out onto the street, she made her way inside. *Bedroom. Gun.* The two words plagued her thoughts as she cautiously closed the door behind her. Nimbly side stepping along the corridor, she glanced into each room as she passed it, only to be met each time by silence and emptiness. No lights were on, nothing appeared to have been disturbed. The bedroom was at the end of the hall, it's door open a crack. Darkness lay within.

Her pistol was in the draw in the cabinet beside her bed. *Just inside to the right.* Her mind walked her through her actions as she reached the entrance to her bedroom. It was humid, and she had begun to perspire both in fear and as a result of the atmosphere. Lucy hesitated, before carefully pushing the door open just enough for her to squeeze through and make a move for her firearm. *Top drawer.* She stepped inside and moved towards the bed. She grasped the knob of the drawer. Before she could open it to retrieve the weapon, a hand slipped out from the darkness and took her by the throat. Her grip tightened around the handle, but as she pulled the drawer open, she was torn away from it, from her gun, and pulled towards her attacker.

Her assailant was a man, that much she could tell. He was big, and strong. Fear set in and her mind was torn between fight and flight; but Lucy was a fighter. *This is my house you son of a bitch!*

'Get the fuck off!' She attempted to overpower him by

grabbing the arm he was using to grasp her neck. As the seconds passed, and she attempted to elbow him with her left arm, only for him to grab it and prevent her from moving. Unwilling to be beaten so easily, she threw her head backwards into his chest and pushed all her weight into him. Her speedy reaction clearly took him by surprise as he began to stumble, thrown off balance. They both stumbled backwards and as they began to fall he loosened his grip on her. Lucy knew that this was her chance. *I need the upper hand.* They hit the wooden flooring with a thud. She took every ounce of fear that had possessed her and moulded it to her own will. But - just as she was about to make her move - her attacker's grip began to loosen and he began to laugh. What began as a light-hearted chuckle soon became a hearty gut laugh. *I know that laugh.* 'You son of a bitch!'

'Luce!' he continued to chuckle, struggling to speak. 'Babe, calm down.'

'You absolute bastard!' she shouted as she threw an elbow towards his groin. With all the shit going on at work – why would he think this was funny?

'Whoa! Babe. I'm hoping to use that at some point in life,' he continued to laugh in response to her act of violence. His incessant joking managed to pierce Lucy's anger and she let out an almighty sigh. It was mainly a sigh of relief, before a smile invaded her face and she giggled gleefully.

'Such a fucking asshole,' she hooted. She let out another sigh and, flopping her arms out beside her, she lay still with her head on his chest. 'You're lucky. I was ready to shoot you,' she admitted. 'If you think you're getting any after that...' She was stopped in her tracks as he began to run his fingers through her hair. One hand glided through her dark locks whilst the other ran down her neck, across her shoulder and then followed the strap of her vest down to her chest. 'Michael. What did I say?' she questioned his act of seduction, although she knew that she would not resist.

'You were really gonna shoot me?' he said as he ran his

fingertips across the silky bronzed skin above her bosom. He then proceeded to slip his hand down under her vest top and beneath the cup of her bra to caress her breast and play with her nipple. 'I do hope you've reconsidered,' he jested.

The excitement of the moment took over and any fear or anger she had felt prior to this now escaped her. Fuelled with adrenaline and dampened by the exhilaration she grabbed at his leading arm, running her hand over his bicep and along his forearm. Running down to his wrist, she waited for him to release his grasp on her breast before enveloping his hand in hers and threading her fingers through his; groping her own breast along with him. Her heart pounded to an excitable beat. Eyes closed, she softly bit at her bottom lip in anticipation.

Mike relinquished his grasp and both of his hands ran swiftly down her sides to her waistline. He grabbed at the bottom of her top, pulling it upwards to reveal her flat abdomen and then up over her head as she arched her back and lifted herself off his chest. He tossed the clothing aside and then flaunted his brute strength by grabbing her by the waist and lifting her up off him; rolling her over above him so that they were then face to face. Lucy took the opportunity to spread her legs, planting her knees firmly down on the ground either side of his waist. Straddling him, she leant forward and kissed him passionately, her tongue caressing his. He lifted himself off the floor, using his elbows and resting on his forearms for balance. Lucy sat up and ran her hands through her hair, pushing it away from her face. Her heart continued to pound inside her chest. She wrapped her arm around to her back and unclipped her black, silken bra, threading her arms through the straps and letting it hit the floor. Mike took hold of her, wrapping one arm around her and using the other to grasp her leg. Again in a feat of strength, he managed to lift the pair of them up and got to his feet. Overwhelmed by the titillation, Lucy wrapped her legs around him, and he started to kiss her softly down her neck.

As he carried her toward the bed, she frantically tore at his shirt, disregarding the buttons as they propelled in numerous directions. She undid the button of his pants just before he placed her onto the mattress. Hastily wriggling out of her underwear she lay bare on the bed, waiting in suspense as he took off the rest of his clothes. Her skin hummed with an electricity as he climbed on top of her, spreading her thighs with his legs and clutching at her hip. His blue eyes melting into her brown, she moaned with passion as he slowly, perfectly, filled her.

Laying naked and satisfied she cuddled up to him. They had both worked up a sweat and needed time to come back down to Earth. Besides, Lucy felt that if she tried to get up yet, her legs would simply give way. Their relationship consisted of spontaneous events such as this. Of course, they had to keep it a secret as the bureau would not approve. Now, although deeply fulfilled by the experience, Lucy's feeling of guilt had returned once more.

'You know if she ever found out she would never forgive me,' she said solemnly. Mike only sighed gently in response. They had gone over this before and he was obviously tired of talking about it, but Lucy needed to vent to relieve some of the weight she felt. 'They got attacked. Krys got hurt, while we...' It pained her to have let her friend down, her team, her family.

'Luce,' Mike responded. 'Krysta knows we have her back. It was bad timing. We'll be more careful in future.' But Mike's over-relaxed attitude did not quell the relentless feeling of culpability that she felt.

'I need some air,' she snapped. 'I'm going for a walk. You coming?' Mike merely grumbled at the suggestion of moving, so Lucy got dressed and left him lying in her bed.

She needed groceries for breakfast tomorrow, so she took to the street, breathing in the evening air. Walking slowly beneath the darkened sky, she took out her phone to check for messages or calls she might have missed. Her only unopened message was from Krysta. *'Hope you're OK hon. Pop by anytime xxx'.* As she read it, she could feel herself begin to tense up again. If it wasn't for another message being received at that very moment, her emotions would have been ready to erupt. She stopped in her tracks as she opened the message. It was not from anybody she knew; there was no sender, nor number displayed. It simply read, 'VM'. The letters were on their own, but on a new line they were followed by reams of a seemingly random combination of letters and numbers. *What the fuck?* Lucy was bewildered by the cryptic message. The only thing that stood out to her were the initials. *Vladimir Markovic?* She pondered the possibility that the rest of the message could equate to code for something else. If this were the case, she would require help with decoding it – that was if, in fact, it meant anything at all. *Claire will know.* Locking her phone, more and more questions continued to circle in her head. *Why have I received this message? What does it mean? Does it mean anything? Could someone have pocket texted me?* It seemed too much of a coincidence that the message contained the initials of the one known criminal she and her team had been chasing for so long. She knew that with their help, she would be able to work out what this meant and hopefully, she could begin to make up for hers and Mike's misdemeanour.

8

Serena

He whistled contentedly. Always the same tune; that one tune that sounded so ebullient as it came from his lips, yet, was always portent to something sickening. She loved it. She herself would not indulge in a habit so puerile, but she could relate to the blissful tone that carried on his tune. She continued to climb her stairs to the first floor, ascending towards the tune, towards her partner. A second sound carried itself on the air. It was originating from the ensuite beyond her bedroom; it was a sound she was all too familiar with. The sound of fear. A gleeful shiver ran down her spine and she listened intently to what sounded reminiscent a distraught and wounded animal.

'Brandt,' she called out, a facetious tone embellishing her words. 'I *do* hope you aren't making too much of a mess.' As she entered her lavish boudoir, she began to undress. Releasing her fiery red hair from its captive up-do, allowing it to tumble down the back of her neck. She then kicked off her crimson heels. She walked towards her open walk-in wardrobe, unzipping and removing her tunic dress carefully. She cared little for man or beast, but she treated her expensive commodities with respect. *Black will do.* She took a pair of fine linen pants from the clothing rail. Slipping them on and pulling them up over her red French knickers, she looked over to the ensuite to see her partner.

Brandt stepped into the bedroom, wiping his hands with a cotton hand towel. The towel that was once a cream colour was now awash with blood and bits of human tissue. He continued to wipe his huge hands as if he were merely drying them after a wash.

'Six fucking bedrooms in this place and you choose mine to do that shit,' she said in annoyance. He showed little interest in her words, but he didn't take his eyes off her. She was evidently unimpressed, stood with her hands on her hips, and her chest laid bare for him to see. He too was topless. Deep, scarred tissue and tribal tattoos smothered his huge, incredibly muscular torso. He did not partake in the materialistic enjoyment of fine clothing or possessions as she did; he wore the same dark pants and blackened boots every time she saw him. He dropped the red-stained towel on the clean carpet and laughed as she frowned at him. Then, he marched towards her with determination.

'You care too much for this shit,' he said as he reached her at the entrance to her wardrobe.

'You care too little, brother,' she said with a clear sense of indignation to her tone, one she exaggerated with the intention of him noticing. *You wish to fight, we will see who burns hottest.* He stood in front of her, exhibiting a sickening grin.

'Your gift's in the tub. There's another in the corner of the bathroom,' he said as his eyes bore into her. A malevolent expression flashed across his face and the scars on his face and chest began to glow.

'Bastard!' she exclaimed, just as he reached forward and grabbed her by the throat. He was strong, but she was fast - an epithet that had clearly slipped his mind. She batted at his arm, forcing him to release his grip. Quickly springing up off the floor, she flung her legs into his mighty chest with a swinging dropkick. She possessed a huge amount of strength herself and the force she exerted onto him, sent him falling backwards. Stumbling, he crashed against her large oak framed bed. His temper flared, and she could see the fire in his eyes erupt into an inferno.

'Don't you fucking dare!' she exclaimed, suddenly realising she knew that look

in his eyes. It was a glint of destruction. He slid the bed across the room with ease, sending it crashing against the entrance to the ensuite as if it were mere kindling.

'Let's see just how hot you are,' he laughed. Serena was infuriated. This was a child's game; one that she had grown tired of centuries ago. He clapped his bear-like paws together and rolled his head, causing an almighty cracking sound to emanate from his neck. A sickening smile materialised across his face, spreading almost from ear to ear, and he guffawed as his palms began to glow. Brighter and brighter they became, along with his eyes and his scars, the dark red brightening to an almost sunshine yellow as the heat in his veins increased. *He will destroy everything!* Her belongings. Her house. She enjoyed what she had, and he was not going to fuck things up. *Not again.*

'You want heat, brother,' she retorted. 'I'll give you heat.' She outstretched her arms and arched her back. Her breasts sat pert upon her chest and her nipples began to swell. She would enjoy teaching him a lesson. Flames spontaneously began to lick up and down her arms, flashing across her chest and then up through her fiery red hair. The white sclera of her eyes began to glow. Brighter and brighter they became. Her irises were ablaze in red flame and the pupils smouldered. As her fury increased, her eyes shone incandescently and the crimson blaze that engulfed her upper body began to burn white hot. She was going to teach him a lesson that he would not forget any time soon - but then there was a loud knock on the door. She and Brandt both turned their attention to the interruption.

'Markovic is waiting downstairs,' announced a scruffy, brown-haired man. He stood in the entrance to the bedroom with his arms crossed in such a way that it accentuated his larger than average, tattooed arms. He seemed to have a cocksure attitude about him that vexed Serena somewhat. She threw her arms down in a sign of frustration. She would have enjoyed the fight that was inevitably about to happen. The flames extinguished and she looked scornfully towards Brandt before turning back to her wardrobe to finish getting dressed. Brandt also looked unimpressed by the sudden end to their sparring.

'If you ever interrupt us again...' Brandt exclaimed, with a grittiness to his words as he forced them through clenched teeth. 'You know what - fuck threats.' Brandt stomped towards the lackey still stood waiting in the doorway. With one hand, he grabbed the man by the neck. The man exhibited a cacophonous scream and frantically reached for a pistol in his belt as his skin crackled under Brandt's grasp. Brandt, noticing this, reached over with his other hand, grabbed the man by the side of his face and in one swift movement tore his head clean from his neck, sending it rolling along the bedroom floor behind him. The man's body slumped to the floor and Brandt stomped off out of the room.

Serena merely rolled her eyes at the sight of her brother's solution to his frustration; however, upon noticing the blood flowing from the dead man she sighed at the thought of having to replace yet another carpet. Swapping her pants for an identical pair, one that was not burnt, she donned an imperial red off-the-shoulder top. Ignoring the whimpering sounds coming from the ensuite bathroom, she stepped over the body in the doorway and left the bedroom, careful to avoid the expanding patch of blood. Barefoot, she enjoyed the softness of the thick carpet beneath her feet. She glided down the stairs, expecting to find her guests in the comfort of her sitting room. However, the room was desolate. *They must be in the study. How dull.* She waltzed through the house to the study to find at least half a dozen men; some of them were standing to attention. *Lackies.*

Others were slumped in chairs about the large wooden table that sat in the centre of the room. Markovic's pointless bodyguards stood rigid against one of the bookcases. Two suited men, no doubt armed to the teeth, stood emotionless and ready to protect their boss. The thought amused her. These men protecting Markovic was akin to a kitten protecting a lion. Pointless. She laughed at them as she walked past, running her hand over their chests as they remained standing still, unflinching even at her touch. Brandt stood at the table, leaning forward with his fists planted on the oaken top. Opposite him, sat in her chair, was her so-called guest, Vladimir. Another one of his men stood beside him - but this one wasn't suited. He wasn't a paid bodyguard. *Perhaps he's a follower. I used to enjoy having followers.* The final person was a girl. Sat in the corner of the room and wearing a floral-patterned dress. Serena took a long look at her, sizing her up, calculating her purpose; the girl did not appear very happy to be here.

'You like the look of Lorelei? She's yours. Think of her as a gift,' Markovic said with a smug look taking over his broad face. He was fairly muscular, but not a huge man. A dwarf in the likes of Brandt's shadow; yet then again, most men were. He was smartly dressed in what Serena knew to be a Kiton suit. It was steel grey, a cashmere and linen blend with a Prince of Wales tone embedded in the pattern. He wore it well with a burgundy shirt – a bold combination but one most likely to be pulled off well by him out of anybody. With one hand rested on the table clenched, his tired looking knuckles showed signs of hard labour, most likely in the form of fighting. In his other hand, he held an Arturo Fuente cigar, yet to be lit.

Serena could tell that her brothers' patience was beginning to wane. He didn't enjoy diplomatic matters such as these. He would rather be putting his fist through some poor soul's skull than attend a meeting to talk logistics.

'Did you leave Christoph upstairs?' Markovic queried,

wondering where his messenger had gotten to.

'In a manner of speaking,' Brandt replied unperplexed, finally deciding to take a seat. Brandt's response seemed to displease their guest somewhat. Markovic took to his feet, put down his cigar and unbuttoned his suit jacket. Removing it, he passed the jacket to the lackey beside him to hold. He grimaced at Brandt to indicate his displeasure and began to roll up his shirt sleeves. The first sleeve revealed a golden watch encrusted with diamond-looking gemstones. He rolled up the other sleeve to reveal a tattoo written in Serbian; 'Cilj Upravdava Sredstva' to which Serena understood to mean 'the end justifies the means'.

'How apt,' Serena smiled as she read the tattoo aloud before she too took a seat at the table, crossing her legs. 'Shall we get on with it then?' She had no time for these males to press their dominance.

'The warehouse was a fucking shambles,' Markovic growled in a tone of annoyance and displeasure. He cut and lit the cigar before flashing a final look at Brandt and taking his seat again. 'Fucking F.B.I-'

'The F.B.I mean fuck all,' Brandt interrupted, swinging back and resting his legs upon the table. 'The ritual didn't work again.' Markovic stared at Brandt. He did not like to be interrupted.

'The ritual was a mess. What the fuck happened?' The anger in his voice caused his accent to come out strong on his words. This time, he turned his attention to Serena.

'I believe the ritual did not work for several reasons,' Serena openly admitted, sitting back in her seat and crossing her arms over her chest. Her own research and recent meeting with the professor had proved useful in determining the exact requirements for the ritual to work. 'Firstly, the victims need to be emotionally linked to the subject. It is not enough for there simply to be twelve of them. Secondly, we were not all in attendance. All the Avunaye need to be present for the initiation ritual to work.

And we have one member who is causing a problem.' This member wasn't the only issue. Even if they got all the others to cooperate, there would still be one of the Avunaye who was not present, and she was yet to determine how to rectify that problem. She had also found a third downfall to the ceremony, another reason as to why it did not and would not work. However, she did not want to lay all her cards on the table now and cause tempers to flare.

'It will be some time before we can try again,' a fact that irritated Markovic as he said it aloud. 'Make sure the preparations are complete next time. As for the pigs - use the kid. Send a message,' he cracked his knuckles. 'Our informant will let us know if the F.B.I make any more moves. You just make sure you are there to take them out. And deal with this *absent member*.'

'Argh!' Brandt let out a sudden exclamation, removing his feet from the tabletop and slamming his fists down on the table, splintering the wood. Serena was unimpressed that, once again, he was damaging her possessions. 'Fuck him! Father said it should work without him!'

'For God sake, you dumb cunt, Matthias isn't here. Quit the father bullshit,' Serena said, exasperated. She knew her words would wound him, she intended them to. Sometimes his allegiance, his blind willingness to follow commands infuriated her. She was also growing tired of these meetings with this insignificant man. But a deal had been struck between Markovic and the Avunaye, one that she dare not break for risk of inviting the wrath of her kin. Her disobedience clearly antagonised her brother, as he turned to stare at her with an incensed glow to his eyes. She knew he would behave himself, however. For, to Markovic, Brandt was merely a dog on a leash.

'We have an agreement. I expect results,' Markovic said. He stood up from his seat once again. He looked to Serena and gave her a nod; he knew she understood what was required. 'I've been informed that I can rely on your brother,

Seymour, for assistance with the next stage of the plan.' He said it with an assured look, receiving a subtle nod from Serena as confirmation; then looking to Brandt, he bore a sardonic smile. Brandt took to the expression with some hostility, slamming his fists down on the table once more, this time breaking through the wood. He stood up from his seat and took up a stance to suggest he was about to tear them all limb from limb. Serena simply sat back into her chair and laughed.

'Brandt,' she sighed. 'Sit down.' She rested her hands on her lap, arched her back slightly and swapped her legs over, crossing them in the opposite manner. In doing this, she caught the eye of the lackey stood beside Markovic. He gave her a cheeky wink, which only made her laugh, this time much harder. Vladimir noticed the man's insubordination and, combined with Brandt's outburst, it caused him to completely loose his composure.

'Give me that!' Markovic exclaimed, snatching his jacket off the man. He threw the suit piece onto the floor, rolled his shoulders and grabbed him by the scruff of the neck. Before the guard could comprehend what was going, on Vladimir slammed his face down onto the splintered table and punched him with some force right onto his temple. A quick second punch knocked the man unconscious. 'I have little tolerance for failure,' he said simply and assuredly, turning now to stare straight at Serena. Holding his cigar between his teeth, he proceeded to continue hitting the out cold lackey, splitting his skin and splashing blood all over the table. He struck the man's head until his own knuckles had split and began to flow with his own thick, red blood and then he stopped. Picking up his light from the table, he re-lit the cigar as though nothing had just happened.

Serena cast her eyes about the room to find that the remaining guards stood unflinching. Despite what had just transpired, they simply stood still. The girl also sat unmoving, still cowering in the corner of the room. Serena was quite intrigued by Markovic's display of authority. *If only you were strong enough to handle me. What fun we could have.* Brandt remained standing, unmoving, yet clearly still irritated. Markovic walked around the table and stood before Brandt. He wiped some of the blood from his hands onto Brandt's chest, before picking up his suit jacket.

'Have the package delivered,' he commanded of Brandt, like a master would a servant. 'Serena, it has been a pleasure.' He took one of her hands and planted a kiss onto the back of it.

Serena did not feel the need to see her guest out. Markovic left swiftly, taking his remaining lap dogs with him, leaving only the dead cronies and the girl behind.

'Aww. He left you behind brother,' she joked. Brandt, who had begun pacing the study, looked increasingly infuriated. 'And you make such a good puppy,' she teased. Brandt took unkindly to her jest and finished off the broken table in a burst of rage, launching it, and the body slumped upon it, across the room. He then took his anger out on several other furnishings, before grabbing the girl by the arm and marching towards the front door. The girl screamed in a piercing terror. She meant nothing to Serena, and so her pleas for help went ignored. *She screams now, god help her later.*

Standing up, Serena let out a sigh. She was unimpressed with the devastation this meeting had left in its wake. Although she had grown fond of the residence, it was not worth the hassle of a clean-up. *Fire destroys all.* She would have no qualms about destroying the house and any evidence it held; it would certainly not be first time, or the last. However, as she walked through the house, hands ablaze, setting alight everything she passed, she remembered that the house was not completely empty. The package that Markovic spoke of resided upstairs, the one that she would now have to deliver herself. She also recalled the whimpering sound that accompanied it in her ensuite.

Making her way up the staircase, now with an inferno fully underway downstairs, she realised she could no longer hear the quiet sob that she had before. *Don't tell me it's gone and died on me.* It wasn't that she particularly wanted whoever it was to be alive, but it was another mess she'd have to clean up. Much to her disgust, however, it would seem that whoever it was that was in the bathroom had in fact escaped. The revelation irked her. Once again, Brandt had left a loose end. So, as the fire continued to grow within the building, she picked up the mutilated body from out of the bath tub, slung it over her shoulder as if it were nothing and left. Walking down the stairs and exiting via the front door, the flames parted before her as though she were Moses parting the fiery Red Sea. Once she had passed through the inferno, the flames licked together again.

The following morning, showered and dressed, she instructed her driver to take her and the package to the predetermined destination. She wore ankle-high black stiletto boots, a black pencil skirt and a red, plunging see-through blouse. The car pulled up in a street lined with trees. Her driver opened her door and she stepped out into the morning sunshine. *How quaint.* She looked up and down the street. Grabbing the body by the ankle, she dragged it from the boot of the car, across the pavement and laid it, face up, upside down on the steps leading up to the front door. Knocking on the door, she waited patiently for an answer. A thundering sound came from within as someone bounded towards the other side of the door.

'Serena!' the young man blurted with a surprised tone as he opened the door to find her standing in the threshold. 'Sorry. Serena isn't it? That's what the professor called you.' She merely smiled sweetly by way of reply. He continued, 'Declan. I'm Declan.' He was all aflutter. She smiled again.

'Declan, darling. Would it be okay if I came inside?' she asked in an angelic tone. 'I am just *burning* to meet your father. Is he home?'

9

Seamus McCarthy

How many more times am I going to have to fucking go through this?! He applied pressure to his forehead with his fingertips.

'She came to *my* house. Threatened *my* family. She left the poor kids' mutilated corpse on *my* fucking doorstep, for Christ's sake!' Seamus was tired, irritable. He wasn't at home when she came to call. He only knew what everyone else knew; what his family had told them already. And still they kept asking the same questions over again like a stuck record.

'It's okay, Seamus. We're just trying to get the full picture of what happened to the kid and why,' Sergeant Joseph McCabe was questioning Seamus about the woman that had come to the door. *But you don't believe what really happened.* Seamus felt exasperated. 'Let's just go over the incendiary device again.' McCabe continued. 'Your wife says the woman was holding something in her hand?'

Seamus interrupted with an outburst of pure frustration, 'Her hand set on fire and the bitch burnt my daughters face!' His exclamation was met by only silence.

'Look. I know this has got to be frustrating,' McCabe broke the silence. Seamus merely sighed in response to the comment and buried his face into his arms on the table. Frustrating didn't even begin to explain how this felt. 'Some parts of the witness statements just don't make sense.'

A knock at the door of the interview room cut Joseph short. Investigating the interruption, the sergeant excused himself and went to answer the door. Seamus' hair was a mess. He looked tired and felt disconnected from reality. The past couple days had taken their toll on him. He hadn't slept properly. Part of him wanted to hit the streets and seek out revenge, another part wanted to grab his family and run for safety in case the red-haired woman returned. Every now and again, when he stopped worrying and the anger subsided, he would struggle to hold back other emotions. Alannah had been burnt; she would no doubt end up scarred, but at least she was alive. Seamus could picture now the body that had been collected from the base of his steps. *The pain that poor boy must have endured.*

Head resting on his arms, he was made to jump as the door to the interview room slammed. Two suits entered the room. Seamus could instantly tell that they were federal as a blonde woman and her male colleague stood in front of him. The woman was injured, arm in a sling. She stood, slightly reserved, behind the man, who seemingly wanted to get straight down to business.

'Officer McCarthy,' the man paused for a moment. Seamus could feel his eyes looking him up and down, sizing him up. 'I'm Special Agent Johnston, and this is my partner Special Agent Rose-Anderson.' Seamus could tell that they didn't make great partners by the strange look she gave as she was introduced. 'We have some questions for you,' Agent Johnston stated. Before he could finish what he was saying, Seamus slammed his hands down on the table in a rage of discontent.

'Enough!' Seamus shouted, feeling himself shake. 'Enough of the same fucking questions!' Before Seamus could continue shouting, he was interrupted. Agent Johnston went to say something in response to Seamus' outburst, but he too was cut off by the female agent.

'Seamus? It *is* Seamus, right?' she asked in a relaxed

tone. 'My name is Krysta.' She sounded sincere. Her voice was soft and unlike all the other interrogators that Seamus had spoken to. He decided to give her his attention. 'How about we get out of here. We could go for a walk, have a chat?'

Seamus couldn't help but question whether she was being serious. In some ways he felt patronised, as though she thought he was a child. In other ways, he quite enjoyed the fact that someone was talking to him without an air of challenge plastering their voice. Either way, he felt exhausted, and knew the fresh air would do him some good. Looking at the expression on her face, he felt that she was being honest and went to accept her invitation. Her partner, on the other hand, clearly did not like the idea.

'Agent Anderson, can I have a word?' he asked angrily.

'Look, Kyle. He isn't under caution and he's clearly had enough. Seamus?' Agent Anderson looked to Seamus for confirmation, who simply nodded in agreement.

'I'm going to have to check in with-' Before Agent Johnston could state his intentions, she cut him off again.

'Go then, check. C'mon, Seamus, let's get some air.'

Seamus breathed in the city air as if he had been imprisoned for years. He hadn't been at work today as he had been granted some leave to be with his family. They'd asked him if he would mind coming in to just go over a few details; he should have known better than to trust that it would have been a flying visit. He'd done nothing wrong, and yet had received the same kind of interrogation he was trained to give other people. The mornings' rain had left a damp weight on the air, but at least it was dry now, allowing them to walk outside. He wore a khaki zip-neck jumper and tan coloured combats. His hair was untidy and he hadn't bothered shaving for a couple of days. Krysta walked quietly beside him; he knew that she would break her silence any second now, but he appreciated the respite, if only for a minute or two. She walked beside him in her work attire, wearing black suit pants and a black blazer, a white shirt and kitten heeled court shoes.

They had probably walked for 10 minutes before she finally worked out the angle to approach him with and spoke.

'Do you know anything about Vladimir Markovic, Seamus?' she asked. It was not a question he had expected to be asked, and certainly wasn't one he had been asked before, so it took him a moment to think of an answer.

'Isn't he the supposed arms dealer that no one can gather any evidence on?' Seamus replied. The look he received indicated that she could see right through him.

'I'll take that as a lot,' she smiled subtly. 'You're a man of the city, Seamus. I know you know more than that.' There was a calmness to her voice even though he could tell she knew he wasn't being one hundred percent honest with her. 'We've been trying to pin Markovic down for some time, unsuccessfully.' The fact of the matter seemed to annoy her somewhat. 'Now there's some new players involved, and I believe you may know more than you even realise. Three weeks ago, you found a man badly burned and in a critical condition.' Seamus stopped walking for a moment and looked at Krysta. He was searching her eyes, her face, trying to ascertain a sense of her true intention. Deciding to see where this conversation was headed, he continued walking. 'This burned man that you found, and you had submitted to hospital. He later somehow fully recovered within a matter of hours and critically wounded one of your colleagues. He escaped to the roof of the hospital and somehow disappeared without a trace.' The calmness had now left her voice and was replaced with one of urgency. *She needs my help.* Seamus realised that this meant a great deal to her. Maybe it was more than just an investigation to her.

'What do you want to know?' Seamus responded to her unspoken request for help.

'Is there anything you might have missed out in your initial report? Can you tell me anything about the burned man or the red-haired woman at your house that maybe you might have held back?' Her plea seemed sincere, and their chat did not feel like an interrogation. They continued walking whilst Seamus told Krysta how he and Samuel Lorenzo had come across the man, beaten and burned to within an inch of his life in the derelict building. She took all the facts in, listening intently. When he finished, Krysta kept walking for a few paces, taking it all in. It was pretty much all what she'd been told already.

'I believe your burned man's name is Adam.' She said reluctantly, unsure if she was supposed to be divulging the information. 'I think there may be a connection with the woman that unexplainably attacked your daughter.'

Unexplainably? There's that word again - does she doubt what happened, too? Krysta had stopped walking at this point and now stood patiently, waiting for his response.

'The woman...' Seamus trailed off and paused for a moment. He hadn't divulged this information to his colleagues. Krysta, however, did not seem as sceptical when it came to his situation. *Maybe she will believe me.* He took a deep breath in. 'The red-haired woman. The one who's hand set on fire and burned my daughter...' He paused again, glancing out the corner of his eye to see what her reaction would be, yet she stood unflinching. 'My son was the one that answered the door to her. He told me that he had met her before, that's why he spoke to her. He said she'd been at the university – NYU - the morning that professor died in a fire.' He could tell that this was new information for her but her expression told him that she was grateful for his cooperation. 'Her name. My son Declan said her name was Serena.'

The pair of them spoke some more as they altered their course and headed back toward the station. They were roughly halfway back when Seamus stopped. He did not want to return there, not yet anyway. He decided he would continue walking for a while and so they parted ways, Krysta thanking him for his assistance. Seamus needed time to process everything that she had told him. One thing plagued him as he marched through the streets of the city, a name: *Adam.*

The day passed quickly as he wandered from block to block and at some point he had subconsciously decided to head to the hospital to check on Moira and Alannah. Before he knew it, he was standing outside the New York Presbyterian Hospital in Lower Manhattan. It was midweek, so the hospital was not as chaotic as when Alannah had first been brought in. He had hoped that Moira would be waiting at her bedside when he reached Alannah's room, but she must have been called away. Every chance she got she would check on their daughter. Alannah was sound asleep when he entered; she had been struggling to sleep during her time here, traumatised by her experience. She constantly had nightmares each time she closed her eyes, so it was quite comforting to see her sleeping undisturbed. The room was filled with gifts and flowers, balloons and get-well cards from friends, fellow students and some of her professors. Some of Seamus' and Moira's colleagues had also wished her a speedy recovery, the precinct having sent a bear which sat at her bedside. Alannah had always been such a selfless and carefree soul; from being a little girl she would look out for those around her, with little thought to wanting or asking for anything in return. Even as a teenager, she had always been courteous and kind and, bar a few rebellious acts, Seamus had always been so proud of her. It was all this that made it so hard for him to understand or accept why someone - no, *something* - would want to harm her without reason. Watching her sleep, he couldn't help but ask himself. *Why? Why my little girl?* He brushed her long dark hair away from her face softly to reveal the gauze that covered the burn. Kissing her on her forehead, he took a seat beside her bed.

He couldn't have been asleep long before he was awoken by his wife. She had come in to check on their daughter and found him snoring by her bedside.

'I didn't realise you were here,' she said, giving him a kiss. 'You should have called me.'

'I knew you'd come by sooner or later,' Seamus replied, stretching in his chair. 'I must have been more exhausted than I thought.' He, too, had not been sleeping well the last couple of nights. Thoughts of what might have happened, and dreams of revenge and retaliation, all plagued his mind at night. The short nap had reenergised him, and he wished it could have gone on for longer. He was, however, glad to see his wife.

'Want me to grab you a coffee?' she asked, caressing his shoulder. 'I've got a few hours left on shift but then we could go get something to eat?' The thought of both caffeine and food brought a smile to Seamus's face. He had not seen much of Moira the past couple days as she had wanted to stay close to Alannah. But, as ever, she couldn't just sit still, so she'd picked up some extra shifts on the ward. She had even slept in the chair next to their daughter the night before.

'That'd be great,' he smiled.

Seamus opened his eyes ever so slightly to find the room in almost complete darkness, bar a couple of solitary blinking lights on the hospital machinery. The blinds had been closed and the door was shut. To his right, the full cup of coffee that Moira must have brought him was sat on the side; it was undoubtedly stone cold now. *Must have fallen asleep again.* He was drowsy and groggy and questioned what the time was. Barely awake, he looked across Alannah's bed to see a figure beside her in the darkness. He smiled slightly that Moira had left the room dark so as not to disturb him. *She always thinks of everyone else.*

'How is she, hon?' he asked. He received no response.

Focussing more clearly, he looked in Moira's direction. His heart sunk and began to pound as the realisation dawned on him that it was not his wife standing on the opposite side of the bed. Eyes now wide open, it was as if his body had received a full shot of adrenaline and he was shocked into a state of full alertness. He stood up quickly and looked across the bed to see the darkened figure of a man stood staring down at his daughter, one hand on her face. At first, Seamus panicked that the man's hand looked to be smothering Alannah's face. But then, he looked properly. His hand wasn't around Alannah's neck or mouth or nose. It looked as though he had removed his daughter's bandage and was now covering her burn with the palm of his hand.

'What the hell are you doing?' Seamus demanded. He was unable to make out any of the intruder's features, the darkness of the room providing a sinister veil to cloak his face. In response to Seamus's question, the man merely turned his head and looked at him. His emerald eyes pierced the veil and Seamus' fears subdued. Confused by the sudden overwhelming feeling of calm despite this unwelcome intruder, Seamus closed his eyes and shook his head. Maybe he was still dreaming? No. He opened his eyes and slowly made his way around the bed to confront the man. His eyes had now almost fully adjusted to the lack of light. He could now fully see the man who stood at his daughters' bedside. He wore shorts and a hooded jumper. He had the hood pulled up, helping to conceal his face in shadows. Seamus noticed, however, that the intruder was wearing nothing on his feet. Shaking his head, trying to recover from the daze he found himself in, Seamus reached out to grab the man. As he reached out, the door to the room swung open. It was Moira.

'What the fuck! Get off my daughter!' she wailed at the sight of the stranger. The man instantly retracted his hand from Alannah's face. Alannah, disturbed by her mother's shouting, opened her eyes to see the stranger before her. She let out a shrill shriek.

'I'm sorry,' were the only words the man spoke. Seamus felt oddly aware of the terrified, yet kind look in the man's eyes before he turned and made a swift dart for the exit. Attempting to grab his arm as he bolted, Seamus missed. The intruder burst past Moira, knocking her back against the frame of the door.

'Seamus!' Moira croaked, a look of terror glazing her eyes. Seamus moved quickly now, past his wife and into the hospital corridor. One foot after another he ran, chasing after the fleeing intruder.

If it were not for the commotion left in his wake, Seamus would not have stood a chance of finding the man that had broken into his daughter's hospital bedroom. Charging through corridor after corridor, Seamus ran as fast as he could, his shoes scuffing the shined floor as he did so. Finally, he caught sight of the man as he turned a corner. He was headed for the stairwell, twenty or so yards away. His hood was still up and his bare feet slapped the tiles beneath them. Seamus knew he could not catch him. Up, down – it didn't matter what route he took, Seamus would lose sight of him in seconds. But knew he had to do something. Anything. His police instincts kicked in just as the man reached the door to the stairwell. His heart hammering inside his chest, he shouted the first word that came into his head, without pausing a moment to think.

'Adam!' The name left Seamus' lips before he could even consider why. But, to his surprise, the man stopped in his tracks, one hand on the door to the stairwell. He remained turned away, his head bowed under his hood. Surprised that the man had halted, Seamus came to a stop as well. *Adam?* He questioned himself. But before he could think any further about the name that had just left his lips, the man moved again and continued his escape, into the stairwell out of sight. Ceasing his pursuit, Seamus was dumbfounded. *Could it really have been Adam, the burn victim I saved just days ago?* He asked himself more and more questions, baffled by them all as he sauntered back to Alannah's room. Bewilderingly, the one that confused him most was that of his own actions: why had he shouted the name?

It was not until he laid his eyes on his wife and daughter that the fear and reality of what had just happened suddenly re-manifested within him.

'Girls!' he called as he entered the room. 'Jesus, are you okay?' Alannah was sat up in bed, her mother embracing her tightly. Moira looked at him. A layer of tears glistened on her eyes. Seamus could not tell whether the tears reflected a fear that resided behind the eyes, or if it was something else entirely. 'What is it?' he asked nervously, almost too scared to know the answer. 'What did he do?' Moira did not respond, she merely continued to stare at him, unblinking. Her face resembled someone in a state of shock, a look of disbelief plastered over her features. Where the tears now filled her eyes, the barrier holding them back broke and one began to run down her cheek. Still, she did not move to wipe the tear away. Confused, Seamus stepped closer. 'Moira?' he asked again, in a cautious but solid tone. This time, his words appeared to register with her. She snapped to attention, blinking rapidly to shake the remaining tears loose and wiping her dampened cheek.

'She's okay,' Moira shook her head. 'I don't...' she struggled to get the words out. 'I don't understand.' Seamus began to become concerned by Moira's behaviour.

'Moira. What did he do?' he now demanded. He was beginning to panic and it wasn't like her to keep anything from him, least of all anything about the kids' wellbeing's. *Did he come to finish what Serena started?* Moira released her grasp on Alannah, taking her shoulders in both hands as she looked at her from arm's length. Seemingly content, she let go and stepped backwards from the bed. She raised her hand and covered her mouth with the back of it as though trying to supress a quiver.

'I need to get the doctor,' Moira said decisively, her nurse's instinct now overtaking her mother's instinct. She turned and left the room, walking past Seamus as though he wasn't even there. Seamus, annoyed that his wife wouldn't talk to him, turned his attentions toward Alannah. Worried for his child, he rushed over to her and got on one knee in front of her. She sat unmoving on the edge of the bed, her feet just touching the floor. For her age, she was short and like any father, he still saw her as the little girl he'd read bedtime stories to.

'Baby? Are you okay?' he asked delicately, trying his best to hold back his nerves and remain calm. She didn't reply. Instead, she remained positioned with her face in her hands. Seamus stood up and grasped her hands to gently pry them away from her face. 'Honey, you shouldn't touch your burn,' he said as he softly lowered her hands. 'Are you-' the words lodged in his throat, an immediate lump having formed. His little girl had looked up at him with swollen eyes, full of tears. He realised now why Moira had seemed so vacant and in disbelief. As he stared upon his daughter's perfect face, he couldn't believe what he saw. Perfection. Not the kind of perfection that any parent sees in their child, the kind that is blind to physical abnormality or wrongdoing. No – this was different. Where just so soon before a painful, ugly wound had infested Alannah's face, now there was nothing. Her skin was completely clear. He could muster no words as she smiled the faintest of smiles. Instead, he allowed his jaw to remain slightly ajar as he was overcome with a sense of pure joy.

Driving as fast as possible, there was only one place he knew he needed to be headed. He'd left his wife and daughter with the doctor and had ran as fast as he could back to his car. He needed to pursue his curiosity – no, he needed answers. *Adam, the red head, Smithy.* So many thoughts littered his mind as he drove. *One person connects them all.*

One person was there when this all started - when Sam Lorenzo and I found the burned man - when we found Adam. He miraculously recovered from his injuries, he vanished. It has to be him. As though he were solving a puzzle, he tried to snap all the pieces together to come to an answer. Only... the edges of the story were there, but the meaty middle pieces didn't seem to fit, leaving gaping, unanswered holes. It wasn't far now. Dante would probably not be home, but it was a place to start; besides, he craved some answers to the questions that plagued him.

It was late when he arrived at Dante's apartment. Seamus banged on the door. As expected there was no answer, but he could swear that he could hear sounds of movement from inside. *Is he trying to make a run for it?* It certainly wouldn't surprise him if the kid was. *Shit. I can't lose him.* Dante was his only lead - he needed this. In a snap judgement, he made up his mind and stepped backward, throwing as much force behind him as possible before barging into the door. It didn't budge. Again, he threw his weight into the door; the sound was loud and clearly disturbed other residents. Cries from several lodgings resounded to the call of 'shut the fuck up!'. Stepping back once more, Seamus kicked the door this time, just below the lock, forcing it to give way. He pushed the door open, driving it through splinters of broken door frame at the hinges. He was quite surprised as he set his eyes upon Dante's home. *Clearly been busy of late.* Seamus looked about the newly furnished living area. The interior of the flat was far from what he had expected, especially judging by the rest of the building. Two large black leather couches sat parallel to one another in front of the largest flatscreen television he had ever seen. A glass slab balanced on an ornamental black panther, the sculpture acting as a table between the two couches. The whole table was covered in money, syringes and what looked like cocaine, among other suspect materials. *The lights are on.* Seamus continued to step his way through the apartment, looking for signs of life. There was no one in the kitchen area that adjoined the living room. Dante's bedroom was also empty; it was a complete mess, but no Dante. Seamus was about to open the bathroom door when all of a sudden, there was a sound from the entrance to the flat. He turned around to find a young boy, no more than fifteen or sixteen years old, stood before him. He was wearing white sneakers and a pair of baggy red and white jogging pants. A jet-black tank top revealed his small, but relatively toned arms. His face was familiar, but the look in his eyes was one of insecurity as his extended arm held up a silver pistol, its barrel staring at Seamus.

'The fuck are you doing?' the boy demanded. He was obviously a friend of Dante's. For a moment Seamus felt nothing as he looked into the barrel of death that looked him in the face. He was calm. He needed answers - if he had to go through this kid then so be it. His recklessness only lasted a second however, as thoughts of his family creeped in and his heart seemed to start to beat aggressively in his chest.

'I'm looking for Dante,' Seamus confessed, slowly raising his hands, palms facing outright to show he was of no threat. The boy continued to stare at him.

'Hey, man, don't I know you?' said the boy, still pointing his firearm directly at Seamus' head. 'Ain't you that cop?' His sudden remembrance of Seamus seemed to anger the boy, his tone becoming increasingly aggressive.

'Look – I - It's okay. I just...' before finishing his sentence, Seamus quickly lowered his hands and lurched forward. He grabbed the gun and the boy's arm, compelling him to point it in the opposite direction, away from them both. He struck down hard onto the kid's arm with the outer edge of his hand, forcing him to drop the weapon. The kid winced at the blow, yet Seamus then proceeded to punch him across the jaw with some force. The boy fell to the ground.

'Enough okay! I'm sorry!' he cried out, but Seamus could

feel an overwhelming rage within him that he could not quell. He grabbed the boy by the shirt, the material ripping in the process. He continued to punch the boy in the face again and again. If it were not for the sudden emergence of another person from the bathroom behind, he may not have stopped.

'McCarthy! Stop!' shouted an unusually timid Dante from behind him. Catching a glimpse of his own reflection in the tear ridden eyes of the child before him, Seamus fell backwards on the floor. *What am I doing?* The kid clambered away from him in terror, stumbling to his feet as he used the wall to steady himself. Seamus' heart pounded ferociously, and his blooded hands shook uncontrollably. He looked at his blood smeared wedding ring as his fist trembled and he was dragged back into reality.

Seamus sat for a couple of minutes, wondering what had possessed him to strike the boy so aggressively. Dante sat in the doorway to the bathroom beside him, resting against the door frame, he's knees tucked up and his arms resting on them. Seamus, still staring at his own hands, couldn't bring himself to look up for fear of being too ashamed.

'You owe me - ' Dante tried to speak but a fit of coughing prevented him from doing so easily. '... a new fucking door'. He chuckled to himself but this only seemed to agitate whatever it was that had been making him cough, as it brought on a whole new fit of splutters. Seamus looked up now. Dante was clearly in pain as he held his chest and abdomen, wincing in agony. He tried to conceal it as if being in pain were a sign of weakness, but Seamus could see straight through his façade.

'What the hell happened to you?' Seamus quizzed. He had now taken a longer look at the teen. Dante was riddled with bruises; the ones around his waist and across his chest suggested that he had some broken bones at the very least. He had a couple of deep cuts across his cheek and his bottom lip was swollen and bleeding. He had one black eye that he could barely open to look at Seamus and his hair, although short, looked like some of it had been forcibly removed as his scalp on the side of his head was red raw.

'You're one to talk,' he began to cough again. 'Beatin' on kids?' Dante raised his eyebrows.

'It was a mistake,' Seamus admitted. 'He pointed a fucking gun at my head. I was looking for you.'

'Well, you found me,' Dante chuckled, ignoring the comment regarding the gun. 'I'd appreciate it if you don't beat the shit outta me though, man.' He smirked. Seamus could see that he was in so much pain, he was barely with it. The police officer inside him wondered if the drugs on the table were an attempt to deal with the pain.

'Look. I'm not here on official duty. But I need answers. I need to know what's going on,' Seamus stated. He was all too accustomed to Dante's games and he didn't have time to barter for information. Even so, his statement did not receive the response he expected. Instead of sarcasm or wit, Dante responded with nothing. His eyes welled up. He seemed broken. As he began to cry, Seamus could see the sincerity in the boy. He moved forward and placed his hand on Dante's shoulder.

'What's going on? What happened to you?' Seamus asked in a gentle tone.

'I'm s-sorry,' Dante responded, fighting through his tears and sobs. 'I told them,' he sobbed more and more as he expressed his remorse for whatever it was he was apologising for. 'He asked for Markovic.' He stopped and continued to weep.

'Markovic?' Seamus' heart dropped in his chest. 'He did this to you?'

'I told him about you - about the body,' Dante admitted, struggling to keep his emotions in check.

'You told Markovic?' Seamus queried; he didn't fully understand what Dante was trying to tell him. The dribs and drabs of information just didn't add up – he needed more.

'I told the big guy,' there was something else that he wanted to say, but it wasn't coming easily. Seamus tried to comfort him in the hope that he would be able to finish what he was wanting to confess. 'I gave him your name... I'm sorry,' he sobbed harder. 'I'm so sorry. I watched, he made me watch.' He repeated the words over and over until Seamus stopped him.

'You watched what, Dante? It's okay, you're gonna be okay now.' Seamus was beginning to tear up himself as he watched Dante struggle, in serious pain physically and emotionally.

'I gave your name,' he said again, this time more clearly. He held back the tears the best he could and tried to compose himself. 'He didn't give you up. He didn't say your name,' Dante grabbed Seamus by the arm and looked him straight in the eyes. 'I watched and then I gave him what he wanted!' He broke down altogether now, but between the pain and tearful gasps he managed a few more words before collapsing in emotion. 'Smithy didn't give your name!'

10

Krysta Rose-Anderson

Having eventually deciphered the coded message that Lucy had received, Claire had been able to deduce a time and place for a meeting supposedly being held between Markovic and his seemingly new-found colleagues. Krysta was sceptical about the method by which they had obtained the data, however. On receipt of the news that they had gained this intel, it had helped to jog her own memory of the message she had received regarding Solomon; Claire was now also looking into that, attempting to work out the source of both sets of messages. The atmosphere within the team was uneasy. Krysta had not long been back at work since recovering from her last trip to one of Markovic's properties, and now there was supposedly to be another. The location of the meet was also not in the nicest part of town, and who was to say that the unknown source that had sent this message was even reliable? Mike and Lucy joked, saying 'it's 'bout time someone else had our backs'. Hale seemed quite unsettled with the plan – but, of course, he would follow orders.

'The intel is undependable at best, I'll be honest,' Solomon sounded above the murmur of the inner-team chatter. 'Claire has managed to decipher a coded message from a currently undisclosed source. The level of encryption required to send this message, and the efforts of Agent

Davenport to decipher it on our end suggests that the source is a high-level hacker at the top of their field. Thankfully for us, Davenport is better. We've also deduced that this is not the first time that this hacker has been in contact,' he said, looking in Krysta's direction. 'Last time it was a warning, so we're going forward and taking this new information as sound. But don't let that fact lower you into a false sense of security – we still don't know who we can trust.'

That word: *trust*. The investigation had already thrown one hell of a large amount of shit their way and the team were reluctant to trust anyone at this point. They were already having to take on some extra members who were not part of the original team. The briefing room contained all of Solomon's team, but also a group of F.B.I SWAT, as well as Kyle and two other agents; agents Travis and Michaels. *Not exactly feeling the trust in this room*. Krysta allowed her eyes to wonder. The room was divided, both literally and metaphorically. She could almost taste the distrust. Word had spread about what had happened at the warehouse, and as such no one really wanted to join in on an investigation that was speedily tallying up a body count. They were also not keen on taking on a mission based on suspect intel from a mystery source, and Solomon clearly knew it.

'Look,' Solomon now stood, slightly deflated with his hands on his hips, glancing about the teams before him. 'I know some of you may not be keen on this one but if we can catch Markovic in the act...' Raising an eyebrow and looking each of the team straight in eye, he paused for a moment. Krysta knew that look and she trusted Solomon. 'We can make huge strides towards getting to the bottom of this shit storm and putting these criminals behind bars once and for all.' His attempt to reassure the group had little effect on some. Of course, the SWAT team and Kyle's lackies didn't know Solomon like she did.

Krysta would have loved to say that her own team were

feeling confident, however, no one was quite sure what they had seen that day out in Flatlands. Krysta herself couldn't remember every detail. She felt driven though; her injury and subsequent time off had given her time to overthink and dwell on things, which was never good. She had always preferred to be physically working a case than sat going through paperwork on desk duty. She had gone over the facts time and time again in her head, so the fact that they were getting out and chasing a lead felt like a good thing, mostly. Solomon went over all the details of the mission, but once he had finished, Kit stepped up to then go over everything once more. *What a jack-ass.* She looked about the room as he rambled on. *No one's even listening.* Krysta could tell that Kyle was only doing it to make sure everyone realised that he too oversaw this operation. His briefing, however, gave Krysta and Lucy the perfect opportunity to have a chat whilst they suited up.

'Things are great,' Krysta blushed in response to Lucy's quizzing of how her relationship with Jake was going. 'He's had to go out of town for a few days. But it's cool, actually, it's great timing what with all this shit happening,' she explained.

'Sounds to me like he's probably had to go back to his wife and kids. You know, to check in,' Mikes' interruption was met with a sharp punch from Lucy to his arm as he strapped up his stab vest. 'Hey! It was a joke!' he chuckled. Krysta would not admit she felt slightly insecure, but the last few weeks had been good. She and Jake had gotten to know each other a lot.

'Ignore him, Krys,' Lucy exclaimed, punching Mike on the arm once more. He laughed it off, but Krysta knew how hard Lucy could punch, even when not trying. 'Glad to hear its going well, but how's it going in, you know... the other department?' Lucy queried not so subtly. A slightly embarrassed Krysta laughed at the question.

'It's all good thanks, Luce,' she replied. However, her and

Jakes' relationship was moving a lot slower than what she was used to. Sure, he was a shy guy but she was used to a much faster pace in relationships. She wasn't worried though. She had always rushed things previously and she thought that might have been the reasoning for them being short lived courtships. 'Hey I forgot to say - thanks for the blue rose by the way. Nice touch,' Krysta said. Her words seemed to be met with confusion however, as the look in Lucy's eyes seemed to question the comment.

'Hey guys,' Paul Hale entered at the opportune moment, taking the focus away from Krysta and her relationship status, for which she was grateful. 'Sounds like you guys are with Solomon,' he said, gesturing vaguely towards Kyle, who was still giving his team talk. 'I get Johnston and his lackies. Yay.' He looked over to agents Travis and Michaels and smiled. Paul had really started to settle into the team recently. He had been out for drinks with Mike on one occasion, although it was still undecided as to whether that would be a good thing for him. He had visited Krysta during her recovery, bringing her some flowers but awkwardly did not hang around for long to talk. Most of the team still knew little about him, but he always seemed pleasant. 'Watch each other's backs out there, yeah?' he said touching Krysta and Lucy on their shoulders and giving them a reassuring shake. He then gave Mike a friendly knuckle bump, before joining Kit and the other agents on the opposite side of the room.

'Right,' Kyle announced, although few took notice. He then coughed loudly to clear his throat. 'Right!' he exclaimed, this time drawing everyone's attention. 'Alpha team, Solomon, Rose-Anderson, Ward and Rodriguez in car one.' He seemed annoyed as he announced the details. Krysta looked to Lucy who gave her a quick smirk and a wink to let her know she was on the same page. 'Bravo team. Agents Hale, Travis and Michaels. You're with me.' The two new agents obviously did not know Kyle as well as the rest of them as they did not exhibit the same look of discontentment that Paul currently had on his face. 'SWAT is going to have our backs on this one as a precautionary measure. Although, hopefully you guys are going to be bored,' he finished, aiming the last comment toward the SWAT team that stood ready to ship out. Kit was then interrupted before he could go on any further, with Solomon giving the final order to move out.

From the blueprints that they had obtained, the building that they were about to enter after reaching their destination was another labyrinth, much like the warehouse that they had been to before. Only one story high, the building had once been a hospital or clinic, but had been converted into a packing and distribution hub in recent years. It was a maze of rooms and corridors that encircled a huge open area in its centre.

'Let's rock and roll!' Mike exclaimed as he exited the squad car.

'Hold up, Mike,' Solomon instructed. 'Wait for Bravo team and SWAT to finish checking the perimeter.'

'And let them take all the glory?' Mike jested.

'More like, so we don't get fucked,' Lucy retaliated.

'Meh. Semantics,' Mike laughed. The second car pulled up shortly after, along with the SWAT team.

'Perimeter is clear, Solomon,' Kit confirmed. 'The whole place looks pretty quiet.' The eight agents stood at the entrance to the building with their backup holding position by the vehicles. Looking into the mouth of the maze, Krysta couldn't help but feel slightly unnerved.

'You sure this is the place Sol?'

'Based on the intel, this is it,' Solomon responded. 'May not look like much but keep your wits about you.'

'I've gotta agree with Krysta on this one Solomon,' Kyle said, drawing several looks of disbelief from the team. 'Maybe the intel was wrong? Doesn't seem to be anything going down here tonight. Or maybe it was decrypted wrong... ' Solomon gave Kit a stern look as he tried to insinuate that

Claire, one of his team, had messed up.

'Look,' Solomon said before Kyle could offend anyone else. 'There's no harm in checking this place out. Even if nothing is going down, we might be able to find some evidence. We'll give it a quick sweep and see what we can find. Just stay sharp.'

The two teams entered the building together, leaving the SWAT team standing resolutely at the entrance. The first thought that crossed Krysta's mind as she entered was how much less of a shithole this place was than some of the previous locations they'd investigated that belonged to Markovic. It smelt a lot better than the sodden stench of the warehouse, and it had obviously been cleaned recently. The foyer broke away into three different corridors. Dead ahead was the entrance to the main central packing area, and to the left and right were openings to the warrens of offices and hallways that surrounded it.

'No lights?' Krysta asked, flicking a light switch in the foyer.

'Looks like the power's down,' Hale responded. 'Torches it is.'

Each of the entrances and exits to the adjoining rooms had some form of emergency lighting above them, providing a dim glow in the darkness, but the fact that the mission felt wrong was only worsened by the idea of having to fumble about in the dark. Kit and Bravo team took off down the corridor to the left, their flashlights flittering like fireflies in the pitch black. Krysta, Solomon and the others moved along the central hallway and into the large cavernous central room. Piles of cardboard boxes and numerous conveyor belt systems ran throughout the area as they pushed forward. They had to move cautiously as the packages and equipment seemed to creep up on them unexpectedly. Krysta couldn't help but wonder what was in the boxes, and as she began to open one, Lucy slipped out of the black to stand beside her.

'I opened a couple already,' Lucy admitted. 'Found nothing but test tubes and a shit load of pregnancy tests.' She stood watching as Krysta opened the box before her. This one was filled with tinned foods. Tinned fruit, beans, fish and other rations. 'The hell?' Lucy questioned, picking up one of the tins. Krysta knew what the boxes were intended for; it could only be one thing as far as Markovic was concerned.

'They're for the girls,' Krysta said, although the words almost stuck in her throat.

'Drugs. Tests. Food.' Solomon said, joining the pair of them with Mike in tow. 'Promised a better life, only to end up belonging to someone, drugged up and eating from a can.' The thought disgusted Krysta and she could tell Lucy felt the same way. 'Krys, with me.' Solomon ordered. 'Mike, Lucy, head back and move through the corridor to the right. You find anything other than tinned food, you let me know.' As Lucy and Mike passed under the orangey glow of the emergency lighting and disappeared into the darkness, Krysta and Solomon continued to examine their surroundings, moving deeper into the void as they went.

The light of Krysta's torch revealed stack after stack of boxes, no doubt containing much of the same items. *How many girls could there be to warrant this much stuff?* Now deep within the darkened cavern of a room, hers and Solomon's footsteps were the only sounds to break the silence.

'Sol?' Lucy asked over comms. 'We may have something here. Some sort of munitions cache. Crates of ammo but no weapons.'

'Hold your position, Luce. We'll come to you,' Solomon nodded to Krysta, indicating for the two of them to head back. Just as Krysta turned on her heels, her feet were taken out from under her. She slipped, hitting the ground with a thud. Shining her flashlight erratically about the room, she saw around her what appeared to be some sort of viscous liquid. She had fell directly into a puddle of it. Looking up at Solomon, whose hand was outstretched, she reached out to grab it and pull herself to her feet. But as her hand passed through the light of his torch, she noticed the red of her palm. Looking closer, the blood was unmistakable.

'Sol?' Krysta said in a panic. Her heart began to race. Clambering to her feet, she and Solomon frantically shone their lights about the floor to ascertain the source of the blood. Krysta had landed in a small pool but to the left there appeared to be a trail leading into the dark. The spatter at first seemed to be erratic and once or twice it threw them off the trail, but eventually the path became clear. They must have followed the droplets and smears for at least another twenty feet further into the structure before they saw her. A girl in a flower-patterned dress.

The girl's dark blonde hair was partially stained red. A small but deep cut ran from her temple down to the crease in her lips; her eyes were closed, sealed with a coagulated mixture of blood and tears. Strands of her hair lay on the floor about her unmoving body as she lay lifeless on the flat of her back. Her flowery dress was torn at her bosom, one of her breasts laid bare. As Krysta looked upon her, her heart filled with sorrow and her stomach gurgled with a sickness she couldn't quell. The girls dress was also torn at her abdomen. Her legs were spread. They were blackened; her skin was cracked and burnt, marked with two large handprints. One leg was out of place, as if it had been dislocated at the hip, and the source of the blood was now evident between her thighs. Fighting the urge to firstly scream and then to cry, Krysta stood in disbelief. What had happened to this girl - no one deserved such a thing. Krysta remained still, unable to move. Solomon bent down to check the girl's pulse, although little hope remained.

'Krys. She's alive!' Solomon exclaimed. He instantly took to the comms, asking Kyle and the team for assistance but his request received no reply. 'Krys, comms must be on the fritz. Head back to the entrance and get SWAT to call for an ambulance. We need to get her out of here.' Krysta had barely waited for him to finish what he was saying before she turned and charged back the way they had come.

Knocking stacks of boxes out of the way, leaping over others, she ran as quickly as she could. But the closer to the doors she got, the more a feeling of doubt began to try and drag her back in the opposite direction. *The doors are open.* The light from outside flooded into the foyer. *Where are the SWAT team?* She began to slow down, calming her pace. She continued forward until she reached the opening and stepped out into the glow of the moon and streetlights. After being in the dark for so long, she found the light slightly disorientating and it took her a moment to focus. There wasn't a sole in sight. She moved towards the abandoned cars; one still had its headlights on. She threw her arms outward in an exasperated fashion, annoyed that their backup had left their post. Krysta went to report their disappearance over the radio, but stopped in her tracks. As she had turned back towards the building, preparing to announce her findings over the comms, her eyes had fallen on the members of the SWAT team. Bound at the wrists and swinging four or five feet off the floor, there were two officers either side of the entrance. Blood ran from their throats, down over their body armour and dripped from their boots into puddles on the ground. *It was a trap.* She grasped at her weapon, summoned the courage to move and bounded back into the building. But before she had even escaped the light from the outside, the sound of gunfire filled the air. She halted for a moment; she couldn't distinguish which direction it was coming from. The sound seemed to be everywhere as it echoed around her. *They were waiting for us.* Krysta began to head back to Solomon when there was a distinctive sound from behind her. The pump of a shotgun and the clink of a shell being loaded.

'Drop the gun. Kick it away, bitch!' Krysta could feel his stare on her back, the aim of his gun. She went to do as he had asked but he must have panicked, as the next sound was that of shotgun fire. She closed her eyes, expecting the pain, expecting the end, but she received neither. She spun around to confront her adversary; there, between her and the shotgun wielder, stood another man with his back to her. The first man dropped his weapon, just before he himself fell to the ground with this stranger stood looking down on him. Krysta did not lower her gun. The second man stood barefoot with the light from the doorway piercing the darkness around him. He wore dirt ridden jeans, but his torso was bare. She could see a faded tattoo on his back; a leafless tree amongst a plethora of scars. One scar caught her eye. On his shoulder, there was what looked like a handprint. Reminded of the girl and of Solomon, she lowered her gun slightly. She needed to get back to them.

'Help me,' she said, the words escaping her lips. 'There's a girl. She's badly hurt.' Krysta continued, not knowing why she was asking this stranger for assistance. But he had saved her life – he couldn't be one of them. He turned to face her. Blood ran down his chest; he'd been shot, but it didn't seem to trouble him. From what she could tell with the lack of light, his hair was a light brown and framed a kind face. Krysta looked him in the face. A guileless look shone in his bright green eyes that - for some unknown reason - felt so familiar.

'Lead the way,' he replied softly. Hesitant to turn her back, she gestured for him to position himself beside her. With this, they both headed off into the darkness, back towards Solomon, towards the din of gunfire.

The unmistakable flash of gunfire lit the way as they rushed into the chaos. Krysta tried to keep as low to the ground as she could, ensuring that at the same time she could move as quickly as possible. He moved beside her, just as quickly and with some ease. They found Solomon taking cover behind an overturned table pushed up against a conveyor, with several boxes stacked up around him to provide some protection. He wasn't alone; he had moved the girl with him, and he had been joined by Lucy, Mike and Kyle. Mike sat on the floor beside the girl. He was grasping at his leg and Krysta could see that he was wounded, but at least he was alive; at least they were all alive. The sight filled Krysta with hope as she and the stranger took up a position beside them all.

'Thank God you're okay!' Lucy exclaimed at the sight of Krysta. Before she could respond, Lucy had turned and was firing her M4 carbine in response to the incessant shooting.

'Mike?' Krysta asked worriedly.

'No worries here, Krys, it's just a graze!' he chuckled in attempt to disguise the pain, but she could see through his façade.

'Hale?!' Krysta asked, looking around but not seeing him.

'Michaels and Travis are down. Hale is MIA,' Kyle responded. He was almost curled up upon the ground where he had gotten so low. He was scared. Normally Krysta would have revelled in this fact, but right now she felt the same way. 'We've taken out a few. Figure there can't be more than four or five left. Where the fuck is SWAT?'

'They're all dead,' Krysta admitted. She straightened up and began assisting Lucy in returning fire, shooting into the darkness towards the flashes of gunfire that were pointed towards them.

'We need to get this girl out of here now.' Solomon stated. Communications were still unexplainably down. *They must be blocking our signal somehow.* Krysta looked around, hoping that something would inspire her into figuring out their next action. Remembering her saviour, she looked around for him too, but he had gone.

The stranger that had saved her had seemingly disappeared into the darkness without her noticing. Krysta didn't have time to dwell. She flew back to face forward as suddenly, a stack of boxes in the distance set a blaze, the fire highlighting the location of two men with automatic weapons. Realising their position had been uncovered, the men attempted to flee but were simultaneously neutralised by Solomon and Lucy. A second fire started far off to the right of the first and another attacker was quickly extinguished by the team. A third, fourth and fifth stack of boxes set alight, each setting a blaze and providing the light the team so desperately needed. Scouring the area Krysta could see no more movement and the gunfire had stopped.

'We need to get the girl and Mike some medical attention. Now.' Solomon ordered; he too had noticed this was their opportunity to move. Lucy and Krysta quickly moved to Mike, helping him to his feet.

'We'll get you a nice walking stick, hey muscles?' Lucy quipped. Mike laughed at the comment.

'Then I'll have four legs,' he smiled and winked before grimacing at the pain in his leg. Solomon and Kyle grabbed the girl, being as careful as they could but knowing that time was of the essence.

'Adam!' A booming voice sounded like a foghorn as the group started to make their escape, the sound reverberating about the cavernous chamber. 'She's mine, Adam!' The team stopped in their tracks. Krysta knew that voice. It was the same booming voice from the warehouse. He began to whistle a playful tune, one that curled her stomach. *Adam!* It suddenly dawned on Krysta that the stranger she met must have been him. He had now saved her twice – what was his deal? Krysta and Lucy frantically searched the darkness for some sort of sign as to where the enemy was. The fires had brightened the room in places, but there was still plenty of shadow for him to hide in. They needn't have searched however, as the owner of the voice chose to reveal himself. The huge man stepped into the light by one of the burning stacks. There he stood, dressed in black boots, darkened pants and a long-sleeved black top, holding his hands out over the dissipating flames, smiling gleefully.

Turning to face Krysta and the team, he pulled a blade from his belt. He tossed it from one hand to the other as he stepped forward a few paces towards them.

'Sol, he has a weapon,' Lucy squeaked. Krysta could feel her trying to pull away with Mike.

'It's not working Adam!' the man shouted. He seemed frustrated. Krysta worried that he would soon lose his temper. His eyes captured the fire light and glowed as if the flames themselves danced within them. 'Serena blames you Adam! Where are you? Come out, come out, wherever you are...' His empty hand formed a fist and emitted a steady radiance of light and heat. 'Father told me to get the job done... but it didn't work Adam!' He was growing more and more agitated and began to walk in and out of the light, kicking anything in his way as he did so. *We need to go.* But she did not dare move; not yet. 'Drop my present!' the last bellow was directed at Solomon and Kyle, who stood holding the girl. Neither of them reacted to his yelling, which seemed to anger him further as he stepped back into the light and began to walk towards them. He could not have been more than twenty feet away from Krysta and the others when out of the black came Hale; hurtling into the man, knocking the blade from his hand and forcing him to lose his footing.

'Go. *Now.*' Adam re-emerged next to Krysta. He was calm, apparently unphased by what was happening. Solomon heeded his words and gave the nod to the team, and then he and Kyle began to carry the wounded girl back towards the entrance.

'Lucy, Krysta! Move!' Solomon's voice carried through the darkness as he vanished from sight. Krysta knew they had to escape, but she did not want to leave Paul behind. He was tussling with the monster that had taunted them, but Hale seemed to be throwing more into the fight than his adversary. Looking to Adam once more, Krysta conveyed a silent plea for help, one that he appeared to be able to read.

She needed only to look into his emerald eyes, and he nodded in response.

'Brandt!' Adam shouted. 'Enough!' He spoke without fear or hesitation. His words were authoritative, demanding of attention from all those around him. Hale and Brandt stopped. Both looked toward Adam. For a moment, Krysta wondered if the beast could be tamed just like that, but Adam's command was only adhered for a moment before Brandt swatted Paul to one side, flinging him several feet away, and then got to his feet and marched towards Adam. Adam turned to Krysta and mouthed the word 'go' before hastily charging towards their attacker. He tackled Brandt with some force, taking the pair of them out of sight, into the dark. Dusting himself off, Hale scrambled to his feet and appeared to be looking for an opportunity to re-join the fight.

'Hale, we need to go.' Krysta called to him, hoping that he would see sense. He turned to her; his vest was torn, and he had only his sidearm. His arms hung beside him, tired and weakened. His face held a resolved look, as if all he had left was his will to continue. Thankfully, after a moment he nodded in defeat and began to limp in Krysta's direction. He stopped in his tracks however, turned and quickly darted towards where he and Brandt had fought; he stooped and picked up the blade that had been dropped before continuing to head towards Krysta.

'Let's get the hell out of here,' he said before handing the knife to Lucy. 'Luce, you need to get this out of here so it can be filed as evidence. Go let Solomon know we're okay and we're on our way out.' He seemed confident that the worst was behind them. 'I'll help Krys with Mike.'

Lucy accepted Hale's plan and tore off towards the entrance. Krysta and Paul grabbed Mikes arms and slung them around their own necks to carry him out of the building. They started to move off into the black, leaving Adam and Brandt behind. Krysta couldn't help but worry about Adam. He had saved her life twice now, and she felt terrible that he'd gone after their attacker yet again. She could hear crashes and thuds but couldn't see anything. Each time there was a loud bang, she would glance behind in fear only to receive no answers. They were almost at the hallway that lead to the foyer, the glow from the emergency lighting a warm and welcome sight. But before they could pass under the dimmed lights, the cacophonous sound of a conveyor crashing against the walls in front of them stopped them in their tracks. Adam came hurtling out of the gloom and crashed against the wall himself with Brandt not far behind him, throwing himself into Adam as he impacted the structure, maximising the damage. Krysta could feel the ground quake beneath her feet.

'You thought it was going to be that easy!' Brandt blasted as he turned to face the three of them. He was wounded himself. Blood rushed down his face and his top was torn, revealing cuts to his chest and abdomen. He spat blood onto the floor and let out an almighty scream.

'Easy? You fucking kidding me?' Mike retaliated. His joking was not received well. Brandt's eyes, scars and hands began to glow a furiously dark red. He went to move towards them but was prevented from doing so; Adam had gotten to his feet and grabbed him by the arm.

'I said... enough,' Adam instructed wearily. He was breathless and barely able to stand, let alone fight anymore. He looked at Krysta and she could see something in his eyes that she couldn't quite understand, a tranquillity that could not have been more out of place. But as soon as she had seen it, it was gone. The heat had extinguished from Brandt's extremities now, making him loose his temper. In one fell swoop, he had placed one hand onto Adams crown, the other grasped his chin, and had snapped his neck. Krysta gasped, feeling sick. Brandt lifted the lifeless body into the air as if it were a rag doll and threw it into the hallway. Knowing they had to move, Krysta pushed off the floor with all her might, throwing herself forward with Hale and Mike in tow. She made it to the hallway, with Mike still propped up between her and Paul. But just as they passed under the lights, she could feel her grip lessening on Mikes arm. He was slipping away – no, something had a hold of him. She turned her head to look at Mike's face; his expression was unreadable. For once, there were no quips leaving his lips, no glint in his eye. Fear was all that he could convey as he slid from their grasp. He moved so quickly that neither Krysta nor Hale could keep hold of him, his fingertips brushing against theirs as they reached out towards the darkness that engulphed him, pulling him back with all they could muster. But it wasn't enough. Mike was swallowed by the darkness, and a whistled tune was all that remained of what filled the darkness.

11

Adam

He could feel every bump in the road. He jolted each time the wheels clattered against a miss placed cobble, with every divot in the grass and every troublesome stone. He was awoken by the sound of the horse's bray; they were pushing it too hard - he could sense the animal's pain. He opened his eyes. It was dark, but the sun was soon to rise. The coolness of the night was fading, and the light of the day would soon pierce the skyline. He was healing still, but felt much stronger than the day before. He had become too complacent and they had found him. This time, Matthias had sent four of them to hunt him down. It had taken all four of them as well, as it had been some time since he had last seen his brothers and sisters and the time had allowed his strength to recover and his powers to grow. But alas, now he needed to heal once more. Brandt had hold of the reins, which explained the regular cries from the horse. Serena rode beside Brandt and no doubt Nahki had gone ahead - but where was she? The cold, hard iron of the shackles that clung to his ankles and wrists pained him as their coarseness chafed against his damaged flesh. Brandt had welded them shut, burning through skin and scolding bone.

Adam looked to Serena, who had noticed him come round. He held his hands up in a plea to have the constraints loosened, if not removed. He knew as well as she did that in his current state there was little chance of him escaping - he needed time to heal. She sat astride a fine mare, snowy white in colour with a braided mane. Serena was dressed finely herself. A low-cut gown of crimson allowed her to flaunt her bosom and revealed a fuchsia coloured kirtle and chemise. He knew she wore the pink for Brandt; too much red would only spark his temper, and she had always been one of the more cunning of The Avunaye, able to easily manipulate some of the others. Yet Adam had always been able to resist the charms of his so-called sister, something he knew had never sat very well with Serena, who was all too accustomed to getting her own way. A blood-red cloak drifted down her back and trailed atop of the horse's rump. Tied loosely about her neck, the hood was kept down to allow her fiery red hair to flow freely. She glanced at Adam to see his plea for a show of mercy.

'You show weakness, brother,' she laughed, a flicker of evil flashing within her eyes. 'Good. You'll break all the easier.' She then spurred her horse to speed up and rode level with Brandt.

'Unusually quiet, Brandt,' Adam quipped. *Maybe if Serena won't help improve me, I can make Brandt do it instead.* Brandt was, of course, so easily angered after all. 'Looking a bit worse for wear, monsieur.' Brandt had clearly taken a beating this time around. Adam tried to remember what had happened exactly, but his mind was always cloudy after a rejuvenation. Short term memories would soon return. Long-term memories, however, could take days, months or even years. He sometimes wondered if his brothers and sisters deliberately prevented him from regaining all his memories, making him rejuvenate every so often as he might begin to remember more and more. Brandt bit his tongue at Adam's jibes and whipped the horse all the harder in frustration, causing the animal to miss place its footing and jerk the carriage.

'Patience brother,' Serena noted. 'We've a two-day ride

to Rouen and unless you wish to walk, I suggest you ease up on that beast.' Brandt said nothing in reply and continued to drive onwards in silence, but Adam could sense his resolve was waning. *Two days to go then*. Adam propped himself against the boundaries of his confinement to try and get some rest. *Two days to be ready*. He was confident; he was healing quickly and with every moment that passed he grew stronger.

The sun rose to its peak and Adam basked in its warmth. It was nearing the end of May and the weather was now kinder, the days were longer and warmer, and the sweet-nutty smell of barley fields scented the open air. *The harvest*. He lay still in the sunlight, breathing it all in; a subtle relaxed smile found its way to the crease in his lips. He needed to be careful. If they were to see that he was recovering well, then they would no doubt snatch life from him once more. Regardless, he lay there with some peace of mind, knowing that his interests were far away from here. They had stripped him of his possessions, clothing, and anything else he may have had on him when they found him. He lay in nothing but a pair of badly torn linen under-pants and what was left of a burgundy woollen shirt. He wondered if he had grown too comfortable, living amongst people.

'I'm fucking starving,' the quiet was broken as Brandt announced his hunger. 'Where the fuck is Nahki?' he asked Serena.

'Finish the red deer, brother,' she graciously replied. 'Nahki will return soon enough.' Brandt continued to grow more restless and impatient. He tore some wrappings from a satchel and uncovered a whole hind leg of venison. Grasping it in his huge hands, he squeezed the meat as it began to cook, blood and juices running quickly through his fingers, staining his beige woollen stockings. He took a large bite from the thigh but was not satisfied with what he tasted; the meat was old and had no doubt began to turn. In a sudden outburst, he spat out the contents of his mouth in Serenas direction and flicked the blood from his fingers, splattering it across her mare's pristine forehead and muzzle. The animal reared in response, almost throwing Serena from its back.

'Are you fucking stupid?' she screamed in anger, her eyes alight and her face almost ablaze with an empurpled fury. Brandt, however, merely laughed at her outburst and threw the meat behind him into Adams cell, as if he were throwing scraps to the hounds. The charred deer flesh and bone fell onto the straw laden floor of the cart and Adam quickly picked it up and bit down into it. Turned meat or not, he wasn't fed often and although at full strength he did not necessarily require food, the recovery process was aided by such sustenance. He was starving. He ate as if he may never eat again; juices from the meat ran down his chin and dripped onto the straw. His teeth sank deep and ran flush with the bone, tearing as much away as possible.

'Aw... Doggy has a bone,' Serena cackled as she dropped back to ride alongside the carriage once more. Adam presumed that she didn't wish to ride by Brandt's side at this moment in time. The look on her face was evidence that she was attempting to extinguish her own temper. Adam took little notice of her jibe and continued to eat, cleaning the bone and filling his stomach.

Darkness fell and they reluctantly stopped to allow the horses some respite from the arduous journey. The animal pulling the cart practically dropped to its knees as soon as Brandt let up on the reins. *I'm surprised it's still with us.* Adam looked at the carthorse; Brandt had taken his anger out on the poor soul, sometimes drawing blood with the reins as he drove. Adam felt sorry for it. If he were in a better position to help it, he would have. If his memory served, in the past he had been able to heal some wounds with a mere touch. *Hopefully a good night's sleep will do us all some good.* Serena had lit a fire and then thrown down some blankets to make herself comfortable. Brandt sat on the other side of the flames, repeatedly passing his hand through the fire with outstretched fingers. He allowed the reds and oranges to dance about his skin, seemingly fuelling the blaze that forever burned within him. Adam's eyes grew heavy, and so he made himself as comfortable as one could on his straw ridden berth and closed them.

Krys, the guy was dead... Now he's... this is fucked up...

It had barely felt like more than a few moments from when he had closed his eyes, when he was suddenly forced to open them again. Searing pain woke him in an instant as the blade cut through his flesh just below his shoulder blade. The knife's entrance, however, was nothing compared to its exit; its razored edge dragging slithers of him away with it as it was removed.

'I'm afraid you don't get to rest now, Adam.' Nahki had returned during the night from his hunt. Brandt and Serena gorged by the fire on what smelt like rabbit. The remains of a hart also sat on the ground beside them. Nahki stood by the cage, wiping the blood and flesh from his weapon onto the cast iron mesh that formed Adams current prison. 'We don't want you getting too comfortable, now do we?' He spoke calmly, as was his nature. He was the youngest of The Avunaye, yet his new-found gifts had made him wise beyond his years. Nahki was confident and calculated, able to supress emotion, as if the change had taken more from him than any of the others. Adam often considered him to now be devoid of humanity, which Matthias had used to create the perfect weapon. Nahki had been a gifted huntsman before the ritual, but now he was something else. He stood staring at Adam, his eyes unblinking. He had very short jet-black hair and his dark skin sparkled slightly in the fire light. Around his neck was a chain of small animal bones with rubies and topaz stones set between them, tied together in an alternating pattern. He wore only a loin cloth made from animal skin, yet he did not seem to feel the chill on the night air. He spun the blade between his fingers and then grasped its hilt; taking a deep breath, he slowly released his grip on the weapon - yet it did not fall from his hand. Instead, the knife slowly sank into his palm, his skin absorbing it until it vanished completely from sight. Adam could remember seeing him do this before - although the last time it was a full-sized halberd that Nahki had brought forth from nothing.

The night passed slowly. Adam had hoped to rest but Nahki saw to it that he got none. The darkness passed eventually, and the morning sun rose again after a night that had felt like a day or two itself. None of them had slept in the end, but at least the others had rested comfortably. The horses reluctantly rose to resume their march; the workhorse whinnied at the thought of being whipped again, but the mare knew better than to misbehave as Serena climbed atop it. Nahki once again set off ahead of the carriage, breaking into a stride and quickly disappearing into the landscape. Adam watched the hunter - or *Mwindaji*, as he was in Nahki's native tongue - vanish from sight. The guilt Adam felt towards Nahki was worse than any of the others. He remembered the day of the ritual; he had not wanted to participate. Perhaps that was why it pained him more so than any of the others; Adam had many regrets, but none more so than the times he had ignored his own conscience and had chosen to follow Matthias blindly. He longed for the memories of his own turning, of a time before all of this. But those memories were locked away deep inside of him, and he could not be sure if he had ever or would ever be able to unlock them.

They continued to travel relentlessly throughout the day. Occasionally, Serena would drop back to make sure that he was not becoming too comfortable in his cage; she would laugh at his current state and once offered to join him in his prison.

'I'll keep you warm, brother,' she suggested, smiling a wicked smile. 'Brandt won't mind... he loves to watch.' Adam

145

refused to acknowledge her perverted insinuations, which in turn annoyed her and so she rode off ahead once more, sulking. Day turned into night once more and then morning came. Setting off again, there was a feeling of anticipation about the group. Today they would reach their destination and Adam would no doubt receive what was coming to him.

He's our only lead... He'll wake up sooner or later and when he does...

Brandt halted the cart abruptly as they reached the bank of a river. It was a large river; Adam could hear its waters flowing for some distance as he sat in the centre of his cage, eyes closed, attempting to aid his recovery. He had often meditated to help his body heal; nightly visits from Nahki ensured that it would take some time to recover completely.

'We're here,' said Serena, stopping alongside. She clapped her hands and smiled with excitement. *What wicked intentions do you harbour sister?* Adam had opened his eyes to see the gleeful look on her face. The water ran steadily, and across its breadth Adam could see a church of sorts. Still in construction, its enormity would no doubt one day prove to be a wonder. Brandt descended from the front of the carriage and made his way around to its rear. He said nothing to Adam as he sauntered around the cage. Adam turned, following his gaze with some curiosity. Brandt stopped at the back of the cage and grasped the cold iron mesh. His hands heated the metal, causing it to glow and soften. Soon it was malleable enough for him to pull it apart and create an exit for Adam.

'There's something you need to see,' Brandt said. There was a distinct malevolence to his words. Adam knew that whatever it was it couldn't be good. Still with hands and feet bound in irons, Adam lumbered towards the opening. Once he was close enough, Brandt grabbed him by the arms and dragged him from the wagon, throwing him to the ground. Grabbing the iron chain that ran between Adams wrists, he pulled him through the mud towards the river. 'Evelina would like a word,' he said as he drew to a halt. Adam looked out across the river as he rose to his knees; he could see a gathering of people in the distance, the people of Rouen.

'Where are my belongings, Adam?' she asked as she walked along the bank to the left of them. She looked more beautiful than ever. Her long golden hair fell over her right shoulder; the gown she wore consisted of several layers of gold toned silk, cascading down like a waterfall. Each layer encapsulated a design of fine intricate patterns of flowers and trees. The sleeveless gown clung tightly to her waist and halted just above her breast; pale gold in colour, it shimmered in the sunlight as rose shaped patterns, created by several crystals or diamonds, caught the sun's rays. Her full, red-rose lips exhibited a gentle smile and her bottle-green eyes spoke only of kindness and compassion. For a moment, Adam bought into the deception and almost forgot the blackened heart that beat ever so slowly beneath her chest. 'My love,' she said softly as she stood before him. 'Tell me where my blade is.' She lifted her gown off the dirt and bent down to look him in the eye. 'You've been awfully busy of late my love, but now it's time to come home,' she said, raising a hand and caressing Adams cheek.

'The blade is far from your reach,' Adam replied, staring into her eyes. 'Matthias is wrong.' Adam wondered if his defiance would force her to lose her temper but for now at least, she remained calm.

'When you try to mend this broken world, Adam, all you do is create more cracks,' she smiled as she finished speaking. Standing, she nodded to Brandt and he grasped Adams arm once more, lifting him to his feet. Smoke began to rise in the distance where Adam could see the towns people gathered near a central pillar.

'What have you done?' he asked in disbelief, wondering why they would choose to set Rouen alight. Evelina grinned. 'Why burn the town?!' he asked. This time anger rode on the back of his words. His spark of emotion only amused her - and Serena too - as she began to laugh.

'Brother, why should we trouble ourselves with a pathetic town such as this?' Serena said, she then chortled. Confused, Adam looked harder in the direction of the smoke. A fire had been lit, but it had not spread. A sense of relief came to him, but then an overwhelming feeling of fear set in as he realised there would definitely be something else coming.

'Lover,' Evelina said, waltzing around him. She stopped to his side and whispered to him. 'As I said, you've been busy instilling hope and faith where it should not be. These mere mortals succumb to fear so much easier.' Her words did not ease his fear. 'A man named Cauchon has so kindly put an end to your meddling.' Adam remained confused, unsure of what she was speaking of and of what it had to do with him. 'Now, lover, one last time, where are my belongings? The blade, the tree. They belong to me.' There was a distinct annoyance to her tone. Her calmness was dissipating, and her patience was wavering.

'Eve,' Adam responded, turning his head to face her. 'Far from your reach.' His continued defiance annoyed her; as she stepped away from him, she clenched her fists in anger.

'You should not pretend to be someone you are not!' She exclaimed in frustration. 'Do you think they will ever be grateful? Do you think they'll ever learn?' She was furious, pacing as she shouted. 'Fear and hate - these are all they will ever be able to fully understand. Do you think they will learn to truly love?' As she questioned him, she appeared to calm down slightly. She stopped pacing and stood in front of Adam, placing her palm on his cheek and looking into his eyes.

'I have hope,' Adam said simply, hoping that maybe she would see sense.

'Hope?!' Serena cackled.

'Do you think *she* has hope now, lover?' Eve said slowly;

a maleficent glint sparkled in her eyes. 'You gave *her* hope, faith. But they feared what she had come to believe. You made them fear *her*.' She smiled wickedly with her eyes as she could see that Adam was coming to realise what she'd done. 'You came to *her*, lover, showed her the way. And now *she* burns.'

The words were like a detonator, arming and causing an explosion within Adams heart. Anger, sorrow and hatred flooded his veins, bringing his blood to a boil. Seeing the rush of emotion stirring within him, Eve wisely backed away. She had done more damage than any of the others had done previously. The emotion surged through him relentlessly, causing him to shake uncontrollably. He looked at his hands as they trembled.

'Now tell us what we want to know and maybe there'll be enough of her left to bury,' Serena said in a cock-sure tone. Her words, seemingly flicking a switch within Adams mind, instantly stopped his trembling. He purged the fear and hatred from his heart, leeching it until all that was left was an undeniable anger. *She was innocent.* He looked at the rising fumes from the pillar to which she must have been restrained. A rush of strength pulsated from within him, and a burning began behind his eyes. The metal of his restraints began to crumble, eroding in moments. His hands were now free to move and the wounds that Nahki had inflicted closed and healed. His breathing was heavy, and his chest hurt. His eyes were sore; the burning persisted as he struggled to dampen his rage. Brandt, seeing the reaction that had begun in Adam's body, once again grabbed him by the arm, his hand already aglow. He held tightly, his grasp melting Adam's skin. But his skin healed just as quickly as it burned. Adam grabbed Brandt's hand, forcing him to release his grip. As he held on, the heat within Brandt's palm diminished. A look of fear flashed across Brandt's face before he swung his other fist and struck Adam across his jaw. The hit made Adam lose his balance and he dropped to one knee. He placed his hands down onto the earth to steady himself and as he clutched at the soil and grass. He felt assured. He felt connected to the earth.

Brandt stepped closer to land another blow, but as he did, Adam quickly arose and threw his hands into Brandt's chest, exerting enough force to send the giant hurtling away through the air. Brandt hit the ground hard about forty feet away from the rest of them. It took him several moments to even begin moving before getting to his feet. Seemingly worried that she was next, Serena engulphed her hands in fire and set the ground before her alight. Her horse whinnied at the sight of the flames and attempted to flee but she held the reins sternly, preventing the animal from gaining its escape.

'Adam! Stop!' Evelina shouted, drawing his attention. The searing pain within his eyes was causing everything to appear green in colour, as though the world around him had gained an evil hue. But as it continued, the brighter everything became and the more painful it was to see. *Must... stop... the pain.* Adam turned to Eve. *She started this.* The thought fuelled his anguish. He stepped towards her, but within a blink of an eye she had already moved towards him. Once again, she placed her hand on his cheek and Adam was forced to stand still. A moment of uncertainty took him by surprise, as if the fire inside was doused for a split second.

Adam of the Avunaye, wake up.

His heart felt as if it exploded once more. 'Why?!' he screamed as he gave into the fury that possessed him and grabbed her by the throat. Yet as he did, the inferno that had fulminated within suddenly went out, as quickly as it had manifested within him. The seething pain within his eyes stopped and the world came back into focus. The head of a spear protruded from his breast, covered in his own blood. Adam released his grip on Eve and dropped to his knees.

'I will always be there in times of despair, Adam, to stop

you. To bring about your suffering.' As Nahki spoke the words, the realisation hit Adam once more that he had failed to protect her.

'I'm sorry!' he shouted as he jolted up from the bed. The lights were bright - they burned his retinas. Everything seemed to be flashing around him. People rushed about; their footsteps pounding the hard floor. So many voices, so many sounds. *Where is she?* He looked about the room, searching frantically. *Where am I?* He was confused. 'Jeanne?!' he shouted. 'I'm... I'm sorry.'

He stood up, causing the voices around him to sound louder. They were talking to him, at him, but he couldn't concentrate. 'Jeanne?!' he called again. He tried to walk but there were people around him, they wouldn't let him move. *I have to help her.*

Anxious and confused, he forced his way through the crowd and into a hallway. Following the lights, he made his way to an open room. 'Where? Where is she?' he asked, disorientated. The voices continued to shout at him. Beside him there was a woman. *Is it you Jeanne?* He stepped towards her, but as he did, she backed away. She lost her footing and fell away from him, scurrying out of sight after hitting the ground. 'Jeanne?!' he called again. Several people attempted to grab him as he continued to search. He couldn't tell who they were, but they were in his way, so he forced them from his path.

It was then that he saw her. The lights continued to hurt his eyes and the world remained blurry; everything still flashed, but he was sure that it was her. Deep feelings of sorrow, regret and grief took him as he dropped to his knees before her.

'I'm sorry,' he sobbed, clutching at her waist until, once again, his world faded into darkness.

12

Claire Davenport

She lost her footing as he marched towards her. Uncertain of his intentions, she had stepped backwards between the desks, attempting to retreat. Everyone seemed to be unsure of how to react to the once-dead man that was now stumbling about the office. Some panicked and moved away, others stood and shouted at him to stop. It was the strap of a brown leather satchel that caught her heel and caused her feet to go from underneath her. As she fell, she attempted to grasp a chair, a desk, anything that would lessen the fall. She hit the ground hard and knocked the back of her head on the smooth flooring. Slightly dazed but still panicked, she scurried backwards, shuffling across the floor away from Adam. He appeared confused, rambling about someone named Joan; he was looking for her. *Who is this woman he's looking for?* Claire watched from behind one of the desks as he knocked several agents to the ground in his attempt to find who he was searching for. Solomon and Hale had both drawn their firearms and were about to shoot him when suddenly he stopped. As he came face to face with Krysta it was as if he had found who he had been looking for. *Don't hurt her.* Claire watched as he stood before her colleague and friend. Claire had always liked Krysta; she admired her and had always seen her as more of an older sibling than simply a work mate. Adam did not hurt her though. Falling to his knees he grasped at her waist and asked for forgiveness. Several times he said he was sorry and begged for her to forgive him. Krysta looked into Claire's eyes, bewildered. He probably would have snapped out of it eventually, but Kyle intervened on the situation with a taser. Adam was carried off, back to his cell.

'Are you OK, Claire?' a voice asked from behind her. She heard the words but was still so intrigued by what had just happened that she didn't acknowledge them, not immediately. 'Claire?' he asked again; it was Malique, one of the data analysts.

'Err.. what?' she replied, her mind still on Adam. *He seemed so distraught.*

'Are... you... okay?' he repeated slowly, as if trying to break through a communications barrier.

'Yes!' she replied, springing to her feet like a jack-in-a-box. 'Yes! Sorry.' Malique had always been sweet and kind. He was reserved and kept mostly to himself, but he had a good heart. 'I'm okay,' She said adjusting her glasses, reassuring her concerned colleague.

'Good. That's... that's good,' he said awkwardly, before timidly turning away and shuffling back to his desk.

'Hey, Claire! All good?' Krysta said, heading over to her. The rest of the team had vanished, following Adam as he had been dragged away. Tensions had been high since Mike's disappearance. They had heard nothing from his kidnappers and leads were few and far between. Their best lead, Adam, had also been confirmed as deceased to begin with, which had made matters worse. During transportation to the morgue in an ambulance, his heart had started beating again. His miraculous resurrection had restored some hope that they might get some information to find Mike. But it had now been a fortnight and waiting for Adam to wake up had taken its toll on some of them. It had seemed to affect Lucy most of all; Mike had been her partner in the field for some time now.

'Yep, yep,' Claire replied cheerily, dusting herself off. 'Glad I didn't go with heels today,' she admitted, looking down at her black dolly shoes. She had tied her brown hair up into a ponytail and wore dark-grey work pants and a long-sleeved white blouse. 'Further to fall,' she giggled, winked and smiled at Krysta.

'Well at least you're okay,' Krysta said, distractedly looking about the office. 'A fair few might have some bruises but at least we're all good.'

'Plus, now we can finally question Adam, right?' Claire asked hopefully. 'Maybe get a lead on Mike?'

'Hopefully. The first word on the road to disappointment,' Kyle interrupted. 'We'll get what we want, don't you worry Claire.' Kyle had a confidence about him, unlike his usual cockiness.

'He'll cooperate. I'm sure of it,' Krysta said, ignoring Kit's presence and talking directly to Claire. The two of them continued to talk amongst themselves until the now irked Agent Johnston decided to move on. They then went their separate ways, with Krysta going to check on the status of Adam and Claire returning to her office.

Claire's office was her pride and joy. Often dubbed her 'woman-cave', it was home to one of the most impressive technological ecosystems known to the bureau. Claire had had a lot of input into its design. From this room she was able to pinpoint locations of people not wanting to be found. She could advise the team with detailed information during real-time missions. Lives had been saved thanks to her skills and she was immensely proud; however, recently she had become more and more frustrated. Sources were drying up; information was becoming harder to obtain. Markovic and his companions had become more and more elusive and despite spending several days and nights looking for some indication as to Mike's location, she remained at a dead end. Yet - perhaps now she had a lead. *He said Joan over and over.* She sat on one of the stools by her main workstation. *Or did he?* She quickly brought up the video footage of the detainment cell where Adam was being held. Opening PRAAT, her speech and language software, she used it to pick out several words that Adam had muttered during his slumber as well as after he had woken up. Slowing down the sounds, listening to the peaks and the dips in the prosody of the words. *Not Joan, Jeanne...* It took a little time, breaking down the video and extracting Adams murmurs, converting them into recognisable words. *Rouen?* Rapidly searching through the web, Claire pieced some of the puzzle together. *Oh my god.*

'Oh my god,' her thoughts escaped her as the information revealed itself. 'He died, then he came back... This isn't too crazy of an idea... Looks good for his age...'

Taking what she had just learnt, Claire hurriedly exited her office, tablet in hand, almost knocking Malique over as she flew out of the room.

'Sorry!' she shouted, not intending to stop, but Malique quickly called her back.

'Claire, have you seen Krysta?' he asked.

'I'm just off to find her,' Claire admitted. 'Why?' she asked.

'I've got Officer McCarthy on the phone again demanding to speak to her. If you see her, let her know he's called again,' Malique said as Claire began to move away.

She headed straight for Adam's cell hoping to find him, Krysta and the team there. But as she arrived, she found the room empty. Grabbing the first agent she came across, she asked where everyone had gone and was informed that Adam had awoken again and was now being questioned in the interview room. Moving swiftly, Claire headed for the room where they would be interrogating Adam. *They have no idea who he is.* She dashed along the hall; she too had little idea, but if her gut instinct was correct and what she assumed was to be true, who knows what might happen?

Claire knew better than to just fly into the interview

room, having been warned for doing so once or twice before. With this in mind she made her way to the adjoining examination room. Claire had always liked the room behind the mirror; she was not keen on confrontation, it was probably the reason she had taken to computer hacking in the first place. Being able to achieve anything from her own safe space was what she loved.

'Claire? You okay?' Krysta asked as Claire bundled into the room. Lucy was stood next to her, arms crossed - although she barely noticed Claire's entrance. She seemed fixated on what was happening on the other side of the glass.

'I'm fine. I'm okay,' she said, slightly short of breath. Claire straightened herself up and walked over to her colleagues. 'How's the questioning going?' She was hesitant to simply blurt out what she had discovered. She was excited, sure, but the fear of looking foolish was setting in. It wasn't like her theory was something normal to come up with. Plus, some of the agents saw her as too immature at times and she didn't want to give them anymore reason to believe it.

'It's fucking bullshit is what it is,' said a frustrated Lucy. 'This guy has been in the thick of it since day one; he was at the last two attacks and we're beating round the bush.' She was clearly worried for Mike and that fear was recently starting to present itself as regular displays of anger. She had twice already snapped at Claire for failing to find any information over the last two weeks, and Claire wanted to avoid any further collisions with her overzealous co-worker. Instead, Claire kept quiet for now and joined the pair at the window onlooking Adam, Solomon and Kyle in the interview room.

'I can't tell you everything you want to know,' Adam confessed when questioned about the whereabouts of Agent Ward, Markovic and the other assailants. Those seemed to be the only words he would say as they repeatedly questioned him for some time, demanding information and threatening him with numerous repercussions. Lucy had begun pacing the room as she grew tired of them getting nowhere. Deciding that the potential gain was well worth the humiliation of being wrong, Claire pulled Krysta to one side and explained what she had found. Although sceptical about what Claire was saying, Krysta could understand why she had been hesitant to share her findings. Apparently taking a chance, Krysta took the tablet from Claire and left the room. *She'll know what to do.*

'Whoa, where's she going?' Lucy questioned in a frantic manner as she realised Krysta had left the room.

'It's okay, Luce,' Claire explained, gesturing towards the glass. Her words were met with scepticism in Lucy's eyes. 'Just watch and see.'

Solomon and Kyle were still going in circles with Adam in the interview room. Kyle had now leaned back in his chair, while Solomon continued to lean across the table toward Adam. His arms rested on the table and his eyes grew tired. Adam, however, had his face in his hands, clearly in some sort of emotional distress.

'How about giving us anything at all!' Solomon exclaimed, banging his fists on the table between him and Adam. At that moment, the door to the interview room opened and Krysta was met by Kyle as she stepped in. Adam looked up now, his eyes having fallen on Krysta and staying there. They spoke briefly in hushed tones, Kyle firstly exhibiting a very confused expression before laughing at her. Ignoring him, Krysta pushed past and handed the tablet to Solomon to view; she then stood against the wall beside the table. Adam remained still. Claire could see him watching Krysta as she walked to stand beside where her colleagues sat. His emerald-green eyes occasionally caught the shine from the bright ceiling lights and sparkled like gemstones. Solomon carefully examined the information on the tablet. He too had a confused and somewhat disbelieving expression on his face as he perused the data he had been given.

'Who are you?' Solomon asked calmly. The icy mood in the room seemed to have melted, having now shifted from frustration to a distinct calm.

'You can call me Adam,' Adam responded in a placid tone, still unable to take his eyes off Krysta. 'I trust you are okay Krysta. To hurt you or scare you was never my intention. I hope you know that.' He admitted. Claire took more notice of him now than she had done previously. He was dressed in a grey jumpsuit. His hands and feet were handcuffed to the table and to the floor respectively, yet he didn't seem at all unnerved by the position he currently found himself in. Claire looked at him more deeply. The only word she could think of to describe this man before her echoes in her mind, annoying her slightly. *Magnificent.* He had short brownish blondish tufty hair. His face was littered with scars which only made him look more worldly. Had he been out on the street, he would probably have been ignored. His was a transcendent beauty that seemed to grow the more Claire looked at him.

'I'm fine. Thank you,' Krysta responded with a slight clear of the throat and shift of the eyes.

Solomon proceeded to calmly ask several personal questions, 'Where are you from?', 'Who do you work for?', 'How are you able to do the things you do?', but to each question Adam simply sat in silence.

'Who is Jeanne, Adam?' Solomon asked sternly, his patience now wavering again. At the mention of her name, Adam's interest seemed to be piqued.

'Jeanne d'Arc,' Adam answered, looking solemnly down at his hands. He exhibited a deep sigh before continuing. 'She is a regret - one of many.' He seemed saddened by the conversation.

'You mentioned her several times in your sleep. Someone called Rouen also,' Solomon continued. 'Why? Who are these people Adam?'

'My regrets often plague my dreams,' Adam said quietly, continuing to stare at his open hands. To Claire and the others, he spoke in riddles. But to him, a sorrow plagued his words which reflected an air of sincerity in turn. 'I could not prevent what happened to her.'

'Well I'm not surprised, seeing as she died in the fourteen hundreds... Do you honestly expect us to believe that you were present for Joan of Arc's death?' Kyle interrupted, finishing his question with a snigger that was laced with a tone of malice. 'Is this some kind of a joke to you?'

'Adam, that was almost six hundred years ago,' Solomon said, attempting to reign Kyle back in and trying to look Adam in the eyes.

'I was present,' Adam said, lifting his head to look at Solomon. 'In fact, it was my fault that she died. She was innocent - I gave her hope. I showed her how to bring peace, but my brothers and sisters...' Adam paused for a moment, allowing Kyle to jump in and commandeer the interrogation yet again.

'Let's talk about your comrades, shall we? Markovic, the beast and this red-haired woman we've heard about.' Adam seemed incensed by the remark. 'Tell us about your connection to them? What is Markovic up to?' Kyle continued to push for information.

'Markovic is a tool. One that, no doubt, my sister Serena is using,' Adam answered; he closed his eyes for a moment and tilted his head as if he was in pain. He looked as though he had a headache. 'I'm sorry. I cannot answer all of your questions - the mind takes longer to heal than the body and I - memories are erratic.'

'Ha!' Kit laughed at Adam's words. 'How convenient. You fucking forgot!'

'Kyle, cut it out yeah?' Krysta interrupted, jumping to Adam's defence.

'Shut it Krys!' Kyle exclaimed in response. His manner

seemed to anger both Solomon and Adam. Solomon stood up, no doubt with the intent of putting Kyle in his place or throwing him out of the room, but before he had the chance Adam beat him to it. Obliterating his restraints Adam stood up and overturned the table between them, sending it crashing against the mirrored glass. Claire almost jumped out of her skin. Solomon, Kyle and Krysta all reacted by instantaneously drawing their weapons. Seeing what was happening, Lucy darted out of the room and left Claire standing, watching, as she fled to assist her colleagues. As Lucy entered the room, however, everything seemed to calm down as quickly as it had built up.

'I apologise,' Adam said in a tranquil manner, raising his hands in submission. 'I promise. I will tell you what I can.'

'How about starting by telling us where the fuck Mike is!' Lucy yelled, reigniting the tension in the room again.

'Can we please get him cuffed again?' Kit asked, his voice cracking as the fear-soaked words left his lips.

'You think there's any point?' Krysta asked in a sarcastic tone. She turned now to Adam, who had returned to his seated position. 'If you didn't want to be here, we couldn't stop you from leaving, could we? Right?' Adam simply looked at her.

'Okay, okay. So how about we start with you telling us how the fuck you just did that?' Kit asked in an irksome tone, gesturing towards the twisted mess of handcuffs on the flipped table. 'Or how you're even fucking breathing in the first place, not so long ago you were literally dead?!'

Adam proceeded to provide some information, however, Claire had a feeling he was holding back. *Perhaps he doesn't trust us.* She wondered what it was that he wasn't telling them. She knew there was something just by the way he kept stopping himself before he went on to reveal too much to the agents. Adam, unaware that Claire was behind the glass attempting to unpick his whole demeanour, went on to explain that he was a member of a group called the

'Avunaye'. This group was made up of a number of people, human by all accounts, with extraordinary abilities. He barely stopped for breath as he divulged that he had lived for an unprecedented amount of time. He explained that he and his siblings had used their power to try and encourage mankind to do better and be better. He was vague on the details, but as he spoke everybody in the room stood in silence, in awe of what he was suggesting. The four agents in the interrogation room and Claire behind the glass stood silently, hanging on Adam's every word. *Could this all be true?* As far-fetched and unbelievable as it seemed, it also seemed... well, believable. The mood, however, changed once Adam unveiled that this brothers and sisters had long given up on saving humanity.

'So why did they turn on us? From what I've seen you seem to want to help?' Krysta asked when Adam finally paused to take a breath. She too seemed to be thoroughly intrigued by it all. Kyle and Solomon were obviously less convinced.

'You did,' Adam said bluntly, in return receiving puzzled looks from just about everyone. 'Mankind. You lost your way. You chose greed, jealousy, selfishness and violence over compassion. The only time we see you unite is when you are confronted with grief. There is no peace among you. Your leaders wage wars over money, prejudice and fear of the future. In short, mankind caused the Avunaye to lose faith in it. Why work to help when you are so self-destructive? Your collective weakness makes you so easily corruptible.' Adam's monologue was not met well by Kyle or Solomon, both of whom took a very defensive stance moving forward. Lucy also became more agitated, staying in the room only to find out what had happened to her colleague.

The interrogation went on for several hours, with each member of the team stepping out for a break every now and then. Claire grew tiresome of standing behind the mirror watching and listening to information that would only be relayed to her in a later briefing, so she decided that she'd be of more use back in her office doing further research. As she sat down at her desk and rubbed her eyes, she noticed that she had had a return on some of her long-term search algorithms. She had finally found a link between the twelve victims from the warehouse. *Finally! Some progress.* A smile of relief spread across her face. Unfortunately, she had also opened an email that brought news of something much less encouraging. The email revealed that Officer Connor Brennan of the NYPD had passed away. The officer had been in a coma for almost two months after he had been hurled against a hospital wall; Adam was now officially a 'cop-killer'.

'Hey, Claire. Whatcha up to?' sighed Krysta as she sauntered into Claire's office dressed in her casual clothes. She seemed deflated, which was unsurprising after hours of interrogation. Claire wondered if maybe the questioning had ended badly.

'Any luck with Adam? Sorry about bursting in like that. It's just – well, you know. Crazy, huh?' Claire said, making small talk.

'What? Six hundred years old? Or more? It's nuts!' Krysta replied, her eyes carrying a glimmer of amazement. She looked at Claire, who smiled at her. 'Is it just me or is he...'

'Amazing?' Claire finished her sentence.

'Yeah! It's so strange, just being in his presence... there's just something... you know?' Claire nodded. She knew what Krysta meant, she felt it too. There was something distinctively calming about Adam, as though questions need not be asked and his words good be taken for gospel always. But she was also a little confused by what she felt towards him. The more she thought about it, the more confused she was.

'I've managed to find a lead on the warehouse victims!' Claire blurted out. The email about Connor Brennan had been sent to the entire team; Claire thought it best not to mention it, despite it being the obvious elephant in the room.

'That's great,' Krysta replied almost dejectedly. The expression on her face suggested that there was something else on her mind. 'I'd run it by Sol tomorrow, we can get moving on it then.' She pulled out her phone, looked at it briefly but then put it away again. She seemed disheartened by what was – or wasn't - on it.

'You're right,' Claire said attempting to move things along. 'Think I'll call it a day, you heading off too?' she asked Krysta, standing up and removing her jacket from the back of her chair. *Maybe she'd like a chat away from work.*

'Yeah, I'm done,' Krysta replied, again looking at her phone. 'Fancy a drink?'

'Ugh. Love one,' Claire sighed. It had been a long day and she felt tense; some relaxation was much needed. 'You can fill me in on the interrogation. And about Jake,' Claire probed, gesturing towards Krysta's phone teasingly. It was clear that Krysta needed to vent.

'That'd be great Claire-bear, I just... I haven't heard from him for a bit, that's all.' Krysta seemed saddened by Jake's lack of contact. Claire knew that he had been out of town for a while, but didn't know the reason for his absence. *Typical guy thing to do.* She herself had never had much time to devote to a relationship, but she knew how often guys liked to blow hot and cold.

'Meet you downstairs? I'm gonna get changed quickly,' she said. Krysta simply nodded in response, smiled, and then headed out of the office. Claire grabbed her phone from beside one of her monitors and made her way to the changing rooms. She felt relieved that the working day was done, and admittedly she was giddy about spending some time with her friend. In the changing room, she slipped off her shoes and changed out of her work attire. Donning a pair of blue denim jeans, a vest top and a hoodie, she put her work clothes into her bag along with the phone. She slipped back into her shoes and was reaching inside her locker to grab the rest of her belongings when the door to the changing room slammed.

'Fucking bullshit!' Lucy exclaimed as she entered the room. The look of surprise on her face suggested that she clearly was expecting the room to be empty. Then she laid eyes on Claire. 'Argh!' she cried, punching her locker door.

'Drink?' Claire proposed quickly and awkwardly. She liked Lucy, but she knew to fear the woman that could put any of the agents in the building on their asses. Lucy sighed in reply as though admitting some sort of defeat, and then finally nodded in acceptance of the invitation. 'Great, meet you downstairs with Krys,' Claire smiled, closing her locker and slipping the set of keys and mobile phone she had in her hand into her jumper pockets.

As she reached the ground floor, Krysta was standing in the foyer waiting for her. A humongous grin was plastered across her face.

'Guess who finally got in touch,' she announced, waving her phone in her hand. *Hm. Not so typical after all.* Claire smiled gleefully in response to the good news.

'Right then bitches,' Lucy came bounding out of the elevator. 'Let's go get trashed.' Krysta and Claire both exhibited looks of concern, to which Lucy responded by saying something in Spanish that Claire took as a remark of disapproval. The three of them laughed before heading out of the building into the evening air.

13

Luciana Rodriguez

She wiped the sweat from her brow as she shifted her weight from her left foot to her right. He had managed to get a couple of hits in, but she was mainly too quick for him. Side-stepping right, she ducked to avoid his swing and then landed a jab to his abdomen with her right fist; she relished the feeling of her power being exerted through the glove, impacting his body. A speedy second jab with her left fist, clenched fiercely, cut across his jaw, knocking him backwards.

'Eh, nice,' Paul admitted, stepping away from her. 'You sure you're hungover?' he questioned, exhibiting a suspicious grin. He was growing tired, she could tell, and like a predator, she took advantage of her preys weakness. It had been thirty-two days since Mike had been taken. A spark of fear had been lit inside of her that day and as each day passed, that spark had developed into flame and a fire had spread throughout her. Her fear for Mike had also begun to manifest itself as a relentless rage, and on occasion, it spilled out and she was unable to contain her emotion. With no leads, her only outlet was to put all her anger and frustration into the power behind her punches in boxing. She bounced, transferring her body mass back and forth, from foot to foot. She had him guessing which way she was going to come at him from next, and then she struck. Feigning a jab to his mid-rift, she quickly landed a blow to his exposed throat, dazing Hale enough for her to kick out and swipe his feet from under him. As he fell to the ground she pounced, swiftly straddling him and punching him square in the face. Paul reacted and blocked a second hit with his forearm.

'What the fuck Luce?' he yelled in anger as he pushed her off him. Aware that she'd taken it too far, she didn't care. His shout meant nothing to her, the adrenaline was still pumping ferociously through her veins.

'Don't be such a pussy,' she jibed, getting to her feet and gesturing with her hands that she wanted to continue. 'C'mon!' she goaded him. 'Twenty bucks says you don't get a hit in!' Her heart pounded and her blood continued to surge.

'Fuck no,' he replied as he too got to his feet. She had never seen Hale this angry before. He leant on the wall and took off his gloves. 'S'posed to be sparring,' he spat, annoyed, touching his nose as if to check that it wasn't broken. He stood in his shorts and short sleeved t-shirt, his tattoo riddled arms on display and a scowl of disappointment expressed on his face. Lucy did not appreciate the look.

'Fuck you, looking at me like a *pedazo de mierda sin valor!*' She took off her gloves and threw them across the mats to Paul's feet. 'I'm tired of you dicks getting uptight about being put on your ass by a woman!'. Hale didn't respond verbally. He simply shook his head, picked up Lucy's gloves and left the gym.

Hale's lack of reaction to her outburst almost drove her crazy. She needed something to take it out on; the heat beneath her skin was verging on unbearable and she just needed a release. She couldn't talk to anybody about Mike's disappearance, and it was taking its toll on her. *Maybe a shower will help cool me off.* She headed to the changing rooms.

She slipped off her shorts and pulled her top up over her head. The water pressure was good, it felt relaxing as it beat down onto her skin like a long-awaited rainfall. She stood unmoving under the downpour, her arms outstretched, her palms against the wall and her head bowed. She closed her eyes and looked up into the spray. Untying her hair, she allowed the water to soak her completely. As she let it wash over her, she prayed that it would carry away her fears and that somehow, Mike would be okay.

'Luce!' A voice called. 'You in here?' It was Krysta. The sound of her friend's voice was like a soft, gentle melody to her ears. Krysta had been a welcome distraction over the past few weeks. She too had man issues, Jake was still out of town so in their own way they kept each other busy and distracted from their individual heart strains. Of course, Krysta was unaware of Lucy's pain. She simply thought her dedication to finding Mike was out of concern for her partner. 'Luce?' Krysta called again.

'Yeah!' Lucy didn't know how long she had been stood under the water, it could have been minutes or hours. Her mind had been working overtime lately and she hadn't slept well since he had gone. 'I'll be out in a minute,' she said, pushing her hair back with her fingers, feeling the water pound on her face once more.

'Sol wants us in the briefing room,' Krysta said. 'Sounds like we're going for a ride.' The thought was a welcome one. Lucy needed to get away from the office, away from the familiarity; everything reminded her of her absent colleague, friend and lover. She turned off the water and headed into the changing room to get dried and dressed, ready to work.

Today she wore all black, much to reflect the feeling of emptiness within her heart. Polished black boots, jet black combat pants and a dark tank top; not the typical office attire but she was hoping to get away from here and get some hands-on work done. As she entered the briefing room, she firstly glanced at Hale. He was stood next to Solomon, feet apart, arms down by his sides. Their eyes met as she made her way to the centre of the room. Hale's face turned into a vague smile, telling Lucy that there were no hard feelings regarding the morning's events. Since Mike's disappearance, he had been available for all the team should they need someone. He was very protective of them all, even Lucy, whom he knew could more than look after herself. Lucy knew that if she needed him, he'd be there - but of course, she would never openly admit it.

Krysta stood waiting at the interactive table with the rest of the team. She wore a pale blue blouse that matched the colour of her eyes, black work pants and kitten heeled court shoes. She pulled Lucy close as she met her at the table, giving her a reassuring squeeze. Hale having left his side, Solomon was now talking to Claire. Claire was noticeably wearing the same clothes as the day before and looked as if she'd spent the night here. Her black pin-striped suit pants were creased, and her white halter neck top had a subtle coffee stain on it; one that she had no doubt tried to scrub out. She looked tired and dishevelled, unlike Solomon. Smartly dressed, he made up for the rest of the team's appearance; pearly white shirt, dark grey pants and a midnight blue tie only accentuated the confidence and determination he seemed to be exhibiting, that which Lucy found most intriguing. *Something must be going down.* With that, Solomon nodded at Claire's final words and then joined the rest of the team, leaving the young hacker clutching at a folder away from the rest of them.

'A little over two weeks ago, Claire found a link between the twelve victims at the warehouse in Flatlands,' Solomon cut straight to the point. Whatever was happening, Lucy had a feeling it was something big; hopefully it was all leading to a lead on Mike. 'The only apparent link between them is a clinical trial they all participated in six months before their deaths. The trial consisted of two blood donations which were taken one week apart. One sample was taken before and one was taken after taking a supposed wonder drug. Now, these trials happened up and down the country throughout dozens of clinics in numerous states and involved thousands of participants,' Solomon continued. 'Claire managed to dig deep and found that all of the participating clinics are owned by different companies, hospitals, foundations, charities, pharmaceutical corporations, shell companies, I could go on.'

'Okay? So... what?' Lucy interrupted. Krysta grabbed her hand and gave it a friendly squeeze. It could have been one of support or her way of saying 'shut up'.

'So.' Solomon said, looking at Lucy. 'We followed the drug.' At this point, Claire chirped up, stepping forward toward the interactive table around which the rest of the team were gathered. She clearly wanted to deliver the news - after all she was the one to do the leg work. Solomon graciously passed the mitre to his eager subordinate.

'The drug was *supposedly* designed to offer several health benefits: you know, reduce cholesterol, increase fertility, all that bullshit,' She was clearly wired on caffeine and her natural quirkiness consistently showed itself as she continued to share her findings. 'But it actually did fuck all. Might as well have been dishing out breath mints!' Claire had definitely over done the whole 'burning the candle at both ends' recently, but all of a sudden there seemed to be a change in her. She stood quietly for a moment, rubbing her eyes, and when Hale enquired as to whether she was okay, she seemed to snap out of her daze and delivered the rest of the information very formally; quirk-less. 'Upon tracing the placebo back to its source through a list of subsidiary companies, I eventually tied it down to one: Brascus Pharmaceuticals.' Lucy looked around at the team. None of them seem too surprised; Ben Brascus was a supposed associate of Markovic, but Lucy couldn't help wondering where this information got them.

'Brascus is supposed to be in bed with Markovic,' Krysta jumped in, practically voicing Lucy's thoughts.

'Right. Well he owns a pharmaceutical lab in Los Angeles that was shut down after the failed trials,' Solomon took over again. 'However, the LA branch have confirmed that there seems to have been activity there for about a month now.' He paused again, looking about the team. Lucy's heart began to race at the news; she knew she mustn't get too hopeful. Her head kept telling her that it was probably just a coincidence, but her heart simply wouldn't listen. 'I've spoken to Deputy Director Stanwell and we have the green light to fly out and pursue the lead.'

'Sol, what about Adam?' Krysta asked, although Lucy couldn't understand why. Adam had not been as much help as they would have liked. He spent most of his days meditating in his cell, and he would rarely speak at all. The only snippets of information he did provide, he seemed only to give to Krysta.

'What about him? He's said fuck all lately,' Lucy expressed, showing her frustration. This pharmaceutical plant was a lead, a good lead, and she wanted to get moving.

'All I meant was that he might have some intel, help us get a better idea of what we're going to be walking into?' Krysta did not seem pleased with Lucy's comment, but there was no time to worry about upsetting her friend.

'Ha!' Claire exclaimed randomly, drawing the attention of the entire room. 'So, tracing the placebo back to its source...' but before she could continue Solomon quickly interrupted.

'Claire, we've gone through that. Are you sure you're okay?' He seemed concerned by her erratic behaviour. She had always come across a little odd, in an endearing way, but this was to an extreme.

'Sorry, yeah,' Claire replied, looking slightly confused. 'A little tired. Where were we?' she asked timidly.

'Adam,' Krysta quickly responded. 'I thought he may be of some help?'

'Actually, you might be right,' Claire announced,

drawing a look of surprise from the team, Solomon especially. 'Adam claims his memory is shot. Whether that's true or not, we aren't getting very far with him,' Claire explained. 'Personally, I get the feeling he is deliberately holding back, however, there's always the possibility that he isn't. Perhaps taking him out with you guys might trigger something for him. Anyway, I've found something.' Lucy hoped this discovery was good; time was being wasted as far as she was concerned. Claire brought up several images on the table. They were hand drawn pictures, sketches. One was of a vase, one of a flower, and there were several landscape drawings of forests and one of a castle. They all appeared fairly random.

'These are Adams?' Hale enquired. 'They're good.' He wasn't wrong. The artistry was amazing. For mere sketches with a pencil on paper, they were incredibly intricate as if drawn from photographic memory.

'You have no idea...' Claire sounded excited. 'When I show you, you're gonna want him designing your next tattoo,' she sniggered at her own joke as she said it. Lucy gave her a puzzled and unimpressed look. 'Michael Scofield?' Claire prompted in response to Lucy's expression, only to receive a couple more from Hale and Solomon. 'Okay... Look. These pictures are so detailed and so intricately done, I have no idea how he drew these by hand. I scanned them into my computer and the damn thing nearly blew up working them out.' Claire moved the images about on the table. She made the paper disappear and took the two-dimensional shapes, placing the drawing of the flower over the vase and then zoomed in slightly. The result stunned everybody. Even Lucy was gobsmacked.

'How?' asked Solomon, looking closer at the screen as if he didn't trust his own eyes. It was Krysta. The two images combined to make a near perfect portrait of Krysta's face.

'What does this mean though?' Lucy asked, snapping out of her dumb-founded amazement.

'The other images include other faces; one seems to be partial blueprints...' Claire continued. 'I think in some way he's trying to share intel, maybe one will show us where Mike is, or at least help...' The idea pleased Lucy slightly, but she wasn't prepared to sit around waiting for Adam to draw the answers she so desperately needed.

'Sol?' Lucy quizzed, turning to her superior. She looked to him to hurry things along.

'Right,' Solomon broke his gaze on the image. 'In light of this, I want Krysta to stay here and help Claire. Talk to Adam, see if you can encourage more drawings or whatever... ' His order didn't seem too well taken with Krysta. She seemed to want to be in on the action. *She was the one who was so concerned about Adam. Serves her right.* 'Lucy, Hale, we'll fly out and meet up with the LA office. From there, we'll coordinate the search of the pharmaceutical plant.'

The team had received their orders and, although some weren't as pleased as others, they all dispersed ready to carry out their instructions. Lucy and Paul gathered up their equipment and joined Solomon at the car before heading to the landing strip. It was going to be a six-hour flight to Los Angeles, Lucy's mind was already racing with the hundreds of possible outcomes from the trip.

As she stared out of the window, watching the odd cloud drift along through the clear blue ether that surrounded them, she prayed that this voyage would bear promising fruit. It was the midst of summer and the time of year she most enjoyed, soaking up the sun and basking in the heat; yet she did not feel as if she could embrace it yet, not until Mike was home, not until he was safe. A car was waiting for them when they landed. The sea scented air filled her senses as she walked across the sun-baked tarmac.

It was a twenty-minute drive to the office. The seconds ticked by in what seemed like ever increasing increments. It was the anxiousness and helplessness she felt that exasperated her as she watched the time pass by, sitting, waiting, inactive. Eventually, they finally reached the Los Angeles main office and were greeted by a burly figure that introduced himself as Special Agent Alonso Hernández. *He has the look.* Lucy laid eyes on the bronzed agent before her. She had once been offered a placement here, but thought of the west coast office as more of a holiday destination. New York was where the action – and her family - was.

'Special Agent Grey?' Hernández asked, scouring round the group as they unloaded their bags from the vehicle. He stood rigid, dressed in black pants and black shoes that gleamed in the sunlight. He wore a tie that was loosened about his neck and the sleeves of his white shirt were partially turned up, presenting his large forearms. He had short dark hair and wore a pair of sunglasses on which the light danced, creating an array of colours. He stood, hands in pockets, meaning business. Solomon stepped forward and shook the man's hand. 'Assistant Director Carson is waiting for you inside,' he explained as he indicated for the team to follow him. 'Also, to give you a heads up, Zane Brown is here.' The news did not appear to sit well with Solomon.

'What is he doing here?' Solomon questioned, his tone carrying an air of exasperated frustration. Zane Brown was the Deputy Director of the C.I.A and was not one of Solomon's favourite people. As they entered the meeting room, he stood at the head of a long table, hands on hips and an almost imperceptible smile on his face. Lucy had only met Zane once, years ago. *He hasn't changed in the slightest.* She looked at him whilst entering the room. He stood next to Assistant Director Carson who remained still, frozen in Zane's shadow the entire time the team were getting settled. Zane was a tall man, taller than anyone else in the room by half a foot at least; Lucy couldn't resist quickly jesting with Hale about getting neck ache simply conversing with the man. Dark of skin, he had short black hair that was neatly trimmed. He wore a suit of Amherst grey that was perfectly fitted to his toned physique. Beneath his jacket, an Egyptian-blue waist coat covered a brilliant white shirt and his ensemble was completed by a sky-blue tie which was patterned with small white leaves. Carson, despite being the head of this office, held a subjected presence, dwarfed by the C.I.A operative beside him. Lucy did not know Carson, but she could tell that he was not accustomed to taking a back seat on his own turf. He looked uncomfortable in his own skin.

'Solomon Grey,' Zane stated, reaching out a plate sized hand to shake Solomon's hand. 'It's been a while.' His words did not illicit an immediate response from Solomon. 'Carson, I'll let you do the introductions,' Zane said, taking his seat whilst keeping his gaze fixed on Solomon. Carson began by introducing Zane to the rest of the teams, before moving on to Solomon, Lucy and Paul. They were joined by a couple of Carson's own agents, Agent Hernández who they had met before, and a Special Agent Philip Matheson. Agents Hernández and Matheson would be joining Solomon and his team for the investigation of the pharmaceutical plant Carson explained, but as he provided details of how he would like the visit to be conducted, Lucy couldn't help but wonder what Zane's involvement here was. This was and always had been an F.B.I case – so why were C.I.A getting involved now?

'Deputy Director Brown is overseeing this op due to its connection to an ongoing C.I.A investigation,' Carson finally explained. As he said the words, however, Lucy couldn't help but sense that Carson was merely reading from a script. *Something is weird about this.*

'Try not to let my presence distract you,' Zane advised, leaning back in his chair. 'The C.I.A have been keeping tabs on a number of Vladimir Markovic's operations overseas and when you contacted this office to request assistance, it was merely flagged and brought to our attention.' His words carried a strange level of honesty that had now captured

Solomon's attention, Lucy could tell. He went on to explain that the C.I.A had been keeping a close eye on Alexei Kuznetsov's - The Jack o' Diamonds - exploits abroad and how recently, there had been a lot of chatter about America and of Markovic. 'Kuznetsov and the Bratva have sworn in. They're now taking orders from the Serbian, Markovic, and we want to know why.'

'We all know of Alexei's connection to Markovic,' Solomon stated shortly. He looked at Zane as if to ask him to make his point known. Zane smiled and then held his hands together, touching his lips with his index fingers.

'The Bratva are taking orders from a Serbian based in New York. The Japanese Yakuza are up in arms about a pair of twins that no-one has any intel on. We have news of a militia forming in Paraguay, millions of dollars being flooded into Iraq and Syria.' He paused for a moment, clearly frustrated. 'Basically... the world has gone fucking nuts overnight, terrorism is on the rise and all of the signs eventually circle back towards the good old U.S. of A.' The room remained quiet for a few moments as everyone tried to absorb what had just been blasted at them. 'We also know about Adam,' Zane said the name sheepishly, but then it was as if a Cheshire grin spread across his face. He directed a stare at Solomon.

'So that's why you're here!' Solomon exclaimed, standing up from his chair. 'You want to get your hands on our perp!' Solomon's uncharacteristic outburst had little to no effect on Zane, who simply sat unnerved in his seat, continuing to stare at Solomon as if to goad him.

'Get fucked!' Lucy scoffed, the words bursting from her mouth before she could stop them. It occurred to her that if the C.I.A got their hands on Adam, the F.B.I would never see him again and the chance of getting Mike back would reduce greatly. 'Sol?' she said, directing her words at him abruptly, looking to her superior for assistance. 'If they take Adam-' Before either Solomon or Zane could say another word, the room was interrupted by the entrance of a woman. She said nothing, walking around the table directly to Carson. The heated discussion on hold, everyone sat silently as she relayed a message, the tension in the room simmering just below boiling point.

'It seems we've run out of time for this little debate,' Carson announced, clearing his throat and sounding relieved to put the previous argument to bed. 'Vladimir Markovic was spotted entering Brascus Pharmaceuticals four minutes ago. Let's get moving.' As Carson finished his sentence, the five agents that were heading out together were already heading for the rooms exit.

The tyres screeched as the car ground to a dramatic halt outside the plant. The building had, despite what the F.B.I knew, officially closed, so there was no activity outside. A single security guard stood at the entrance who, upon being confronted by five armed F.B.I agents, quickly stepped aside. The team swiftly moved through the foyer, passing under a huge banner displaying Ben Brascus and his vision for the future, checking the nearby offices and a canteen. Thus far, there was no sign of life.

'Claire?' Solomon said over the comms. 'We need directions to the main factory floor.' Lucy stuck close to Paul as they headed down the corridors that Claire directed, the other two agents falling in behind them and Solomon leading the way.

'Sol?' Lucy asked as they made their way towards the main production area. 'What's the deal with you and Zane?' She was curious. Something big must have happened in the past to create the obvious tension between them.

'I've been paired on three ops with Zane,' Solomon answered quickly, continuing to move. 'We never made any arrests as there were never any survivors. He's good at finding perps, no one can deny that. I've just never known anyone to never ask any questions. He's a killer.' Solomon said no more on the subject as they continued their search.

Lucy knew that their line of work was a lot greyer than simply finding the bad guys and killing them; information was key and therefore taking prisoners was usually the best method. They scoured the factory floor, the loading bays, nearby production offices, yet still, no sign of anyone. No sign that anyone had been here for a while. There was no one in the building.

'Claire!' Solomon hissed, sounding thoroughly irritated. 'Are we sure Markovic is here? What if Carson's intel was no better than the shitstorm we were given before?'

'Intel says he hasn't left the site. We've had satellite surveillance running the entire time, I've seen it with my own eyes, sir,' Claire responded. The team stood still, gazing hopelessly outwards from where they stood to the peripheries of the large production area.

'Sol? It's Krys,' Krysta's voice sounded across the comms, a scintilla of hope. 'There's a basement laboratory that wasn't on the city's blueprints,' she said, drawing looks of confusion and disbelief from everyone.

'Then how do you know it's there, Krys?' Lucy asked the obvious question that was on the tip of everyone's tongue. There had been no sign of a basement entrance, and they'd never discussed the possibility of one either.

'Adam drew the blueprints,' her response was paired with a heavy sigh and met with silence. Lucy looked to Solomon, who stood with one hand resting on the butt of the M4 that was strapped across his front, his other hand scratching at his temple; he was unsure.

'She's right Solomon,' Claire announced, coming back onto the comms to confirm Krysta's findings. She described an entrance at the rear of the factory, concealed within the room's décor. In truth, although Adam hadn't been forthcoming with spoken intel, he had always tried to help them on their missions before. Lucy nodded to Solomon, reassuring him that she was prepared.

They must have passed it at least twice before, a third

time even as they looked for it. It was well hidden; a seam in the wall opened to an elevator that contained just the one button, presumably that took them to the basement. The five agents stepped into it and rode it down until it stopped. The elevator opened into a small room that stood empty. It had one door on the opposite wall that was made of glass or a Perspex and was labelled 'Quarantine'.

'Only one way to go,' Lucy said, bullishly pushing her way out of the elevator, eager to explore. The other members of the team seemed more reserved, hesitant even.

'Luce, it says *quarantine*,' Solomon pointed out.

'Markovic has got to be in there,' Lucy persisted. He was so close – possibly Mike, too. She didn't want to give up now, not when there was so much at stake. She knew that Solomon was searching for a way to dissuade her, but from the look in his eyes, she knew he had nothing.

The team proceeded to step into the small narrow corridor beyond the door, Solomon stepping past Lucy and leading the way. Hale stayed close to Lucy following the other two agents, Matheson and Hernández.

'The door won't open,' Solomon said, attempting a couple of times to push open the door at the end of the corridor.

'We're in a decontamination chamber,' Agent Matheson deduced, scanning the walls and ceiling. 'You'll need to close the door behind us before it'll open,' he turned to Paul and Lucy as they held up the rear. Lucy turned and began to push the door shut. As she closed it, a sudden feeling of dread scurried over her body, a fearful chill as she shut them in. The door closed and locked and, as Agent Matheson had predicted, Solomon was now able to open the door before them.

They passed over the threshold into a spacious laboratory. Lucy recognised some of the equipment on show; test tube racks, flasks, beakers and other receptacles filled with different coloured chemicals. There were numerous desks, each littered with paperwork, microscopes and petri dishes. The workstations were spread out like that of a classroom, and up against the outer walls sat countless fridges and larger pieces of equipment. Lucy could see at the other end of the room there was a partition, separating the laboratory from another room, possibly another laboratory.

'What is all this stuff?' Lucy questioned as she rummaged through some of the paperwork on one of the nearby desks and then peered into a microscope.

'Well they're centrifuges,' Agent Hernández said, pointing to some of the equipment. 'What?' he quickly said in reply to Lucy's look of surprise. 'I know stuff,' he said, smiling. The large bronzed agent seemed chuffed with himself.

'He's right,' said Hale, holding up some papers in his hand. 'Thermal cyclers, electrophoresis and molecular biology equipment,' his voice carried a distinct level of concern. 'They're growing cell cultures, testing DNA.'

'Altering it, it seems,' said Solomon. He too was now investigating some of the literature. It was at this point that they heard a crash from the next room. They instinctively raised their weapons in response to the noise, straightening up quickly. Solomon signalled for them to move towards the partition. Agents Hernández and Matheson stood either side of the sliding glass door that provided access to the room beyond. On Solomon's command, Matheson slid it open and Solomon, Lucy and Hale, followed by the other two agents, made their way inside, weapons at the ready.

'For fuck sake!' a well-dressed man screamed, throwing a steel tray and all the utensils on it across the room. Lucy knew exactly who it was.

'Markovic!' she instinctively shouted. 'Freeze!' Lucy's shout startled the two-armed security personnel that stood either side of Markovic. The man himself merely turned towards the F.B.I agents and smiled. He did not seem at all concerned by their presence. Lucy could feel her finger reaching for the trigger of her rifle. She was angry, and she was scared.

'Drop your weapons!' shouted Solomon and Matheson simultaneously, neither receiving any reaction from Markovic or his men.

'You really, really, should not have come here,' Markovic goaded, straightening his suit jacket. No one moved. 'Solomon Grey,' he said smiling confidently, as if knowing who Solomon was altered the hierarchy of the room somehow.

'I said drop your weapons.' Solomon said once more. Once again, the men stood unflinching.

'Luce,' Hale croaked, attempting to get her attention. Lucy struggled to pull her gaze away from Markovic's smug face long enough to look elsewhere. Again, Paul repeated her name, so she quickly glanced over to him to see him nod towards the back corner of the room. There, in the corner of the room, under a dimly lit light, sat an operating table with a covered body laying upon it. Fear flooded Lucy's mind as she looked at the large body on the table. She pictured Mike under the cover. With Markovic unwilling to back down and his men still holding their firearms, Lucy slowly sidestepped towards Hale. Markovic glanced back at the table after seeing Lucy move and then looked at her with a smile.

'You don't want to look at him. It's not a pretty sight,' he said as a smile crossed his face, without a glimmer of remorse. The word 'him' shot through Lucy like a bullet to the heart. Her breathing hastened, her heart raced. Part of her wanted to rush over to the table, the other part of her wanted nothing more than to turn and shoot them all. 'Just so you know, it was slow and very excruciating. I could barely watch,' Markovic said, almost gleefully.

'You son of a bitch!' Lucy screamed, turning her weapon on Markovic. Hatred and anger began to fill her veins as she moved her finger toward the trigger of her gun.

'Lucy! Stop!' Solomon shouted. Hale quickly took the opportunity whilst Markovic was distracted by Lucy to move toward the table. He stood next to it, facing the enemy. The team were now almost surrounding the criminals, yet they remained confident. Paul slowly reached for the cover that hid the body, never once taking his eyes off Markovic. He gave it a tug, just enough to uncover the corpses head. Time slowed as the sheet rolled over his face, uncovering his identity. Lucy saw his dark hair, his broad face. His beard ran from his sideburns and as she looked, her heart stopped. A tear ran down from her right eye, caressing her cheek; falling from her chin it was absorbed by her Kevlar vest. She did not recognise his face. A look of pain and despair had possessed it and would remain there forever more.

'Sol,' Hale said. 'It's not him. It's not Mike...' Lucy knew it already, but hearing Paul say it seemed to make it real. Suddenly time restarted, and she took a huge gasp for air. The body wasn't Mike, but that just left the question, where was he?

'Where's Mike?' she asked Markovic. There was a pain in her voice. Markovic took note of it and smiled again.

'I would be more concerned about where you are,' A voice sounded from nowhere. The team looked around the room for its origin. 'Only the God of Death can grant you peace, for without death, there can be no re-birth and so he, Lord of the Underworld, now king of the living.' He spoke riddles; his words were as eerie as his voice that brought a sick sense of dread to Lucy's stomach and an icy chill to her bones. Markovic was not at all concerned by the mysterious voice. In fact, Lucy could swear he appeared even more confident now. Lucy's comms crackled with a wave of static: they were cut off from the outside world. Suddenly, there was a distinctive beep. Everyone looked to Lucy as the sound emerged once more. Even Markovic's interest was captured. It was Lucy's phone. She shouldn't have brought it, but since Mike's disappearance she had always wanted to stay connected to the world, to anyone. She looked at the message briefly: GET OUT NOW! RUN!

It was from their unknown source, Lucy could just feel it. Upon reading the message, she began to back up slowly towards the exit. Hale, taking one look at Lucy, proceeded to do the same.

The dim light that hung above the body began to flicker. A shadow appeared to form beneath it, stretching out from the table as if the corpse had stood up; yet it lay there, unmoving. Shadows converged and from them, a man appeared as if from nowhere. He was dressed in a black monk's habit, a dark tunic covered with a scapular and cowl. It had a hood, yet he did not wear it up. Instead his purple hair flowed freely, strands of it falling across his pale-grey coloured skin. His eyes were of a blue-grey tinge that matched his lips. He was the most frightening thing Lucy had ever seen - at least that was what every fibre within her was currently telling her. Shrouded in darkness, it was as if death itself had entered the room.

'The plague of man, spawn of lust-' he said, scouring the team as they backed away. BANG! Hernández, overcome with fear, fired his weapon at the mysterious figure. However, his bullet, piercing cleanly through the man's clothing and flesh, did not seem to bother him.

'Run!' Matheson shouted, moving back to the door. Lucy was the first out of the room, back out into the lab, followed by Hale and Solomon. Matheson and Hernández exchanged gunfire with Markovic's men before managing to get out themselves.

Lucy's adrenaline-filled heart pounded as she moved to the first desk. Crouching by it, she covered the retreat of those behind her. Paul did the same at the next desk, allowing Lucy to move on and Solomon after. She made it to the door of the decontamination corridor and turned to see one of Markovic's men coming out of the room from which they had just escaped. She quickly took aim and fired, hitting him in the lower neck, above the collar bone. She then hurried into the corridor and made a run for the exit, forgetting that it would not yet open. Hale and Hernández came in next, followed by Solomon. Matheson managed to get one foot into the corridor but then for some unknown reason stopped. He stood in the doorway, trembling. Lucy moved down the corridor, pushing past her colleagues to help him, but as she reached the open door it slammed shut with Matheson falling backwards, back into the lab. She tried to push the door open, but it would not budge. The purple-haired man stood on the other side of the windowed door, one hand holding the door shut, his other hand rested on Matheson's cheek. The agent looked through the door at Lucy. The sheer look of terror in his eyes overwhelmed her. He was on his knees, crying; tears flooded from his eyes as he placed a hand on the window that stood between them.

'I'm sorry' he said, barely able to speak through the tears. His voice was muffled anyway as it sounded through the glass. Lucy banged frantically on the door with both hands, pounding against the window. Matheson took a deep breath and then looked Lucy in the eye. She could see something dark stirring within them, just below the surface. 'I can't do it any more...' and with those words, Matheson took his sidearm, placed it under his chin and fired. With the door between them and the lab being shut, Hale had managed to open the exit. Unable to move, Lucy knelt helplessly until Solomon grabbed her and pulled her backwards. As she was dragged away from the mystery figure, she started to move her feet independently, the fear, the feeling of dread that had incapacitated her suddenly began to lessen, allowing her to think, to move once again. As they piled into the elevator, she looked back to see those blue-grey eyes staring back at her, a stare full of pain, of despair.

Of death.

14

Nahki

He was frustrated and angry, that much he knew. Yet, for a mere mortal, Vladimir often surprised Nahki with his unpredictability. Most men in his position, constantly being hounded at every turn, would snap; they'd lose their temper, attempt an ill-advised act of vengeance. Yet Markovic showed much restraint. He was livid, but he had almost complete control of his emotions. Nahki had little comprehension of what Markovic felt at this point in time. He could recall a time, before his rebirth, when he did feel as all men did; yet the anamnesis of what it was to feel was gone. Joining the Avunaye had made him stronger, faster, wiser. It had given him the knowledge to be able to do incredible things, and it had rid him of any weakness. He felt nothing. He did not suffer at the hands of anger or rage; he was not confused by the touch of love, nor held back by remorse or grief. The absence of all emotional constraint allowed him to become a weapon. A hunter without distraction or hesitation; calm, calculated and unshakable. The lack of any mortal tether had also given him clarity; for he understood his abilities, how they worked, and was close to surpassing some of his older siblings regarding his power. A secret he knew he must keep - at least for now. Nahki sat, perched on a rafter away from the action. Dressed in nothing but a pair of brown shorts and his necklace of precious stones and bones, he waited, listening, learning.

'Two fucking weeks!' Markovic ranted, holding up two fingers to emphasise his words. He was surrounded by men and women that worked for him. Associates, ring leaders of gangs, thugs and lawyers. He had been caught in the act at his plant in Los Angeles. The F.B.I had him standing next to a corpse with brother Seymour in tow. The evidence was truly stacked against Markovic. He had barely escaped that day. Luckily for him, the Avunaye were not as foolish as mere men and Seymour had constructed an escape for them.

The room in which they now resided was fashioned as an old European style wine cellar. Casks lined the outer walls, every now and then a barrel would sit on a tilt, tapped, its contents ready to be poured. A large round wooden table sat in the hearth of the room on a stone clad floor. This room, however, was above ground. In fact, it stood within an eleven-story building that, unknowingly to most, belonged to Markovic. It was a safe house of sorts on the outskirts of Manhattan. 'Two fucking weeks they've been seizing everything they can, squeezing the fruits of my labour!' Markovic slammed his hands down on the table at which they all stood around. Nahki, like a hawk, continued to watch from afar, waiting for the herd to thin out. 'They've been squeezing and getting juice, fucking juice! If there's one thing I won't tolerate its fucking disloyalty. Which of you bad, puss filled fruit, has been leaking your juices to the fucking F.B.I?' Markovic's metaphors were often lost on many of his compatriots, but he always made sure they received the intended message. 'Maxine,' he said calmly. Several of the on-lookers turned to stare towards a short-haired blonde woman, dressed in a blue suit jacket and black pencil skirt, who stood amongst them. Nahki could smell the fear that was injected into the air as her name was called. 'Maxine. How long have you worked for me?' he asked. She stood silently, shaking. Markovic walked around the table towards her. The jet-black shirt he wore had the sleeves rolled up, his unique tattoo on display. Markovic stood before the woman, and with his left hand, he tapped his fingers on the surface of the table as he waited for a response.

'Thr...Thr...' she stuttered as she continued to tremble nervously. 'Three years.'

'Three years,' Markovic repeated, nodding in confirmation. Nahki could hear the malice in his voice. 'Three years you have worked with your colleagues, looking after my affairs,' he stood looking at her, speaking slowly and clearly; if not for Nahki's enhanced hearing, he would not have been able to hear him from where he sat.

'Y-Yes,' she responded, tremulously. She continued to quiver in Vladimir's shadow.

'Yes?' he asked her, yet she had no answer. 'You were assigned to kill all connections to me regarding Brascus Pharmaceuticals. Yet I am now finding myself surrounded by F.B.I agents with my pants around my ankles.' He retained his calmness despite the heat in his words, which now began to gain a stronger and stronger twinge of his Eastern European accent as he grew more perplexed. Maxine did not know what to do; she merely stood still, like a dear in the headlights. Markovic allowed her some time to respond to his statement, but all he received was silence. He was finally done waiting. He reached behind him and pulled out a silver desert eagle pistol that he had stuffed into the back of his pants. He placed the gun on the table in front of the cowering woman. 'I am not a fan of guns myself. Usually, I am liking to settle issues with my hands,' he cracked his knuckles as he spoke, one by one, each knuckle sounding loudly. 'There is just one bullet in this gun Maxine,' he said, softly. 'I want you to pick it up, go on." She hesitated at first but then lifted the weapon up off the table slowly. Despite being almost empty, the gun still carried some weight, which clearly took Maxine by surprise. 'Now Maxine, you have two choices,' Vladimir said, crouching down beside her and uttering the words directly into her ear as the woman began to shake even more violently. 'One: you will take the gun, place the barrel in your mouth and pull the trigger,' he paused for a moment, watching the tears as they began to fall from her face. 'Two: you can take the gun and point it at another person in this room, someone who - in your opinion - has wronged me more than yourself.' As he said it, the silence that filled the room began to fade. Every soul present was now scared. Nahki sat, intrigued. The fear was palpable. Holding the gun, Maxine looked to her left and then to her right. She looked to one man in particular, a dark-skinned man in a navy-blue suit. He was shocked and terrified.

'Maxine?' the man said, surprised by her actions as she slowly began to raise the weapon towards him. Tears streamed down her cheeks as she contemplated what she had to do to survive, her hands trembling both with the weight of the weapon and her sheer fear. Yet before she could pull the trigger, Markovic moved forwards, grabbed her around her neck and with one swift movement he snapped the life from her. The lifeless body fell to the ground with a thud and the man she had pointed the gun towards, let out a huge sigh of relief. Markovic picked up the gun off the floor, and without hesitation he cocked back the slide and shot the bullet into the man's head, his blood and brain matter splattering all those nearby.

'Stop fucking up!' Markovic screamed manically, slamming the gun down on the table. 'Now get out...' Like the obedient servants they were, the crowd left the room at his command, leaving just Markovic, Nahki and the two dead bodies. Markovic pulled a heavy wooden chair, dragging it across the coarse stone floor and placed it by the table. He sat down besides the two bodies that lay on the ground and then looked to Nahki.

'Why are people so...' he asked, struggling to think of a word that would best express exactly how he felt.

'You're flawed,' Nahki responded, jumping down from

his perch. Nahki could sense Markovic's disgust with being compared to the rest of them. But he was just like them, as far as Nahki was concerned. Mere human; the base of their kind. Nahki understood that he himself was human. He was not deluded, of course he knew this, but he was ascended, he was more. So much more. 'You scrounge around for a lifetime, searching for power, purpose, love; yet all the while ignoring that which surrounds you.' Nahki enjoyed preaching the 'verse of the Avunaye' as his family called it. 'For over fifteen hundred years now I have watched people. I have learnt much, yet as a species, you have not changed much. You'll see, when our agreement comes to its conclusion, everything will be accessible to you; you'll finally see what the world is truly like and why things must change.'

'You talk of knowledge and power as if you have it all... Yet you require men like me to do your own bidding. You cannot achieve it alone.' Markovic had a pitiful look on his face, as if he were, for a moment, looking down on Nahki. This did not please the once-Bantu tribesman.

'You think less of us because we use you?' Nahki questioned, scoffing at Markovic's thoughts. 'There are rules we must follow. Unfortunately, we are not all indestructible. Our lives are not indispensable like yours,' Nahki looked at the palms of his hands *One day things will change, and then nobody will be able to stop me, not even Adam.*

Nahki continued to give Vladimir a lesson in history, of how the Avunaye had influenced mankind for generations, starting wars, ending wars, furthering and stinting mankind's advancement as they saw fit. Just as he began to reminisce about the second siege of Constantinople, his sister entered the room.

'Serena,' Markovic hastily said, cutting Nahki off mid-sentence. 'Finally.' He stood up to greet her as she stepped over his deceased employees.

'Charming place you have here,' Serena said, looking about the room and grinning at the bodies. She was wearing a light, white blouse that tied at the neck and had a small oval opening displaying her cleavage. A top of that, she wore a thin vermillion coloured summer blazer that matched the colour of her heeled shoes. Her loose-fit, straight legged pants were a cream colour and she wore her bright red hair down, straightened. She looked to Nahki as she took a seat at the table and crossed her legs. 'A room full of wine and not a glass in sight,' she said, raising her eyebrows. 'And what were we discussing brother? The good old days?' she chuckled as she sat, awaiting a drink. 'Believe it or not Vlad, I have a few centuries on young Nahki here. The stories I could tell you.' She ran her finger in circles on the table until Markovic dutifully poured a glass of red wine from one of the barrels. She smelt the wine, breathing in its quality before slowly taking a sip. 'So. I'm here, what is it you wanted?'

'I have a job for Nahki, and once it's done, I'd like your assistance with overseeing the procurement of some items we require to further our plans,' Markovic said. 'Your brother, Seymour – he assures me that his work is ongoing and almost ready for testing. But I'll need you to help make sure the final stages will go... smoothly.' Nahki knew they'd get dragged into this deal sooner or later. So far, Brandt had been the only lap dog. *Serena will not like this.* Nahki looked at her, awaiting some reaction to Markovic's request.

'As long as you don't expect us to get directly involved,' she said. Her unexpected acceptance surprised Nahki somewhat.

'My men will handle most of it. It's more... your presence I require, more than anything else,' Markovic admitted. The Avunaye had explained to him several times about their rules as part of the deal. Bound by blood, they were unable to directly involve themselves in mortal conflicts; they could defend themselves and influence others to do their bidding, but the rule helped to prevent any of them simply wiping out humanity. Matthias had always made it clear that until

Adam crossed that line, none of them could. Of course, there was always 'grey areas' to every law, ones that they could take advantage of. Brandt, for example, enjoyed taking a hit or two before lashing out in an act of self-defence.

Markovic explained the details of what was required of them and then he left the room to attend to other matters. Nahki had been charged with paying an informant a visit. The information he would obtain would pinpoint where Markovic's men need to go, with Nahki and Serena in tow.

'Well brother. As I'm not needed right now, I am going to make myself useful,' Serena said, standing up from her seat, glass in hand. 'I think I'll pay a visit to the beach, soak up some sun, maybe I'll find myself a new rich husband.' She laughed at the thought before making her way out, stepping over the bodies that were steadily growing colder. Nahki knew that he was best to wait until the evening to find this informant of Vlad's. Until then, he figured he would check in on their guest.

Vladimir sure has strange taste. Nahki walked down the steps from the ground floor of the building to the basement. The ground floor was designed to be perceived as an eastern travel company, dealing in travel and property sales. The basement felt like a completely new world, as if he had stepped back in time to the dark ages. A coarse, solid oak hand rail lead him down the wooden steps. A cold limestone floor awaited him at the base of the stairs, with a flame flickering from a wall sconce, the only source of light. The air was damp and musty; Nahki could smell the scent of death which clung to the orifices of the structure. A narrow corridor ran from the stairs along to a heavy ligneous door. Nahki knew that Markovic had been moving him from place to place, attempting to stay out of reach of the authorities, but this place was no doubt the strangest location he had been.

As Nahki pushed open the large door, he was greeted

by two armed men. Both were wearing khaki coloured combat pants and dark green tops. Their faces were hidden from view by balaclavas, concealing their identities from their hostage. Nahki entered the small room; there was no window, no source of natural light. Cold, hard, stone flooring lay throughout, running up to the rough sandstone walls that formed Markovic's very own dungeon. Nahki asked the men to leave, to which they dutifully obliged. He closed the door behind them and sat down on a wooden stool, just by the doorway. With the door closed, the room was in darkness except for a small flame that flickered from a burning candle.

'Can you keep a secret?' Nahki asked of the darkness. 'Of course you can,' he said, a slight smile crept to the corner of his mouth. 'That's why they continue to ask you questions.' Nahki stretched out his right hand toward the candle and the light that it emitted grew brighter and brighter until the entire room was visible. 'There you go. Now you can see me too,' he said, talking to the half-naked man clinging to the arenaceous rock that formed his cell.

He was barefoot, his feet blistered and sore. The only clothes he had were a pair of black pants, combat style. His back was bruised, no doubt from sleeping on the hard unlevel floor and his front was black and blue, distinct signs of the torture he had endured in response to his unwilling stance on giving up information. Burns and cuts riddled his upper arms and the creases of his elbows were covered in scattered scratch marks. They had been injecting him with something, Nahki surmised; he had been trying to claw out whatever it was from under his skin. His beard was soiled with dirt and blood, as was his hair. He tried to hide his face, the new light clearly hurting his eyes.

'If you've come to kill me, get on with it. I can't afford anymore therapy sessions,' he said, stroking the wall he rested against. There was a mixture of emotions to his tone. Nahki sensed fear, but his wit and his sarcasm hinted that he still clung to a glimmer of hope.

'Michael,' Nahki said, grasping the prisoner's attention. 'I'm just here to talk. It would seem you're far too important for me to simply kill.' The nearly broken man before him had clearly anticipated another beating of sorts; Nahki could hear a change in his breathing, a slight relief.

'You,' Mike said, turning to look at Nahki. He squinted; his eyes not quite adjusted yet to the light. 'You're not my type.'

Nahki smiled, 'A sense of humour? I *am* impressed. Usually it is the humour which is the first thing to go during torture such as what you've endured.'

'Torture?' Mike coughed, spitting some blood from an open cut on his lip. 'They've yet to crack out the feather duster.' His jest was lost on Nahki. This attempt to feign courage would only hold out so long. 'So, if you're not here to kill me, then what?' he questioned Nahki's intentions.

'Like I said, I'm just here to talk,' Nahki replied.

'So, not physical torture then. Just mental,' Mike smiled, although even smiling seemed to hurt, his face and jaw were fiercely bruised. 'Here I thought you lot were all about the killing.'' Nahki had come here with a purpose and it was not to exchange sarcastic comments.

'You really know nothing,' Nahki moved his stool closer to the prisoner as he spoke.

'Enlighten me,' Mike said, pulling his legs up to his chest away from Nahki. He was retreating. 'I've got all the time in the fucking world.'

'Actually, quite the opposite,' Nahki admitted in a matter-of-fact tone. Mike was mortal and would age and die. *If he is not killed within the next few days.* Nahki, however, would live forever should he not be killed himself, and, if his knowledge continued to grow, maybe even then he could escape death, perhaps much like Adam. 'Do you know the story of Adam and Eve, Mike?' he asked. Mike looked at him, perplexed by such a question.

'I believe it's part of the Genesis story?' Mike was clearly not religious and right now he was no doubt wondering what Nahki was getting at.

'Let me tell you a different version of the tale, one that I have come to learn over the past fifteen hundred years or so.' He had Mike's attention, whether he comprehended what Nahki was saying or not. 'The story goes, God created Adam and then, using Adam's rib, he created Eve as a companion,' Nahki went on to recite the story of Adam and Eve as written in the Book of Genesis. Mike spent most of the time looking puzzled and repeatedly asked Nahki what his point was. 'Well, the story is pretty close,' Nahki smiled at the dumbfounded expression that possessed Mike's face. 'God, in all his wisdom, creates Adam in his own image. His own image of power over life and death and creation, the works. He granted Adam the knowledge to mould the world as he saw fit and to protect his creation. Adam resided in the garden of Eden. There sat the tree of knowledge, the key to creation, knowledge of everything. The tree bore fruit, apples, that granted Adam with the knowledge he needed to continue God's work and further creation. So, removing a rib from his own flesh, Adam was able to create Eve, a companion, a mate, enabling him to continue to create life, for the human race was said to have been born, not simply manufactured.'

'Where are you going with this?' Mike asked again. 'You really expect me to believe that Adam is... *the* Adam?' he scoffed at the notion and then began to cough again.

'Taking Adam's rib,' Nahki continued, ignoring Mike's interruption. 'Eve forged a blade, inter-twining bone with a branch from the tree of knowledge. You see, Adam and Eve had children. As their children grew and had children of their own, Eve began to realise that mortality would eventually take her and her children, but not Adam, who was moulded by God. Possessed by jealously of Adam's immortality and fear of death, she took the blade and made twelve sacrifices, before plunging the knife into her own heart. In doing so, she was granted the knowledge she so desperately sought to escape her mortal fate. Craving their parents' abilities, their sons, Cain and Abel, fought to the death, with Cain claiming the blade as a prize. Horrified by what had become of his creations, by the malice and corruption that had possessed his loved ones, Adam banished everyone from the garden and he hid the tree of knowledge from the world.'

'That blade?' Mike said slowly, considering the truth to Nahki's story.

'You've seen it,' Nahki said matter-of-factly. 'In fact, I believe it currently resides in the F.B.I headquarters.' The thought of it being in their possession and them having no clue to its importance amused Nahki a little.

'What has any of this got to do with me?' Mike asked.

'Well, actually, very little I'm afraid,' Nahki answered honestly. 'But you see, Adam's blood flows through each of our veins. Meaning that we're all connected in some way or another. The Avunaye cannot simply act on their own impulses because, simply put, Adam has not yet crossed that line. He's taken a back seat as humanity has unravelled itself,' Nahki continued to explain.

'But if he is all powerful, surely he'll just stop you fuckers from killing whoever you want,' Mike lifted himself up slightly, elevating his chest and attempting to broaden his figure.

'He's the one you should be worried about Michael,' Nahki said, drawing a look of confusion from the captive. 'We have thus far contained Adam's powers over the centuries, each time he dies he loses a piece of himself, memories... If he were to ever fully recover, no-one would be safe. Not me, not you, not your friends or your loved ones...' He paused for a moment, carefully studying Mike's, knowing each face he was picturing. 'You and your team are just unlucky, wrong place... for the longer Adam is around you, the more danger you are all in.' Mike's expression changed; no longer confused, he was fearful. More than that, there was a spark inside of him now, a spark of determination. Nahki had planted a seed of doubt that would grow; if Mike wanted to protect his loved ones, he now knew that Adam would have to die.

Nahki left Mike to stew in the knowledge that his friends and colleagues were in danger and headed across town to his own residence. As a hunter, one who created his own weapons from his own flesh, Nahki needed very little to survive. He kept a third-floor flat on the Upper East Side of Manhattan; close enough to his prey, yet far enough to remain inconspicuous. The apartment was almost void of all things, with no furniture to speak of - no table or chairs. Nahki occasionally required food but would venture out to obtain it. His bedroom contained no bed, but within the built-in wardrobe there were several different disguises that allowed him to blend in, and when required, get close to his targets. He had decided a formal attire would be a prerequisite for what he needed to achieve. He took a dark grey suit jacket, matching waistcoat and pants from off a rail. A pair of dark brown shoes and a powder blue shirt completed his outfit. He buttoned the shirt, all except the final button, covering his necklace. He was not accustomed to clothing, but he had learned to live with its restrictions. With this, he closed the door behind him and headed out into the city.

A bar named 'Twin Dice' was his destination: the informant that Markovic required him to meet would be there. The journey involved walking through many of the cities run-down streets; avenues littered with people drawn outside as the night took hold. *The darkness brings out the worst in many.* He continued on towards his objective. Nahki's inability to sympathize with how mortal man felt meant that they were truly worthless to him, merely obstacles.

The bar was set off from the main road. Nahki walked through a stone archway between two buildings and followed a set of steps down beneath the city streets. The underground nature of the establishment would no doubt attract a number of unscrupulous characters, or maybe it was just the girls that brought them in. The steps lead down to a set of cast-iron doors manned by a large man named Deryk. Upon seeing Nahki approach, Deryk hastily opened the door for him and tried not to make eye contact. It was not Nahki's first visit and the outcome of his last would no doubt forever live within the doorman's memory. Inside, the bar produced a distinct mood; the smell of smoke, alcohol, sweat and sex bombarded Nahki's senses, and dimmed lighting allowed for dark deeds to be concealed. The bar was set into an alcove on the far side of the establishment, with a dozen tables scattered between it and the entrance. Naked, intoxicated girls either danced on the tables, lay incapacitated on top of them or were dragged off to the VIP booths set off to the left of where Nahki stood. They weren't willing participants, but they were serving the needs of Markovic's paying guests; they knew better than to disobey. The room Nahki sought lay to his right, through another heavy metal door, this one guarded by two men; one was bald, riddled with tattoos and piercings, the other short haired and his stance suggested that he was most likely ex-military. Seeing Nahki approach, they quickly opened the door to let him inside and then closed the door behind him.

It was a storeroom of sorts. Crates of counterfeit booze lined the shelves within a cage along the wall to the right of the entrance. To the left sat a table and three empty chairs. In the centre of the room sat a woman on a stool; she had blonde hair bar a thick streak of black that ran down the right side of her face. She wore a tight tank top; it had clearly started off beige in colour but was now tarnished with stains of blood, creating an almost tie-dye affect that was trivial in comparison to its true nature. She also wore black jeans and heavy-duty black safety boots such as those worn by construction workers. Sat with her elbows resting on her knees, she was leant forward, wiping her fingers on a piece of cloth and cleaning the blood from the knuckle dusters she wore on both hands.

'You must be Nahki,' she said, her tone baring a gravel that was unexpected. She looked Nahki up and down and smirked: 'Nice threads.' she said, his suit clearly amusing her.

'I hope that doesn't belong to my guy?' Nahki said, gesturing toward the blood-soaked rag she was holding.

'One of the girls...' she replied simply, standing up from her stool. 'Markovic doesn't tolerate disobedience.' She threw the rag onto the back of one of the chairs and looked Nahki in the eye. He could see that she had probably learnt firsthand that stepping out of line did you no favors; she had a thin scar that ran from the corner of her mouth across her right cheek. 'I'm Sinead,' she said, walking over to the liquor cage. 'Your guy is currently getting a lap dance, but my boys will bring him in soon'. She opened the cage and shifted a couple of bottles around. Reaching to the back of the shelf, she grabbed a half empty bottle of bourbon. 'I keep the real shit hidden,' she grinned and winked mischievously. 'Fancy a drink?' Nahki waved away the invitation, receiving a look of disappointment from Sinead. She shrugged her shoulders and took a swig from the bottle before returning it to its hiding place.

'Hey, Raven?' a man stuck his head into the room. Sinead looked over in response. 'Bringing this guy in now,' he said, before his head disappeared out of the entrance again. Nahki walked over to the table and grabbed two of the chairs; he carried them to the center of the room and, kicking the stool out of the way, sat them down facing one another a foot or two apart. Two men entered the room, dragging a third between them. Nahki recognized the ex-service looking doorman from outside the room, the other man was dressed the same and was presumably security personnel as well. They both wore creased light-grey suits with white - or at least off-white - shirts with black ties and black shoes. They were armed, their holster straps showing under the suit jackets each time they moved their arms. The second man had dark slicked-back hair that was tied up into a top knot. A single earring in his right ear and the evidence of a tattoo on his neck, partially hidden by the collar of his shirt, were notable characteristics. His broad face, however, was easily distinguishable, looking as though it had been broken before. It was home to an off-set nose and crater-like scars on his chin and cheek. The two men dragged Nahki's informant over and sat him down on one of the chairs.

'The prick's had a few...' said the resolute doorman before turning and heading back out of the room to his post. The larger, crater-faced bouncer decided to stay for the show and headed over to the table to take the remaining seat.

Nahki's informant sat still, slumped in the chair. His mousey-brown hair was a mess and his face was riddled with sweat. He wore blue jeans, tan coloured walking boots and a red and grey polo shirt. *How the fuck am I supposed to get information from him if he's trashed?* Nahki stood over the man, with his hands on his hips. He looked over to the bouncer at the table and scowled.

'Sinead?' he asked calmly. 'Do you have a defibrillator to hand?' She looked puzzled, but seeing that Nahki was serious, she speedily left the room, only to return moments later with a bag.

'Apparently we do. What you thinking?' she quizzed.

'I'm a busy man. I don't have time to wait for him to sober up, so...' Nahki stopped speaking and undid the button on his own right jacket sleeve. His idea was rash, but he had spent more time than he would have liked to around these people already. He rolled up the sleeve and then did the same with his shirt sleeve. Holding his arm at a right angle, he ran the fingers of his left hand along his right forearm. As his fingers slowly moved along his skin, they lifted the hilt of a blade up from under the surface of his flesh. Grasping the haft, he pulled a knife clean from his arm. Dumbfounded, Sinead went back to the cage to find her bottle of bourbon again.

Nahki took the blade and made a small cut on his palm before quickly tearing the inebriate's shirt at the neck. Making a small cut with the knife on the man's upper chest, he then placed his palm onto the cut, mixing their blood.

'Get the kit ready,' Nahki instructed, pulling his hand away and pointing to the bag. As she hurried over to the defibrillator, the man in the chair began to jerk in his seat, his arms and legs flailed and his head rolled back and forth. He began to shake vigorously and suddenly started to scream as he woke from his stupor.

'The fuck you done to him?!' shouted the bouncer, standing up from his seat, trading his usual vacuous expression for one of concern.

'Gave him the rush of his life,' Nahki answered, smiling. 'Now shut the fuck up and sit down!' The bouncer resisted compliance for a moment before sitting back down hesitantly. 'Sinead? Ready?' Nahki asked as she frantically prepared the portable defibrillator. Suddenly, there was a silence in the room as the man stopped shouting. He desperately clutched at his chest, the muscles in his neck pulled taut and his face ran aflush with blood under the skin. He struggled, wrestling with the pain within before losing the fight and slumping into his seat, lifelessly. 'Now would be a good time...' Nahki said, stood, arms crossed. It only took one shock to kick-start the man's heart, much to the relief of everyone in the room. He was suddenly wide-eyed; Nahki could hear the flow of his blood, pumping fiercely through his veins. *You're going to feel rough in the morning.* Nahki didn't care for the man's wellbeing, yet he was grateful that he had survived the process thus far.

'What the fuck just happened?!' the man exclaimed, panickily looking around the room whilst rubbing at his chest.

'Ha! Think you almost died,' Sinead quipped. She was sat on the floor, legs apart, holding herself up with her arms.

'What the fuck?!' he said, still in shock. He didn't look to be able to focus, his mind and body racing, bursting with life.

'Enough!' Nahki shouted, taking the seat opposite the man. 'I'm here on behalf of Vladimir Markovic. I hear you have some information for me?' he prompted, whilst rolling his sleeve back down. The world seemed to have come rushing back into focus for the man as he attempted to straighten himself. 'I am Nahki of the Avunaye and you have some information to give me.' Nahki spoke slowly but sternly, he had wasted enough time already.

'Okay,' said the man. 'Hunter's Point, on the corner of... of 45th, opposite the park,' he spoke clearly, yet he delivered the words as if he had a twitch. The effect of Nahki's blood lingered within him.

'You're sure?' Nahki asked. He believed the man, but he could literally taste the fear emanating from his pours.

'I'm sure,' the man nodded, this time in a defeated tone.

'You're useful Officer Reeves, don't look so scared...' Nahki said, looking him in the eye.

'W-what are you going to do?' Axel stuttered. He was nervous, anxious, terrified. He was no doubt still buzzing inside from the intoxication, which would only make every emotion worse.

'Bring the city to its knees,' Nahki replied, standing up from his seat and dusting himself off. 'Mankind has lost its compassion. You only seem to care, truly care, when you are grieving a loss. We are going to help you find your way again.' Nahki moved towards the door but before he reached the exit, Sinead grabbed his shoulder.

'What are you going to do?' she repeated the informant's words. Her senses, too, were overflowing with fear.

'Start again,' Nahki simply said, before leaving the room

behind.

Nahki walked through the city as the cool night faded away and the warm sun rose. The people of the dark retreated to their homes and the chaotic nature of civilization burst out onto the world. He ventured through Union Square Park and walked along Broadway until he stopped outside of a coffee shop. He had arrived just in time, as calculated. An old friend would be inside, grabbing their predictable morning coffee. He could smell him on the air, yet, there was someone else with him today. Nahki recognized her scent but he had not yet had the privilege of an introduction. He stepped into the bustling establishment. People moved back and forth, grabbing their drinks from the counter to take away; the two he sought after sat together in the corner of the shop. Both dressed in their work attire, they were no doubt on their way to the office. Nahki took a deep breath in, learning what he could from the smells that filled the air. The gentleman was drinking a black coffee from a mug, whereas she had one in a paper takeaway cup. She tore at a freshly baked croissant as they talked amongst themselves, occasionally moving a stray strand of blonde hair that continued to fall across her face.

'Solomon Grey,' Nahki said, stepping towards the pair. Solomon turned in his seat; he smiled as if to suggest a welcome, yet the fakeness was clear as his eyes gave away his true feelings.

'Zane?' Solomon said. 'What brings you here?'

'Work... as always,' Nahki replied. 'But I heard they did a great morning tea here.' Nahki's response seemed to receive a look of caution from Solomon, but the woman simply smiled as she attempted to chew and swallow her food as quickly as possible.

'Zane Brown, this is Special Agent Rose-Anderson. Krysta, this is Zane Brown, C.I.A.' Solomon said suddenly, as if just remembering that she was there too.

'Call me Krysta,' she said, holding out a welcoming hand. Nahki took her hand and gave it a gentle shake, keeping eye contact. 'What brings the C.I.A to our neck of the woods?' she asked. Her words gave away her caution, she had obviously heard of him, and if Solomon was her source it could not have been good.

'Here to collect,' Nahki said, a wide smile spreading across his face. 'The paperwork will probably be waiting for you when you reach the office.'

'Sorry – I don't - collect what?' Krysta said naively, turning to look at Solomon for answers.

'He means Adam,' Solomon said. His words brought a concerned look to Krysta's face. 'I'm afraid you're too late Zane,' Solomon said, holding a straight face, but Nahki could see the Cheshire grin that was desperately wanting to show itself. 'He's gone.'

'Gone?' Nahki asked. If it was true, it was an unfortunate result, although not entirely unexpected.

'He said it would be too dangerous for him to stay any longer,' Krysta admitted. Her honesty appeared to draw a glare from her superior.

'Sol, it's okay, we're all friends here,' Nahki was having to play the part, but in truth his skin was crawling. Adam's disappearance could cause problems. The longer he continued to remain alive, the stronger he became, and for Markovic's and Matthias' plans to work, he would need to be manipulatable. 'You realize how much shit this is gonna cause right? Him going missing on the F.B.I's watch?'

'He didn't exactly give the team on duty a choice,' Krysta added defensively, coming to the defense of her superior, for whom she clearly cared for. 'We have him on tape. He turned into a huge fucking wolf and sauntered out of the cell before leaping out of a window and practically vanishing.'

Adam's powers were indeed growing, Nahki surmised. With nothing to do but recover, his healing process must be working on overtime. *The faster he heals, the harder he is going to be to put down.* The two agents were looking at him, seemingly waiting for a response of shock or amazement.

'Well, I'll be needing everything you've managed to get on him then. I imagine I'll need access to files etc. I guess we'll be seeing a bit more of each other Solomon.' Nahki touched Solomon on the shoulder, rubbing salt into the wound. 'Nice to meet you Krysta,' he nodded. *No doubt our paths will cross again.* He turned away from the two of them and headed for the counter.

'Zane Brown,' he said to the barista, a wry smile creeping to the corner of his mouth. 'Looks like it's going to be a beautiful day.'

15

Seamus McCarthy

'Hey dad! Go long!' Declan called, stepping backwards, holding a football close to his ear, preparing to let it fly. The hot summer weather was drawing to a close and the city was entering the fall. It was mild out; the sun seemed to counter-act the cool breeze and his son wore his dark blue sleeveless top and grey jogging pants for their trip to the park. It was Seamus' idea to get out of the house. He had desperately needed some fresh air and a chance to clear his head. He wore his running trainers, a pair of black shorts and a grey top with long sleeves as he had often felt the chill on the breeze these past few days. He ran away from his son. Knowing just how far Declan could throw, he knew he would need to cover some ground and quickly. He looked back over his shoulder to see his boy let loose of the ball. Seamus watched it as it hurtled through the air, attempting to calculate where it would come down. He was paying so much attention to where the ball was that he missed his footing and as he was about to prepare to catch it, he found himself beginning to fall backwards. Upon hitting the grass, with the ball landing a mere foot and a half away from him, Seamus, for a moment, lost his temper.

'God damn it!' he exclaimed, punching the soil with his right hand, his knuckles colliding with a large stone that lay just below the dirt's surface, hidden within the sea of green.

'Whoa dad, it was just one missed pass. Don't give yourself a heart attack,' Declan jested, grabbing at his own chest and playfully falling to the floor.

'Yeah alright,' Seamus said, half-heartedly laughing at his son's mockery of him whilst shaking off his throbbing hand. 'You'd better go long!' he said, climbing to his feet and picking up the ball. 'I'm talking way long... way out there,' he said, smiling as Declan began jogging away slowly. As he grasped the ball in his hand, he noticed some blood on his fingers. Where he had hit the stone, the impact had split the skin on his knuckle and his blood ran freely down the back of his hand. He stared at it for a few moments, the sight of the blood on his hand drawing a flashback to Dante's flat and reminding him of how he had lost his temper that night.

'Hey old man! Any day now!' Declan yelled across the park, his voice snaring Seamus' attention and ripping him from his daydream-like state. He squeezed the ball slightly between his hands and then cranked his shoulder back, pulling back his firing arm before whipping it forward in a swift jerk motion, releasing the football and launching it into the air. The ball soared upwards but not as far forwards as he had hoped, meaning Declan had to run towards it to catch the pass. Diving to catch the ball, Declan missed it by a hair, with it landing right at his outstretched fingertips.

'Has anyone ever told you that you both suck at football?' The voice belonged to his daughter, Alannah. She and Moira had left the two budding sportsmen to their ball game and had gone for a walk to take in the colourful scenery. Fall brought a multitude of new and vibrant colours to the world, changing the cherry blossom pinks to shades of blood orange, before the winter months stripped them bare. Seamus looked at his wife and daughter as they approached. Moira wore her black fur-lined boots, skinny blue denim jeans and she had donned a thick, fluffy white jumper to protect herself from the fall winds. Her dark curled hair shimmered in the sunlight and as she laughed at Alannah's comments, she brightened the world for a moment. Alannah trudged beside her mum in a pair of dark oaken-brown walking boots, black leggings and a multi-coloured, flower-patterned, long-sleeved dress that hemmed just above her knees. Her long dark hair flowed freely whenever the air caught it, revealing her perfect, untouched face. Seamus tried not to think of what had happened, but each time he laid eyes on his little girl, he would feel this empty pit in his gut that he couldn't ignore. He had spent so much time since that day searching for answers -working side by side with Sam Lorenzo - that today was a rare occasion for him and his family. Time spent alone with Moira had become scarce and the kids had hardly seen their father as he pursued one theory after another. He had spent so much time with Sam that the kid had become like one of his own. Seamus had spent so much time at work and out on the streets with Sam that the young cadet had become the envy of his loved ones. But today was different. Seamus had promised, not only to his family but to himself, today was all about them.

Seamus and Declan continued to throw the ball to one another as Moira and Alannah mocked their lack of sporting ability.

'You think you can do better?' Seamus said, looking to his wife, smiling. The squint in his eyes seemed to give away his true intention.

'Don't you dare!' Moira said, pointing at him sternly, exhibiting a worried smile as she tried to anticipate Seamus' next move. Declan playfully goaded his father to do what he was thinking of doing and Alannah merely laughed joyfully at the sight of it all. Seamus tossed the ball to Moira gently, allowing her to easily react and catch it.

'Oh! Defence!' he exclaimed as he began to move towards her, insinuating that he was going to tackle her.

'No!' she said in reply, struggling to keep herself from grinning. 'No, no, no!' she continued whilst speedily stepping

she wore knee-high brown leather heeled boots and dark blue jeans, a thin white blouse was mostly covered by a black western-styled denim jacket, its silvery buttons shimmering when they caught the sunlight. Her hair was slightly curled, and she wore it down, occasionally pushing strands of it behind her ear as she stood, unknowing how to respond.

'I'm Jake,' said the man, cutting in and breaking the awkward moment of silence; he offered his hand as he introduced himself. He was tall and well built. He wore a beige coloured Seattle coat, a black woollen top, black pants and a pair of large tan coloured suede boots. His interruption annoyed Seamus and his hand gesture went ignored. Seamus had a purpose and continued to stare at Krysta.

'Seamus. Now is really not the place,' she said, realising that he was not backing down. 'I can't discuss cases out here, especially when I'm off duty, well not even when I'm on duty...' Each word prodded at Seamus' patience, but he could sense that he had knocked her off balance.

'Well I can't get hold of you when you're on duty. Look, I just want to know what's going on with the Adam case,' Seamus said abruptly, his tone carrying his desperation.

'For god's sake Seamus, you promised!' said Moira. She was clearly furious, stood holding two hot dogs, one for Seamus, whilst Declan dug into his food. Alannah stood solemnly next to her mother, quietly expressing a look of disappointment.

'It's okay, Mrs McCarthy. We're leaving now. Apologies for interrupting your afternoon,' Krysta said, jumping on the opportunity to escape the situation. Seamus, however, was unwilling to let her slip away so easily.

'This is my daughter, Krysta,' he said, pointing towards Alannah, ushering her to come over to him, but instead she remained rooted next to her mother. Krysta looked over the to the girl and smiled. Her smile, however, quickly dissipated as she got a clear look at her and then confusion flashed across her face. 'That red-haired bitch burnt my daughter, you remember right?' he said angrily, his own words seemingly fuelling the fire that burned within. 'Well, Adam paid my daughter here a visit in hospital... he put his hand on her and healed her face,' he said, snaring Krysta's attention. 'I want to know why! How?... What the hell is going on?!' His exclamation and frustration drew a sigh of disbelief from his wife. Jake moved closer to Krysta in response to Seamus' display of emotion, placing a hand on her lower back.

'Just let it go Seamus, for fucks sake,' Moira said, begging for him to stop.

'Look Seamus,' Krysta said stepping closer to him, enabling her to lower her voice. 'I don't know why or how he did it,' she said calmly. 'I don't even know where he is now. This is a federal investigation and I will not...' she seemed determined to shut him down, however, the word 'now' screamed inside of Seamus' head and he stopped her before she could finish what she was saying.

'You don't know where he is now?!' he asked, trying to piece everything together. 'You knew before? Don't tell me you had him in custody?' As Seamus said it, he could tell that he was right from the look in her eyes. 'And you lost him?!' he exclaimed in disbelief, rubbing his face. The look on her face was one of admission, of guilt. *You lied!* His temper began to flare. *I trusted you!* Seamus was about to lose control when suddenly Jake placed his hand on his chest.

'Seamus, we're leaving,' Jake said sternly, yet calmly, attempting to disarm the situation.

'So are we,' Moira said subduedly. Torn between preventing either party from leaving him standing there empty handed, Seamus conceded defeat and simply watched Krysta and Jake walk away. When he finally calmed enough within, he turned around, only to realise that his family had also left him; the hot dog that Moira had bought him sat on the ground where she had stood.

That evening had climaxed with Seamus and Moira arguing about his obsession. Seamus left the house and walked to the nearest bar for a drink. He knew it would not help the situation, but he struggled to care at the time and he needed some air. After two drinks, he returned home to find that everyone had already gone to bed, so, guiltily, he decided to lay down on the sofa and eventually fell to sleep himself.

Thankfully, the next day was a working day. Moira had already left for work when he awoke and the kids were heading out themselves, so there were no arguments or awkward silences to deal with. He looked at the time. *Shit I'm gonna be late!* He decided to skip his morning shower and headed upstairs to get dressed. His back was stiff due to the uncomfortable sleeping situation and his legs felt as if they craved exercise. He had not been for his usual morning run for over a week now, his life becoming less of a routine and more resembling chaos. Moira had ironed and hung his uniform up for him, the sight of it gave him a twisted feeling in his gut as he recalled their argument the night before. He quickly donned his clothes and hastily groomed his hair before heading out into the city.

'All those times you was early McCarthy. I knew it'd never last,' Sergeant McCabe laughed as Seamus hurried into the precinct. Seamus tried to ignore the rounded man's chuckle, but then he was called back. 'Seamus! Chief wants to see you and Lorenzo now.' That was not what Seamus needed to hear right now. He had only ever been summoned to the chief's office once before in the past and that was to receive a commendation for his hard work and example; he doubted this visit would be for the same. He glanced across the room to see Malek and Axel leering. Seamus' growing obsession with the case had made him a bit of a recluse and his friends and colleagues had begun to act awkwardly towards him. Seamus, however, couldn't help but notice how they both looked: Malik with an aura of confidence and Axel, his opposite, tired and infirm. *Fuck.* He fastened his belt and altered his course for the chief's office. When he reached her door, he found Lorenzo there waiting.   'Hey   kid,' Seamus said to the cadet, although these days Sam was more like a partner. The young man stood confidently, feet apart and hands behind his back like a soldier.

'Hey Seamus,' he replied, smiling. 'Good weekend?' he asked with an attentive look on his face. Seamus didn't want to bore him with the details of his topsy-turvy days away from work, so he gave a simple nod in reply. 'What you think the chief wants with us?' Sam asked of his mentor and friend. He suddenly seemed less sure of himself.

'Not sure,' Seamus responded honestly, taking up a position alongside the cadet. 'Nothing to worry about though, I'm sure.' He hoped that his words reassured the rookie.

'Captain Wu is in there at the minute,' Sam said. 'Pretty quiet though.' It was quiet, Seamus realised; with any luck that was a good sign. It was never a good day if the chief was in a bad mood.

What could the chief and the captain want with me and Sam? Seamus started to get anxious the longer they kept them waiting. As the minutes passed by, he almost stopped breathing as he contemplated a hundred different scenarios in his mind, yet, he was finally able to relax as the door to the office opened and Chief Pérez's voice sounded, calling him and his partner inside.

The pair stepped into the office, Seamus closing the door behind him before joining Sam, who was stood before the chief's desk. Captain Daniel Wu stood beside the desk, nodding to Seamus in acknowledgement as he took up position. The captain stood silently, feet together; two gold bars sat on each wing of his white shirt collar, denoting his station. His surname sat below his captain badge that was capped with a crown and rested on a bed of laurels. An experienced officer, he was a good and honest man, often providing those younger with words of wisdom. Proud of his eastern heritage, he wore three small coloured pins on his breast, one red, one yellow and one green. He had short black hair and a candid face; Seamus could only hope that his inclusion in this rare meeting was a good sign. Chief Valentina Pérez sat in her chair the other side of the desk. She also wore a white shirt, with a black tie. Her long dark hair was tied up, exposing her smooth, honey coloured skin. She had soft brown coloured eyes and full cherry blossom pink lips that aided in the illusion of a light-hearted woman, for when tested, her fiery commitment to her department and to her city knew no bounds.

'McCarthy, Lorenzo,' she said, her way of greeting officers she rarely had dealings with. 'I'm not one to beat around the bush, so I'll get right to the point,' she said, not holding back. Her stare pierced through Seamus' defences with ease. *Shit, here we go.* Seamus' worst fears about this meeting came to a head as he understood his standard of work had dropped in recent weeks since Adam entered his life.

'Think of yourself as Sergeant material?' she asked the question, but gave no time for him to answer. 'Applied twice, missed out twice: both times to a detective. Think you're good enough to skip detective grade and jump straight up the ladder?' Again, the question seemed rhetorical and so Seamus bit his tongue. 'Four months ago I might have agreed with your bold self-examination, but according to Captain Wu and Sergeant McCabe, you've lost focus.' Seamus stood unflinching. She was right, but to show sign of fear or weakness right now would be like baring his jugular to a wild lion and hoping it didn't kill him. 'An almost unbelievable level of attendance, commitment, punctuality, praises from colleagues, civilians... yet, beyond any understanding, it almost seems to change overnight. Firstly, you rescue one 'John Doe', then there was an intruder in your home. I will admit this must have been traumatic, but you must remain professional. It appears that ever since these incidents you have struggled to cope. You've let yourself and this precinct down and I need you to snap out of it.' She paused for a few moments looking Seamus, and then Sam, up and down. Maybe she was waiting for one of them to break, to try and defend themselves. Seamus caught a glimpse of Daniel as he tried to remain unmoving. The captain stayed quiet; he would not do anything until called upon. 'Cadet... Samuel Lorenzo,' she said, checking a piece of paperwork in front of her, no doubt to ensure she had the right name. 'Think McCarthy is sergeant material? You've spent enough time with him recently.' Seamus looked to Sam who was currently expressing a look of clear bewilderment. *Is this a test? What's her angle?*

'Speak Lorenzo. I won't bite. From what I hear you're normally very vocal,' she smiled, probably attempting to ease Sam's nerves.

'I believe so ma'am,' Sam said formally. He clearly hadn't been expecting to be put in this position. 'He's a great officer and teacher ma'am, he's committed, he's good at what he does, I couldn't have asked for anyone better to be paired with ma'am, he's...' but before Sam could finish, she interrupted.

'That'll do Lorenzo,' she said, probably regretting her encouragement of the young cadet's vocality. She turned in her chair and stood up. She looked out of the window behind her desk, seemingly contemplating her next move. '108th precinct have requested assistance with a homicide investigation. They've had their budget cut and are short on resources at present. McCarthy?' she said, turning to face Seamus, indicating that the attention had shifted from Lorenzo back to himself. 'Tomorrow and Wednesday you will assist 108th with their investigation as a detective inspector. Lorenzo, you will assist in the capacity of an officer. Should I hear good things, when you return home, we will look at making these promotions permanent. It's not sergeant, but it's a step up and when the next sergeant's position becomes available... you catch my drift?' She looked to Seamus for an indication of his understanding.

'Yes ma'am,' Seamus said simply. He knew that there was no need for thanks, she was an intuitive woman and she'd know what this opportunity would mean to him.

'Fantastic. Captain Wu will provide you with the details you'll need. Good luck to you both,' her words were a dismissal. Captain Wu broke his stance first, providing the sign that Seamus and Sam were required to take their leave and continue with their daily duties.

'Bryan Miller. Age thirty... seven. Shot in his doorway. Wife and eight-year-old kid weren't home at the time,' Officer Sanders informed Seamus and Sam not long after their arrival. They had left early that morning, hoping to beat the traffic and get a head start on the day. Neither of them had gotten much sleep. They were both too nervous and excited, taking on these new and hopefully rewarding roles. Seamus was feeling good; he and Moira had had a good evening, one without argument. The news of a possible promotion had almost instantly relieved the tension that had been created by the weekend's events. It seemed Moira was almost now thankful of Seamus' commitment to the case. 'Initially chalked up as a mugging or gang shooting, only the guy was shot twice in the chest and once in the head. Long Island thugs are not usually so precise. Plus, nothing was stolen,' the officer continued to give his theory on the incident as they examined the scene. The case gave rise to many questions, but a lack of manpower meant that this riddle would most likely go unsolved.

'Where did he work?' Seamus asked. His curiosity had been snared. He was determined to make the most of this opportunity. He wore his usual work shoes for comfort, but instead of his uniform he had donned a pair of dark grey pants with a jacket to match, a clean white shirt and a dark blue tie that had once belonged to his father.

'Not far from here. Some storage place on corner of 45th,' Officer Sanders divulged. With no suspects and very little evidence to work with, Seamus was beginning to wonder if he had been called in simply to aid with the paperwork. Regardless, he would do his best.

'Seamus,' Sam said, edging in on the crime scene. 'You ask me, this is bullshit. Sounds like a hit.' Sam wasn't wrong; something was off about this case, but Seamus knew better than to let it distract him from the work he was expected to do.

'Lack of resources Sam, they'll probably never solve this one,' Seamus didn't want to quash the young soon-to-be officers thirst for truth or justice, but he would need to learn that there were limits to what could be done in some cases. The victim's neighbours had seen nothing. He apparently had no enemies, no one looking to cause him harm, nobody had a motive. Yet for some reason, he looked to have been professionally killed.

The morning passed slowly as Seamus made arduous notes about the crime scene. It was a grateful respite when Sam suggested that they stop to take a break and grab a coffee and something to eat. There was a local deli nearby that the pair quickly visited. Upon returning to the scene, Sanders was frantically packing away his kit into his car.

'Whoa, where's the fire?' Sam joked as he stood watching the chaotic movements of the frenetic officer before them. Sanders did not reply to Sam's comments, prompting Sam to look to Seamus; he shrugged his shoulders in a plea for assistance.

'Officer Sanders,' Seamus said, attempting to sound as assertive as possible. 'Care to tell us what the hell you're doing?' It wasn't curiosity that urged him to get to the bottom of what was going on, more a sense of anxiety; Seamus couldn't afford for this job to go wrong.

'Look, you two head back to the station and crack on with the paperwork,' Sander's graced them with a moment of his time to explain himself. 'Call just came in, shots fired,' he finished bundling his things into the vehicle and began to climb into it. 'You two have been ordered back to the station. I've gotta respond to the 10-10.' Upon finishing the sentence, he slammed the door shut, turned on his blue light and sped off up the street.

'Maybe we should assist,' Sam said, watching the car disappear into the distance. If this was any other case then Seamus would have agreed, but they had been given the order to return and so that's what they were going to do.

'We have orders kid. We're on their turf, better to do as asked. We want those promotions remember?' Seamus felt bad for saying it, but it was imperative that this opportunity went right, his family needed it and he knew Sam needed it too.

They climbed into Seamus' car feeling rather subdued and Seamus started the engine. Sam sat quietly in the passenger seat, adjusting his radio to listen to the incoming communications.

'What?' he said in response to Seamus' frown. 'I can at least listen to what's happening.'

'We have a 10-20 in progress at the scene of the shooting' an attending officer announced over the airwaves.

'Sounds like someone is eager to rob the place, old fashioned bank robbery?' Sam queried. His face lit up with intrigue and there was a clear excitement to his tone. Seamus could understand the kids desire to get stuck in.

'Suspect fleeing the scene' another announcement confirmed as Seamus put the car into drive and pulled off, heading back to the station. *'Suspect is female, red hair, heading east on 45th.'* Seamus hit the brake so hard that Sam had to hold his hand out to prevent himself from colliding with the dash. Seamus' heart boomed with the sudden injection of adrenaline. He looked to Sam for any manner of

confirmation that he wasn't simply hearing things.

'It could be...' were the words that Seamus wanted to hear as they left Sam's lips. Seamus pushed down hard onto the gas pedal and spun the wheel to perform a U-turn, before tearing off in the same direction as Officer Sanders had gone.

Seamus was driving so fast that he almost didn't stop in time when a group of pedestrians stepped out onto a crosswalk. Thankfully, it was perfect timing.

'Seamus, look!' shouted Sam, staring out his window. On the corner of the street next to the one they sat upon was a mass of plain-clothed officers. Several police cars blocked their direct path to the source of the commotion, but Seamus didn't want to go to where the shooting took place, nor the robbery. He felt angry and had only one thing on his mind, and that was her. 'Sir, if I was running from the scene of the crime, I'd be heading for the park. It's lunchtime, gonna be crowded.' Sam was thinking clearly, for which Seamus was grateful; all he saw at the minute was red.

'We'll pull up ahead, and then head into the playground on foot,' Seamus decided; they'd need to be quick though, he couldn't let her escape. The idea that it may not be Serena never crossed his mind. As they drove past the emptied tennis courts and soccer pitches, Seamus thought of his daughter and how Serena had hurt her. *Of course she'd chose a public place with kids*. Pulling up at one of the entrances to the playground, Samuel and Seamus quickly exited the vehicle, checked their sidearms and headed into the rather crowded recreational area along one of the pathways leading off from the sidewalk. *There's too many people*. Seamus was scanning the faces of everyone he passed.

'Huh. Maybe we should've gone back to the station, we get mixed up in all this shit and Pérez is gonna have our asses.' Lorenzo was concerned. A sense of fear and doubt clasped to his words. *Maybe he's right*. Seamus couldn't help but doubt himself as their search continued fruitlessly.

'Freeze!' exclaimed an officer from amongst the crowd of people. Seamus couldn't quite see what was going on through the hoard of civilians.

'Seamus! Look!' Sam shouted, pointing to the outskirts of the playground. There stood a man dressed in a pair of beige pants and a leather jacket. He had some sort of neckerchief that covered the lower half of his face and thick curly brown hair. He was being handed a case of sorts and as he took it, he turned and moved for the nearest exit. As passers-by moved from Seamus' eyeline, he saw the person that had handed over the case. She stood staring in his direction, her fiery red hair waving ever so slightly in the breeze. She smirked.

His legs began to move seconds before his mind had made the decision. With Sam in tow, he started to push his way through the crowd towards her. Each time he caught a glimpse of her, he could swear she was looking straight at him, as if she were waiting for him. She stood there, unnerved, confident; dressed in a pair of merlot satin pants, woven at the waist and a white off the shoulder peplum top. *Why is this bitch just standing there?!* Seamus was beginning to close the distance between them to a matter of feet. Just as he was about to reach touching distance, she turned with such speed and grace, and then began to flee. He couldn't let her get away - who knew when he'd have the opportunity again.

'Sir, something about this don't seem right,' Sam panted as he ran alongside his partner in pursuit of Serena. Seamus didn't care; the woman who had haunted him for months was 10 feet away and she was not going to escape. They ran out of the playground and across the street. Marginally missing several pedestrians, Seamus and Sam tore around the corner of the block and continued the chase down the road. She seemed to glide effortlessly across the tarmac, dodging all traffic before turning left at the next bend. Without thinking, Seamus ran across the street, forcing one car to break sharply and another to swerve. He made it to the corner to see his target enter a tall building on the opposite side of the avenue.

'McCarthy!' Sam called as Seamus darted out into oncoming traffic once more, determined to catch his fiery prey.

'Sam, it'll be fine! C'mon!' he exclaimed to his wary partner. He couldn't stop, not now; the need for justice swelled within him. He reached the door to the building; it had clearly been forced open. The broken pieces that lay on the ground forced hesitation for a moment as Seamus wondered what other tricks this woman had up her sleeve. He took to the stairs and saw a flash of red and white, just one flight up through the metal mesh that ran down the centre of the dog-legged staircase. Sam was still following him as he pushed on up one flight after another, taking the steps two at a time. It had to have been at least eight stories up that Seamus could swear he saw someone else running alongside Serena; a dark-skinned man. But as he reached the last set of steps, a longer set than its predecessors, he saw only her as she reached the climax and disappeared into the hallway beyond.

Seamus took a moment to catch his breath, which subsequently gave Sam the chance to catch up.

'This chick can *run*,' Sam quipped as he bent over to exhale. 'Feel like we're chasing Usain Bolt's half-sister,' he joked as he gasped for air. Seamus wasn't going to give up now. Receiving a groan and a look of discouragement from the cadet, he again pushed on up the stairs and into the hallway beyond. At the end of the hall he saw her, standing by a window, looking out onto the city.

'Nowhere left to run!' Seamus exclaimed, before taking a deep breath, removing his weapon from its holster and taking the safety off.

'I wouldn't be so sure...' she said smiling, looking down at the streets far below. Seamus inched towards her, aiming his gun high on her chest. Aiming for her heart. 'How is your darling girl?' she asked, turning to face him head on. The words burned inside of him, scolding his heart and bringing his blood to the boil.

'Shut your fucking mouth!' he said, teeth gritted, finger on the trigger. 'You don't talk about her!'

'Seamus!' sounded Sam. He had finally caught up and stood at the hallway's periphery, his firearm at the ready. 'We should take her in,' he said with trepidation, as if he didn't trust Seamus to do the right thing.

'It's okay, Sam. I got this,' Seamus replied, looking back at his colleague for a second. But a second was all it took. Quicker than a heartbeat, Serena moved to Seamus, grasped his gun wielding hand and his throat and pinned him against the wall. Panicking, Sam shouted for her to freeze before firing his weapon, the bullet missing her by a fraction of an inch. Serena, holding Seamus by the neck, forced him to turn his head towards Sam; the young cadet stood quivering in the hallway, arms raised, gun pointing at her. He was so afraid. She pressed her lips against Seamus' ear.

'Look, and you shall see,' she said softly. Behind Sam, Seamus noticed something weird on the wall that ran along the hallway. It was distorted, moving, shimmering. Suddenly the dark-skinned man stepped out from inside the wall. He was bare chested, wearing nothing but a pair of torn denim shorts and a necklace with red stones. He made no sound, smoothly running one of his hands down his opposite arm. As he did, a sharp point appeared from his wrist and extended into a long shaft. As the tail end of the spear left his skin, he spun the pole, grabbed it with both hands and then thrusted it forward, spearing Sam through his back. The head of the weapon protruded from the kid's chest. Sam dropped his gun and looked down at the silvery tip, his blood dripping from its point. Looking at Seamus with a vacant expression, he was unable to speak, his eyes welling up with tears and a distinct look of terror on his face.

Seamus tried to wrestle away but he could hardly breathe or move, such was her grip. Inside he was screaming. SAM! He writhed in agony but was unable to express his thoughts and emotions. The spear-wielding man swiftly withdrew his weapon, with it vanishing back into his skin and Sam slumping to the floor.

Serena lightened her grasp on Seamus' throat allowing him to let out a cacophonous cry. He could feel the pain and anguish building up inside, helpless to help his friend. Marching towards Seamus with intent, the man was ordered to halt.

'Nahki, stop!' she commanded, using her thumb to turn Seamus' head towards her. She looked into his hate-filled eyes and smiled. 'Not this one,' she said. She continued to stare as Seamus tried everything he could to move. 'Adam,' she stated simply, drawing Seamus' attention and halting his struggle for a moment. 'Oh my,' she tutted and smiled, a glint of intrigue in her eyes. Releasing her hold on him, Seamus dropped to the floor, letting go of his gun. Serena and Nahki simultaneously moved towards the window and threw themselves out of it, plummeting down to the pavement below.

Gasping for air, Seamus crawled on his hand and knees down the hallway toward Sam. He felt as if his head was about to explode as the tears welled up within his eyes and the pressure built up within. Reaching the body, he rolled Sam over and dragged him up onto his thigh. He grasped at the young mans blood-soaked shirt, biting his teeth together, trying to hold back the sea of despair. Sam's lips trembled as the spark in his eyes began to fade. He wanted to speak but there wasn't enough time. The second hand of life had stopped ticking.

'AH!' Seamus screamed until his breath ran out and he cried as if his heart was tearing within his chest. 'No!' he exclaimed, gripping Sam tighter. He pressed his face against the top of Sam's head to try and muffle his wail. As his strength lessened, he loosened his grip on his partner, and he sat diminished, staring at his bloodied hands.

'Seamus? What the fuck are you doing here?' he didn't recognise the voice to begin with; he was mentally absent. 'I have an officer down!' she spoke on her radio, relaying their location. 'Seamus! What are you doing here?!' she asked again, with Seamus finally coming around and acknowledging who it was.

'Krysta?' he said, still in shock.

'She's gone, Sol,' she said over her comms. 'The package has gone, too.'

Seamus sat in the interview room, staring despairingly into space. No one came to see him for some time, leaving him wrought with guilt. The emptiness inside swelling up and tearing at him from the inside out. Finally, the door opened, and Krysta walked in with another agent. He was tall and balding, with a neatly groomed goatee.

'Seamus, this is Special Agent Solomon Grey,' Krysta introduced the man. 'We realise that you might not feel ready to talk but we need to ask a few questions.' Seamus was starting to get a grip on reality again. The hole inside him that was brimming with remorse was now beginning to fill up with a mixture of emotions, some of which he didn't quite understand.

'Sam,' Seamus choked, the name almost sticking in his throat. 'Cadet Samuel Lorenzo, where is he?' he asked, he wanted to know if his friend was being cared for properly.

'He's...' Krysta paused for a moment, seeming to choose her words carefully. 'They're going to take care of him Seamus. Seamus? What happened to Samuel?' Seamus struggled to convey his story, breaking down on every other sentence as he remembered the day's events.

'Seamus, there was a package. Do you know where it is?' Solomon prodded, almost unsympathetically.

'Sam said we should have gone back to the station,'

Seamus said, staring at his hands again.

'The package Officer McCarthy?' Solomon asked again.

'Fuck the package!' Seamus shouted, slamming his hands down on the table and rising to his feet. Suddenly, he felt hot, anger flooding his veins, enraging an inferno inside. 'Sam died! That bitch and some fucker called Nahki!' he stood up and punched the desk; then he kicked his chair away. The fury craved revenge.

'Seamus!' Krysta called to him assertively as he became more and more agitated. 'They stole the casing for a bomb!' she sounded as if she was pleading with him. Her fear grasped his attention amongst the din of his internal ire. 'The victim whose murder you were investigating with the 108th, he worked at a homeland storage facility. They have the casing for a tactical biological warhead.' Her words, or at least their honesty, struck home with Seamus, dousing the flames of hatred that had consumed him.

'There was a guy in the park, in the playground. Serena handed him a case,' Seamus revealed dejectedly. His city, his family, it was all under threat and he didn't understand why. His mind raced with questions. *Why did she mention Adam? Is he behind this? Why didn't I just follow orders? What is their obsession with me?* But one question repeated louder and louder within his mind:

What have I done?!

16

Adam

He caught a glimpse of his reflection in the wing mirror as he leaned into the back of the truck to grab another bag. He didn't quite recognise the bearded face that stared back at him, but he could never mistake those eyes, his eyes. The face he had chosen to wear was familiar in feeling, more of a muscle memory; it was the one that they recognised but it was not truly him that they had ever seen. His beard was unshorn, the colour matching his russet hair. His skin was tired, worn by the weight he carried inside. The dark blue plaid shirt he wore had holes in the right sleeve and two buttons were absent from the front, leaving a grey t-shirt beneath exposed. He paused for a moment and searched the fathomless blue eyes before him, locating a remnant of emerald-green within their depths.

'Joel?' a voice sounded. 'Are you coming?' she asked. He shook his head as if to release himself from a daydream and grabbed the bags of groceries. He smiled and nodded in reply as he carried them to the entrance of the house where she waited. She wore a mustard-yellow jumper, keeping the chill off. Her hair was a brown-blonde with odd strands of grey the only thing to insinuate her age; it was tied back, out of the way, widening her kind face. 'If you can just take them through to the kitchen that would be great,' she said, stepping past him onto the porch. 'I'll just grab my bag from the car, and I'll be right behind you.' Adam took the bags into the house, passing the sideboard covered in mail, and the reems of picture frames that hung on the walls. The staircase ran down to the vestibule, its wooden banister serving as a coat rack of sorts. Straight ahead, down the corridor, was the kitchen. Sunlight from numerous windows reflected off the laminate flooring. In the centre of the room sat an island where the rest of the shopping already sat, waiting to be unpacked. 'Thank you, Joel,' she said, entering the room and touching him on the shoulder. 'It's funny how a simple thing can be so difficult in times of...' she paused and took a deep breath. 'Well, you know,' she said before mustering a quarter smile.

'I know,' Adam reassured her. He placed his hand on her shoulder to help tame her emotions. She seemed grateful for the reprieve.

'John's always working these days. He tries to convince me that he's not doing it simply to distract himself, but I know better,' she admitted, beginning to unpack some of the food. 'Where would I be without you Joel?' she smiled as she said it.

'It's my pleasure, Mrs Holmes,' Adam nodded, assisting with the un-bagging. The Holmes family lived in a small village about two hours' drive west of Manhattan. Well respected in the community, John and Margaret had always worked hard to provide for their daughters.

'How many times do I have to tell you to call me Maggie?' she said hoping to break the sense of formality that Adam often created between them.

'Always at least one more, Mrs Holmes,' he said, smiling as he continued to help placing items into cupboards and passing the fresh food to Maggie to put into the refrigerator. Her husband, John, worked as an accountant and would often travel for work, leaving Maggie to tend to the needs of the house and look after the store that they owned in the heart of the village. Adam met her for the first time shortly after leaving the custody of the F.B.I and had made a few return trips since, helping where he could with her daily chores and routines.

'Are you thinking of staying long this time, or just passing through as usual?' Maggie queried, seemingly enjoying his company and grateful for the help. Adam simply shrugged in response; he couldn't stay but the conversation would often become awkward once she started quizzing him about where he's going or what he does for a living. 'One of these times hopefully you'll be able to meet our girls,' she said optimistically; her smile laden with a sense of hope but her eyes held some doubt that she'd rather not admit. He could tell that the subject was hard for her but needed to talk about it and she had grown to trust him.

'How are they?' he asked, whilst remaining assiduously attentive to her emotional state. She had so much love for the girls, it was apparent in her words and expressions as she spoke of them. She picked up a picture of the family from off the side as she spoke, a slight tremble crept into the tone of her voice. Adam placed his hand on hers and relieved her of her doubts and fears, providing some peace, at least for the moment. 'I had better be getting on Mrs Holmes...' he said, taking the picture from her and returning it to its resting place. 'I have an old friend to visit before I head back towards home.' He looked at the photo for a moment before saying goodbye. The family were dressed up ready to go out or attend something nice, it appeared. Forever captured in the moment, John stood proudly with Maggie. He wore a tuxedo and Maggie was dressed in a pearly white two-piece. Their eldest, Clara, had bobbed blonde hair and was dressed in a soft pink off-the-shoulder evening dress. The younger daughter, Lorelei, stood with a huge smile on her face, one that Maggie said could light up even the darkest of rooms. Her blonde-brown locks fell gracefully down one side of her open, joyful face and nested on her shoulder. She wore a colourful dress, one that accentuated her personality. A yellow, western-styled one-piece dress, patterned with blue flowers.

Adam left the Holmes' residence and headed towards the village's exit. He was angry inside, his guilt pained him. *You never care for the damage you cause.* He berated himself as he marched along the road. He felt restless and needed a release. It was necessary for him to be in the city by nightfall and he knew he wouldn't make it in time by walking. He kicked off his boots and ran, letting his legs take him onwards. His beard began to fall away and drift off into the breeze. His hair changed colour and the green returned to his eyes. Grasping at his shirt as he bounded across asphalt and then dirt, he tore it away and left it lying on the ground in his wake, revealing a torso of scars; his skin marked with memories of past lives. As he gained speed, he found himself bounding forwards and soon he planted his fists down onto the ground, the stones trembling beneath his touch. Using his hands and feet he continued at pace across grassland and roads alike. He felt a glow within as he gave into his inner wildness, the animal within forcing its way beyond the confines of its human boundaries. His jaw widened and his teeth sharpened. Canines protruded from bone and the flesh of his face began to peel away, revealing a layer of tawny coloured fur. A soft, buff coloured coat developed down his neck and along his torso as his rib cage shifted and narrowed. Tufty ears erected from a now rounded head and a long slender tail outstretched from his rear, ending with a black tip. Fists transformed into large front feet with retractable claws and his feet became the same only smaller. As the change reached its conclusion and he opened his large green-beryl wide-set eyes, he slid to a halt. He purred in his new form and then announced his return to nature with a thunderous growl, before setting off again towards his destination.

Quickly and stealthily he moved into the city as the sun

set. He managed mostly to move unseen, startling only a few witnesses to his magnificence as he went. He pushed onward until the large stone place of worship stood before him; supported by its eight granite columns, the impressive structure humbled even he who had seen so much. The service had finished and there would be few people inside, so Adam sauntered into the cathedral via the western entrance. There were several gasps and a single scream as he waltzed into the building, waiving his tail behind him. He halted in the centre of an aisle and sat down, stretching out under the west-end of the naïve, scratching at the hard floor.

'It's okay everyone!' a voice called from ahead of Adam's position. 'He's friendly,' the man repeated as he walked towards Adam, attempting to reassure the people hurriedly moving away towards the exits. His excellency, Bishop Timothy McCauley was the dean of the Cathedral of St. John the Divine and was a friend to Adam. 'You know, it's not often folk around here see an oversized... cougar, is it? Just walk into their church after mass.' He seemed torn between his emotions; Adam's entrance had caused some disruption, but Adam knew his old companion would be pleased to see him. Timothy perched himself on a nearby seat and scratched at the little hair he had left on his head. He was of average height and build, with almond coloured skin and a warm round and inviting face. He was wearing a black choir cassock with a deep red stole hanging down either side of his neck. 'You do realise how hard I work to encourage people to come in here, right?' he teased, frowning as Adam playfully rolled onto his back and opened his huge mouth, bearing his enormous sharpened teeth. 'Oh, it's like that is it?' he said, standing and letting out a small sigh. 'Well, you should know that we don't allow animals inside so,' he waved towards the doors and began to walk away, leaving Adam to his own devices. Adam rolled back over and stood on all fours. He let out an almighty growl and then began to change back into his human form. 'Adam!' Timothy turned to look at him in disappointment. 'Any louder and the windows will smash!' he said almost half-jokily. 'Ten thousand pieces of glass in that one,' he pointed up to a large rose-shaped stained-glass window above the doors before chuckling to himself and continuing to walk away. 'You'll be needing some clothes. Hurry it up – you might not have four legs now but I know you're not slow.'

Once his transformation had completed, Adam hurried after the bishop. He decided to be in his true skin, he had nothing to hide from his friend.

'You know, they think me strange keeping spare clothes stashed behind here,' Timothy said, reaching behind the alter that stood prominently in front of several statues of known saints. 'I always justify myself in saying that you never know who might walk in through our doors, and what they might need.' He laughed as he spoke. Adam took the grey hooded jumper and matching coloured pants and got dressed.

'Thank you,' Adam said, grateful of his companion's aid.

'Yes, well. A massive cat is one thing, but you, in all your... glory... not sure we want anyone walking in to see that,' Timothy quipped. 'You'll confuse the sisters! What brings you here this time Adam?' Adam sensed some concern and contorted his face in an air of confusion. 'Oh come on now, you rarely visit baring good news. So? Come on, what is it?' he sat down on the shallow stone steps leading up to the alter.

'The city is not safe right now, my friend,' Adam admitted, taking a seat next to Timothy.

'When is it ever?' his wise friend quickly stated.

'I'm serious,' Adam said turning to look at the aged man beside him. 'It's going to get worse, a lot worse. I can't protect everyone.' Adam looked solemnly to the marble steps on which he was perched; saying the words aloud always made them more real and didn't always lighten the burden.

'That's where the Lord comes in. You can do incredible things Adam, and you have a good heart. But you're still human, just like the rest of us.' The bishop tried to reassure him by placing his hand on Adam's shoulder. Adam smiled at the sentiment. Where Adam calmed souls with his touch, sadly the old man's attempt had little effect, but Adam appreciated the thought.

'I've recently spoken to an Imam and a Rabbi who said similar things,' Adam admitted. He had travelled a lot recently, searching for advice in many places.

'An Imam, a Rabbi and a Bishop...' Timothy pondered for a moment. 'My, my - you've been busy.'

'Imagine if you all walked into a bar...' Adam stopped; his face expressionless.

'HA!' Timothy hooted. 'Was that a joke?!' he slapped a hand across his thigh in disbelief. 'I never thought I'd see the day *you* made a joke,' he chuckled to himself. 'You've been in the company of us mere mortals too long!' he said flippantly.

'I think I have found someone who I can talk to. I mean, besides you,' Adam changed the subject. His time in the F.B.I custody had helped him connect with Krysta; she made him feel more at ease, more human.

'Well, whoever they, are I hope they can help you realise that you're not alone in this fight, that you don't have to worry about us all. And hopefully they'll help pull that stick out your ass.' Timothy stopped to see Adam's reaction. Adam simply looked at him, questioning his meaning. 'You know what I mean... don't look at me with that gormless look on your face...' He raised an eyebrow and gave Adam a look that put an end to the conversation.

'I feel more like a mortal human these days Tim,' Adam confessed. The Bishop's curiosity piqued. 'I feel everything, from everyone. I feel love. I feel others joys, their pain, their fear... but I too feel. I feel fear too.' Timothy smiled for a moment, likely thinking that Adam was joking once again;

but as the realisation that he was not came to him, he looked to Adam for a reason.

'What do you fear Adam?' he asked. Adam sat for a moment in silence before looking to his friend.

'I fear that this is it,' he answered, his reply too cryptic for the older man to understand. 'I fear that this is heaven, that this is our paradise, and we're abusing it.'

The two of them sat quietly for a while, reflecting on Adam's words as well as enjoying each other's company. As they sat, one of the large bronze doors on the western side opened and closed. A man stepped into the building; he wore a blue denim jacket over a black hooded jumper and a pair of hole-riddled jeans.

'Duty calls,' Timothy said. Using Adam to support himself, he lifted himself off the flooring and got to his feet. 'Hello there,' he said, walking towards the visitor. Adam watched as his friend walked open armed to invite the stranger into his life. *There is a light within humanity, a compassion within each of them. If only they could all find it within them.*

'How can we help you?' Timothy said as he stood face to face with the man. The hooded visitor did not reply at first, he was looking around the huge room, perhaps in awe of its wonders.

'You know, I've never been in here before,' the man avoided the bishop's question, staring up at the ceiling before looking toward the bishop. 'All my life I lived round here, but not once been in,' he smiled.

'Newcomers are always welcome,' replied Timothy softly, putting his hands together.

'That's nice,' the man said, clearly lacking interest. 'I'll be sure to pass on the invite. Now, father, I've been sent to collect this month's... donation,' he said earnestly, his words seemingly unnerving Timothy.

'It's not yet the end of the month,' Timothy said. His tone was full of fear; it seized Adam's attention.

'Markovic said it's due, so it's due,' the man said, cocksure, in reply. Not once did he blink or break his gaze on the old bishop. Adam rose from his seat and began to walk slowly towards his friend. His movement appeared to displease the would-be debt collector and he became agitated. 'I suggest you just hand over the money and there won't be any trouble,' the man said knavishly.

Adam halted in position behind Timothy. He remained calm on the surface, but he was a rage with emotion inside. The shear sound of Markovic's name angered him and the idea of him taking money from a place of peace and worship only made it worse.

'Adam, it's okay, really. Just a misunderstanding of dates I believe,' Timothy said cheerily, holding his hand out to dissuade Adam from coming any closer.

'There's no misunderstanding,' the stranger said, reaching into his pocket and revealing a pistol. He held the gun sturdily and pulled back the hammer. 'You pay up... or you pay,' he said raising the weapon toward the bishop.

'Timothy...' Adam said, gritting his teeth as the fury burned inside. He stared at the gunman, his green eyes aglow. Adam knew that he could not simply disarm him, only in self-defence could he act. To interfere would be breaking the rules and would allow his brothers and sisters to do the same, which could cause catastrophe. The fact that he had all the power but needed restraint often tortured him.

'Adam, it's okay, I will sort this matter out,' Timothy said, noticing that Adam's fists were clenched and that he was shaking ever so slightly.

'McCauley is it? I don't like being kept waiting. I was told you was tough and that I'd probably have to use a bit of force,' the visitor admitted, his finger primed on the trigger of the gun. 'I don't like how your friend here is looking at me,' he said, diverting his aim towards Adam now.

'Please, I'm sure we can come to some sort of

arrangement,' Timothy pleaded. Adam could see it in the man's eyes, hear it in his heartbeat; his mind was already made up.

'You already have an arrangement priest!' the intruder yelled as he pulled the trigger. Adam could hear every action as the weapon operated. The pull of the trigger released the firing pin which struck the primer, igniting the gunpowder. Time stood still as Adam sensed the pressure build within the pistol and force the bullet down the barrel and out of the muzzle. He contemplated dodging the projectile as it hurtled towards him, but the hatred inside grounded him to the spot until the tip of the bullet tore through his top and pierced the skin of his shoulder. In that moment he knew that the choice had opened up to him. He could act out of defence, to teach this man a lesson, or he could yield. He almost made the decision that his friend would have suggested, however, the gunman showed no sign of hesitation as he began to turn his aim towards Timothy.

'Adam, no!' screamed the bishop as Adam instinctively pushed him out of the way and grasped the shooter by the throat. He lifted him up off the floor as if he were weightless and carried him over to one of the pillars, slamming him against the stone foundation.

'You take pleasure instilling fear, preying on the weak!' Adam said, teeth bared like an animal. His heart pounded ferociously as his temper flared. 'Do you want to know real fear?' he exclaimed. 'Let me show you just how deep the depths of despair are.' His eyes pained with an intense burning as he used his ability, the power he held that would usually instil peace and tranquillity, he now used as a weapon of fear and hatred.

'Adam! Stop!' Timothy yelled, grabbing onto Adam's raised arm that pinned the hapless human against the granite. Glaring angrily at his friends face, Adam saw the terror in his eyes as the bishop struggled to stop him. The look of trepidation he saw was enough to bring him to his senses, but unfortunately the damage had already been done.

Releasing the stranger from his grasp, the man slid down the pillar and onto the floor. His body trembled as he lay there, hands, feet, head, all shaking uncontrollably as if he were experiencing a fit. The emotion that had flooded his body and mind was too much for him and soon his body stopped shaking and he remained deathly still.

'Adam, quickly, help him,' Timothy said, dropping to his knees besides the body. He looked up at Adam and saw his hesitation. 'I know what he did was wrong, but we do not get to decide who lives and who dies,' his friend pleaded with him. Adam was a mess with emotion, a moment ago he would have happily killed him, but now he must save him. Adam dropped to his knees and placed his palm on the gunman's head. Closing his eyes, he tried to shut out the world; he had healed others before, he could do it again. Adam placed his other hand on the man's chest and tried again, but nothing happened. 'Adam? What's wrong?' the bishop asked worriedly.

'I... I don't know...' Adam replied, lifting his hands off the man. He had not healed anyone since his rebirth, perhaps the ability had not yet returned to him. Like his memories, not everything recovered the same each time he resurrected.

'I'll get him to the hospital,' Timothy said, attempting to lift the body up off the floor, but it was too heavy for him. 'I'll call an ambulance,' he said in defeat. 'Adam you had better go before anyone comes,' his friend advised earnestly. Adam was unsure what to do. The man was a criminal, but he did not deserve what Adam had done to him. 'Adam, get out of here,' Timothy almost sounded angry as he said the words. He was more likely disappointed, but Adam wasn't sure which would be worse.

'I'm sorry,' Adam said, shaking from the core with guilt.

'I know you are,' the old man said calmly. 'but you must go.'

Tearing through the bronze door of the cathedral, Adam ran down onto the sidewalk. He was disorientated, unable to stop seeing the fear in his friend's eyes before him. He looked up and down the street, not sure which direction to head in.

'AH!' he screamed as he slammed his fists down onto the concrete, smashing the slab beneath him.

'Hey, you! You okay?!' shouted two police officers that saw Adam's outburst from across the street. They began to cross towards him. *They won't understand.* Adam wondered if he should ask for their help, but decided against it. He was scared. Was it his feeling, this fear? Or did the fear of his friend still linger on his skin, within his heart? He stood here in his true form, riddled with scars, a blood-stained top with a wound that was nearly healed, and his eyes continued to emit their green glow. He looked to the officers as they carefully crossed the street. One was thin and carried a rugged appearance, the other was shorter and had a warmer expression on his face. But Adam couldn't trust them; he needed to run. *Run now. RUN!* His feet obeyed. Turning, he ran off down the street, but his sudden decision to flee clearly alerted the officers as they decided to pursue him.

'Hey! Stop!' they shouted, but Adam could not heed their request. Instead, he bounded onward, faster and faster until they were nowhere to be seen. He continued to run, down one street and then the next. The city was aglow with streetlights and people moving from here to there. Several times, Adam had to halt in his tracks so as to not crash into anyone, as doing so would surely cause more harm. He stood beneath the tallest building, looking up at its enormity, pondering whether he'd be better off up there, out of the way. The summit of this man-made edifice scratched the heavens. *To know such peace.* Adam stared upward. His attention was then caught by the flashing of a red and blue set of lights. Their colour illuminated the walls of the buildings around him. Adam could hear the officer within the car from which the lights originated. The two officers he had fled from had called in his disturbance. The body of the man had also been discovered. They had no doubt marked Adam as a suspect and his description was being relayed for all to search for. *I'm so close.* He decided to continue to flee from the law enforcers. Before the officer was completely out of his vehicle, Adam charged towards the car. He bounded up to it and, placing one foot onto its bonnet, he leapt into the nights air.

Hurtling through the air over the street below, he hit a building on the opposite side with force, pushing his grip into the structure, grabbing hold. He then proceeded to climb, each time throwing himself upward and smashing his hands into the wall to force a new grip until he reached the top. The skin on his hands and feet had been torn to shreds by the impacts but they quickly healed, leaving stains of dried blood over perfectly formed new skin. Leaving the sounds of a siren below, he moved onward, leaping from rooftop to rooftop until finally, he had reached his destination.

Timothy was right, having someone to talk to, to connect with, was important, but Adam knew he would have to be careful. Anyone he got close to would instantly be in danger from those who didn't understand, those who were susceptible to greed, fear or hatred. She would need protecting from everything that would do her harm. Lowering himself down the fire escape, he stopped at her window, which was ajar. *She needs me as much as I need her.* He opened the window fully and climbed into her apartment; she had no doubt left it open for the cat that he often assumed the form of. Adam pulled the window down, returning it to how she had left it, and as he did so, he could hear a key within the lock of the door behind him. She was home.

17

Krysta Rose-Anderson

God, I hate paperwork. She was sat at her desk. She had been holding her fingers above the keys of the keyboard for a full ten minutes now, primed to type but unsure what to write. For over a month they had frantically worked, searching for information on where Markovic was held up, where and when this potential bomb threat was going to happen, and of course, they had still made no further progress in their search for Mike. Krysta couldn't help but fear something huge was about to happen, and it wasn't going to be good. Nothing felt right recently; Lucy had almost given up hope on finding Mike alive. He had been kidnapped, yet no ransom had been asked for, nobody had turned up on the shores of the river. Nothing happening had been worse than something happening. Kyle had spent so much time with the team since the threat of a biological weapon came to light that Krysta was ready to request for a transfer. She was also starting to feel ashamed of her recent use of Seamus. After cadet Lorenzo's death, if it wasn't for the F.B.I stepping in, Seamus would have been stripped of his badge. Instead, he had just served a month's suspension, during which Krysta had been ordered to use his clear obsession with the case to find out as much information as she could. He had lost the opportunity of a promotion and confessed that his home life was on the verge of imploding, yet Krysta had been ordered to utilise his connection to the Avunaye, Adam and Markovic as much as possible, no matter the cost. She could see that the more he got involved, the more unlike himself he became and for that she carried a weight on her heart and conscience.

Outside of work she had been happy, which probably also added to the guilt she felt with all that was going on.

'Argh!' she grumbled in frustration, gaining a few strange looks from her colleagues and startling Malique as he shuffled through the main office. 'Sorry, Malique, didn't mean to make you jump,' she smiled. She was feeling more restless than anything else and was struggling to sit still and work.

'No, not a problem,' he replied. He had a weary look about him, and he could barely bring himself to smile. Malique was never the chattiest of people, but Krysta could tell something was wrong.

'Everything okay, Malique?' she asked curiously. He paused for a moment. He wore a bright white shirt that was buttoned up to the top, no tie and a lab coat. He fidgeted with his short, curly black hair and his caramel skin wrinkled slightly with lines of worry.

'She's under a lot of stress,' he said nervously, almost as if someone else was listening.

'Who?' Krysta asked. Malique had always kept to himself socially. Right now he and Krysta were probably having the most extensive conversation they'd ever had, but she was intrigued as to why he was acting so anxiously and it was a welcome distraction from the pencil-work she had been attempting to do.

'Claire,' he admitted quietly, almost at a whisper. 'She just went nuts at me for labelling a piece of code incorrectly.' Krysta was taken back a little by his words, she'd gotten to know Claire pretty well, they were good friends, but she'd never seen her shout or get angry or frustrated before.

'*Our* Claire?' Krysta queried in disbelief. Malique quickly nodded in reply and then hurried off back towards the lab.

Deciding to investigate Malique's accusation of Claire's current mood, Krysta got up from her seat and started to head towards Claire's tech room. It had been cold and wet this morning, so she had worn a thin black rib-knitted jumper with lace sleeves and white ruffled cuffs over her white blouse, to keep the chill off. A pair of wide leg black pants and small heeled shoes completed her attire. As she headed to see her friend there was a tap on Solomon's office window, and her superior signalled for her to come in.

'Sol? What's up?' she asked, entering his office. Solomon stood, perched on the edge of his desk. He seemed relaxed, which was nice to see - if a little unusual. He had recently been more than a little stressed. Increased C.I.A involvement in the Markovic case had caused the deputy director to apply more pressure on Solomon to make progress. Christopher Travis' and David Michaels' deaths, along with Mike's continued absence had brought a shadow over Solomon's position; his capability was being questioned. The pressure would be enough to make anyone tense, but he stood with a pleasant expression.

'How's the report coming along?' he asked with a relaxed tone. Krysta doubted whether she should brandish the truth, but something about his relaxed nature put her at ease.

'Not great...' she admitted honestly. 'Struggling to sit and type if I'm honest,' she said openly. Solomon nodded in reply.

'Needs to be done though. I'll trust you'll get it finished?' he asked, to which Krysta, imitating her mentor, nodded back. 'How's Seamus McCarthy coping? You mentioned he was struggling in your last update. Is he going to keep it together?' Krysta knew it was important, but something suggested that this wasn't the reason for him calling her in.

'Yeah. He's - he's a soldier, you know?' Krysta said, answering his query. She knew Seamus wasn't handling everything too well right now, but Solomon didn't need all the details. He stood up straight and unbuttoned the cuffs of his beige coloured shirt and then proceeded to roll up the sleeves.

'What are your plans for thanksgiving? Not long now - what is it? A week or so?' Solomon asked. Krysta was stumped by the question, it felt so out of place. *Perhaps he's finally cracked under the pressure...* She smiled a bewildered smile at him.

'I know we have a lot going on, but I thought it'd be nice for you and the team to join Lu and I for dinner. The kids are spending it with their grandparents,' Solomon explained, no doubt reading into Krysta's expressions. The invitation was nice. She had contemplated spending it with Jake and Lucy; her friend especially could use the company over the holiday.

'I think it would be a great idea for us all to spend it together,' Krysta said, getting the feeling that was the response Solomon was hoping for. 'Besides, I haven't seen Lulu in ages, would be nice to catch up.' Krysta had always held Solomon as a father figure, so naturally, his wife Lulu was sort of a mother to her, one that she got on very well with.

'That's great,' Solomon smiled and rubbed his hands together. 'I'll invite the others one by one, maybe play the whole 'you're in trouble' card to shake them up a little. What you think?' he laughed. Krysta chuckled with him, again, thinking how nice it was to see him a little lighter-minded.

As she exited Solomon's office, Krysta still had hold of the door handle when she heard a voice. The sound pierced deep into her bones, like cutlery scratching at a china plate, and she clung to the handle, tempted to take refuge back inside the office. Failing to act quickly enough, her opportunity to escape was lost as he called out her name.

'Hey, Krys,' he called from across the main office area. *Maybe if I ignore him, he'll get sucked into a black hole.* She stood still, like a deer in the headlights of oncoming traffic, unable to prevent the impending situation she would find herself in.

'Krysta... Hey, I was hoping to catch you,' said an exasperatedly ebullient Kyle as he approached.

'And now you have. However, I'm just in the middle...' Krysta said, hoping to dissuade him from talking anymore; she wanted to see Claire. Kit, catching her mid-sentence, quickly interrupted.

'That's okay, Krys, it won't take long,' he said. As the words left his lips, the distance to Claire seemed to lengthen monumentally. She looked at him with a sarcastic smile and a glare that only she knew the true meaning of. He stood with his hands on his hips, his thumbs resting on his belt. He was wearing navy blue slim-fit suit pants with a pair of tassel-less mushroom grey coloured suede loafers. Atop his off-white shirt he had a matching blue waistcoat and his ensemble was completed with a dark-blue bow tie. His attire warranted a glance, which was most likely the reason he chose to parade the office dressed as such. However, the laughter that Krysta was holding back would no doubt not be the reaction he expected to receive. As he raised a hand and lightly touched his mousey-blonde hair, making sure it remained in place, his eyes indicated he had something to say.

'What do you want Kit?' Krysta gave in and conceded to his stare.

'Well, as you asked...' he said with a smirk. 'I was hoping to get your report on what you've found out from our friend Seamus McCarthy.' *It just had to be that.* Kyle was constantly trying to outshine Solomon of late, in any way he could; Krysta often thought that he was probably pushing for complete control over the case.

'It's almost ready,' Krysta clenched her teeth through the lie, hoping he'd move on.

'Try and make it a better read than your report on

Adam. That time you spent with him during the L.A. mission...' Kit placed his hand over his mouth to imitate a yawn as he slowly backed away and left Krysta to continue on her way to see Claire.

'Argh!' Krysta bawled, releasing some of her built up frustration as she entered Claire's techno-haven of an office. Her friend sat on a stool at her main terminal, squinting at the screens in front of her. 'You'd find those a lot easier to look at with your glasses on, honey,' Krysta said with a smile as she approached. Her colleague sat leant forward, leaning her chin on her palms with her elbows resting on her knees as she stared unblinking at the data on screen. 'Claire?' Krysta asked as she failed to receive any response from her previous comment. Suddenly realising someone else had entered her chamber of solace, Claire jumped as she snapped out of her trance-like state. She then smiled gleefully as she saw that it was Krysta by her side.

'Oh god, Krys! You made me jump!' she giggled loudly whilst brushing her hair back behind her ear. She wore her hair down, which was slightly kinked and greasy due to a lack of attention. The bulk of it flowed down, draped over her right shoulder. She was wearing the same black blouse as the day before, as well as the same stone-grey tartan mini skirt. Her shoes however, seemed to be missing as she sprang out of her seat, bare footed.

'Uh, hon?' Krysta said with an air of hesitation. She was worried for Claire but tried to not let her concern show too much. 'Aren't they...?' she pointed at Claire's creased clothing.

'I know, I know,' Claire replied with a childish giggle. 'I pulled another all-nighter, but...' Before Claire could complete her sentence, Krysta interrupted.

'Hon, you know you don't cope well without sleep,' she stated. Since Mike's kidnapping, Claire had worked through the night on several occasions and the team had come to notice that a sleep deprived Claire was, to be polite, less effective than a well-rested one.

'I know, I know - but wait!' she said, scurrying off to another screen and typing something on the keypad. 'Ah! Where'd it go...' she said, moving to a third terminal. 'Slippery little sucker this one,' she chortled at her own words as she continued to look for something.

'Claire seriously. Are you okay?' Krysta asked, starting to become more and more concerned. 'Malique said you went nuts at him, he's pretty shaken up to be honest...' She was hoping to reign her friend back down to her plane.

'Malique?' Claire questioned, looking up from her screen. 'I haven't seen Malique since... yesterday morning I think...' she scratched at her head as she pondered.

"He said you lost your temper with him, this morning... " Krysta stated, bringing Claire's current state of mind into question.

'Nope, honestly, Krys. I haven't seen him, wasn't me,' Claire quickly shuffled over to Krysta and grabbed her hand. 'That's not important - this is, let me show you,' she said, pulling Krysta over to the screen she was working at before springing away to close the office door. Claire's mannerisms were seriously starting to unnerve Krysta. Her friend was always, had always, been quirky, but this was bordering on eccentric. 'I worked out the code,' she said smiling before pointing at the information in front of them both.

'What code?' Krysta queried, looking at the seemingly random formation of letters and numbers sprawled across the screen, not understanding their meaning.

'I trust you, that's why I'm showing you,' Claire rambled quickly. 'Our mystery friend, the encrypted messages, the texts...' She had a glint in her eye that told a story; she had finally succeeded. Krysta looked at her colleague, awaiting the answer. 'I had to write like two thousand lines of coding to break it down into a tri-hexagonal algorithm.' Claire was explaining, regardless of whether Krysta was able to understand.

'Claire?' she asked, hoping for a simpler explanation.

'It's my frickin' code,' Claire replied, with a look on her face that could only be construed as pride. 'Well not my code, but the one I wrote for the bureau after I joined.' Krysta didn't understand what Claire was trying to say.

'What... what are you saying?' she asked, still confused.

'The messages, they come from someone within the F.B.I, within these headquarters.' The look of pride faded as Claire could see the worry within Krysta's expression as she processed the information. A feeling of dread enveloped Krysta as she sat staring at the code on Claire's monitor, as if somehow, it now made sense to her. Scenario after scenario played through her mind. The team had their suspicions over who the messages had been coming from; they had always come at times of urgency, as warnings, or when they were struggling for a lead. One thing was more troubling than anything else, they had all been connected to the Avunaye. *If the messages are directly connected to the Avunaye, then maybe they've infiltrated the F.B.I? But why warn us?* Krysta sat unmoving for a while, almost catatonic.

'Krysta!' Claire clapped, hoping to get her attention. Claire called out her name three or four times before she managed to snap her out of the daze she was in. 'Krysta, we need to be careful. I told you because I trust you, I don't know who else I can trust.' She was scared, the information Claire had uncovered was huge - but it was also dangerous. Whoever the source was, they had gone to great lengths to hide themselves, to cover their tracks and could potentially become a threat if their cover was blown. 'Krys,' Claire said, her voice trembling. 'What do we do?' Her inexperience shone as she sat worriedly, hoping for Krysta to provide all the answers. However, Krysta wasn't sure herself. Her team, her family, one of them may not be who they seem. She felt... lost.

After agreeing with Claire that the information was best kept between themselves for now, Krysta was called into a meeting with Solomon, Kyle and Hale. Their pursuit of

Markovic was finally bearing fruit. Hale had led two operations over the last few days and now firm connections could be made regarding weapons racketeering, illegal substance manufacture and the trafficking of young girls. They had evidence linking Markovic, evidence that would hold up in court. Also, the girl from the converted medical facility, Lorelei Holmes, had finally started to make some progress and according to her doctors, could wake up any day now. With her testimony and any information that she could provide on Markovic's exploits and his dealings with the Avunaye, they just might be able to piece together what the end game was and where Mike might be. Paul stood quietly next to Krysta as Solomon and Kit took it in turns to run through the findings from each mission. Arms crossed, he was wearing khaki coloured combat pants and a dark green short sleeved t-shirt, his tattoos on show running from his biceps to his wrists. Clean shaven, his short dark brown hair was neatly styled; he had been one of the few during this time of chaos to never let his standards slip. He stood firm, listening intently even though he already knew the intel that was being recited by his superiors. Hale had been a rock, one that had not weathered in the slightest, and had provided much needed support for Lucy, Krysta and the others when they needed it. Every now and then, Krysta would look at him and he would remain focused, yet if she was lucky, he would smile at her with his deep blue eyes, reassuring her of his ongoing support.

'Anything we missed, Agent Hale?' Kyle asked. Kit stood with his hands on his hips, awaiting a response.

'No sir,' Hale confirmed quickly. Krysta's mind drifted for a moment and she couldn't help but think that Kyle lacked a mirror whilst getting dressed this morning, the thought making her smile. She looked around at the three people she stood with, the information Claire had given her at the forefront of her mind. To think that either Solomon or Paul could be anything other than what she knew them to be, pained her somewhat. She unfortunately would not be surprised if Kyle was mixed up in it, but she doubted that he'd have the ability or nerve to undertake such a task. She didn't want to question any of their motives or their allegiances. *Maybe Claire was wrong to tell me. Someone isn't who they appear to be, but who?*

She reached the door of her apartment with her hands full. Having stopped on the way home to grab some food, she would now have to put down the warm, sweet smelling containers of Szechuan barbecued beef, steamed vegetable dumplings and spring rolls that were currently giving the corridor such an edible aroma, so she could open the door. Taking out her keys, she unlocked the door and pushed it open before picking up her food and entering her humble abode, kicking the door shut behind her. Quickly placing the containers on the marble counter that separated her kitchen and lounging area, she took off her coat and kicked off her shoes, grabbed a fork from the draw and headed over to the coffee table where she proceeded to curl up on one of the sofas, ready to eat. Feeling a slight draft, she realised that the window was still partially open. She quickly got up again to close it and keep the warmth in; the nights were growing longer and they were now very cold. As she latched the window, the reflection of a man behind her caught her eye and, panicking, she span around to confront him, her heart almost bounding out of her chest. He stood in a dark grey hooded jumper and matching coloured pants; his feet were bare, and his hands hung by his sides, each appearing to be covered in blood. Hastily preparing to grab her firearm and defend herself against the intruder, she noticed his unmistakably emerald-green eyes, shining from within the darkness of his hood.

'Adam?' she asked, instinctively knowing it was him as she lowered her guard.

'I didn't mean to frighten you,' he replied softly whilst

lowering his hood to reveal his face. His hair stood short and tufty, a mixture of ash brown and spring honey colours scattered throughout. Several scars littered his brow, cheeks and chin; some flesh coloured, some pale blue and a couple with a hint of violet. His eyes were like deep gemstones, pools of endless green, but at present they held a worry that was clear to see. Looking down at his crimson stained hands, Krysta could not help but wonder what had happened. Again, she looked into his eyes, a calming glimmer of eternity rippled beneath their surface. He was beautiful. 'Krysta...' he said softly, before remorsefully looking at his hands and screwing them up. His voice was almost two toned, velvety, yet with a mysterious coarseness. 'I can explain...' Yet before he could say anything else, there was a knock at the door. Adam looked at Krysta, his expression one of a desperate sadness as she stepped around him and walked towards the door. Another knock on the door brought a haste to her step. *What do I do?* She grabbed the door handle and opened it to find two police officers stood outside. Holding their peaked hats down by their sides, they each had on a thick overcoat to keep off the chill of the evening air. One was shorter than the other; he had his coat open to show his uniform underneath, the edge of his badge catching the light of the hallway lamps. The taller of the two had a slim build and a dubious look about him, his weasel-like face felt familiar to her, but she couldn't put her finger on where she knew him from. The shorter officer had mousey brown hair and a much kinder face, however, he looked tired, emphasised by the darkened skin beneath his eyes.

'Good evenin', miss,' the tall officer said, looking her up and down before exhibiting a perverted smile. The other officer merely lifted his hat up slightly and made a small nod to acknowledge her.

'Evening officers. Can I help you?' Krysta asked. She was trying to disguise her nerves, knowing that Adam was standing within the apartment.

'There's been a death this evening miss, up at St. John's Cathedral. We're asking everyone in the area to remain vigilant and report anyone acting suspiciously,' the officer said, running his hand through his slicked-back jet-black hair. Krysta knew of the Cathedral but knew it to be a way up town.

'It's a bit far to come all the way down here, the Cathedral is up town?' she questioned. *Surely their search area isn't that big.*

'There's a suspect miss, fled the area earlier this evening and has been sighted nearby,' said the shorter officer.

'That's why we're looking down here and not up town...' the shifty looking officer said sarcastically; Krysta did not appreciate his tone. 'Please let us know if you see or hear anything,' he quickly added, trying to add some professionalism to his arrogance.

'I...' Krysta paused for a moment as she looked back towards Adam and contemplated whether she needed the two officers' help. Adam may well be the suspect they're after; would she be safe letting them go? Her hesitation seemed to begin to arouse some suspicion from the brown-haired officer. 'I'll be sure to call should I see anything,' she said before smiling courteously and began to close the door.

'Hey, aren't you...' the smaller of the officers said, just as he and his partner began to turn away. 'You're that F.B.I agent, aren't you?' As he said it, Krysta remembered where she had seen them both before. The taller officer expressed an awkward posture, clearly remembering what an asshole he had been the last they met. Krysta did not answer his question, she simply smiled again in response and continued to close the door. However, the smaller officer quickly stepped forward, placing his foot in the doors path to prevent her from doing so. 'How's that investigation going? All those dead bodies, that was one messed up place...' he said, placing his hand on the door. 'You catch that monster yet? What'd they call him... the beast? That was it...'

'Investigation is still ongoing,' Krysta said, her tone questioning his action. 'I can't really discuss it.' She hoped that would end the conversation and the officers would leave, but she could feel the resistance against the door. Questioning herself as to whether she should just ask them to leave, Adam moved beside her, hidden from the officer's view by the door. He placed his hand on the wood, slightly overlapping her own and out of the corner of her eye, Krysta could see his eyes shine brighter. The officer gave in and gestured a form of goodbye or goodnight, and he and his partner then turned and moved on, allowing Krysta to finally close the door.

She leaned back against the closed door and after sighing with relief she looked at Adam. So many questions burst into the forefront of her mind, with one racing to the edge of her lips.

'How? How did you...?' she stumbled at asking the question, awash with emotion, she was partially mesmerised by him. Part of her screamed with fear of the unknown, worried about what he was capable of, but she was also intrigued by his capabilities. 'Your eyes... and then... how?' Adam took a step backwards away from her, his action drawing some concern and she stood up straight, off from the door. 'I'm sorry, I didn't mean to...' before she could say anymore, he raised a hand.

'It's me who should say sorry, I brought this to your home.' He looked at his stained hands once again.

'What happened? Was it at the cathedral?' Krysta asked cautiously, her curiosity peeking.

'A man came. He threatened a friend of mine...' Adam paused, he seemed to find the words hard to say. His eyes brimming with remorse.

'Your friend, did he...?' Krysta needed to know. 'I mean - the blood... on your hands,' she pointed to them.

'My own,' he replied, his answer calming the pounding

within her chest a little. 'I lost control,' Adam confessed. As he admitted it, he closed his eyes and took a deep breath as if the confession brought him some relief.

'Lost control?' Krysta wanted to know everything. She felt a certain level of trust towards him, but she wanted to know exactly what she was dealing with.

'It's hard to describe, let me...' Adam reached out a hand towards Krysta and she flinched slightly. He presented his palm, open and waiting, waiting for her to take it, yet she hesitated. *What's going to happen?* She contemplated taking hold of his hand. She started to move forwards. As her fingertips reached his hand, she winced in anticipation; mere millimetres away from contact, she could feel something: a gravity, a connection. As her skin touched his, a pulse surged up through her fingers, her hand, her arm. It raced within her until it reached her heart and like a dull, unsharpened blade, it tore through. Her legs felt as if they were crumbling beneath her, tears flooded her eyes and an unstoppable grief possessed her completely. She pulled away and reached out for the counter to help prevent her from falling; the connection was severed but she still felt the overwhelming ache that accompanied the feeling of remorse. She wasn't going to make it. As her legs gave way and she headed for the floor, suddenly Adam was there to catch her. He speedily picked her up, one arm supporting her head and the other her legs. In a blink of an eye he was putting her down on the sofa. Still dazed by what she had felt, the only words Krysta could muster were: 'Thank you.' to which Adam replied again, with an apology.

It took a few minutes before the world came spinning back into focus and Krysta felt like herself once more. 'You... you can control emotion,' she said calmly, looking up at him as he stood looking worriedly down at her. 'I'm okay,' she said, hoping to offer him some relief. 'It's wearing off, I think.'

'I didn't mean...' Adam struggled to get his words out again. She could tell that he was holding back on what he truly wanted to say. She could feel it, as if she was still feeling as he did.

'It's okay, you can tell me,' Krysta said softly. She had felt his pain and his remorse, and now understood that what happened was an accident.

'It wasn't meant to be that strong... you have a very open heart Krysta,' he smiled as he spoke and she couldn't help but see the beauty in his expression, which almost floored her yet again. 'I can feel what you feel, or I can let you experience what I feel...' He was looking at her, searching her eyes for something. He could control others emotions, she knew it, maybe admitting it worried him. 'The man at the cathedral... he preyed on people, inflicting fear. I lost my temper, lost control. I made him feel the fear that he so easily forced on others. But, I couldn't...' He gritted his teeth and looked away from her as if disgusted with himself.

'It's okay,' Krysta said softly. She could see he was in pain, the connection between them dimming to a mere flicker. She reached out without thinking and grabbed his hand to soothe him. As their skins met, he turned to look at her. A feeling of calmness rushed through her veins and she could feel his pain lessening but there was something else, buried, a confusion. He involuntarily opened a door within himself and she could feel him trying to pull away. For a split second she felt as if she was in a long tunnel; there was an immense, terrifying darkness behind her, and ahead, a closed door. She reached out and pushed the door open and stepped over its threshold. That was when it hit her. A need, a want, but also more than that. Blinding lights flashed past, voices cried out in pain, fear, agony; thousands, maybe millions of faces flashed before her. Then it stopped. She found herself back in the hallway with the darkness and this time standing in the doorway was a woman. It was her reflection. The feeling of love, a love more than love possessed her as she looked upon herself and she could hear the beating of his heart in time with her own, and then the darkness engulphed her as she fell in a swoon.

She must have been out cold for a little while before coming to. Brushing her hair out of her face, she saw Adam sat perched on the other sofa, watching her with a distinct look of concern.

'I should go,' he said as she sat up and straightened herself out, yet he did not move. His words seemed more of a question of whether he should go or not. Unsure of what she had just felt from the second blast of emotion, and still feeling a blaze of emotion that she couldn't be sure was her own, Krysta did not respond for a few moments. Instead, she quietly reflected on what had happened and tried to find her centre.

'Does that happen every time you touch someone?' she finally asked, ignoring his intent to leave. She wanted him to stay.

'You... You caught me a little off guard. I'm sorry, it won't happen again.' She was increasingly becoming lost within his eyes as she tried to think of what to say next.

'Why did you come here Adam?' she finally asked, surprising herself that she hadn't asked the question sooner.

'Company,' he answered, simply and honestly. Krysta was taken aback. She had assumed that he was here to warn her of something, or perhaps he had some information for her. Yet all he seemed to want, as he said, was someone to connect with.

The pair talked for some time, Krysta finally tucking into her now cold takeaway. She had now begun to ignore the emotion inside her, tucking it to one corner of her mind.

'What's it like?' she asked vaguely. Somehow, she felt as if he knew what she wanted to know.

'What?' he said, his eyes suggesting he was toying with her. 'Death? Immortality?' He exhibited an almost blank expression, one that Krysta wasn't sure of. 'Immortality is... lonely,' he said, and she realised that the look in his eyes was one of woe. They continued to talk about history, art, war and evolution. Krysta came to see that beneath his worry, he held such passion.

'What about the Avunaye?' Krysta asked, looking to gain some insight on his siblings. He confessed that his memories were still recovering; a lot of his more recent ones had returned, but much of his past was a blank page. What he did say about them, however, he said with an absence of hatred; they were like him, beneath their flaws. They were family.

'Markovic plans to use some kind of biological weapon any day now,' Krysta said, interrupting Adam as he spoke of his brother Brandt. She needed help, her team needed help, and she hoped that Adam may be able to provide some. She told him that the team had come across a purple-haired man in Los Angeles and of the blood work that was being carried out within the lab. Adam remained still, listening intently, perched on the sofa as she spoke.

'His name is Seymour. He'll no doubt be assisting with the weapon you spoke of,' Adam said. He seemed pained by his words, as if he felt a level of betrayal towards his sibling. 'You've lost your compassion as a species, they intend on forcing you to find it again, the only way they know how. Humans – mortal humans - need to learn to reach out with open hands instead of closed fists.' He stood up and walked around the sofa to the window; he was agitated.

'Is everything okay Adam?' she asked. He was shaking as he stood looking through the glass to the world outside.

'Stop the bomb,' he said, before opening the window. Krysta leapt up out of her seat and hurriedly walked around it to stand beside him. He turned to look at her, the pain returning to his eyes, like a shadow within their green purity that cast itself upon her soul. 'Close the window after I leave. It's going to get cold, especially with the snow.' Krysta looked out of the window questioning his comment. It had been clear skies all day and there was no snow forecast. As he climbed out onto the fire escape and then up onto the rail as if to leap off, Krysta juddered forward, her hand outstretched, worried that he would fall, unsure of what his next move would be. But just then, a single, unique white flake fell from the heavens and landed gracefully on her hand. He turned to look at her one last time as she stood half hanging out of the open window. His bright, moon-lit, green eyes changed to a deep yellow, and from his skin sprouted an array of large feathers. He tore through his clothes as he transformed and then, with outstretched wings, he took off, leaving Krysta staring out into the night sky.

18

Michael Ward

The sun's rays reflected off the red and yellow veneer of his teammates helmet. The flickering light danced before him, flashing like strobe lights on a disco ball. The summer warmth had made the game interminable, but this last throw could see them snatch victory from near defeat. He was on the offensive, the quarter-back, with the weighted expectations of those in the stands as well as those on the field poised on his shoulders. Beads of sweat ran down his cheek and dripped from his chin. His firing arm felt heavy, but he was ready. He breathed in the sweet perfume of the cut grass and mentally tightened his grip on the leather of the ball. Calling out the play, his companions shuffled about before him, righting their positions, following his command. He decided on his own manoeuvres and restarted play. Receiving that which the entire opposition sought after, he moved backwards, buying his team time to get into positions. Red and yellow clashed with white and blue, fierce battles being fought ahead of him and to the left and right; he could end this war with a crank of his shoulder and the release of his iron-grip. A fiery blur hurtled down the line to his right, heading for the end zone. He pulled back his arm, his bicep tensed in the heat, but as he let the missile fly, heading directly to its target, he was hit in the side by an opposing warrior. The impact hit hard and he winced at the pain. He had been tackled many times before but this time it was different, this time it burned. As the pain seared throughout his veins the smell of burnt flesh overwhelmed his senses. Reality had returned.

'AH!' he screamed out in agony as the fiery pain persisted and the flames licked up and down his body.

'There you go sweetie,' she said, glad to see him coherent again. 'You must stop passing out baby,' She pursed her soft lips against his ear. Her heat was intense, every inch of her radiated against his skin as he hung, chained in the centre of the room, wearing just a pair of badly singed pants. She pushed herself against him. 'Say her name, baby,' Each and every visit Serena had made ended in the same manner. He could barely picture her face, nor could he taste her lips. Her perfume had long since left his senses. All he had left was her name, and Serena wanted to take that from him too. 'Baby, say her name.' She caressed his chest and nibbled gently on his ear lobe. Suspended from the ceiling, his hands were bound above his head and his toes only just touched the cold, hard flooring below. Sweat and blood covered his skin as he struggled to remain conscious. He needed to stay awake, for each time he passed out Serena would make sure he woke up again, screaming.

'Her name...' he whispered drowsily as she ran her hand over his chest and up into his hair, listening intently, with a sense of excitement. 'Beyoncé,' he hissed, spitting up blood, some onto the side of her face. 'Or was it Cher?' He chuckled as much as his beaten body would allow and gained a small sense of relief from seeing Serena's displeasure with his continued resistance. 'Red is your favourite colour, isn't it?' Mike said in jest, the corner of his mouth forming into a forced smile.

'Michael, you disappoint me,' she said as she stepped back away from him, having wiped the splatter of blood from her cheek. 'You best pray you didn't get any of that on my clothes...' She stood with her hands on her hips as she looked him up and down, unamused by his remark. She was wearing a black ribbed knitted midi dress that hugged the shape of her body. It had long sleeves and popper-front fastenings. Her shimmering red hair flowed freely, straightened, but with a natural kink. The dress had cut-away shoulders, revealing a touch of her golden skin and she wore ruby stilettos with twisted straps that entangled her ankles and lower calves. Mike couldn't help but wonder if she always made this much effort to torture people.

He did not know how long he had been in this room for now. So far, they had moved him to several different locations during his time as their hostage. This particular room was dark and rank; it reeked of his own pain and fear. He hated to admit it, but he had all but given up hope of being rescued. In the dark he had conversed with the shadows and contemplated the unthinkable to end his suffering. *She wouldn't even recognise me now.* A tear seeped from the corner of his eye. They had kept him fed and watered. For reasons unknown to him they seemed to want him to stay alive, at least for now. He had tried to stay positive in the beginning and he had attempted to work out each day to keep up his strength, but time had beaten him down, reducing his hope and positivity to nothing more than a desire for this nightmare to end soon. At least once a week he would be visited by one of the Avunaye. Nahki would question him and play mind games. Mike tried to take in as much as he could, any information he could take back to his team that would help them but like his body, his mind was so weary. Brandt would come only to break his spirit. He would say very little, not that Mike could hear him over his own screams once Brandt laid his hands on him. Serena was the worst. She would bring the light to his darkened existence. Her flame would chase away the darkness and bring hope, only for her to strip it away, slither by slither, chastising him. She would both remind him of what he had to fight for, as well as what he had already lost, and still had to lose. In his weakened state she had used the thought of Lucy against him, preying on the occasional deluded sense of reality he had, pretending to be the one he most desired.

'Imagine if she was to find out about the nasty things we've gotten up to in the dark,' she stepped closer and placed her hands on his abdomen. 'You're not the first to mistake me for someone else, Michael,' she ran her fingers along his waistline, brushing the top of his pants. He knew what she was doing, and he wrestled in his chains; trying to escape her, she merely laughed at his attempt. 'Show me your strength,' she said, slipping a hand into his pants and grasping his flaccid penis. 'Baby, just think of her,' she whispered as she caressed him, attempting to arouse. He fought as hard as he could to stop his body from participating as she would want, but as his genitals flinched and he felt a rush of blood flow to his shaft he lost hope and cried out in anger and frustration. 'There we are, that wasn't so hard was it? Well, I suppose it is now.' She giggled at his displeasure.

'No!' Mike shouted, tears falling from his eyes. He had to do something to make her stop, and so he spat, intentionally this time, a thick cocktail of saliva and blood. She instantaneously halted her foreplay as the crimson slobber hit her cheek and she turned away from him. *This won't be pleasant.* He awaited retaliation. Wiping her face, she stepped further away from him, disappearing into the darkness. He could hear her footsteps, but he couldn't see her. It was unlike Serena to be shy or quiet, a fact that seriously unnerved Mike at present.

'What the fuck are you waiting for?!' he shouted into the black, tired of the games, tired of waiting for what he thought to be the inevitable outcome to his time as hostage, their plaything. 'Just fucking kill me already!' he yelled emotionally.

'Patience Michael,' her voice sang softly from the

shadows. He looked for her, following the sound of her voice and then her position was made clear as her fiery eyes began to glow a deep dark red. 'I've learnt to be patient over the years. The last time I...' she paused for a moment, her stare fixed on him. 'You'll find that I don't anger as easily as my siblings. Even when those silly Greeks mistook me for Helios, I...' she started what could easily have been mistaken for a conversation, all the while her eyes continued to emanate a glow that slowly grew brighter. '*Selene*, they called me: Goddess of the moon. Whilst Helios the God of fire and the sun? A man? Ha!' her tone was one of annoyance. 'Even after I punished them, they denied to re-write their history, the stubbornness of humanity. Humanity! Even that word is recklessly used. You class yourself above the animals of the planet, your ability to speak, to think, to build, despite other species showing all of these same characteristics in one way or another and yet you're stupid enough to kill each other, to persistently attempt to halt your own development, to reduce your own numbers, and why...?' As she continued her eyes sparked and the heat she emitted rose and rose. 'You fight over colour. Over beliefs, possessions and most foolishly money! Ones and zeros define so many of you that you forget what was given to you from the beginning, what you all seem to take for granted.'

'Is this going anywhere fast?' Mike said, interrupting her. 'It's just, my arms are fucking tired.' The interruption silenced her and the flames in her eyes dimmed and then extinguished. Darkness and silence filled the room once more as Mike hung, unmoving, waiting.

'Michael,' she moved so quickly towards him that he could feel the air pressure shift around him. 'My love. Time to play.' As she whispered the words her hand set alight next to his face. The heat was intense. He turned away from the flames, looking away from her, striving to escape the heat but there was no escape. His screams resounded throughout the room as she continued her foreplay, resuming where she had left off.

It was a muscle spasm in his leg that caused tender flesh to chafe against the fabric of his pants and awoke him in a fit of pain and fear. The pain was intense but as he came to, he realised that he was alone in the room and this fact eased him slightly. Pushing himself up off the cold floor, he sat leaning against the hard brick wall. It was at least a minute before he was observant enough to realise that he was not in complete darkness. Staring across the room his eyes were fixed on the flame that flickered atop a half-melted candle. The light it emitted almost caused him to weep as he struggled to calculate the odds of this being reality or dream. He held a mix of emotion within him, the light offered hope, but the flame reminded him only of despair. The dull pain between his shoulder blades reassured him that it was real as he tried to move. Each movement sent a flourish of pain throughout his neck, shoulders and back, but the candle held such beauty that he needed to get closer to it, before it ceased to burn anymore. He crawled across the floor, dragging himself through his own blood and urine. The stench of his prison had once bothered him, but now the worst smell he could contemplate was that of burning flesh. The white candle sat on a single-seated wooden bench that sat next to the door to the cell. Mike could not decide whether the bench was new to the room or not as he had rarely seen any of it. In the darkness, he had imagined what it might be like and to his consternation he had been rather accurate. The floor was of an unforgiving rough concrete, it had provided no comfort in the dark and even now in the light, its uncompromising coarseness grated against his skin. He pulled himself up against the smooth wooden seat and stared, besotted, at the orange flicker at the end of the wick. The candle was over half melted already, its liquid had seeped out from the pool at the candles peak and flowed down to its base, cooling and setting as it went.

Globules of hardening wax clung to the candles' side like small waxy stalactites. Mike ran his finger over their smooth surface, down the height of the candle to the growing moat of wax that resided at its base. There was something... As Mike ran his fingers over the wax that had set on the bench, he could feel something harder just below the white, slippery surface. As he broke the crust, he realised that what lie beneath the wax was a key. *A key? For what?* He was unable to begin to believe that it could possibly be for the door beside him. *A trick, a joke, a trap.* These explanations cycled through his mind as he sat, key in hand, staring at the lock on the steel plated door to his prison. As he held his means for escape, he thought of Lucy, of seeing her again, touching her, feeling her touch him in return. He also began to think of how she would react when she saw him, or what was left of him. Serena had done an exquisite job at chipping away at the man that had been taken captive until all that was left was this frail shell. Afraid of how much might have changed while he'd been gone, he clenched the key in a fist and squeezed it hard, hard enough for its rough metal to break the worn skin of his palm. He closed his eyes and searched the darkness for the spark, the spark that he used to have, the flame that the fire goddess had tormented and extinguished. He gritted his teeth in frustration as he struggled to find courage to free himself. *Why is this so hard?!* . For so long he had craved the light, but, fear and shadow had tamed him. He sat watching as the candle grew smaller, the fire reducing it to nothing.

There was a knock on the door and then the sound of a key entering the lock. Mike moved away from the exit as quickly as he could, afraid of who it might be. *If they find the key, they'll kill me.* He grasped it tighter in a panic. The heavy door opened and, in its doorway, stood one of the guards. He had muddy black boots on and wore a long-sleeved dark-blue jumper under a black ribbed gilet. This one had visited

Mike before, not long after he had arrived at the first location that he had been held. At this point, Mike's spirits had not yet been broken and he had resisted his first couple beatings; the scar that lay beneath this man's right eye was testament to that. He had a shaved head and dark skin that absorbed the light from the candle.

'Where the fuck did you get a candle from?' he asked angrily, kicking over the bench and snuffing out the light. Darkness closed in around Mike, the only light coming from the hallway behind his visitor. 'You don't get to have light motherfucker, not unless we give it to you!' he directed his anger at Mike, kicking at his legs as he cowered against the wall of his confines. Mike stayed silent, holding onto the key and hoping that he would soon be left alone with the darkness once more. 'What you got there?' the guard asked, instilling a flood of fear into Mike's heart as his clenched fist betrayed him. Mike remained quiet. The guard stepped closer and kicked him again, this time he hit Mike's hip, the pain causing Mike to curl up even more, a sign of submission. *Please go away. Please, please go away.* The guard kicked him again, this time hitting his lower back, the jolt from the pain caused Mike to open his hand and drop the key. Instantly the guard realised what it was that Mike had in his possession and he bent down to grab the key off the floor. Panic swept over Mike like a sandstorm in the dessert; the key was his only chance of getting back to Lucy. The darkness of the room may have had a grasp on him, holding him back, but the light beyond the door was worth fighting for. He had finally found his spark.

'Fuck off!' Mike exclaimed as he too reached for the key and got to it first. Without hesitation he grasped it in his hand and thrust its point upwards at the guard as he bent over before him. The guard let out a cacophony of sounds as he writhed in pain. Mike took his chance and grabbed the man by the throat, squeezing as hard as his weary body could, pressing his thumbs harder and harder against his wind pipe until the sounds stopped and the light within his captor had diminished. Removing his key from the lifeless man's eye socket, Mike hobbled to the door frame, clutching it with his aching hands. Then, he dragged himself out into the light.

Accustomed to the dark, the lights that lined the hallway dazzled him. He was forced to look at the route ahead with squinted eyes, his path a little blurred. To his left was a set of stairs that lead upwards, there was more light glowing from the top of them. To his right, the corridor ran a little further, at the end of it was another door. Shrouded in uncertainty, for some unknown reason this door called out to him. The stairs to his left were pathed with light and screamed '*exit*', yet despite being the obvious choice, Mike couldn't help but think that there was no doubt more trouble at the summit and he was in no shape to fight more guards. He just couldn't risk it. Moving along the corridor towards the closed door, he could hear voices behind him. *Shit!* He tried to hasten himself. Using the wall for balance and support, he shuffled towards what he hoped would be his way out. *One foot in front of the other.* He staggered forwards, dragging the knuckles of his toes on the hard flooring as he went. *Almost there, Luce, I'm almost there.* He drove forward, his legs heavy from lack of use. As he reached the door, he leaned into it, pushing the handle down, but the door failed to open. Mike dropped to his knees and slammed his palm down onto the doors cold, steel surface. It was locked. He tried the handle again and again, just in case it was just stuck, but only achieved the same result. Hope began to dwindle. He ran his fingers over the handle and down to a hole where the doors' key must go. Banging on the door once more, he let out a sigh of desperation and began to weep.

'I need a fucking key,' he sobbed aloud to himself. He looked back down the hall to the stairs and contemplated his options, crawling back into his cell being one of them. 'I just need a key,' he whimpered in self-pity, before a thought came to him. *Maybe the guard has a key?* The thought lifted his spirits a minute amount, but it was enough to enable him to act. As he began to turn, he felt the metal between his fingers and suddenly it dawned on him. 'You have a fucking key!' He cried, elated. Tears of sadness turned to ones of joy as he turned back to the door with his key at the ready. Sliding the bloodied key into the dark opening beneath the doors handle, Michael could hear the locking mechanism within. As he turned the key, he listened ever closer as levers within shifted and the bolt disengaged, allowing him to pull down on the handle and open the door.

Exhausted and bemused, Mike looked upon the closet before him. There was a small shelving unit with three shelves, only one of which was in use. On the shelf sat two containers of bleach and leant against the shelving's frame was a mop handle, its head resting in a bucket on the floor. *Why give me a key for this?* He knelt in the entrance.

He chuckled: 'Want me to clean up my own shit?' He spoke as if someone else was there to hear his words. Exhaling, he sat back on his heels and looked upwards at the ceiling, the time for praying was almost at hand; he had never been one for religion. *Try anything at least once.* He clung to the last fibre of hope. He stared at the ceiling, looking, hoping for some kind of divine sign when he saw it. Built into the ceiling of the closet was a vent, a large vent that Mike surmised must be for ensuring airflow down to the basement or wherever he was. No matter what the vent was for, it would hopefully serve him well. Pulling himself to his feet, he grasped onto the shelving unit to help him walk, his legs still too weary to hold his full weight just yet. The vent was reachable, but he would need to climb onto the shelves to get up to it. It was about as un-sturdy as it looked, he found as he put some of his weight onto it. He would need to be quick; the shelving wouldn't hold him for long. Thankfully, the vent looked as if its cover should come away easily enough. Climbing up the wire mesh shelves, he used his arms to lift the rest of him up at each stage. Balanced on the last but one shelf he reached up towards the vent, hoping to be able to remove the cover from where he was, but his fingertips barely brushed against the metal. *One more shelf.* He coaxed himself forwards as he struggled with the final push. Lifting himself onto the top level of the unit, he reached up and removed the vents cover, revealing a space large enough for him to climb up into. Pulling himself up to the venting, the shelf that currently held his weight began to creak. The metal posts that formed its frame began to buckle. In a panic, Mike pushed off from the shelving in an attempt to get all of himself up into the metal tunnel that would aid his escape. In doing so, his weight proved too much for the shelves below and the unit began to topple. He had become so accustomed to pain that he did not notice at first, but as he hung, half in and half out of the vent, the shelving was suspended, balancing on two legs. The wire mesh that served as the highest level of the unit had given way and his foot had broken through it, but as he attempted to free himself from it, the ends of several wires of the mesh pierced the flesh of his bare foot, hooking him. He attempted to pull himself up and out of the wiry snare he found himself in, but one slither of metal had dug in deep alongside the little toe of his right foot. He would not be able to get back up here again now that the shelves had collapsed, but he would also not be able to hold himself up here for much longer. Something would have to give. He pulled timidly once more and felt the wire scrape along the bone under the skin of his toe. The pain was intense but his resolve to be free was stronger and so he bit down, gritted his teeth, closed his eyes and pulled himself up as fast as he could, leaving the unit to fall onto the floor below, taking a small piece of himself with it.

He wanted to cry out in agony but managed to keep it to a dull groan. He knew that the sound would only be carried by the vent he was in, a fact that could result in him being caught. Dragging himself through the vents ,he took a number of turns whilst crawling up and along, all the while the walls closing in around him, in this claustrophobic maze. He was part way along a lengthy stretch of tunnel when he heard his voice, carried on the air.

'Cardoza, you have twelve days to pull this off. I take it that will be enough?' It was Markovic, he was talking to Kryln Cardoza. Mike knew this not to be good. If Cardoza was here, then the likelihood was that they were planning a something terrible. Mike knew he had to get out and warn the others.

'Twelve days until this city bleeds; we will be needing the blade back to complete the ritual.' Mike recognized the voice: it was Nahki.

'The blade resides within the F.B.I. headquarters,' a third voice said; judging by the accent, Mike presumed it belonged to Cardoza. 'I will send some of my men to retrieve it,' he said assertively. Mike could hear a chair scraping across a hard surface.

'It is time we took care of the F.B.I. and other loose ends.' Markovic sounded confident. 'We have confirmation of their whereabouts - send teams to each of these locations. Tomorrow night we take care of them all and reclaim the blade.' Mike's resolve peaked as well as his panic, his team was in danger. He began to crawl again, desperately looking for an exit, when Nahki spoke again.

'We won't be able to get involved, you know that, but once the blade is back in our possession, we can move forward with our plans.' His words were emotionless as always, as if he were a robot, not a human.

'Cardoza. See to it that it is done. Start by killing that runt in the fucking cellar,' Markovic ordered and Mike knew his time was up. He needed to escape now, before they realised he was missing from his cell. He crawled on his belly using his arms to drag himself along as fast as he could until he reached the end of the vent, an exit beneath him leading into a corridor below.

Dropping down into the hallway, he knelt for a moment; behind him was a lengthy corridor with several rooms coming off from it. Ahead of him was a door with a large lever-like handle spread across its width. He headed for the door, hoping it was an exit from the building, from this hell. He needed to get back to his team, to his family, to Lucy. He grimaced as he got to his feet, the pain in his right foot was worst of all. He stepped forward with a limp, dragging his injured limb as he went. One step turned to two and soon he had managed to force himself to the door. Placing his hands on the handle, he felt cold. He could feel the air around the door; it was freezing, whatever awaited him on the other side. As he applied pressure to the door, a glow began to spread around its edge. He could tell it wasn't sunlight, but it was light none the less, and light meant hope. As the door opened, it met some resistance; something on the ground was holding it back. The outside world shone with a majestic glow, snow covered the ground and for the first time in a long while Mike tasted the city air. His feet numbed as he walked out into the snowy night, the cold concealing the pain he had felt. He basked in the chill of the nightly breeze and caught falling flakes in his palms as the tears froze to his cheeks. Each extraordinary and unique crystal; the attestation of his deliverance.

19

Luciana Rodriguez

'That's about all I can remember I'm afraid,' sighed Lorelei; their questions had been few but specific and she had provided as much information as she could. She was recovering well but due to the extent of the damage done to her, it was going to take a lot of time before she would feel anything remotely close to herself again. As Lucy stared at the girl lying in the hospital bed, she was surprised at the small feeling of envy she had. This girl had been badly injured and had suffered in more ways than she dare think of, yet she had spent the best part of the last six months in slumber. Asleep, she had the chance to dream of things, to escape reality, whereas Lucy had had to consciously deal with Mike being missing and regrettably, the coming to terms with the likelihood that he was dead.

'That's fine, Lorelei, get some rest my darling,' Lorelei's mother said, sat at her daughter's bedside. 'Can we call it a day?' she asked, looking at Lucy and Krysta. She had a kind face. Lucy could tell that she really wanted them to leave her daughter in peace, although she'd never say it outright.

'No problem, Mrs Holmes. Thank you, Lorelei, you've been very helpful,' Krysta said in reply. Lorelei had given details of several buildings they had taken her to, including a residence of Serena's that they'd be able to investigate. Lorelei merely smiled in response, before closing her eyes and trying to make herself more comfortable. Her brown-blonde hair was lifeless and flat, and a scar ran from her temple down to the crease in her lips. Despite her injuries, and her current inability to move about and walk, her spirits were high. Her mother sat dutifully by her, watching her every movement and fussing constantly as loving mothers do. Her spirits were not quite at the level of her daughters, it would seem. Her hair was no doubt once the same colour of Lorelei's but was now mottled with signs of age and stress. She wore it up, brushed tightly back into a ponytail with its ends resting on the collar of her thick brown winter coat. Lucy stood still, simply staring at Lorelei as Krysta went to leave. She couldn't help but consider the idea that this girl before her was a trade for the one she loved. She had been found as Michael had been lost and now as she had awakened from her sleep, perhaps, somewhere out there, Mike had closed his eyes for the last time.

'Luce, come on,' Krysta beckoned, tugging at her arm, urging her to leave Lorelei and her mother alone. Snapping out of her daze, Lucy turned and followed her partner out of the room. 'You okay, hon?' Krysta asked as Lucy stood looking back into the room through the window.

'Yeah... Yeah, fine,' Lucy replied, internally shaking herself out of her current slump. She looked at Krysta and forced a smile to hopefully reassure her friend. Lucy had worn her favourite suit to work today to try and brighten the cold, miserable excuse for a day that she'd awoken to. It was a grey-pink, windowpane, chequered, tailored jacket with matching suit pants. She wore black v-cut court shoes and a white jersey blouse. Her dark hair had been curled, but she had tied it up into a rough bun, leaving a few strands to fall by her golden cheeks. Krysta, dressed in slightly less formal attire, was wearing a loose fitted burgundy buttoned shirt with dark pants. She had donned her F.B.I. jacket and stood assuredly in her black military-style boots. Her golden hair was down, exhibiting its natural wave.

'Poor girl has been through hell,' Krysta said, looking back through the glass pane into the hospital room. 'I'd best update Claire with what Lorelei has said, hopefully produce some leads as to Markovic's whereabouts.' Krysta took out her phone and called the office. She relayed the details of Lorelei's captors' premises, different buildings she had been dragged to, people she had met, names she had heard, anything that she could remember that may help with the investigation. As Lucy listened to Krysta, she realised how out of sorts she had been, some of the details seeming like it was the first she'd heard of them. She sighed within herself and tried to encourage herself to concentrate. *Focus Luce, focus.* She continued to listen to Krysta's conversation with Claire. She used to be on top of her game, especially at work; she wanted to return to where she had been, but everything felt so difficult.

Once Krysta had finished updating Claire, she and Lucy turned their attentions to one another. Lucy knew their friendship had taken a knock recently and that she was mostly to blame, but it was time to get things moving again, back to where they used to be, where they should be in her eyes. They spoke and laughed about their recent get-together over thanksgiving. Solomon had managed to get the entire team together to eat, drink and celebrate the holiday. His wife Lulu had put on an amazing spread and they had all been able to relax, if only for a short while.

'Not sure Solomon will ever forgive Hale for falling off his chair and smashing that priceless lamp,' Krysta laughed as they reminisced.

'If you ask me, he did him a favour... That lamp was hideous!' Lucy replied, laughing with her friend; the pair both unwinding as they conversed.

'Speaking of Paul, I happened to see that you two are getting on rather well lately,' Krysta said, fishing for gossip as friends do. Lucy, however, was not keen to take the bait, any thought of starting anything with anyone while the case into Mike's disappearance was still unresolved felt too uncomfortable.

'He's a good guy, he's just being supportive, that's all,' Lucy replied, purposely adding a hint of sadness to her tone to urge Krysta to change the subject. 'Anyway, what about you and Jake?' Lucy said quickly, feeling like the moments awkward silence they shared was a moment too long.

'You jumped him yet?' her question instantly putting Krysta on the spot as her friends' cheeks blushed. Lucy had succeeded in moving the conversation along.

'Actually, he *is* coming over tonight,' Krysta responded with a coy smile. Lucy merely shook her head.

'Honey, you have way more restraint than I do,' she said honestly, to which both of them laughed in acceptance to the truth.

'Fancy running into you two again,' a voice sounded from down the corridor. Lucy recognised it but couldn't quite put a name to the voice until she turned to see who it was.

'What would the deputy director of the C.I.A. be doing wandering the halls of this particular hospital?' Lucy asked as Zane approached them. She stood, arms crossed, awaiting his reply. He was more casually dressed than the last time they had met; he was wearing dark brown leather Chelsea boots, a pair of azure-blue coloured pants, a white buttoned shirt with its sleeves rolled up and he was carrying a black overcoat.

'I was here to see Miss Holmes. Although, I imagine you beat me to it,' Zane said. He was attempting to act okay with missing his chance, but Lucy could sense an anger about him.

'Better luck next time I guess,' Lucy said sarcastically. He was full of himself; she could tell even with only meeting him twice; but he was undeniably attractive. He smiled in response to her quick jest and Lucy caught a glimpse of a necklace he had around his neck, otherwise concealed by his shirt. 'Nice neck piece you have there,' she said, directing attention to it. Zane quickly pulled his collar together and changed the subject of conversation.

'At least this trip wasn't a complete waste, it is of course a pleasure to see you both again,' he tipped his head slightly as a courtesy.

'I'm surprised you made the trip to be honest,' Krysta said; she had told Lucy of hers and Solomon's coincidental meeting with Zane. Krysta had told Lucy that she couldn't shake the feeling that he had been looking into their team for some reason. Solomon, of course, had little praise for the man.

'I'm pretty thorough, you'll come to learn that about me,' he said in response. Although he was talking to Krysta, he did not take his eyes off Lucy; she could feel his stare piercing through her until he diverted his gaze to Lorelei's room. 'I'm sure you can fill me in on any progress you've made. Mind if I walk you both to your car? Or perhaps you require a ride?' His tone became slightly condescending, but his mannerisms were almost demanding of them as he suggested heading for the exit.

'We're fine, thanks,' Krysta said turning to Lucy. 'Ready to go?' she asked, ignoring the presence of the deputy director.

'Actually, hon, I think I'm gonna stay for a bit,' Lucy said in reply. 'Grab a coffee and hopefully speak to Lorelei's mom before I head off.' Lucy wondered if perhaps Lorelei's mom had picked up on anything that had been left out of their interview, any clue that would help with her missing partners case. She was desperate.

'Okay, if you're sure then no problem,' Krysta replied reluctantly. 'Want me to hang around for a bit?'

'No, you go, I'll be fine,' Lucy said quickly, remembering that Krysta was meant to be meeting Jake this evening. 'Have fun. And definitely don't do anything I wouldn't do,' she said grinning.

'That doesn't leave a lot!' Krysta laughed.

'Exactly!' Lucy replied, winking at her friend. The pair said their goodbyes and Krysta began to leave.

'Let me walk you out,' Zane said, walking backwards alongside Krysta as she headed for the exit. He gave Lucy a subtle yet mischievous look before turning around and leaving with her colleague.

The overly noisy machine dispensed a beverage that was luke-warm and bitter at best, but coffee was a necessity right now, however it came. As Lucy drank from the tepid recyclable cup, she was greeted by another requiring a caffeine fix: Lorelei's mother, Maggie. She smiled at Lucy before instructing the machine as to how she wanted her drink, but Lucy could see through the polite façade that she tried to mask her pain with. The look in Maggie's eyes was one she knew all too well herself, one of fear and weariness, for she had seen it many times staring back at her in the mirror.   'She's incredibly brave, your daughter,' Lucy said, interrupting the silence. Maggie took a sip of her drink and then took a deep breath in, composing herself.

'She... She's the strongest person I know.' She smiled a fake smile again as she struggled to get the words out.

'You have two daughters, right?' Lucy said, trying to keep her from breaking down; it was a difficult time for her and she was alone right now.

'Clara is my eldest,' Maggie said, nodding in reply. 'Hopefully she and my husband will be here later,' the thought clearly reassured her a little. Lucy couldn't help but feel for her.

'Must have been difficult, waiting for Lorelei to wake up,' Lucy said, carrying the conversation. 'It's when family is needed the most, I guess.' As she said the words, she couldn't help but think of her own, distant family, but then again, she had two families, and her team had always been there for her.

'And friends,' Maggie added. 'And complete strangers,'

she said smiling, yet this time her smile was different, real.

'I can imagine your local community has helped,' Lucy said, assuming that was what she meant by strangers.

'Well, yes. Then there's Joel, he's been a Godsend,' she said, again with a smile. 'He just showed up one day in July and every now and again he pops by just to help and listen.' The thought of this Joel seemed to relieve some of her stress.

'You'll have to give me his number. Sounds like someone we could all do with from time to time,' Lucy quipped. Maggie's expression told another story, however.

'That's the most amazing thing. I don't have his number, he doesn't even live locally,' Maggie said. 'He just showed up one day, said he was just passing through. Truth is, you'd think me crazy letting someone I know nothing about into my home, my life, on occasion. But he has this amazing way of helping you see the light at the end of the tunnel. Know what I mean?' Lucy wished she had someone like that in her life right now, but it did seem a little strange. Her F.B.I. trained senses tingled. The two of them spoke some more of this Joel, Lucy managing to get a good description of him from Maggie without her realising what she was doing. While they were talking, Maggie received a phone call from her husband and so she left Lucy standing with now stone-cold coffee-tinted water in her cup as she went to meet up with the rest of her family.

Following Maggie's departure, Lucy sent the details of this Joel character to Claire to look into. Something felt off about the whole idea, but if her gut feelings were wrong, if nothing else, this stranger deserved a commendation or something for his help. The chances of Claire finding any information on a mysterious backpacker whose name may or may not be Joel were minute, but if anyone could, it'd be Claire. Deciding to see if Lorelei was still awake and willing to answer a question or two, Lucy turned to head back to her room, only to turn right into a man that was passing behind her, heading for the dispense machines.

'I'm so sorry,' Lucy said quickly as she shook off the collision.

'That's quite alright. Agent Rodriguez, is it?' the man said; the mention of her name instantly drawing Lucy's attention.

'Officer McCarthy?' she replied awkwardly. He was probably the last person she would have expected to bump in to, and considering how stretched his and the F.B.I.'s relationship had become, she felt like turning and walking away rather than getting into anything right now.

'Call me Seamus,' he said in reply. He was not in uniform, which made Lucy question his being here. He was dressed in tan coloured boots, darkened by moisture from trudging through snow. His blue denim jeans had a hole in on the left knee and he wore a dark brown leather jacket to keep the winter chill off. He was clean shaven, and his hair tidily combed over to one side, although it could do with a trim, especially around his ears as it crept over the tops of them. 'I was hoping to catch my wife, but it seems she's a bit tied up at the moment,' he admitted freely, answering Lucy's unasked question. 'You must be here to see the Holmes girl, right? Krysta here too?' he asked curiously. Despite the bureau's treatment of him, he still occasionally called for Krysta, hoping to share information, unable to let the investigation go. Lucy sympathised with him a little, she too had lost someone, although she didn't have the closure of knowing he was dead like Seamus did. Regardless, losing a partner was incredibly painful, especially when there appeared to be no reason as to why it happened.

'Krysta already left. I'm just checking in on Lorelei before I go myself.' She hoped that would end this awkward encounter, but instead he merely stood there with a look of sorrow. The lights above them flickered and the pair both looked to the ceiling in curiosity.

'Want some company?' Seamus asked in a broken tone. In truth, it seemed that he was simply wanting some himself.

'Seamus...' Lucy said with a discouraging tone, hoping he would take the hint, but the lost look in his eyes pained her. She decided to simply nod in acceptance of his offer and the two of them walked off towards Lorelei's room in silence. As they reached the room, a doctor was just exiting.

'Everything alright doc?' Lucy asked, hoping to still be able to question the girl.

'Just a check-up,' the doctor replied. 'All's well, she just needs some rest. I'd advise holding off on any more questions,' she said, clearly recognising Lucy's intentions. The lights flickered again.

'Strange...' the doctor said in response, before taking her leave. Unfortunately, the doctor's suggestion was not what Lucy was hoping for. But she would have to oblige; the girl had been through enough already. The lights flickered again before turning off completely, the corridor and surrounding rooms now bathing in the emergency lighting.

'What the fuck is up with these lights?' Lucy asked, looking up and down the darkened empty corridor. Seamus had no response, but he seemed concerned. A door at the end of the corridor opened and light from a torch entered.

'We could all do with one of those.' Said Seamus. Another light appeared.

'Hey! Down here!' Lucy called, requesting aid from the torch bearers.

'Lucy...' Seamus said, placing his hand on her shoulder. 'There are four lights.' There was a sense of fear in his voice. Seamus' words forced Lucy to see what was right in front of her; the lights were now moving down the corridor in formation. *Fuck!* Lucy screamed within herself as she opened the door to Lorelei's room and ushered Seamus inside. Time slowed down as she too stepped partially over the threshold, dropped to one knee and took her sidearm from its holster. Their movement was caught in one of the torch lights and, breaking formation, there was an almighty crash as a hail of bullets flew past Lucy and shattered a window further down the corridor. *Silencers?!* She returned fire, her weapon alerting everyone to what was happening and awakening Lorelei to the hell that was erupting in the corridor.

'Seamus,' Lucy whispered loudly. 'Get Lorelei into the bathroom, low as possible. Do you have your firearm?' she knew that the chances were slim with him being dressed in his civilian clothes, but she hoped he'd surprise her. Unfortunately, Seamus shook his head in response as he lifted Lorelei from the bed, who whimpered in pain as he moved her. *Fuck! Shit! Fuck!* Lucy attempted to formulate a plan to survive. 'F.B.I!' she shouted down the corridor in the hopes that they'd give up or that it'd turn out to be some kind of mistake. In response, there was another flurry of shots that splintered the doorframe behind her, and she was forced to retreat into the room, firing a couple of rounds back at her attackers as she did. *Breathe.* Lucy told herself as she positioned herself under the window, against the wall that housed the entrance to the room.

Seamus appeared from the bathroom, closing the door behind him and quickly tipping the bed over on which Lorelei had lay, to provide some form of cover. His face was a flush with fear. Silence filled the air as Lucy struggled to hear even the faintest of screams or sounds of rushing about in nearby wards and other corridors. These assailants weren't Markovic's usual gangbangers, she realised. Lowering herself even further, Lucy lay on the floor against the wall, aiming her weapon at the doorway; time was against them, yet time was all they had. Their attackers were moving along the corridor cautiously as far as she could tell from the occasional flicker of torch light that shone about the doorway. Their echoless footsteps didn't aid her in any way. As the seconds passed, the room seemed to grow darker. She tried to reduce her breathing to remain as quiet as possible, but the harder she tried, the more the fear within hastened her heart. She looked to Seamus to see how he was fairing; he knelt, mostly concealed by the bed. The look on his face, however, was unknown to her. There seemed to be a calmness about his expression, yet in his eyes it was as if a rage was pounding beneath the corneas, trying to break through. Lucy was momentarily mesmerised by them, which drew a look of confusion from Seamus, but then all attention fell to the window above where she lay.

Fingers of light stretched out across the room, touching everything they could. A pane of glass separated their world of fear from their pursuers and the rays of torch light reached out to grasp them and pull them into the eternal shadow. Lucy knew she must bide her time, they were close enough now to hear; from the silence came sound. *Four of them... Tap, tap, tap.* She listened as one of them scurried past her, only the thin partition between them. The light appeared to move past the doorway, but then it turned and looked into their hiding place. *Tap, tap, tap.* She listened again and then... Lucy pulled her trigger, firing a round straight through the foot of one of the assailants and following suit by swiftly discharging a second round straight to his temple as he fell into the room. The sound alerted everyone to their location and thus chaos ensued. A second stepped up to the entrance and sprayed bullets about the darkness, hoping to extinguish any lives that remained. Seamus hit the deck and covered his head as debris scattered everywhere. Lucy counted. *One, two, three.* On three, she pushed off from the wall, sliding across the debris riddled floor and fired into the torchlight, again and again, until the light fell to the ground with a thud. Her heart pounded ferociously within her chest and then suddenly it stopped dead. The white hand pierced the veil of the window and bathed her in its glow. She barely had time to realise that her clip was empty when from behind her Seamus flew from his hiding spot and threw himself through the windowpane and collided with the attacker.

Lucy, getting to her feet, ran out of the room to assist Seamus; forgetting about the fourth light. She saw Seamus and a masked attacker wrestling on the ground; she did not see the butt of a rifle until it impacted with her temple, knocking her back into Lorelei's room. Dazed, she reached out to grab hold of something, anything, to steady herself,. Clinging to a crater riddled wall, she managed to prevent herself from falling. She reached forward and grabbed the barrel of the rifle with one hand and slammed the palm of her other into the attackers' hand that was primed to pull the trigger. She punched them in the face as she pulled the rifle from their grasp, but she pulled too hard and, losing her grip, the weapon flew across the room. With little time to think Lucy then had to divert the silvery blade that intended to plunge into her away from herself. Failing to hit his mark, number four slashed at the air around Lucy's throat, shaving any micro-hairs from her neck. Forcing herself to concentrate, Lucy managed to block another attack, hitting down hard onto his arm, causing him to lose his grip on the weapon. She clenched her fists as tightly as she could; she could feel the strain within them, and the wrath. She landed a powerful blow to the side of his chin and then another to his abdomen. Dodging a swing of retaliation, she quickly landed two more powerful blows to his face, knocking him off balance. Her hands screamed out in pain but the fear of losing and the drive to survive pushed her on. She kicked him in the side of his left knee forcing him to kneel and then swung her tired fist to land another hit to his head, only for her attempt to be blocked. Before she could attack again, he hit her hard in her side, and, as she winced at the pain, he hit her again, this time his hardened fist impacting with her cheekbone.

Stunned, Lucy staggered backwards; she caught sight of Seamus and number three still beating each other, their fight having moved down the corridor. She clenched her fists and raised her hands up, but he chopped her hands to the sides and grasped her around the throat with both of his hands, squeezing hard. He slammed her against the wall as she tried with all her might to pry open his grip and fight back. Yet the more she tried the more the shadows crept in. Air was hard to come by and her head felt like a lead weight. Her arms felt anchored as she tried to punch out at him, at his masked face. Each gasp for air allowed him to restrict her further. She looked into his eyes as the darkness began to envelope everything. So much hatred resided in them, that for an instant, she felt an ounce of pity for him.

'Cardoza sends his regard...' his sentence ended in a gurgling sound as blood splattered across Lucy's face. The silver blade protruded from his open mouth and his hands fell from her throat. Gasping for another breath she pushed him away from her, and as his body slumped to the ground, in his place, stood the ghost of the man she loved. Confused and struggling to breathe, she stared at the bearded, haggard man before her, recognising him as the man she loved. He was naked from the waist up, his torso bruised and scarred. His feet were noticeably bare and bloodied. Thinned by mistreatment and malnourishment he was a shadow of his former self. He stood unmoving; his tired eyes glazed with tears as he looked at her. A loud crash sounded from beyond the room as Seamus and one of the attackers continued to tussle. The noise startled Mike somewhat and he turned away from Lucy and fled out to the corridor. Still in disbelief of what she had seen, Lucy rubbed her sore, bloodshot eyes and stumbled out of the room behind him. He had exited the room and gone to assist Seamus by grabbing the man from behind, wrapping his arm around his neck and constricting him like a snake until he passed out from the lack of air. Releasing the man, Mike collapsed to his knees and began to weep. She couldn't tell if it was sadness or joy, she didn't care; rushing over to him, she knelt before him and looked into his eyes. It was him. It was really him. Tears filled her eyes and her heart felt as if it was about to explode from her chest. She grabbed his frail hand and went to embrace him when he spoke.

'Cardoza...' he said in a debilitated tone. 'The team...' These were the only two other words he could manage before collapsing into Lucy's arms. There was no time to be elated with the return of her colleague, her friend, her lover; Lucy was now stricken with fear that the same was happening with her family, her team.

'Seamus,' she said frantically. 'Call it in.' She hurriedly took out her mobile and selected Krysta's number from the list of contacts. No answer.

20

Claire Davenport

There was no light peeking through the slats of her blind, she noticed, as she slowly opened her eyes at the sound of her alarm. The world was still in darkness, yet it was time to rise; a fact that Claire would never get used to whenever winter reared its head. Carefully slipping a finger out into the morning from under her thick seasonal duvet, she quickly retracted her hand upon realising the difference in temperature between being in and out of bed. *Argh!* The alarm continued, awaiting her touch to silence it. She pulled the soft, heavy cover up over her face as she drew the courage to reach out from the safety of her warm and comfy sleeping place. *Man up Claire.* She contemplated staying put and forgetting the world for the day. Despite the allure of her more than commodious resting place, duty called. A night in her own bed had given her the opportunity to get a decent sleep, which should help her with the day ahead. She spread her legs under the covers, then closed them again, performing star-jump like motions as she lay flat, psyching herself up before tearing the quilt off like a band-aid on a wound and hurriedly putting an end to the repetitive drone emanating from her bedside. Sat on the edge of the bed, barefoot on her bedroom carpet, she pulled the hood of her soft woollen onesie up over her bed-styled hair. A gift from Krysta the Christmas before, her onesie was midnight-blue in colour and was patterned with star constellations, mapped out by shining silver sequins. As she stood up, still adjusting to her woken-upright state, one word came to mind. *Coffee!* Bouncing out of the bedroom and down her stairs, she made her way to the kitchen. Her kitchen was a mixture of slate grey and bright white, with the cupboards and doors coloured white and the walls grey. Her worktops were a sapphire blue-black marble and the majority of her kitchen appliances were silver. To her left stood a large fridge-freezer, and next to it a petite breakfast table with two chairs. To her right sat a kitchen counter with two pull out black stools, the counter separating the cupboards and cooking station from the rest of the room. She placed a pod into her coffee machine and took one of the two mugs that hung from a little, white wooden tree that sat on the back worktop. Once made, grasping the mug with both hands, she breathed in the deeply satisfying aroma of her freshly made beverage and, as it filled her senses, it was confirmed; she was awake.

Thankfully, the drive to H.Q. was quick and easy. A commute-hangover was not what she wanted, and so the decision to go home the night before seemed justified. Upon arrival she set straight to work in the lab. They had been running several tests recently on the unusual blade that they had obtained from Brandt just before Mike was abducted. For some time after Mike's disappearance, the blade had been kept under lock and key. It was presumed that Markovic or the Avunaye would likely trade Mike for it, or perhaps it was simply wishful thinking on the team's behalf. Forged from a mixture of wood and bone, the age of the weapon could not be determined, something that astounded Claire and made her even more eager to unlock its secrets. *Meh, here he comes.* The sound of Malique's voice resonated within the nearby corridor as she sat examining the latest set of test results. He bundled into the lab dressed in his long, white lab coat with a take-away coffee cup in each hand.

'Claire, I've got your coffee!' he said as he hurried over to her, almost spilling the drinks as he went. 'Just the way you like it,' he said smiling, as if he was a child, handing an apple to his teacher. 'With an extra shot of espresso.'

'Oh,' Claire said, intrigued by what he assumed was the way she liked her coffee. 'That's new, but thanks.' she said, taking the cup from him. She had always had her coffee as a caramel latte: a caffeine fix with a little sweetness.

'That's a good one,' he said half chuckling with a somewhat stupid expression on his face. Claire looked at him puzzled. 'Yesterday you said you'd changed how you liked it,' he said almost shrill, as if losing his patience.

'You know I love my caramel latte too much to change, Malique,' Claire said in response, 'I've no idea where this idea came from,; she said holding up the beverage. 'But it's okay, thank you for the thought,' she said, smiling. Malique's eyes widened as if he had just blown a fuse and then with an awkward sigh of exasperation, he turned and wandered off to his own station. *Weird.* Claire shook her head and chuckled slightly.

Eye deep in her work, Claire didn't even notice the rest of the morning disappear – in fact, if it wasn't for Solomon entering the room, she would have never noticed the time. *That explains the tummy gurgles.* The prospect of food entered her mind.

'Solomon,' she said, smiling as he walked into the lab and straight over to her desk. However, the smile was soon stripped from her face as Kyle entered after him but a moment later. Solomon wore his usual work attire, black suit pants and jacket, black tie, black boots and a white shirt. He seemed agitated at first glance; Claire presumed he was tired of being followed around. Kyle had once again pieced together quite the ensemble to wear to work; a three-piece mint green suit made sure he stood out. He wore a gleamingly white shirt underneath with a burgundy tie tucked in under the waistcoat. The pants sat an inch or so above his brown shoes, revealing his naked ankles. 'Agent Johnston,' she muttered. 'To what do I owe the pleasure...?' Solomon raised his hand slightly, pre-empting any sarcasm from Kyle.

'Claire, we're here for an update on this blade,' Solomon said. From his tone she could tell he was in a hurry, but it felt as if he had something else on his mind. 'Krysta and Lucy are at the hospital interviewing the Holmes girl, no doubt they'll be in touch if they need anything. But for now, what have you got for us?'

'More questions,' Claire said quirkily. Truthfully, everything she discovered recently just raised more questions. 'The blade consists of human bone and wood; the two are intertwined and somehow fused together so that they both run from hilt to tip. Despite every attempt to carbon date it the results are all inconclusive.' Solomon drew a puzzled figure whereas Kyle seemed very intrigued as Claire went on. 'Despite being human, the bone shows no signs of cellular breakdown. In fact, if I had to guess, I'd say it is in a constant state of rejuvenation, which is also feeding the wood and preventing it from, well... dying...' Saying it out loud seemed to amaze Claire all over again, as well as her colleagues.

'Claire!' Malique called as he shuffled over to them. 'I have the results. You're not going to believe this.' He was giddy, almost forgetting his true, shy nature as he delivered the news. Malique then realised Solomon's and Kyle's stares and he hurriedly tootled back off to work.

'So, what's Malique found?' Kyle asked impatiently as Claire looked at the findings. She stared at him for a second, trying to convey her displeasure with being hurried by giving him what she considered to be an evil stare. *What did Krysta ever see in you?*

'Okay, so - wow,' she said increasing the already high

level of anticipation in the room. 'They pretty much have a symbiotic relationship,' Claire's own astoundment and continued pauses seemed to frustrate Kyle, though she barely noticed.

'Okay? So?' he said impatiently.

'Solomon,' Claire said, ignoring Kyles presence altogether. 'The two elements of the blade mutually benefit one another. It's as if the wood is providing the cells in the bone with what it needs to regenerate and then in return the bone passes this on to the wood to keep it sustained, and around it goes!' Claire was very excited with the discovery. Taking a moment to gather her thoughts and calm down a little, she explained to her superiors the advancements that could be made in medicines and beyond if they could utilise what was happening within the artefact. Kyle's eyes lit up at the idea of human enhancement, Claire could almost see the dollar signs in his eyes.

'Type up the report, I want it on my desk by tomorrow morning,' Solomon said, seemingly pleased with the results she had achieved. He and Kyle then left the room and Claire's stomach growls hastily returned.

She had a mouth full of chicken burrito when her phone rang. It was Krysta calling, no doubt with an update from the hospital. Claire answered the call with her food still in her mouth and greeted Krysta with several mumbled sounds that could barely be construed as words.

'I'm sorry, Krys, mouth full!' Claire said once she had finally chewed enough to swallow. 'Go ahead, I've got a pen at the ready,' she reached for a stylus to enable her to quickly note down everything Krysta said onto her touch screen table. Krysta relayed the information that Lorelei had provided. 'That girls got some memory,' Claire said, whilst jotting down all the details. It was nice to hear her friends voice, she sounded good, which made Claire smile. 'That's brilliant, Krys, I'll get onto this right away and see what I can dig up,' She felt on edge talking to her colleague, nervous even. *Perhaps it's the knowledge that we share a secret.* Claire thought as she said goodbye to Krysta. Claire had still not been able to discover who the inside-hacker was, the potential mole within the bureau, and it troubled her. *Right, let's get back to work.* She finished off her burrito and began dissecting the intel that Krysta had supplied, creating multiple search algorithms to do the hard work for her. Some of Lorelei's descriptions were great; Claire was quickly able to find information on a house fire in which could possibly be the building where Lorelei said she was gifted to the beast by Markovic. It was a breakthrough, one that might go a long way to working out where else Markovic and the Avunaye had popped up. Fuelled with intrigue and excitement, Claire continued her fact-finding crusade, delving deeper into the web, spreading her reach out across cyberspace.

She was so engrossed in her campaign for answers that she almost missed a call from Lucy. She wanted Claire to investigate a mystery back-packer named Joel that had been visiting the Holmes family. It was a bizarre request, but Claire was a sucker for a mystery and she knew Lucy's gut feelings were rarely wrong. Claire had even once nicknamed Lucy 'The Bloodhound', but only in her head, as she was too shy to say it aloud. Besides, Lucy was not the type of person you wanted to upset with a name that she might take offence to. Initialising yet another search on her mainframe, Claire attempted to continue looking into the information from Krysta, but she was interrupted once again by a returning Solomon. She smiled at Solomon as he entered the room, yet the constant breaks in concentration were starting to grate on her patience. She was beginning to feel a little tense. *Claire, just tell him what he wants to hear and maybe he'll fuck off.*

'I'll make sure that report is on your desk first thing boss,' she said, hoping to answer his question before he asked it, thus shortening his stay.

'That's okay, Claire,' he replied casually, a sign that this visit was for something else. 'Krysta and Lucy been in touch?' he quizzed, taking a seat. *Argh! He's sitting down, not good, this is going to take some time.* Claire tried to smile again to hide her true emotions.

'Yeah,' she replied in a tension filled tone. 'I'm actually neck deep in utilising all the information, got a result already!' She hoped her admittance to being snowed under would appease any further conversation, but luck was not currently with her as he began to talk about how nice it was for all of them to get together at Thanksgiving. He was right, it was nice, Claire had thoroughly enjoyed herself, possibly drinking a little too much wine; but now was not the best time to chat about it.

'It was great to have a break from all the chaos, wasn't it?' Solomon stated. Claire replied with an instant 'yes' hoping that was the final question, but then he began talking about the food and Paul's jokes. He kept talking and talking, with each word prodding the beast within her that just wanted him to stop. She felt as if she was at breaking point, ready to scream at her superior regardless of the consequences. Yet, just as her lips separated and the sounds began to form in her larynx, another voice sounded, saving her from the torment of small talk.

'Claire!' Malique called, his voice a welcome interruption. 'You need to come and see this.' There was a sense of urgency to his call, combined with excitement and what could be interpreted as a hint of fear. Claire and Solomon rose from their perches and made a dart towards the other section of the lab. Passing through a security door, they entered the room where the blade was being kept and studied. The item itself resided in a sealed compartment and attached to it were a multitude of sensors to assist in the study of it and record any findings. It was these sensors, or rather what they were currently finding, that had gotten

Malique all excited and one look at the data told Claire exactly why.

'When did it start?!' she said, almost shrieking with fascination.

'Only a moment ago. I came and got you as soon as it started,' Malique replied, again with a hint of fear to his tone; he was guarded, to which Claire dismissed as another over-reaction, much like the coffee incident. The temperature of the blade was increasing, and as it did so it began to break the sensors, preventing further recordings from being taken.

'We need to move it, Lab Two should do,' Claire stated, realising they would require heavier duty equipment to work out what was happening within the blade. Requesting assistance to help move the artefact to the other laboratory, two more assistants entered the room at Claire's command.

'Keep me informed of what's happening Claire,' Solomon said, looking at the blade, a look of fascination stirred in his eyes and he turned to Claire. 'I've got other matters to attend to, let me know of any changes.' Solomon then backed away a few steps before turning and leaving the room.

As he stepped back through the security door, there was a loud crash. It sounded as if it originated on one of the lower floors, but after the thunderous noise, the vibrations could be felt by all. Claire panickily turned to Solomon, who in turn turned to look at her. He moved to re-enter the room, however, as he attempted to do so, the door between them locked, a light flashed, and the alarm sounded. Solomon banged his palms on the glass in frustration as he looked Claire in the eyes. His usual manful demeanour was lost, and worry materialised within his deep brown eyes. He shouted something to her, but the thickness of the glass prevented her from hearing a thing. She attempted to read his lips and thought she had gotten the gist of his message: 'stay put and I'll go and see what's happening'. *I'm not going to just sit around waiting.* Claire turned to look at Malique and the pair of assistants.

'Malique, keep an eye on the blade,' she said confidently as she headed over to a computer terminal. Normally used solely for research purposes, the terminal wouldn't usually have access to the building's security matrix, but Claire knew exactly how to use it to serve her own purpose. *Need to see what the fuck is going on out there.* The confidence she exhibited to the others that she was trapped with was a façade, inside, she was shaking, trembling with fear.

'Claire, what's going on?' Malique asked, his words quaking as they left his quivering lips. She chose to ignore the question. She wasn't sure herself and she didn't need everyone panicking, especially when she was doing enough of that herself. *Got it!* She had hacked her way into the security camera footage and scanned the images for a sign of what was happening. Suddenly a camera in the stairwell switched off.

'That's not good...' she said aloud by accident, her words grasping the attention of all the others in the room.

'What? What is it?' Malique asked, before rushing around the desk to see for himself. 'W-W-Why are the cameras out?' he asked, his voice mimicking that of a small child.

'I don't know,' Claire answered honestly. She was scanning all the cameras closely, but thus far all she had seen out of place was her own colleagues rushing about.

'People are running about with guns. That... what does that mean?!' Malique asked, again with the annoyingly high and fearful tone.

'I don't know,' Claire snapped, although she could take a guess at what was transpiring. *We're under attack.* Her hand was shaking. Lights flashed on two of the cameras and Claire knew it to be gunfire; whoever was attacking them was moving fast. The second-floor cameras went out, quickly followed by the third and fourth.

'Claire?' Malique asked, but before he could say

anymore, another loud crash sounded and the building shook once again. The other two assistants stood by the blade, speechless, but the expressions on their faces said everything for them. 'Three more floors and they're here Claire. We are safe though... right?' he asked. 'That door and the windows, they're all bulletproof... right?'

Shut up! Malique continued to incessantly ask questions, to which she had no answers. The loud crashes were no doubt security doors being blown open, doors much like the one into this room. Claire didn't need someone constantly talking at her, she needed a second to think. As floor six's cameras went blank, her mind seemed to seize up and she struggled to think coherently. *Try to remember your training, is there another way out of here?* She dialled several numbers on her phone but they all provided a busy signal. *What do I do, what do I do?* She watched the camera windows switch off one by one, without any sign of who was doing it. She grasped at her hair as she tried to purge the fear from her thoughts so that she could concentrate. *Think Claire! Think!* She screamed inside, but then the first camera on this floor turned blank and her thoughts stopped completely.

Stepping away from the screen, she turned to face the entrance into the room. She backed up, moving away from the door until she bumped into the containment unit that housed the blade. Malique stood next to her and the two assistants stood behind them, all of them simply waiting, doing nothing, ceasing any form of movement as they anticipated what was to come next. *It's almost time.* Claire shook her head, confused, but it did not matter; time was up. Her attention was stolen by the figure that now stood at the glass that separated her from the commotion within the building. They were dressed all in black, wearing tactical gear much like the SWAT team that operated out of the headquarters. A dark mask covered their face, a hole for their mouth and a pair for their eyes were the only chinks in their armour. For a moment, Claire could feel her heart stop, only for it to then race as she began to panic. The figure stood still, watching and waiting, their next impending action weighing on Claire's resolve. She wanted to scream at them to just hurry up or go away, but she couldn't muster the words.

A few more moments passed until finally they moved. Raising an arm, they placed something on the glass of the door and then stepped back. As they retreated, Claire realised what it was, and she hurriedly turned and attempted to usher the others to find some cover.

'Get back!' she screamed, shoving Malique and her other colleagues backwards towards the tables behind them. The device detonated; the force it generated pounding on Claire's back as she tried to take cover and sent her flying into her team, knocking them all to the ground. She turned on the floor and tried to clamber backwards away from the enemy that was crossing over the threshold into the lab. One masked intruder stepped over the debris and a second followed. Once in the room, they both stood still. Armed with automatic rifles, they were waiting for something, and then a third and a fourth person entered. It was the fourth to enter that turned out to be the one that they needed to fear, the leader of their group. There were no distinguishing features between the four of them, apart from slight differences in height and build. It was the stockiest of them that walked towards Claire and her team, who cowered against the outskirts of the room. They grabbed Claire by the forearm, their grip biting down hard, pulling her away from Malique and the others into the centre of the lab. One of the assistants shrieked, her scream a cacophonous noise that pierced the ears of all to hear it. The sound offended Claire's captor and they let their grip on her arm go, raised their weapon and put a bullet in her head. As her lifeless body hit the ground, silence filled the room. *Oh my god, oh my god.* Claire's mind rampaged as she knelt shivering alone. Seconds felt like minutes as she resided there, staring at the ground, fearing for her life. Malique was soon dragged beside her and her assistant beside him. Malique was silent, kneeling, unmoving; tears ran steadily down his cheeks.

'Please! Please let us go!' her assistant pleaded as the four intruders stood unflinching before them. *What are they waiting for?* Claire looked up, scanning their masked faces, searching their seemingly emotionless eyes.

'Who is in charge?' the larger of the four asked. He had an accent, maybe European or Hispanic, Claire couldn't quite decide. '*Who* is in charge?' he asked again sternly, his question this time was directed at the assistant whom remained quiet, unsure of what to do. His inaction displeased the attacker and he swiftly raised his weapon and shot the man in the head. The sound of gunfire rippled through Claire's head, echoing again and again. She closed her eyes so tightly that they ached, hoping that when she reopened them it would all be over. *Claire, it's almost time.*

'Who is in charge?' The man asked of Malique this time. His tone was unchanged, killing the lab assistant meant nothing. Claire knelt still, waiting for Malique to say her name, hoping he would so that maybe he would survive. 'Who is in charge?!' he said again, a hint of impatience creeping into what had been such an inexpressive voice. His question received no answer and Claire could hear him raise his gun once more.

'Me!' she shouted without any more thought. 'I am.' She opened her now tearful eyes to see Malique's face become awash with relief. Her honesty was met by two of the other three stepping forward and grabbing her, one clutching her arm and the other grasping a handful of her hair. The apparent leader struck Malique across the face with the butt of his weapon and then diverted his attention to Claire.

'Cardoza? You know this name?' he said, to which she responded with a nod. *These must be Kryln's men.* 'He wants the abort codes for your security network.' He had asked for something that Claire could never give. She knew that the codes would enable them to walk out of here, and worse, it would give them access to the entire F.B.I. mainframe in the process. She bit her tongue. 'The codes?' he said, taking a knife from his belt and pressing it against her cheek; he applied a little pressure, just enough to draw blood.

'Stop! Please!' she yelled, afraid. 'I...'

'THE CODES?!' he screamed at her ferociously, saliva hitting her in the face. Claire felt paralysed.

'I...' she said trembling; but as she looked into his eyes, she caught a glimmer of her own reflection, a reflection of someone she almost didn't recognise. 'I... I would appreciate it, if you did not spit at me,' the words left her lips uncontrollably, with a confidence that was not hers. *Sit back Claire, I'll take care of this.* The voice was there again, but this time it was as if she had lost control of her own body.

With her free arm, Claire forced her knife wielding attacker backwards and grabbed the one that had held of her hair.

'We like our hair,' she said, or the voice said, Claire wasn't sure which. But with one rapid movement, she hurled the two masked assailants across the lab, throwing them against the walls as if they weighed nothing. The third aggressor raised their weapon but, before they could shoot, Claire flew towards them and within a blink of an eye, she disarmed them, breaking both of their wrists and grasping them by the throat. She lifted them up off the floor as high as she could before flinging them against one of the windows, knocking them out cold. The question master lunged at her with his blade again and again, but she moved unnaturally fast, avoiding his attacks. The voice inside laughed as she made Claire toy with him. *Stop it!* Claire screamed inside her head and suddenly she stopped. She threw a single punch and hit the man in his chest, sending him crashing through the open doorway and onto the floor beyond. Claire could feel the smile on her face although it was not her own. She felt the enjoyment, the feeling of release but could not understand what was happening. She looked at Malique who had managed to scuttle away and under a desk during the commotion, the fear in his eyes returned from when he had been at gun point, only now it was directed towards her. *Malique it's me, Claire!* She shouted within, but he could not hear her.

'My name is...'

'Carmen!' a voice boomed from outside the room. Broken debris crunched under the weight of his footsteps as he stooped to fit through the entrance. 'So, this is where you've been hiding, sister,' he said, looking down on her with his red-hot fiery stare. He wore a charcoal grey long sleeved ribbed jumper and black pants. His top was stained in places with dark, rustic, red-brown stains of blood. His muscles were taught and his hands a glow as he stepped toward her. Claire screamed within, demanding control of herself once more, wanting to flee from the beast before her, yet she remained still.

'A moratorium from the violence, brother?' she said in a deprecative tone. She stepped to one side, placing herself between Brandt and the blade. *He's after the blade!* Claire shouted inside, receiving but a smile from the current controller of her body.

'Interesting choice, this vessel of yours,' Brandt said looking her up and down. 'She'll break easily,' he said with a wicked smile. *Enough!* Claire yelled with all her might and as she did, she could feel her fingers again. Her legs, her toes, her body. Her sudden control unbalanced her however, and taking advantage of this, Brandt swatted Claire out of his path with a single movement of his arm. Then, smashing its containment, he reached in and grasped the blade.

'You kept it warm for me,' he grinned, before turning and walking out of the room, whistling as he went. Claire and Malique cowered on the floor. Claire looked to her colleague full of fear and remorse. She then looked at her own hands, scared and confused. *See you again sweetie.* The voice within her faded, causing her to jump and then begin to weep uncontrollably. Malique, seemingly losing the fear he showed towards her before, etched closer and wrapped an arm around her. His embrace comforted her a little. She looked around at the destruction and as she did, she saw Kyle standing at one of the windows looking in. He was looking straight at her, expressionless. He did not look scared or relieved, but there was a glint of something there that left Claire feeling very unnerved.

21

Krysta Rose-Anderson

'Poor girl has been through hell,' she said to Lucy as she looked back through the window into Lorelei's room. She and Lucy had questioned the girl with a few but specific questions that had provided them with a lot of information to move forward with. Krysta had noted down everything that Lorelei had to say, hoping Claire would be able to utilise some, if not all of it, into helping the case. Pulling out her phone she explained to her friend that she was going to call Claire to pass on the information, however, Lucy seemed side-tracked, as if her attention was elsewhere. *It's a good job I made the notes.* Krysta thought to herself as she dialled Claire's direct number. Answering the call with a mouth full of food, Claire seemed to be in high spirits; her bubbly and quirky personality shining through as bright as ever, but as Krysta passed on all the information she and Lucy had gathered, there was a definite awkwardness to their conversation. The knowledge of a mole or double agent within the bureau had put a little strain on their relationship recently; it was a huge secret, a burden that they had both struggled to bare.

After hanging up on Claire, Krysta turned her attention back to Lucy. Their friendship had also been turbulent of late, Krysta knew that Mike's continued absence troubled Lucy, as it did the entire team, but there was something more, something that Lucy felt she couldn't - or simply didn't want to - share with her. Krysta sometimes wondered if Lucy had an issue with Jake; she had not been in a relationship for some time, at least as far as Krysta was aware, and perhaps the subject was a sensitive one. Krysta wanted nothing more than for things to return to how they were before. She even contemplated playing matchmaker for her friend, insinuating that there might be something between Lucy and Paul as they laughed about the recent Thanksgiving antics. The suggestion, however, appeared to make her uncomfortable as she deflected the topic of conversation back onto Krysta. Trying to contain her excitement, Krysta explained that she was seeing Jake this evening; they had arranged for him to stay for the evening and to get breakfast in the morning, a new step in their relationship that had Krysta emotionally flying above the clouds. Laughing in response to Lucy's admittance to having little or no restraint when it came to the opposite sex, their conversation was timely cut off by the arrival of the deputy director of the C.I.A.

He stood confidently in his blue suit pants and white shirt; a black overcoat slung over his forearm to help brave the cold winter weather outside. Zane's arrival here unnerved Krysta a little. Ever since she had bumped into him at the café with Solomon something hadn't felt right; Solomon had made his feelings towards the guy clear, which had probably contributed to Krysta's unease around him. Krysta subtly questioned his being there, a question this silver-tongued operative had no trouble answering, but it was more to do with his mannerisms that unnerved her further. He spoke to Krysta but did not break his gaze on Lucy, and what was more, Lucy appeared interested. *Not quite what I had in mind Luce.* She tried to measure the chemistry between them.

'Actually, hon, I think I'm gonna stay for a bit,' Lucy said in response to Krysta's attempt to get them both out of there. She was surprised by Lucy's answer, considering how distracted she'd seemed all day. Thankfully, Zane decided it was time for him to leave as well as Krysta said her goodbyes to her friend, one less thing for Krysta to worry about, the thought of these two hitting it off made her skin crawl.

'Let me walk you out,' Zane said, walking backwards beside her as she made her way towards the exit. 'Don't want the elevator?' he said as she continued to walk past the confined metal boxes in search of the stairs. Part of her hoped he'd take it himself regardless, but instead he continued to walk with her as she made her way down towards the ground floor. 'The silent type is not what I would have put you down for,' he said, breaking the silence as they descended the steps. Krysta merely smiled at him and carried on walking. 'Stuck up, narrow minded, slightly blind to the obvious, but shy? Nah,' he chuckled as he insulted her, and it proved to be the last straw for Krysta as she halted her march.

'What?!' she exclaimed, stopping in her tracks and turning to face him. 'Where do you get off?' she said, but before she could say anymore, he shh'd her. *Asshole!*

'I don't like awkward silences,' he grinned whilst holding up his hands as if to surrender. 'You seem to have a problem with me...' He stared her directly in the eyes, unblinkingly. *Where do I begin?* Every action he made seemed to infuriate her further.

'Stuck up? You don't even...' Yet again he interrupted her.

'And I'll never get to know you if you don't speak, now will I? At least now I know you have some fire in you,' he laughed again, the sound grating on her nerves. 'Let me guess... Solomon told you I'm not to be trusted so you figure you have me all worked out?' he began to seem less confident in himself as he tried to answer his own questions. 'Our line of work...' he crossed his arms, a stance in which Krysta recognised as a way to protect himself as he spoke. 'Sometimes you have to switch off, and sometimes it's hard to switch back on.' As he offered an excuse for what he assumed Solomon had said, Krysta could sense that he was feeling vulnerable right now.

'I...' Krysta said awkwardly as she stood searching for the right words.

'Apology accepted,' he said, smiling again. His smile riled her; an apology wasn't even close to her lips. She couldn't believe how self-assured and cheeky he was. Mystified by the array of mixed emotions and ever-changing opinion she had of him, Krysta was at a loss for actions or words. 'Well, Special Agent Rose-Anderson, I would offer you a lift in my very nice car, but I imagine you'd refuse,' Zane said, donning his overcoat. 'So, I'm going to leave you now and head for the car park, have a lovely evening and let Solomon know I'll be popping by the office soon.' He smiled, but his mannerisms confused her a little. She couldn't tell whether he was being sarcastic or genuine for a change. He had been such a prick but then appeared honest, sensitive and open. *Argh!*' She waved a half-hearted goodbye. Generally, she was good at reading people, but this guy perplexed her completely.

It was cold out and the breeze carried an icy touch that bit harshly at her skin. Krysta quickly zipped up her jacket and hailed a taxi. As the driver started off, she took out her phone and messaged Jake. *'Fancy cooking or take out? X'* the message was read and it was almost instantly replied to with *'I'll cook, if you can grab some...'* the words were followed by emoji's for some spaghetti or pasta of some sort, tomatoes and peppers. The tomatoes had little goofy faces that made her laugh. *Tonight will be perfect.* She sat back in her seat and stared out of the window, watching the city pass by. She instructed the taxi driver to redirect to a nearby food market so that she could obtain the ingredients for the perfect meal.

She received a few mixed looks as she zipped through the market grabbing what she needed, her F.B.I. jacket turning a few heads. Krysta couldn't remember the last time she had smiled so much at passing strangers. As she reached the checkout with a basket full of foods, she recalled the saying that *'you shouldn't shop whilst hungry'* and smiled at the mixture of goodies she had plucked from the shelves almost obliviously. Having exchanged pleasantries with Mrs Tchaikovsky, an elderly woman that lived on the ground floor of her apartment building, she exited the market and got into another taxi to head home.

Stood in the glow of a nearby streetlight, one hand holding her bag of groceries, the other fighting off the evening's numbingly cold embrace, she fumbled with her keys until she eventually grasped the right one and slid it into the lock. She was greeted by a cherry and peony perfume as she entered the foyer and bounded up what usually felt like arduous sets of stairs, until she reached her floor. Today, she was excited to return home.

Successfully locating the right key and navigating it to the lock on her door, she bundled into the apartment and dumped the groceries on the countertop. *Right, one hour.* She loosened the laces on her boots and kicked them off, finding her way to the sofa at the same time. She scanned the apartment for things to do before his arrival. *Washing up to go away, clutter to clear up.* Then it dawned on her. *Window!* Getting up from her seat, she realised that the window was fully closed, leaving no way for her frequent feline visitor to pop in. Yet, before she managed to open it, she saw the state her bedroom was in and hurriedly rushed over to it to collect all the dirty washing that lined the floor, covered her bed and for some reason, hung from her window blind. She took off her jacket and placed her badge and sidearm in her bedside draw. *The mirror is not kind.* She caught a glance of what she saw as a tired, bedraggled version of herself.

'I need to clean myself up, let alone the house,' she said out loud, pulling at her cheeks as she looked in the mirror. The final straw was smelling her own armpit, this causing her to head straight for the bathroom, undressing and flinging items of clothing onto the floor as she went. She brushed her teeth whilst quickly running a brush through her hair, as there was not enough time to wash it, she surmised. Spitting out the contents of her mouth and ditching the brush, she turned on the shower, ensuring it was warm for her when she was ready to jump in.

The hot water streamed blissfully over her naked skin and the delightful scents of orange, berries and tea perfumed the room as she washed away the days stresses and allowed herself to begin to unwind. Having little time to spare for pampering herself she hurriedly shaved her arm pits and legs in the shower, resting her feet up against the glass of the door one at a time as she prepared for the evening ahead.

Dried and standing by her bed, dressed in a black laced bra and French knickers, the question of *'what to wear?'* reared its head; a question that seemed to become more difficult to answer the longer she stood looking at her options. *Argh!* She struggled to decide, yet the situation was unthinkably made worse by a knock at the door.

'Shit!' she said, realising the time. 'One second Jake!' she called, grabbing her black cotton bed robe. Donning the garment, she closed the doors to her bedroom, concealing the mess, and skipped to the door. 'You're early,' she said with a beaming smile as she opened the door.

She attempted to slam the door shut, but they were too quick. One of them kicked the door hard, forcing it back open and exposing the entrance to her home to all of them. Krysta stumbled backwards, turning, trying to sprint across to her bedroom; her gun was in the draw, waiting, but as she moved, an arm wrapped around her waist and hurled her backwards. She crashed against the bookcase and lost her footing, falling onto her knees and knocking the nearby table over, smashing the plant pot that had resided on it. *Two of them, no three.* She tried to think how many she had seen in the hallway. They were dressed in black, wearing some sort of body armour. Their faces were covered by black ski masks. The one that had caught her was carrying a sidearm and a large blade held in a holder on their belt. Krysta darted forwards, getting to her feet; she pushed him backwards, forcing him to hit the sofa behind him, tumbling over it. She had gained a second. Quickly moving towards the kitchen, her way was blocked by a second figure. They underestimated her will to survive. She hit low and hard, and then hit high. Again, she hit him in the face, so hard she could almost map out his facial features in her mind's eye. He stumbled on the step up to the raised kitchen flooring, falling to the floor, and as he did the third one moved towards her from the doorway. Leaping onto one of the stools, Krysta slid across the counter and reached for a kitchen knife. As she turned to face the third assailant, her bag of groceries came hurtling through the air towards her, swiftly followed by a man. He led with his knife wielding arm, the razor-sharp steel narrowly missing her as she backed up against the kitchen sink to dodge his attack. Cherry tomatoes scattered across the floor and a red pepper burst under the attacker's foot as he made another advance. She managed to bat away his leading hand and sunk her small kitchen knife into his upper thigh, thrusting her shoulder into his chest to push him back.

'AHH!!' he screamed, teeth bared. 'Bitch!!' He lunged forward, grabbed her forearm and with his free hand, he batted her across her face, forcing her to stumble to the side and crash into the kitchen counter. It stung. The pain was like a shockwave that rippled through her skin, her skull, her teeth.

'AHH!!' she screamed back at him, the animal within coming to life. She spun back around and kicked out with the flat of her foot, hitting the hilt of the kitchen knife, sinking it further into his leg and causing him an immense amount of pain. This time he attempted to stab her in retaliation but, as he tried, Krysta quickly disarmed him.

Prying the weapon from his grasp, she thrust it down below his chin, just above his vest, into his flesh. His final action was to shove her forcefully against the counter before dropping to his knees, gurgling in his own blood.

Her spine impacted against the immovable counter as she crashed against it once more. *Two left.* Some blood dripped from her lip. As she turned to face the second, a wire noose was quickly strung, lassoed around her neck, and she was pulled backwards. He pulled quickly from the other side of the counter and with such force he took her breath away and a panic set in. She kicked out at the adjacent cupboards trying to land a foot on something she could use to launch herself up onto the counter and relieve some of the pressure on her throat. She clawed at the cable as it constricted and she tried to reach behind her to maybe grab her attackers' hands, arms, anything, but he avoided her masterfully. *Now!* Her insides screamed as the second man moved to hold her still. She took the opportunity to spring up off one leg and thrust the foot of her other into his body in order to throw herself backwards across the counter and into the one strangling her. They crashed to the floor with a bang, but thankfully the hold of the cable loosened, and she was able to gasp for air. As she wrestled against the grasp of the man now lying under her, her other assailant made his way around the island and was coming for her. She hurriedly clutched at the man's sidearm beneath her and pulled the trigger in the hope that the safety was off. The bang was a welcome sound but caused the man below her to roll her off him fiercely as the bullet shredded through his calf. Taking the cable from around her bloody and aching neck, she threw it to one side and clambered on her hands and knees around one of the sofas, heading for the coffee table. She received a swift kick in the ass, and, falling forward, she hit her face on the corner of the table, cutting her cheek and sending a reverberating pounding through her head.

'What the fuck is going on here?!' a strong voice

sounded from the entrance to the apartment. Krysta couldn't quite see who it was as she lay on the floor looking up at the man who had kicked her. He had turned to look at whoever had just entered, paying Krysta no further mind. 'Get in, kill the bitch, get out!' the voice said. He had a thick accent, possibly Spanish as far as she could tell, but who was he? 'Three of you... fucking hell you useless cunts!' he exclaimed angrily at the fact that Krysta was still breathing. She needed to act fast, but she struggled to get moving as she attempted to shuffle back away from her attacker. 'There you are,' he said, standing over her. He was huge. A towering man with a shaven head. He had a tattoo of a cobra that ran down his left cheek, continuing down his neck and under the collar of his top. He had dark skin and menace in his eyes. He wore a dark green jumper that clung tightly to his enormous figure and a pair of camo-patterned pants. 'Markovic sends his regards,' he said with a sickening smile before he reached out with his huge bear like paws. Krysta tried to fight him off but he had so much strength that he easily grabbed her by the arm and by her thigh, picked her up and threw her against the doors that separated her bedroom from the rest of the place. Her body smashed through them as if they were made from paper and she crash landed on the bed.

Dazed, it took her a few moments to realise where she was, how close she was to her gun, her phone. She lay on the bed, her legs laid bare, small cuts across her thighs from the splintered doors. Her head pounded and the drumming intensified as he stepped closer. Her outstretched hand hit the top of the drawers, her fingers feeling their way across its surface and over its lip. She grasped the handle of the top drawer and pulled it open, only for the bear of a man to grab her wrist and throw her hand away.

'No!' she screamed as he plucked the gun from the drawer. He laughed as he taunted her with it before throwing it aside.

'You won't be needing any form of protection tonight miss,' he guffawed and waved over the two masked men from the other room. She knew what he meant and the thought sickened her as she tried to cover as much of her naked skin as possible. She scrambled up the bed, hugging the headboard, grasping it tightly as if it provided some form of security, of protection. Her heart pounded fiercely beneath her chest and her lungs began to ache as her breathing raced uncontrollably. She was torn between fighting against her body's state of panic and fighting against those who meant to cause her harm: she was overcome with an undeniable state of fear. 'She's all yours boys,' he said before striking her hard across the face. His huge hand sent a bout of pain like an arrow through her cheek to the opposite temple. *No, no, no!* She felt the first touch on her ankle. *Please no!* She tried to move, but the world was clouded in pain and the fear of what was about to happen constricted her, pinning her down, as if gravity itself had now become her enemy. She could feel their eyes on her and almost hear their sick, perverted thoughts.

'No,' she whimpered as she tried to lash out at one that had grabbed her knee. He caught her hand and squeezed it hard, pushing it down against the mattress whilst he pulled at her leg, attempting to separate it from its twin. She felt the mattress move as the second masked man climbed onto it and grasped her other leg; tensing her leg muscles as hard as she could to keep them together; the strain pained her. She tried to lash out again with her free hand, thrashing as much as she could, but they were too strong. Blood ran from her lip and cheek whilst tears streamed from her eyes.

'Hold up boys, what the fuck is that?' Cardoza said moving towards the living room; something had caught his attention. The men halted, much to her relief, but they did not let go and she knew that they would continue from where they were as soon as he gave them the opportunity. She tried to take advantage of their pause, but they did not release her, their grips did not wane. 'Ha!' he laughed. Krysta wanted to see what he might be looking at, but the fear inside fought against her decision to open her eyes fully, for she would see them looking down on her. 'This little fucker is going nuts, think he wants in on the action?' He laughed again and then Krysta could hear it. Scratching. The sound of small paws clawing at the windowpane.

'No... please...' she said, hoping to be released, hoping they wouldn't hurt her friend, begging for a miracle.

'Let's put this little guy out of his - ' Before Cardoza could finish his sentence, there was a loud crash as the window smashed. 'Well fuck me,' he said with a tone of disbelief. The men were unsettled, their grips loosening. Whatever it was, Krysta could only pray it was here to save her. 'I've heard all about you, señor,' Cardoza said in a cock-sure manner. 'All bark and no bite as long as we don't attack you.' He sounded confident. Krysta fought against the fear to open an eye. Her heart pounded harshly as she saw the two men on her bed waiting patiently to rape her; she saw Cardoza stood beside her sofa, but the figure beyond him was blurred, a shadow.

'Please stop.' She knew that voice. He asked them calmly: it was Adam. More tears fell from her eyes, some of hope and relief as someone was here to help her, to save her.

'Let me think... *fuck you*,' Kryln said before stepping to one side, allowing Krysta to see Adam clearly. 'Darlin', this mother fucker wants the boys to stop, but I'm afraid I can't ask them to do that. See, they're so excited. I mean, fucking look at you, my cock's fucking solid at the thought, fuck knows what theirs are like!' He looked at her and then looked at Adam as he stood there unmoving. 'Hell, I'd even bet that Adam here wouldn't mind watching the show, seeing as the cunt is unable to intervene n' all.' Cardoza's smile turned her stomach, it was as sickening as the image before her, with these creeps touching her. She looked at Adam in distress, trying to beg for his help with her thoughts, hoping he'd hear them. Adam stood, fists clenched, his eyes fixated on her; ever green, they shone brighter and brighter.

'Please... Stop,' Adam asked again, this time struggling to speak as he gritted his teeth. She could see his hands shaking as he struggled to fight his own nature.

'No,' Cardoza replied plainly before walking past Adam towards the exit. 'I got places to be, but, boys! Give Adam here a good show.' He then left, taking with him any sense of hope she might have had as she looked at Adam who was remaining still. The two men returned their full attention to her, taring open her robe and spreading her legs, hurting her hips in the process. One of them rested his knee on top of hers and leaned over to grab both of her wrists; allowing his comrade to let go and begin undoing his belt. *NO!* She screamed inside, resigning to the idea that it was pointless doing it aloud. *Adam...* Her eyes ran dry, the tear ducts seemingly empty. He pushed down hard on her thighs as he moved into position. She wriggled and writhed, attempting to break free of their grasp before they could take her, but her struggle only encouraged them more.

'I said stop,' Adam said once more, yet this time his voice was different, it was wrathful. She could no longer feel their disgusting touch on her skin, but she refused to open her eyes as she heard the screams. She had never heard such a combination of terror and pain, and despite the sound indicating her safety, it frightened her to her core.

22

Claire Davenport

Yesterday. The day haunted her like a bad dream, one that had awoke something inside of her, something she didn't understand. Yet, like the worst of dreams, she was struggling to piece together what was real, what had actually happened, and which parts her mind had made up to fill in the blanks. One thing was for sure. The unsettling feeling of strength, of power, lingered in her hands, leaving her anxious and afraid; a fear of if what she recalled, what she felt, was real. Fearful that her voice would again return. She stood in the elevator, neither travelling up nor down. She was mesmerised by her own reflection captured by the metal panel that surrounded the controls. The face staring back at her was her own, yet she searched it for any sign, any irregularity that might indicate that it wasn't truly her after all.

'Going up?' a gentle voice asked. An elderly man had joined her in the elevator. His question snapped her out of her current trance and made her jump. She was still very much on edge since the attack and had thus far eluded contact with other people. 'I'm sorry if I scared you,' he said, reacting to her jitteriness. 'I should know better than to make people jump,' he chuckled. 'Doc says my own heart might give out at any minute. He smiled a kind smile and waited patiently for her response. 'Hey, miss, I aint getting any younger,' he quipped after giving up on waiting for Claire to reply. His mild humour seemed to do the trick, however, as she began to feel more at ease.

'Sorry, I'm... I'm going up, yes. Visiting some friends,' she said, smiling back at him and leaning in to press the button for the floor she needed. As the elevator reached her floor and the doors opened, the old man bid her farewell. Yet Claire's response of: 'we hope everything goes well for you," startled her. If fear was a blade, it had struck her directly in the chest. Panicking, she looked down to each end of the hall for what she needed. *Doors, walls, no, no.* She looked erratically at her surroundings. *Window!* She rushed to a nearby room, heading straight to the nearest window. Staring closely at the reflective surface, she did not notice the puzzled faces on the inside of the room gawking back at her. She saw the pair of wayfarer-style glasses perched upon her face and a pair of hazel coloured eyes that housed a million and one questions, but currently not one answer. *Get a grip Claire.* Letting out a large sigh, she straightened her specs and went back out into the hall to look for Mike's room. She had dressed comfortably, wearing a pair of queen pink coloured running shoes, dark grey jogging bottoms and beneath her thick black fur lined gilet she had a grey hoodie, two vest tops and a long-sleeved t-shirt to keep her warm. Her wavy brown hair was down and she had neglected to apply any make-up, hoping that she would feel more like herself without it.

'Oh my god,' she said, the words almost sticking in her throat as she fought off the urge to begin blubbering as she laid eyes on Mike. He was alive, a fact that she still struggled to believe even now as she looked upon him. A lot thinner and paler than she remembered him, Mike lay in the bed, connected to machines and drips, all aiding in his recovery. His eyes were closed, his beard untidy and he was cut, bruised and broken, but the squiggly line on the ECG stood out to her, assuring her that her friend had beaten the odds.

Beside him sat Lucy. She looked at Claire as she entered and smiled a smile that Claire had not seen for some time, one full of hope and relief, one full of joy.

'Hey,' Claire said softly as she walked towards the bed. In response, Lucy jumped up out of her seat and rushed over to her, embracing her tightly as if to check that she was really there.

'Hon, you have no idea how relieved I am to see you! I heard about what happened at the office.' Claire was happy to see her colleague safe and sound, she too had been through a traumatic ordeal.

'What, that?... I hear you took on an entire hit squad, solo. Some G.I. Jane shit, ha!' Claire said, full of praise for Lucy's heroics.

'It wasn't quite like that, I had help,' Lucy admitted, looking back at Mike.

'So I hear,' Claire responded. 'And how did Seamus get caught up in all this?' she questioned, before stating how fortunate it was that Mike turned up when he did.

'Claire, I believe...' Lucy paused for a moment. 'I think Seamus was a target too.' She expressed a worried look before turning to sit back down. Lucy went on to explain how she didn't believe that Cardoza would send four men just to eliminate a barely mobile girl in a hospital bed. Judging by the fact that the office and Krysta's apartment were both attacked as well, she assumed that she was a target too, but still, she felt four men seemed excessive. She was adamant that they must have known Seamus was here also. His constant presence in the case had earned him a place on Markovic's hit list.

Lucy looked as if she had spent the night here; her clothes were dirty and looked as if they'd been slept in. It was unsurprising really, seeing as Mike was here along with Krysta, who too had spent the night in hospital after her ordeal. Lucy had no one to go home to, so she no doubt felt safer staying close to her colleagues. As Claire looked at

Mike, the nickname 'Muscles' was lost on him after six months in hell, but she looked forward to hearing his voice again, providing some witty comment or hilarious joke. The thought made her smile.

'Have you seen Krys yet?' Lucy asked. She was sat attentively at the bed side, much like a loved one would. *Could it be?* Claire noticed subtle mannerisms that Lucy was displaying towards their colleague.

'Erm...' Claire tried to shake away her investigative thoughts for a moment and answer the question. 'Just about to head there now - now that I've seen you two are on the mend.' Claire was glad to be moving on, she was getting carried away with her thoughts.

'Great, I think Jake has left now, so she'll be grateful of the company. I popped in on her earlier this morning. She's... okay, I guess, but what can we expect.' Lucy was sincere as she spoke of her best friend, yet she seemed to cling desperately to the bed beside her.

'Glad you're okay Luce. I'll catch you later,' Claire said, edging backwards out of the room. *Is there something between those two?* Claire stopped in the hallway and closed her eyes. *It's just my imagination.*

Considering Krysta was going to be allowed home today, and that she had only spent half the night here, Claire was in awe of how many bouquets of flowers attempted to brighten her room. An array of different coloured tulips, lilies and roses sat atop every available surface, their scents perfuming the air, laying waste to the standard clinical smell that lurked the halls beyond. She found Krysta lying in her bed; her legs were covered by the sheets, but Claire could tell that she was curled up in the foetal position. Her hair was flat and lifeless and her skin was missing its usual glow. Her attackers hadn't gotten what they wanted, but Claire could tell that they had taken something from Krysta. '*It's fear,*' the voice sounded, causing Claire to momentarily loose her smile. '*That's what you can smell, beyond the flowers.*' Claire tried to ignore the inner chatter and decided to walk over to her friend.

'Krys?' she said, displaying her best sympathetic smile. Her once-lifeless colleague was revived at the sound of her voice.

'Claire!' Krysta exclaimed, hurriedly sitting up in bed and stretching out her arms, calling for a hug. Her face was tired, bruised and cut, but she had a familiar warmth in her eyes that reassured Claire that her friend was still in there. Like a child, Claire leapt up onto the bed beside her and wrapped her arms around her. 'I'm so glad you're okay,' Krysta said, squeezing her tightly. There was a tremor in her voice: she was still on edge.

'Me?' Claire said in response. 'All I had to deal with was a few angry bastards shouting at me. It's you Krys, what you had to go through...' Claire loosened her embrace so that she could look her friend in the eyes. 'We're so glad you are okay, after... you know'. The subject of attempted rape was not one that Claire wanted to bring up and she imagined Krysta would rather not discuss it either. She stroked her friends cut cheek. 'Is it gonna scar?' she said sorrowfully, to which Krysta shook her head. 'Good, I'm glad,' Claire responded with a grin. 'No nicknames like scar face or Harry Potter required then!' Thankfully, Krysta chuckled at her ramblings and then the pair hugged one another once more.

'Claire, there's something I need to tell you,' Krysta said, slowly letting go of her. It wasn't quite fear that Claire could hear in her voice, it was something else, but she couldn't quite put her finger on it. As Krysta looked Claire in the eyes once more there was despair in her expression. Claire looked at her, silently asking what it was that plagued her so. 'I told everyone I didn't know what happened to the two guys in...' Krysta averted her gaze for a moment, looking noticeably uncomfortable, taking a deep breath in before continuing. 'In my room...' There was a quiver to her voice. Claire placed a reassuring hand on her friend's shoulder and simply nodded to acknowledge she knew what Krysta was speaking of. When the response team had finally reached Krysta, she was trembling in Jake's arms; he had arrived a while after the attack and tried to comfort her as best he could. The two attackers in her bedroom, the ones that had attempted to rape her, their corpses were indistinguishable. Whatever had happened to them, it appeared at first glance, according to initial reports, that they had been torn apart, every extremity ripped asunder. 'Claire,' she said calmly. 'It was Adam.' Her words seemed to hit Claire like a hard punch to the chest, almost knocking the wind out of her, causing her to gasp audibly. She couldn't understand it, why she was feeling what she was, but her confusion soon turned to fear as the once absent feeling of strength started to trickle back into her veins.

'Adam?' she asked in a squeaky tone. 'You sure?' Quickly realising that she was questioning her friend, Claire quickly added, 'Of course you're sure, I mean, he saved you,' she gave a half-hearted smile. Krysta, however, did not smile in return. In fact, she seemed even more worried.

'I didn't see what he did, I only heard the screams...' she confessed, tears forming in her eyes as she recalled the sounds. 'After, he... he apologised.' Claire looked at her puzzled. 'He said he was sorry, because it would now only get worse.' Her face screwed up and a couple droplets fell from the corner of her eyes and slid down her cheeks. Claire took the initiative and quickly embraced her again, holding tighter than ever. She closed her eyes and breathed in the smell of her friend, and as she did, something stirred deep within that confused her. It was like the voice in her head, the feeling was there, inside, but it felt foreign. Her skin tingled and she felt her heart hasten. A warmness quivered between her thighs that made Claire jump off the bed. Krysta stared at her puzzled, and the voice in her head simply laughed at her reaction. Claire shook her head in disbelief and tried to fasten up her already fastened gilet zip.

'Hon? You okay?' Krysta asked. *Am I? Am I?!* Claire took a deep breath. She raised a hand to steady herself as she prepared to answer Krysta's question.

'Yes, yes. I erm, I need to get back to the office actually... 'cus... 'cus the mess, lots of work to do, reports and stuff...' Her words petered off as she tried to work out what was going on inside of her. She gave Krysta a kiss on her forehead. 'We'll see you later yeah?' she said, trying to hide her anxiety.

'We?' Krysta asked, half accepting her friends exit. Claire hadn't even realised that she'd said 'we' and panicked.

'I...' she said smiling. 'Or we, if someone else - someone real - came with me, also, we, me and them, ha!' She could feel her body growing more and more awkwardly tense until she turned and quickly took her leave. Confused, Claire left the room and hurried down the hall, clumsily bumping into people as she sought the exit.

Upon arriving back at the office, she avoided everyone and made her way straight to the locker room. *Breathe Claire, breathe.* She looked into a mirror above one of the sinks. She placed one hand either side of the basin and stared into the reflective surface with intent.

'I am Claire,' she said, trying to steady her breathing. The journey from the hospital had been horrendous; traffic was heavy, meaning she had had plenty of time to think and to listen. Afraid she was going crazy or having a breakdown, she was desperate to rationalize what was happening to her. She took another deep breath and splashed her face with some cold water. 'I am...' She wanted to say her name but there was something holding the word back, as if a gate had been closed. 'I...' she said, her once flat palms slowly curling up into fists, pressing down on the hard surface either side of the sink. 'I am...' she tried again and cried out in frustration as she struggled to finish the simple sentence. 'Argh!' she exclaimed, pressing down harder with her fists. 'I am...' she strained, her face almost changing colour as she tried to force the words out of herself. 'CARMEN!'

'*Finally,*' the voice inside her said. Claire frantically looked around the room, looking everywhere for the source of the voice. '*I'm not out there, Claire-bear, look in the mirror,*' it said the words so calmly and sternly. Desperate to find out what the fuck was happening to her, Claire turned back to the mirror, slamming her fists down and fracturing the hard granite surface.

'What's going on?' she asked angrily of her own reflection, only to then look at herself and fear the worst. 'I'm going insane,' she said with a whimper.

'*Claire, shut the fuck up,*' the voice said, it was now irritated, which only made Claire feel even more overwhelmed.

'Oh... my god,' she said, starting to pace up and down the room. 'Not only am I hearing voices, but they're being dicks to me! Fantastic!' She briefly contemplated the idea of post-traumatic stress, then low self-esteem. Nothing seemed to make sense.

'*Think Claire, think,*' said the voice. '*My name is Carmen,*' the voice was so clear now, not like a whisper, more like someone was standing next to her, talking to her. Claire struggled to fight against it, part of her wanted to listen. '*Claire-bear, do what you do best, I'll be waiting.*' Finally, there was silence within her head and Claire looked at the damage she had caused in incredulity.

'Do what I do best?' Claire said, clearing the clutter from off one of her computer screens within her sanctuary. There were a number of people moving in and out of the room as she typed frantically; the investigative teams were still gathering evidence and construction workers were formulating plans for the work that needed to be done to repair the building. Every now and then Claire would hear someone speak and she'd look up to check that it wasn't just another voice in her head. 'Do what I do best...' she repeated aloud as she scoured through information about schizophrenia and dissociative identity disorders.

'*Claire, I said what you do best... you're not crazy and I am very real,*' the voice said, but Claire was still not sure about what it was hinting at. Claire continued looking at medical journals until suddenly, as if acting on their own, her hands lead her to her research regarding the Avunaye, the data on several suspected sites for where Mike might have been held, and finally the algorithms she had written to discover who this mole or informant was. Regardless of whether or not they had thus far aided the team, whomever it was, they had managed to bypass all of the F.B.I.'s security; security that Claire had personally helped to design and implement, and what was more, it had started to look like they had even used Claire's own coding to engineer a back door into the system. '*Finally, the penny drops,*' Carmen said as Claire put all of the pieces of the puzzle together. The answer was staring her in the face, literally, as she looked at her reflection in the glassy surface before her.

'Son of a bitch!' she yelled aloud, jumping up off her seat and then quickly covering her mouth with her hand.

'Claire?' Solomon's voice called from outside the room. 'I thought I told you to take the day off?' he said disappointedly, as he walked into her safe haven. His frown said everything, but Claire knew he would not really be that surprised by her presence here. 'Are you okay?' he asked sincerely. 'Did you find something?' he questioned, nodding towards her screen.

'*Don't tell him,*' Carmen said, almost sounding scared. *What am I supposed to say?* Claire decided to talk to the voice within the privacy of her own head. *I can't exactly say 'Hey Solomon, I'm the informant. Well not me, the voice inside my head is!'* Her prolonged silence seemed to concern Solomon as he raised an eyebrow. 'I'm fine,' she said nervously before following up with an excuse for her outburst. 'Just can't believe what a mess they made...' she said hurriedly, before exhibiting a half smile and pointing around the room.

'Hmm...' Solomon murmured, seemingly unconvinced. 'Don't work too hard, and make sure you make an appointment with Singh,' he said, before glancing about the room. 'Oh, and Zane Brown is around here somewhere. The C.I.A. aren't too pleased about the artefact being stolen.' He stood for a moment, hands on hips, as he looked around at the aftermath of the attack, before turning and leaving. Claire was dreading seeing Doctor Singh, especially now she was actually having mental issues; the thought of this secret was already feeling like an un-carriable weight. *What do I do?* Claire slowly continued sifting through data. *Someone is going to notice something.*

'Relax Claire-bear, I've got your back,' Carmen responded to her troubled thoughts. Part of Claire felt reassured with someone looking out for her, but the realization that it was literally all in her head reared its ugly face and she resumed her anxious state. *Is that supposed to make me feel better?*

'*I get it, I'm one of the Avunaye. But trust me, I'm not like the others,*' Carmen said; she sounded sincere. *No, you're inside me, that's pretty different.* Claire began tapping a stylus on her screen. *Holy crap... one of the Avunaye...*

'*It's complicated but you can trust me. You can trust us, we can look out for one another.*' Confused by the flood of emotions she had whirling inside her, Claire didn't know what to think, but the voice, Carmen, had saved her and Malique during the attack, that much she did know.

'Okay... for now, I guess. You *have* had my back so far, I think,' Claire said aloud, stopping her continuous tapping as she began to calm down.

'That's good to hear, but who would you be talking to?' the man's voice came from the entrance. Stood in the doorway was a well-dressed man, dark skinned with short black hair. He leant against the door frame with one leg crossing the other. He wore a white shirt with the cuffs fastened by ruby red cufflinks that shimmered with every movement of his hands. A Marengo coloured waistcoat and suit pants looked to conceal an exemplary toned physique and his ensemble was completed by a burgundy tie patterned with small white diamonds and a very nice pair of burgundy leather shoes. He looked to smile with his big brown eyes, but the rest of his face was inexpressive, almost inscrutable.

'I keep forgetting that door is open...' Claire said, trying to hurriedly think of an excuse for her soliloquy. 'Just keeping myself company. You must be Zane.' She smiled as she finished speaking, hoping that would be sufficient to have the subject changed. She had heard enough about this deputy director to know that it was him. *Lucy did say you dressed well.* She recalled her colleagues' descriptions.

'And you must be the infamous Claire Davenport.' He stood upright from his position, placed his hands behind his back and slowly began to walk towards her. 'Rough day you had yesterday,' he stated, looking about the room and at the lab beyond it.

'That's certainly one way to look at it,' She'd have to admit to herself that she was nervous as she accidently flung her stylus up in the air.

'*That voice...*' Carmen whispered, there was distrust in her tone.

'Can I... Can I help you?' Claire said, adjusting her seating position and then instantly readjusting it again.

'I'm interested in what happened, the loss of the blade, the appearance of the so called '*Beast*',' he said, coming to a halt on the opposite side of her desk. 'We're aware that Cardoza's men were present and that he himself supposedly made an appearance at your colleague... Krysta's apartment.' He spoke with a blank tone, direct and to the point, but emotionless. His eyes homed in on hers, unblinking, like a human lie-detector, or an android. 'What I'd like to understand is how two lab-tec's fought off an attack team and survived a meet-and-greet with Brandt, our hot-tempered foe.'

'Expelliarmus!' Claire replied instinctively to his questioning. She then coughed to prevent herself from laughing in his face as he looked at her completely bewildered.

'Come again?' he said, not understanding her attempt at humour.

'It's a spell... I disarmed them... with my wand...' she said the words but could tell that with every syllable his patience waned. 'It'll all be in my report,' she quickly added, smiling and then looking down at her desk awkwardly.

'I'm off to visit Agents Ward, Rodriguez and Rose-Anderson next. I don't suppose you have any information regarding their attacks you'd care to share. Give me a head start?' He seemed genuine, or so she thought. He was so hard to read - Carmen didn't seem to trust him, and Claire felt as if she was balancing on a knife edge. She simply adjusted her glasses and shook her head in denial. She had no idea if the feeling of mistrust was her own or coming from her unwanted tenant, but regardless, she took heed and did not divulge what she knew.

'I look forward to reading that report,' he said with a subtle air of charm. He then walked to the exit before turning back and saying. 'Next time, try... stupefy,' he winked whilst maintaining his stoney expression, which made his comment all the more hilarious to Claire who laughed until she almost fell off her seat.

'*I wish you'd pay attention to your stomach,*' Carmen said, as it gurgled with the need for food once more. It was well into the afternoon and, as per usual, Claire had neglected to eat as she worked like a beaver. She had two targets at present; the first was to work out when and where the impending terror attack on the city would occur; the second was to figure out what on earth was happening to her, how it was possible and potentially how to reverse it. It was, however, proving hard to concentrate on her own issues when

Carmen seemed to be threatened by the idea of eviction and repeatedly tried to distract her. She would need to eat though, if she was going to be able to get anywhere.

'Fine, I'll go out and grab something to eat,' she said in reply to Carmen's third suggestion that the rumbling in her abdomen meant that she was hungry. She stood up and locked her computer. Heading for the door she grabbed her gilet and slipped it on.

'C'mon! Girls gotta eat!' Carmen sounded again, testing the patience of her host.

'God!' Claire responded in frustration. 'Fucking eating for two,' she said with a heavy sigh. 'No, no, no!... I meant...' she attempted to explain to the gobsmacked colleague that happened to be passing her doorway as she whined about her incessant guest. Claire wondered what was going to go wrong next as she watched the woman walk away and no doubt begin the rumour mill. Carmen laughed hysterically within. She passed by Solomon's office before heading down to the lobby. Thinking of asking if he'd like anything picking up, she changed her mind when she saw that he was deep in conversation with Kyle. Whatever they were discussing, Claire believed it to be a heated exchange judging by their body language.

She bought herself a ciabatta with chicken and caprese salad and a steaming hot caramel latte from a nearby shop before trudging through the layer of snow on the ground. It was snowing constantly, but lightly; every now and then a flake would land on her cheeks and caress her skin as it disappeared. Any sane person would have eaten inside, but Claire wasn't feeling completely that right now. She stood, food in one hand, coffee in the other, looking at the large black granite sculpture that resided in Foley Square. It was something she had seen a hundred times before, but suddenly felt different to her as she watched crystals from the heavens glisten on its dark surfaces, as if she was seeing it with a new pair of eyes, a new understanding of what it was and why it stood there. Braving the relentless cold, she moved on and found a seat within the nearby park that wasn't completely white with ice and snow. She sat quietly and ate her sandwich without interruption. Perched on the edge of the bench, she watched as people rushed about to get from place to place, avoiding the cold and the damp, but completely oblivious to the beauty that nature was providing. She knew that she should have been freezing by now, despite the layers of clothing she had on, but an inner warmth flurried from her core, a feeling of heat dancing on her skin beneath her clothes. Like sparks attempting to light a fire, the electricity fought off the chill to a comfortable degree.

'It's you, isn't it' Claire said aloud accusingly in response to what she was feeling. *It's your warmth.*

'It's our *warmth, Claire,*' she replied, her tone soft and gentle. '*I'm not like the others you've met, Claire-bear, hopefully you'll understand that in time.*' Claire could almost swear that she sounded dejected, and as she sat peacefully viewing the world around her, she came to understand why. '*My brothers and sisters have always meddled and orchestrated things surreptitiously, but I'm afraid that with Adam's recent transgression, the world is about to change and if we are to survive and help protect those you care about...*' Carmen stopped. Claire knew what she wanted to say, she could feel the panic and trepidation that Carmen felt, and those feelings seemed to translate themselves into words in a way that Claire did not understand, but something inside of her urged her to have faith. She stood up from her seat and looked for a waste bin to put her rubbish into, and that was when her phone began to ring.

'*Withheld number*' it read, yet Claire answered it the same way she would answer any call. At first there was just a muffled breathing on the line but then the voice sounded. They were using a distorter to hide their true voice, but their message was short and clear.

'I know who you are, or should I say, what you are. I wonder how your friends, your colleagues would react if they found out. Secrets always come with a price, Claire. There's a trash can to your left.' They hung up, but their voice lingered with Claire as she desperately looked around at the people in view, looking for someone on a phone, or someone looking at her, but to no avail.

23

Seamus McCarthy

'10 days 'til Christmas and they're hoisting you up outta here to some unknown location? Dude, I need to get myself shot at more often.' Malik laughed until he realised that no one was laughing with him. 'You fuckers are far too serious. 'Carthy's probably gonna be put up in the fuckin' Plaza.'

Far from it. Unfortunately, the budget for the victim and witness assistance program didn't quite stretch that far. No, Seamus and his family were being moved to a secure location for the time being after the attack at the hospital two days ago. Moira, Declan and Alannah would no doubt be arriving there any minute, having been picked up by the F.B.I. earlier that morning. Seamus was being picked up from the station after meeting with the chief.

'Hey, Seamus, don't worry about it,' Axel said, no doubt noticing that Seamus was deep in his own thoughts. 'You'll be fine. Moira and the kids too,' Axel smiled. However, it didn't seem to matter what expression he made lately, he always looked so weary. It was as if he had the world on his shoulders; he had lost a little weight and looked debilitated. 'You know where you're headed yet?' he asked, sniffing as if he had a cold. 'No better protection than your family,' he tapped on his shield as he spoke. Sadly, no matter how much Seamus trusted some of his co-workers, he knew they would never be able to stand up to what was no doubt coming for him next, and confiding in any one of them would just put more people in harm's way. The red-haired woman and the dark-skinned assassin still plagued his dreams. The recent attack at the hospital had stirred up the memory of Smithy, and of Sam. Seamus often woke in the night with the hallucination of having blood-soaked hands.

'No idea, Axe,' Seamus replied truthfully, although Axel appeared to be slightly perturbed at the lack of an answer.

'I swear, every fucking day you look more and more like a crack head,' Malik said, gesturing towards Axel's current appearance. 'We do have random drug tests bro...' he added, air-quoting the word random. Seamus wanted to tell Seif to shut the fuck up, yet he had to admit that the thought of his friend taking drugs had crossed his mind, withdrawal or addiction could both explain the progression of his colleague's slovenly mien.

'Fuck off,' Axel said in reply, following up his defence with a bout of coughing and more sniffling. 'Nothing more than a summer cold or flu that just won't fuck off, that's all,' he tried to brush it off but they had all told him to go and see a doctor at some point or other over the last few months.

'Hate to break it to you Reeves, but summer is long gone!' Sergeant McCabe's jolly tone bounded across the room as he approached the group of officers stood in the cafeteria. Whereas Axel was shaving off the pounds, the sergeant was certainly doing the opposite. Axel had no retort for McCabe's jibe and instead decided to take his leave. 'Something I said?' McCabe joked. Stood with his hands on his hips, the sergeant's shirt over-hung his belt by an inch or two and he would occasionally and instinctively run a hand along his belt to make sure his keys and gun were still there. He was clean shaven as always and his thinning brown hair was combed neatly into a side parting. His full cheeks held a huge smile between them, however, when he was thinking, he would often suck in his bottom lip and his brow would drop.

'Relax sarge,' Malik piped up after the exit of his colleague. 'Axel aint been himself last few days.' Malik's concern surprised Seamus somewhat, he rarely cared for anything than himself, certainly not others feelings. Since Sam's death, Malik had often quipped about how Seamus had thrown away his only chance of promotion, as if that were all he had lost that day at Hunter's Point. Malik looked at him now and Seamus could almost see the cogs at work behind those beady brown-yellow eyes of his.

'Anyways, today is about hot-shot McCarthy, right? Fighting off ninja assassins 'n shit,' laughing as if it was all a bad joke. Seamus bit his tongue in an attempt to stay in control, but Malik always knew what button to push and he would always inevitably push it. 'Seems you made an impression with the feds though, what with them pulling your ass out of the firing line and all.' *Gunna shut this mother fucker up.* Seamus clenched his fist impetuously. Thankfully, McCabe stepped between them at that very moment and reminded Seamus that he had a meeting with Chief Pérez.

'Yes, sarge,' he replied before heading for the exit. McCabe half smiled at him before sucking in his lip and wandering off towards one of the chiller cabinets. Seamus could see Officer Seif move to follow him, so he hastily left the room and headed for the stairs.

As far as Seamus knew, the protection from the F.B.I. was a done deal, so the need for this meeting was unknown to him. As he climbed the stairs to the Chief's office, he pondered as to whether he was in more trouble than usual. Ever since returning to work, after the loss of Cadet Lorenzo, it felt as if the chief considered Seamus to be on his last chance. The memory of her telling him to not fuck up the chance of becoming a detective had replayed in his head a number of times.

'Take a seat, McCarthy,' she said, as soon as he entered her office. To Seamus' surprise her tone was not one of anger or annoyance, she seemed quite at ease, or at least as at ease as he had ever witnessed. 'Captain,' she said, indicating that Captain Wu was free to take a seat also. She was formally dressed, her merited golden stars stood out pinned to the collar of her white shirt. She wore a black tie and had donned a black blazer. Her peaked cap sat on the desk; for now, at least, she wore her silky, dark hair down, coming over her right shoulder. For a moment she simply stood and looked at Seamus sat before her, her stare scanning him like a robot, calculating his every measurement before taking a seat herself. 'I'll try to keep this brief as I have an important meeting with the Commissioner and the Mayor.' She sat back in her chair, relaxed, or at least that's how Seamus perceived her. 'I imagine you can guess what the meeting will be about McCarthy,' he remained silent and gave a quick nod. 'So far the F.B.I. have kept us at arm's length throughout this investigation, however, a terror threat on this city endangers us all and they will be requiring assistance. They simply do not have the manpower.' She spoke calmly, yet there was a definite authority to her tone. Seamus briefly looked at Daniel sat beside him, unflinching and utterly attentive. 'Now,' she said, slightly changing the mood within the room. 'I don't want to hear anymore wild stories of people with unnatural abilities, *nor* do I want to be kept in the dark any longer.' She looked at the captain and then at Seamus again. 'Somehow, McCarthy, you have wound up smack in the middle of this shit storm and this department has paid a price. We have lost some good people...' she paused for a moment, seemingly searching for the right words. 'But we also have a great family here and two key ingredients to a great family network are trust and loyalty.' She turned in her chair slightly, facing Seamus more than the captain. 'You've shown loyalty to the badge and to the city, McCarthy, and I would like you to continue to do so, especially in these troubling times. Our family is on the ground and to keep them safe, we need all the information available.' The conversation had taken a strange turn that Seamus had not expected as she looked to him with intent. 'I trust that as far as the terror threat is concerned, that I and that this department know as much as you do.' She was so calm that it caused a shiver to flurry up and down Seamus' spine. She was literally asking him if he knew anything about the attack. Seamus sat speechless for a moment, but he couldn't help but feel offended that she was suggesting he might be hiding information. He hoped his silence would suffice as confirmation that they were all on the same page and thankfully she was very adapt at reading people. 'I would like to keep it that way. You will soon be placed into protective custody with the F.B.I., joining your family at their safe house. Any new information that comes to your attention, I would appreciate you passing onto Captain Wu by whatever means that doesn't jeopardise you or your family's safety.'

Pass on sensitive F.B.I. intel? That should be fucking easy. Sat between a rock and hard place, Seamus' mind struggled to consider his options, he struggled to think at all.

'Officer McCarthy will do his duty, Chief,' Captain Wu said. He could no doubt see that Seamus' emotions were running amok within him. Seamus thanked him with a glance.

'Right then gentlemen,' she turned in her chair and stood up from her seat. Her actions spoke a thousand words; Seamus understood them to basically state that this conversation never happened. He only wished that to be true. Seamus left her office, still bedazzled with what was requested of him, but he was swiftly pursued by Daniel.

'Seamus, wait a second,' he said, closing the chief's door behind him and hurriedly moving to stand at Seamus' side. 'Pérez has a way of sand-blasting simple things.' He was trying to defend her, but Seamus was starting to feel incensed and he wasn't sure why it was hitting him so hard.

'Simple! Dan, what the hell is simple about that?!'

Seamus asked.

'Hey, keep your voice down,' Captain Wu demanded, but his trustworthy glow had been tarnished by his silence in the meeting and Seamus was struggling to see past his own fiery haze. 'How is relaying - or better yet, spying - on the F.B.I. a fucking simple thing?' Seamus asked with a riled tone. The captain tried to find the words but Seamus' patience gave way and he decided it was time to go. 'I will do my job, to protect and serve,' he stated, before walking away from his once faultless mentor and headed for the stairs. *You just make sure you do your job, cap.*

As Seamus reached the exit to the stairwell, he could hear a ruckus coming from one of the nearby corridors. He was not far from the holding cells and the custody room, so the noise was not uncommon, but this sounded different, as he could hear the familiar voices of some of his colleagues shouting as well. Deciding to investigate the commotion, Seamus quickly headed towards the din. He turned the corner to see an officer on the floor and two others currently tussling with a large, muscular man. He had clearly been arrested for some reason, Seamus noticed the pair of handcuffs hanging from his right wrist. *What the hell is going on here?* Seamus rushed to check on the officer that was down. She had a pulse and was breathing, but she was unconscious. The brutish criminal was dressed in dark blue jeans, torn at the knees and a leather jacket that had had its arms removed, allowing him to show off his large upper arms. His head was shaved, and he had a tattoo on his left cheek of a bird of some sort, as far as Seamus could see. Dragging the downed officer away from the fight and shouting for aid, Seamus moved to assist the others in detaining the man. After pushing one of the officers against the wall, the callous brute landed a blow to the other officer's face knocking him over. He then turned his attention back to the first one and grabbed her by the throat.

'Let her go!' Seamus yelled, swiftly moving towards the man whilst taking out his baton. 'Let the officer go!' he repeated before striking the man's arm with his baton, forcing him to let go of the female officer he had pinned. Seamus went to strike the man again, this time on the back of his leg, only for him to be quick on his feet and avoid the attack. Swinging and missing, Seamus caught a glimpse of the anger within the man's expression right before taking a blow to the nose. Pain thrusted itself upwards and inwards throughout his face and head as he stumbled backwards a few paces. Shaking his head, Seamus opened his eyes just in time to avoid a second hit. He could feel the warmth of his own blood as it slid down the inside of his nostrils and spilled out over his lips, rolling down his chin and dripping onto his shirt. The sensation, the smell and the taste of the blood ignited a spark within him. The anger and disappointment of his chief's request, the constant, unshaking guilt he felt regarding Sam, his inner turmoil towards his family's safety, combined with the physical pain he now felt; Seamus could feel a void inside him, a well of fury urging him to claim retribution. Seamus couldn't be sure how quickly he gained the upper hand or just how many times he had punched the man in the face, it was all a blur. All he knew was that the large man now lay face down, unmoving on the hard floor with a bloody nose, his hands cuffed behind his back and the female officer, whom Seamus had rescued, stood staring at him with a look of shock, as well as disgust, on her face. Seamus looked behind him to find, to his surprise, Malik Seif sat on the floor nursing a cut and a fresh bruise on his cheek.

'Too far you bastard!' Malik exclaimed, looking up at Seamus. 'The fuck is wrong with you, 'Carthy?!' Several other officers had found their way into the corridor to witness the aftermath of whatever Seamus had done. Seamus looked down at his sore hands, confused and shaken. He couldn't remember even swinging a punch. Looking up and down the corridor worriedly, imagining what his colleagues must be thinking, he noticed someone hidden at the back of the slowly amassing crowd, a face that stood out from the sea of officers. *Please be my ticket out of this mess,'* he tried to ignore the looks that he was receiving from his colleagues whilst walking towards the man that had caught his eye. He had short dark-brown hair and was wearing a light blue shirt with the sleeves rolled up, showing off his ink laden arms. He had beige coloured pants and was carrying a thick black jacket.

'Seamus,' he said, leaning towards him with an outstretched and welcoming hand, introducing himself. 'Special Agent Hale. Time to be going.' Seamus was grateful for Hale's apparent sense of urgency; he wanted nothing more than to be elsewhere right now. 'Hope you look better than the other guy,' he said, looking at the state of Seamus' face before he turned and lead the way out.

They were heading out of the city. The journey seemed to be lasting forever as Seamus sat looking out of the window, watching the streets that he proudly called home flash by. He was nervous and it was made all too obvious as he constantly checked the mirrors to make sure they weren't being followed. It wasn't just him at stake, if anyone found him then his family would be at risk; he had put them through so much lately, that this, all be it a temporary situation, felt like another screw up on his behalf. Agent Hale didn't attempt to put his mind at ease, in fact he didn't say much at all. Sat in the driver's seat of the S.U.V., he concentrated on delivering Seamus to the safe house. He was calm and possessed a modest confidence Seamus surmised. In all honesty there was little to do but to inspect his driver. Hale's tattoos stood out and drew Seamus' gaze for a good portion of the journey. On his right arm, at least from his elbow down to his wrist, he exhibited an array of incredibly detailed and eye-catching pieces of artwork. Appearing from under the light blue sleeve of his shirt were the ends of a spread of feathers, no doubt the rest of the wing covered his upper arm; below the tips of the angelic plumage resided a variety of intricate flowers including roses, lilies and orchids, each magnificently shaded with a selection of words written on some of the petals, to which Seamus assumed were written in Latin. Tattooed around his wrist was a serpent with its head resting on the back of his hand, its scale covered body coiled around an apple. His left forearm was just as impressive with a complex range of clock faces, all with their hands displaying different times, and tribal art that weaved in between them.

'Quite a lot of ink you've got there,' Seamus said, attempting to break the silence as the drive went on. Agent Hale simply nodded in reply and the quiet resumed. Snow had settled on the ground but as of yet had not caused any disruption to the roads in and out of the city. They left Manhattan in its Christmas preparation via the George Washington bridge and drove for about an hour. Seamus knew they were heading through New Jersey, but Hale did not let on to any specifics regarding their destination. In fact, he barely batted an eye lid when the car suddenly ground to a halt at the gates to a driveway. Seamus looked about puzzled. The gates sat at the entrance to a drive that lead to a house set back away from the road. The building had a large front garden with two trees, allowing him to see most of the residence from where they sat.

'Wow!' Seamus said slightly gob-smacked, he had fully expected some kind of hovel or at best a dingy flat. 'You sure this is the place?' he asked. He was answered by the gates opening automatically; they drove up along the wide drive to an open parking area. Beyond the residential car park Seamus could see what he presumed was a swimming pool, mostly covered up and under a layer of white. The building's façade was more like that of a castle, with turret-like bays standing out either side of the front entrance. It had double doors with a large square window above them and a fanlight above that.

Agent Hale knocked twice on the front door; the door opened and standing in the entrance was a large man, wearing a jacket with the letters F.B.I. written across the breast.

'Seamus?' Hale said as Seamus stood gawking at the vestibule beyond the doorway. 'It's fucking freezing...' Hale moved in closely behind Seamus, urging him to hurry up and step over the threshold. The floor had a marbled look and feel, it was of an off-white colour with a dark grey criss-cross pattern spread across it. A curving staircase ran from the corner of the room upstairs, and there was an archway to his left that appeared to lead to a dining room. Another, squarer entranceway seemed to lead through to a couple of other rooms; Seamus moved toward this one to investigate further.

'Dad!' Alannah's voice sounded from the connecting kitchen as she ran to him and embraced him strongly. After hugging him she realised the state of his face and gasped. 'Mum is going to kill you,' she said quietly. He knew that his bruised and blood-stained appearance would not go down well. Moira was already irritated with the idea of having to leave her job and home behind, temporarily or not.

'Think she'll notice?' Seamus joked, smiling at his daughter's warm face. Alannah had clearly made herself at home already, dressed comfortably in a thick red hoody, black leggings and a pair of fleece lined slipper boots. She smiled in response and skipped back off into the kitchen where Declan and Moira were sat at a central island. The kitchen had a dark oaken laminate floor and contained bronze coloured wooden cupboards and island, which was topped with a mottled caramel coloured marble identical to the other kitchen surfaces. Declan raised a hand to coolly welcome his father, whilst Moira let out a sigh, exhibiting a look of disappointment that had become all too familiar of late. Light poured in through the many windows within the kitchen and adjoining eating area that housed a reasonably sized breakfast table. The white ceiling was covered in scattered spotlights that would no doubt light up the dark like a blanket of stars. Seamus moved towards his family, but before he could say anything, Agent Hale entered and explained the living arrangement and the rules they would have to abide by to stay safe. The rule of 'no contact with the outside world except for in an emergency' brought an instant look of emotional distress to the kids' faces.

After doing his duty and joining Seamus and Moira for a much-needed coffee, Hale left the family to settle into their new accommodation. An F.B.I. agent stayed in the house to help ensure they were looked after, occasionally stepping out into the cold for a smoke. As the day grew dark, Seamus sought out the master bedroom and its ensuite to clean himself up and to get changed out of his soiled uniform. Stood shirtless, wiping the dried blood from his face, he was joined by his wife. She was wearing a brick-red, high neck marbled poncho with a black long-sleeved t-shirt underneath, blue denim jeans and her feet were bare. Seamus looked at her reflection in the mirror for a moment as she stood silently waiting for him to turn and face her. She had tied her dark curly hair up into a messy bun and her face displayed a tired and concerned look.

'What happened this time?' she said, her tone a clash of concern and annoyance. Seamus knew that the truth would no doubt land him in the doghouse, but she could always tell when he wasn't being honest, so he really didn't have a choice.

'A detainee got out of hand, injured the arresting officers. I stepped in to help.' He kept it short, it was the truth, just without the gory details.

'Your nose?' she questioned, looking at his facial contusions. Seamus tried to refrain from laughing or making a joke as he remembered the look on Malik's face.

'He hit me,' he said simply, only for Moira to sigh.

'What?' he asked in reply to her sign of exhaustion, only he instantly regretted saying anything at all.

'You were nearly killed in an attack at the hospital.' She sighed again and placed a hand on her forehead in frustration. 'We barely see you, we get hoisted up out of our home and carted off because you've pissed someone off royally, and then you turn up battered. Fuck, Seamus! When do you stop to think about us? About me and the kids?' The temperature in the room was rising and he could tell that his wife's temper had sparked. Another argument was inevitable. He needed to find the right words to defuse this bomb before it blew up.

'Everything I do, I do for our family,' he said, cutting the wrong wire.

'Everything you do?!' she shouted and then took a deep breath, seemingly in an attempt to calm herself; but the fire had already been lit. 'I married a police officer, I get it, I understand what comes with the territory. But don't stand there and say it's all for us! We've been to four of your colleagues' funerals!' Holding up four fingers as she spoke. 'You become obsessed with this Adam, the red-head, our daughter got attacked Seamus! For fucks sake! And you pursue it further, pissing your promotion down the drain and that poor young boy...' she paused as her emotions started to get the better of her and Seamus was grateful for the break in the verbal assault; the mention of Sam stirred an anger inside him that he so desperately wanted to keep buried. 'It was all for us?!' she said, tears beginning to run down her cheeks. Seamus was at a loss for words. He could neither excuse his actions over the past months, nor could he provide a lucid explanation for what he had been feeling recently or how gradually, whatever was wrong with him, was getting worse. Deciding to say nothing, he quietly stood looking at Moira, hoping that his wife, the one person who knew him more than anyone, would be able to read the thoughts he was trying to convey with his eyes. He hoped that she who held his heart could now see into his soul and know how much he loved her and that deep down he was a good man. *See me Moira.* He watched her patience withering away. *Baby, see me, please!* She looked upwards, wide eyed and bit her lip before another tear ran down her face and she turned and left the room.

The lounge housed two large corner sofas, pushed together in a U-shape that looked comfortable enough to sleep on. *Another night on the sofa.* He slumped down onto the cushions. He grabbed a blanket from off the back of the sofas and switched the T.V on using the remote. Sat in his bed shorts and t-shirt, he quietly watched the news, disinterested in what the report was, just watching it for the lack of something better to preoccupy him. It wasn't long until he heard someone moving about just out of sight from where he was slouched. Sloth-like, he slowly moved his head and turned it as far as his neck would allow without moving anymore of himself.

'Moira?' he said into the evening gloom, but it was not his wife that was wandering the ground floor. It was his son Declan's face that appeared into view, coming from the kitchen with a snack in hand.

'Doghouse again bruiser?' he said cheekily to Seamus as he flumped himself down beside his father. 'So... I got a text from Sophia, who said that she'd been told by Alec, who heard from David's dad that you bust Officer Seif's nose...' he said with a glint of intrigue in his eyes.

'Don't tell your mother...' was all that Seamus said in response, his words prompting a triumphant 'ha!' from his son before he shoved a handful of potato chips into his mouth. Seamus held back on his own self-jubilation in an attempt to set a fatherly example.

'Stick the game highlights on,' Declan said, with half a mouthful. His 19-year-old son sat in his boxer shorts and a hoodie, NYU purple in colour. He was very much like his father, similar facial features and hair colour, just a younger, fitter and less stressed version. Seamus looked on at his son with a sense of pride as he switched on the highlights of the Giants vs Cardinals game and watched the boys interest become snared. 'No way!' Declan said as his team failed to advance on the first down.

'Ugh...' A voice sounded from behind them in response to Declan's disbelief in the current state of play. Alannah had found her way downstairs too, and sat down beside Seamus dressed in a festive-themed onesie. In her hands she had a bag of sweet popcorn and a pack of Oreo's.

'Do you two snack like this often? Or is this a one off?' Seamus asked, looking at the amount of, what he would deem, trash-food his kids were currently delving into late in the evening. Declan and Alannah glanced at one another before both shaking their heads and struggling to excuse themselves due to having too much food in their mouths. Seamus sat back in his seat and watched as his son made his best impression of the Giants coach and as his daughter laughed at her brother's frustration. For a moment he forgot that they were practically adults themselves and found himself reminiscing of times when the four of them would partake in a movie night, he and Moira snuggled up on the sofa whilst the kids dined on popcorn on the rug. *Maybe Moira is right.* His heart warmed with memories of simpler and happier times. He looked at Alannah as she sat eating yet another cookie. Her long, dark hair was tied back, allowing her near perfect face to bask in the glow of the light from the television. Seamus looked at her and smiled but the smile soon disappeared as he began to think how different it might have been. *Maybe I have brought all of this chaos upon us.* Alannah caught wind of his inner-distress and inched closer to her father, curling up against him. The scent of her hair eased his pain slightly and he tried to focus once again on what was good in his life. As the evening moved on and night descended, Alannah bid the two of them goodnight and gave her weary father a kiss on the cheek before heading off to bed. Declan followed suit once the highlights finished and once more Seamus was alone. He contemplated going up to see Moira, to try and say some of the words he should have said earlier, but doubting his capability to say the right thing and not wanting to upset her further, he stayed put and silently conversed with the darkness.

It was a little after 2am when he woke to the sound of buzzing. Picking up his phone, he had just missed a call from an unknown caller. He noticed they had tried three times, as Seamus looked at the call log wondering who it could have been. His curiosity was short lived as his phone began to vibrate again as he held it. Wanting to find out who it was calling him this early in the morning, he swiped the screen and held the phone to his ear.

''Carthy?! That you?!' the voice shouted down the line. Seamus recognised it, but for a moment he couldn't put a name to the voice. ''Carthy? Please answer!' They sounded desperate, perhaps in need of help. Seamus contemplated asking them who they were when suddenly their identity dawned on him.

'Dante?' he said drowsily. 'How...?'

'Nevermind how I got the fucking number dude, you gotta come meet me,' he said, cutting Seamus off. His plea sounded genuine. Seamus' senses were waking up quickly now.

'Meet you? What - its 2am. Dante, what is it? What's wrong?' Seamus asked, trying to kick start his own brain into processing quicker than that of a tortoise.

''Carthy, please man... I can't talk over the phone. Just meet me where all this crazy shit started. You got two hours man then I'm gone before the bastards kill me.' They were the last words he spoke before hanging up. Seamus couldn't even sound off a syllable before the line went dead.

Two hours... it's not enough time. How the fuck do I get to Manhattan without a car, without getting stopped...? He needed to get moving but there were so many obstacles in his way, the biggest being his wife. *If Moira catches me leaving...* he didn't want to think about the repercussions of his actions, but if he stayed then what would happen to Dante? *He said they'd kill him.* Whilst he contemplated who might be after Dante, he began to picture the look on Sam's face when... Bombarded by feelings of guilt and sorrow, Seamus remembered how scared Dante was that night when he broke into his flat. *I have to go...* He felt half-pulled by duty and half by the need for redemption.

After creeping up the stairs, he slipped into the master bedroom. Moira lay on the bed wrapped up in the covers, her head laying on one pillow, with the other held tightly in an embrace. In that moment, Seamus' resolve waivered. What he would give for all the worry and complications to disappear right now so that he could climb into bed beside her and hold her close. He chose to quietly open one of the cases left on the floor and grabbed a pair of his jeans and a thick woollen turtleneck jumper. He thought it best to put them on outside of the room to reduce the risk of waking her, but as he went to slip back through the partially opened door, he looked back at his love and prayed once more that she'd forgive him for everything. Making it downstairs unnoticed, he donned the clothes over the top of his night wear, the thick grey jumper hugging him tightly. *Back door.* He put on his running shoes. The front would be too risky, the officer that was watching the house would be on patrol and Seamus couldn't get caught. He headed through the kitchen and made it to the French doors that overlooked the patio and garden. He grasped one of the handles but it was locked. *Shit...* He checked the lock for the key, but it wasn't there. Surmising that it must be close by, he began to look around.

'Looking for this?' Moira's voice came from the archway between the kitchen and lounge. Seamus turned around to see her standing there. The light was dim, and he could barely see her face, yet he knew the expression she was currently displaying, her disappointment was practically tangible, as if it rode on the air.

'Moira...' he said walking towards her, but she simply held a hand up in response, asking him to stop. As he got closer, he could see that she was crying again. She placed something down on the cold hard surface of the island and slid it towards him. It was the key. 'The kid needs my help...' he said, attempting to explain.

'And no other officer will do,' she murmured in reply. Seamus knew he could call it in, he could tell the officer outside, he could call the F.B.I. But it was the nagging feeling that this was all his fault that held him back. His hands were drenched in blood and no amount of washing would ever clean them. He needed to atone, to make it right again.

'Moira...' he said, hoping that she'd try to understand, but she knew that his mind was already made up and, holding a hand over her mouth, she turned away and walked off into the darkness.

Chasing after her and arguing about it isn't going to save Dante. He reassured himself as he snuck out of the house and managed to escape the confines of the property onto the road unnoticed. He headed east until he came to a fork in the road. There were headlights in the distance, *Please give me a ride.* He didn't have time to waste, sticking his thumb out. The car drove straight past him as he stood on the side of the road waving; it didn't even slow down. *Come on!* He had no idea which direction to run in to get any closer to his destination. It had taken them just over an hour in the car to get here and he had roughly an hour and a half to reach Dante. Another set of lights appeared further up the road and Seamus was so determined to hitch a ride that he stood in the road and jumped up and down, waving his arms. The lights did not appear to be slowing down as they approached him. *Maybe they haven't seen me yet.* But as the vehicle drew closer, he became less and less optimistic.

Stepping out of the way of the speeding car, Seamus had all but given up hope on this one when suddenly he heard the screech of rubber on the tarmac and like a ship dropping anchor, the car ground to a swift halt. Seamus couldn't believe his luck at first as he looked at the beast of a vehicle before him. Midnight blue in colour, the two-door coupé roared from the front as its impressive sounding engine turned over. The passenger side window wound down and a voice called out from inside.

'Need a ride there, stranger?' A ride was exactly what Seamus needed and after confirming with the driver that Manhattan was the destination, he jumped on in.

'I've gotta say, this is a nice car,' Seamus admitted just after they had set off on their way.

'Thanks, she's a beauty,' the driver replied, prior to offering a hand to shake. 'Edgar.'

'Seamus,' he responded, shaking the man's hand and thanking him for his help.

'I'll get you to Manhattan in forty-five,' he said, possibly picking up on Seamus' jitteriness. 'Hope you don't mind me asking but, it's pretty late to be heading into the city, alone, with no ride. Everything okay?' He sounded sincere but Seamus couldn't tell him the truth and so he simply said he was helping out a friend. Edgar seemed to take him at his word and concentrated on the drive, occasionally making small talk, but not overdoing it. He was dressed smartly, wearing a black silky shirt under a royal blue suit jacket with a darker blue checked pattern. He had a handsome face with a neatly trimmed short-boxed beard that met his textured, short, silverish-brown coloured, crew-cut hair at the sideburns. Seamus surmised that he was fairly well off due to the impressive watch about his wrist.

'What brings you to Manhattan today?' Seamus asked, before realising that he sounded like a shop assistant and shaking his head.

'Heh,' Edgar said, seeing Seamus regret his tone. 'I keep

a place in the city. I work a lot, but tomorrow - tomorrow I have a date, so figured I'd make a trip out of it and head over early.' He smiled and Seamus couldn't help but think that this guy no doubt went on many dates. Their discussion from then on was fairly brief, covering work and the weather. Edgar was apparently in stocks and shares, confirming Seamus' initial impression. Seamus got Edgar to drop him off a block away from where Dante wanted to meet. 'You sure you wanna get out here? This neighbourhood isn't the friendliest,' Edgar said, showing some concern for his passenger. Seamus confirmed and climbed out. He stood by the side of the road and listened to the throaty roar of the V8 engine as it sped off into the night. He jogged round towards the building Dante said he'd be waiting at, the building where Seamus and Samuel had found Adam; where it had all began.

Months had passed since Seamus' last visit, but the street was still in the same poor state as it was back then. Darkness clung to everything, with very few streetlights working. Where there was an ounce of light, sinister shadows stretched, clutching everything in their path with their darkened talons. The sounds of partying adolescents from nearby blocks carried on the air, with the occasional feral cat fight in amongst the crashing of trash cans, kept Seamus' senses primed. He was tense, scared, his emotions balanced on a high wire. Soon he stood at the foot of the steps to the darkened, derelict apartment building. Its appearance in the early hours were more menacing; its broken, crumbling exterior created a tale of fearful shapes and eerie obscurities that caused the imagination to run wild. As Seamus placed a foot onto the first step a voice sounded from behind him.

"Carthy, you seriously thinking I'd be inside that death trap?' It was Dante; he had been hiding in the shadows waiting for him. 'Fuck, I got enough peeps trying to shank me without putting myself in shit like that.' Dante stood there twitching, like a junkie needing a fix; he couldn't stand still, looking nervously up and down the street repeatedly. He was dressed in black, with the hood of his top pulled up over his head.

'Dante?' Seamus said stepping towards the boy. 'What is it? Who's after you? What info did you have for me?' Seamus needed some answers, a reason to justify leaving his family to come here. Dante shook his hand in the air in response to Seamus' bombardment of questions.

'Just listen, then I'm gone,' he said stepping in towards Seamus as if to whisper to him, as if the street had ears. 'Twice Dice, you know it yeah?' he said softly, looking at Seamus, with eyes filled with desperation. Seamus simply nodded to confirm. 'There's this woman - Raven or summin - I heard her tell this dude, *'nine days, get out of the city'* and there was summin about 'The Big Party' which I figure must be the one in Times Square, right?' His face was riddled in fear, divulging the information seemed difficult for him. He was scared for what it meant, what would happen to him. Seamus had seen the same look about him when he was battered and bruised, lying on his bathroom floor.

'Dante, I have a contact at the F.B.I... she can help you,' but Dante cut him off before he could continue.

'*Fuck.* No one can protect me from Markovic or that - that giant.' As Dante spoke of Brandt Seamus could see the fear in his eyes transform into terror, almost powerful enough to stop his heart. 'Nah, I'm better off a hundred fuckin' miles away from this place! Further even!' He didn't wait to hear Seamus' attempt to convince him to go into protective custody, he simply took off at some pace away from the streetlights and into the dark of night. Seamus took out his phone to call him but to no avail, he had withheld his number. He then thought of calling Agent Rodriguez. He had a certain level of trust in Lucy, something forged from their survival. *C'mon, pick up, pick up.* The phone continued to ring out. She was no doubt asleep, but he needed to pass on the intel Dante had given him. Every second counted. *Fuck it.* He decided to send her a message instead. *'Lucy – Xmas Eve – times square – Se..'* His thumb slipped across his phone and his fingers lost their grip as he felt a sharp stabbing pain on the right side of his lower back. He had dropped his phone before he could press send. He clutched at the right side of his abdomen, feeling the wet of his own blood as it soaked into his jumper. Before he could turn to see who it was, there was an unfamiliar voice from behind him, a females voice, one filled with malice and animosity.

'Markovic sends his regards,' she said, as she removed that which had pierced his flesh. The cold steel slipped out of him as easily as it had gone in, leaving his warm blood to flow freely and quickly. Seamus dropped to his knee as he turned to confront her, but she was gone. She had driven deep, and he began to feel weaker. Thinking of Moira, Declan and Alannah, he searched the snow-covered pavement for his phone. Grabbing it with his blood covered hand he fell over and rolled onto his back. He wanted to call his wife to say how sorry he was, to tell her and the kids how much he loved them. He was so sorry for everything he had put them through, but as his head grew lighter and his eyes heavier, he saw the message he had began to write to Lucy and managed to press send.

He was struggling to stay awake and the phone had slipped from his hand. He lay there, looking up at the sky, as the stars slowly faded away. Blinking again and again, in his fight to remain conscious, the stars themselves seemed to be falling from the skies. Shining white pieces of heaven showered down upon him as he began coughing up blood, their icy kisses caressing his face. As the world turned darker, all beauty was lost, the purity of the white darkened by the red of his life.

24

Serena

She knelt at the foot of the steps leading up to the temple. The pain was excruciating, like a raging inferno it burned inside her. She clawed at the stone steps, warmed by the sun now at its highest.

'Athena!' she cried out, her voice one of pain and suffering. 'Help me...' she begged as she looked up at the temple's magnificence. The large earthen columns rose high up from the precipice of the acropolis. Its entablature encapsulated an impressive frieze that detailed the story of the goddess she now prayed to for mercy. The sun's rays beamed down on her skin, penetrating to the womb and feeding the flames she bore within. 'AHH!' she wailed, her body writhing in pain, so severe that even tears could not form in her eyes. She was naked, her skin tainted with the bruises and stains of her soon to be previous existence; her long golden hair was awash with the blood of the slain. The settlement at the foot of the acropolis was once home to those that now lay on the floor within the temple. Four of them had raped her the past night, each taking a piece of her as they forced themselves on what they considered an object of beauty. Her cries through the night went ignored. Once free, she was shunned by the people she had once called her neighbours. She had fled to this holy place to seek aid and to pray for a swift and painless end to her life, only her prayers were answered by another. Instead of the gods, he had come and lit the spark inside. She believed him to be of the gods, as when he appeared to her he was just a man, yet before her eyes he grew to the height of two men at least, towering above her, looking down on her. He called himself Matthias, and he had held out his hand and offered her justice and hope, with the promise of a new life. He had carried her into the temple where, twelve of them, those who had ravaged her, those who had turned their backs on her when she needed them most, knelt, hands bound, awaiting justice.

'Let the fire burn bright,' She looked up to her right to find one of the five who had delivered her justice, looking down on her. As hard as stone, his nigh on perfect physique soaked up the sunlight, the scars across his flesh a glow with the heat. 'Call me Brandt, sister,' he said, offering her one of his huge paws. His eyes sparkled as if they too held a fire within them. She took his hand, but instead of hoisting her to her feet, he simply held it, squeezing slightly. Serena was puzzled and looked to question his inaction when she felt the immense heat radiating from his grip. 'Feed the rage, feed the fire,' he said, with a mischievous smile. The heat broke the skin of her hands and stung the raw flesh beneath. For a moment, it was enjoyable, the warmth seeping into her blood stream and permeating throughout her body; however, it soon grew increasingly uncomfortable, as her flesh began to melt, she could feel her palm welding itself onto his.

'Ah!' she shrieked and tried to pull away, but he simply squeezed a little harder.

'Brandt, that's enough,' said a voice, so dulcet. It took Serena by surprise as to the authority it carried. Brandt instantly let go, like a petulant child he shook Serena's hand off and stomped off up the steps. The pain in her hand began to melt away and the amalgam of emotions she had swirling within her seemed to subside, slowly being replaced by a sense of peace. An angelic blonde stood before her, her golden locks falling gracefully about her shoulders, her lips a subtle pink and her skin was a glow with the light of day and her eyes sparkled like emeralds. She wore a silken white chiton dress that hung over her left shoulder and draped across her torso, leaving her right breast uncovered. Torn at the hips, the dress fell between her thighs so that as she moved, her legs were laid bare. Around her waist she wore a belt of large golden medallions and her forearms and shins were protected by fine golden bracers and greaves. She also held out a hand, yet this time Serena felt compelled to take it as an unrecognisable feeling of trust enveloped her. She lifted her sore, damaged hand and placed it into that of the woman before her, instantly feeling her flesh begin to heal and regenerate.

'Athena?' Serena asked naively as she was helped to her feet.

'No, my dear,' the heavenly woman said in reply, smiling with closed lips. 'My name is Evelina, my dear Serena. I am your family now.' Evelina grasped Serena's hand tightly with both of her own and, pulling her up onto the same step as her, she pressed Serena's hand against her bosom so that she could feel her heartbeat. 'You are one of us now, my love. The same blood surges through our veins. You feel a fire inside, a burning, a yearning from your soul to understand what you are, who you are. Listen to it my love, hear its words and you will find the answers you seek are within the flames.' Confused, Serena was unsure of what she spoke of, but there was an unshakable trust between them, a feeling that somehow, despite meeting her for the first time, they were somehow now reunited.

Two days passed within the temple and its grounds. The six of them stayed together, the others seemingly waiting for Serena to find herself before they moved on. She had barely slept but it did not seem to ware her down; she had rested enough in her previous life. She had gotten to know a little about her brothers and sisters and the one who had delivered her from the depths of despair, the one Brandt referred to as 'Father', yet for now she continued to call him Matthias. She had spent most of her time thus far learning from Evelina and her beautiful sister Carmen. Carmen had a confident, outspoken personality that suited her slender yet muscular appearance. She harnessed the build of a warrior, yet her soul-searching stare proved to be her greatest weapon. Hair of yellow and brown, her diamond shaped face was only comparable to that of Evelina's. Her full pouty lips let slip almost every thought she had and her honey coloured eyes were ageless. Masked in beauty, Serena could swear that when she looked into Carmen's eyes, it was as if she was looking through them and not her own, a strange outer-body experience that made her feel like a captive within her own skin; it would always make her hairs stand on end. Her newfound brother Adam was one of secrecy. Of all of them, he seemed to keep to himself the most, offering subtle pieces of advice from time to time. The others seemed to keep a watchful eye on him, except for Carmen, who clearly looked upon him with admiration. Carmen's sexual advances towards Serena, Brandt and Evelina were frequent, yet for Adam, she acted like a doting daughter, something that did not sit well with Evelina.

'Can we please fucking leave this place already?!' Brandt exclaimed on the eve of the third day. He was restless, never sitting still for long, the stone of the temple now bearing many wounds as a result of his impatience and frustration.

'Only when Serena is ready,' Evelina said calmly, giving Brandt a look to put an end to his tantrum. Serena instantly felt the pressure on her return, try as she might she could not hear the flames inside her, she did not yet understand. Unpredictably, Adam stood up and walked towards her.

'You won't age or die of natural causes. You'll understand the world and its workings like never before, and you will come to see that knowledge is power. You will tower above mere mortals, but will be unable to act against them except for in self-defence.' He stood before her robed, his hood hiding most of his face with his bright green eyes shining in the dusk. 'The world cannot know you. Fear, passion, despair, emotions that drive every beast, every bird and every insect, these will remain but shadows within you.' His words felt like a warning rather than advice, but despite their lack of coherency, Serena took note of every syllable. Evelina, however, did not seem to appreciate his input. She took Adam by the hand and dragged him a few paces away from Serena.

'Evelina...' Carmen looked to say in protest, yet of what, it was not clear; Evelina simply glared back at her in response.

'Enough!' Matthias stepped in, his bronze coloured torso laid bare, glittering in the twilight. 'She just needs a nudge.' Serena wondered what he meant but as she stood unmoving, the five of them disappeared and the night rolled in like a swift wind, adding a chill to the air. Suddenly she was alone. She looked for the others, but could not see where they had gone. A noise emanated from within the temple atop the steps. Serena looked up expecting it to be her brothers and sisters, yet there stood four men she recognised all too well. As they began to descend the steps towards her, her heart began to race in fear. She pictured what had happened before, she could feel them touching her skin once again.

'No, no... No!' she uttered in trepidation, searching for her newly adopted kin. But she had been abandoned. The four men continued to walk towards her, the looks on their faces matching those she recalled from three nights ago. Malice and lust filled their eyes as they surrounded her with intent. The fear inside her grew like a black hole, swallowing everything she was until all that was left was the smallest of sparks. Tears streamed from her eyes as she fell to her knees in an act of cowardice, but before they could drip from the edge of her face, she felt them lift off from her skin and evaporate. The spark inside exploded and her every fibre was suddenly engulphed in feelings of rage, hatred, disgust, avarice and retribution. She rose up and looked upon her attackers, the inferno inside her breaking through the boundaries of her skin. She stretched out her arms and watched as the flames danced along her flesh, warming her, making her feel safe. She then fixed her gaze upon her attackers and as she saw the look of terror in the eyes of the four men before her, she smiled. The flames grew hotter and larger, turning her tunic to ash but leaving her unharmed, and as she projected the fire onto those who had caused her so much pain her golden hair changed to crimson and like a phoenix, she was reborn. The four hostiles disappeared into the flames and her brothers and sisters were once again beside her, looking on at her with pride and awe.

'Time to go,' Brandt said, rubbing his hands together and exhibiting a large grin.

'Serena, it's a lie, he's not your father. You can do good in this world...' Adam tried to march over to Serena as he spoke, but he was held back. 'Serena! The knowledge is not yours, stolen not rewarded, your freewill be forfeit.' Evelina took out a blade from her belt and to Serena's surprise she thrust it into Adam's chest. She then turned to Serena, saying: 'All is well my love. All is well.'

You will tower above mere mortals but will be unable to act against them. She remembered Adam's words as she listened to Markovic, Cardoza and Brandt fumble through the finer details of the up and coming event. *Unable to act... Oh Adam...* she smiled as she thought of how things had changed. She looked at Brandt and knew that he had not come to realise, as she had, the change within them. Something had happened, a monumental event in time, for a tear had emerged in the rulebook of their existence, pages had been torn asunder and now the game could be played as she saw fit. Yet, despite her newfound freedom, she had her orders from Matthias, as did Brandt; to disobey him would no doubt lead to their demise. *I wonder how many of the others know...* She sat painting her nails. The frost-bitten wintery gloom that had descended on the city upset her somewhat. She craved heat, the warmth of the sun. Usually she would have escaped to a much more desirable climate, but orders were orders and she just couldn't wait to get it over and done with. *Four more days and I'll be gone.* At least, that was what she kept telling herself. However, there seemed to be something else holding her to the city, an interest she'd like to deny but struggled to ignore. She was painting her nails red, a deep, dark shade to match that of her lip stick. Dressed in black, high-waisted, skinny jeans, a white, V-neck, rib-knit, long-sleeved top with a carmine coloured shawl-collar wrap-coat, she had reluctantly substituted her fashionable heels for a pair of snow trudging brown ankle boots. Her scarlet and crimson coloured hair hung down over her shoulder in a fish-tail plait.

'Serena, come. Join us,' Markovic said, whilst lighting a cigar. He sat cross-legged on the sofa in the adjoining room, with Brandt sat on a chair opposite, and the barbarian Cardoza pacing around them. Vladimir looked at her with some concern in his eyes as she slowly rose from her seat and walked through to join them, blowing on her nails as she went. He was dressed in a grey suit with a midnight blue shirt, open at the neck. Brandt wore his usual grubby black pants with a dark-grey long-sleeved top that buttoned at the neck and Cardoza looked, as he often did, ready for a military coup. She sat down next to Markovic, the cigar smoke masking many smells, but she could still smell his fear, whether he showed it or not. 'Serena,' he announced, placing a hand on her thigh. 'The device is ready. Seymour's virus has been perfected so that it can be dispersed as a gas. On Christmas Eve, Manhattan will bleed.' He spoke clearly and assertively. He cared little for the people of the city, or of the world for that matter, so, what was he afraid of? 'The world will grieve, and, in their grief, we will have peace.' He was pleased with the plan, with the idea, so what bothered him?

'So, at what point do you live up to your end of the deal?' Cardoza asked, stopping his incessant pacing.

'When all is done,' Brandt added in an irked tone. Serena smiled at her brother; it was about time he said something.

'When all is done?! All is fucking done, we have risked...' Cardoza attempted to rant but was instantly cut off.

'*You* have risked?!' Serena exclaimed almost laughing at Kryln's suggestion. 'The Avunaye have risked everything to fulfil this plan, all we asked was that we were to go unnoticed! Yet we have your authorities investigating our very existence.'

'Maybe if you'd lift a pretty finger!' Cardoza retorted angrily. His outburst infuriated Serena and she noticed the heat building within in Brandt's eyes.

'Enough!' Markovic ordered, slamming his fists down onto the table before him, shaking it almost to breaking point. 'The cop is dead. Sinead saw to it,' Serena looked at him as he spoke to try and interpret if he was lying or not. 'As for the F.B.I. and anyone else involved, they'll be dead by Boxing Day. The testing phase of Seymour's virus showed a 37% kill rate. Of those who survived, 22% carried the virus and were highly infectious and a further 19% showed signs of mental degeneration and increased rage, causing them to harm themselves and, or, others. The city *will* bleed.' He sat back and took a long pull on his cigar. He was assured, and as far as Serena could tell, he spoke honestly.

'Then, by New Year's... Father will initiate you,' Brandt added, surprisingly keeping his temper in check. *If Brandt were to be nudged, who knows what fun we could have...* Serena presumed her sibling remained unaware of his newfound free will. Both Markovic and Cardoza seemed pleased with

Brandt's response, yet the undeniable scent of concern still lingered in Markovic's pores. *Or is it distrust?* Serena watched him like a hawk. After all, the ritual did not work before. *Perhaps he doubts us.* She couldn't blame him; he had good reason to doubt them as she knew full well that the Avunaye would not, or rather, could not, live up to their word with these two neanderthals. *Even if we wanted them to join us, if what Brandt says about Carmen is true... There are too many obstacles.* The four of them continued to discuss the plan and the preparations for the big day. It would seem that Officer McCarthy's final act was to alert the F.B.I. to the location and date of the attack, ensuring their presence at ground zero. After the attack, Nahki was tasked to ensure that the rest of the Avunaye make it to New York for the ritual.

'What of Adam? He will no doubt try to fuck everything up.' Markovic showed concern, perhaps his worries were to do with Adam after all.

'He won't be a problem, we have the means to keep him under control,' Serena added, smiling, hoping that would convince him. The Avunaye knew that the possibility of Adam attempting to thwart the plan was more than likely and so Serena had already called in a favour to make sure her brother did not interfere. Once Markovic and Cardoza began discussing what they'd do once part of the Avunaye, and Brandt began telling them war stories, Serena knew it was time to leave and get some air.

Sat in the back of the vehicle, she pondered for a while of where to spend her evening. Something nagged her, a deep sense of something was pulling her back to the city and so, directing her driver, she sat back and waited patiently for him to take her to where she felt she was gravitating towards.

'Washington Square Park ma'am,' her driver said, as he opened her door for her. 'Not the best weather,' he pointed out as the snow fluttered down. Serena gave him a sharp stare to let him know that his opinion was not required.

'Wait by the car until I return,' she said, causing the driver to express a distinct look of distress. 'I won't be long,' she said, fastening her coat a little tighter before heading into the park. Blanketed with snow and lit by the glow of numerous lampposts her path was crisp and untouched. The surrounding trees that had provided so many colours in the spring and summer now stood baron, trembling in the cold and dark, pillaged of their leaves by this bitter season. She walked through the sparkling layer of powdered snow, leaving footprints behind her that were gradually re-filled and disappeared from sight. The warmth of her body meant that despite the steady fall of flakes, not one managed to touch her, each evaporating a couple of inches from her skin. The unspoiled path she tread led her to the frozen fountain, a brightly lit archway and a beautifully decorated tree. She stood, looking up at the forty-five-foot pine that had been intricately decorated with thousands of tiny lights. Its snow-covered branches helping to reflect some of the illumination creating a glow warm enough to pierce even the coldest of hearts.

'Such a beautiful representation of the hope they all carry within. A hope that, despite their countless flaws and unwillingness to change, there lies more to life than merely existing,' she spoke aloud, knowing that he was listening.

'You almost sound sincere, Serena,' he said, stepping out from the gloom, cutting through the icy rain as he walked towards her. His green eyes caught the light and shimmered like brilliant jewels. 'You've never been cold on the outside, yet I can feel something stirring beneath that icy, hardened barricade that surrounds your heart.' Serena tried to ignore Adam's comment, she despised his empathic ability.

'My feelings are my own, Adam, brother,' she stated, warning him to not test her patience. 'I was reminiscing earlier, about my initiation.' She looked at him knowing that the subject would make him uncomfortable. He was half naked, wearing only a pair of worn out jogging pants, yet he did not seem affected by the cold either. 'Do you recall what you said to me that day, when I found my fire?' she asked, partly wondering how much of his memory had returned. The disheartened look he gave her suggested that he did not remember yet. 'You said that I would not be able to act against the mere mortals, except in self-defence...' She smiled and held up a hand, playing with a flame between her fingers, watching it jump from one to another. 'Tut, tut. What *did* you do Adam?' she asked, looking him in the eye, searching for an answer. He was inconsolable with the knowledge of what he had done, the glow of his eyes flickered like a dying candle and an unspoken request for forgiveness emanated from every inch of him. His magnificence was tarnished, and for the first time, Serena could see his humanity; his flaw.

'Since - for as long as...' he tried to speak but Serena could sense a mix of emotion within him. He was sharing his feelings and she did not appreciate the intrusion.

'Speak Adam! For Christ's sake, put all these damned feelings into words! Say what you want to say! Pity? Grief?' Serena exclaimed, frustrated with Adam. 'You killed! You made the decision to kill outright and now you want forgiveness?' She laughed at his pathetic state, to which he did not react. 'What was it that you killed for after all this time?' she questioned, although she could feel the answer flowing through her like a wave crashing against the shore. 'Ha!' she cackled, holding her abdomen as she laughed. 'You think... love?' She laughed from the gut, almost falling over. 'How very *human* of you!' She looked at him shaking in the snow as the cold began to bite, his mousey-brown hair covered in flakes. She could hardly believe that he had been reduced to such standards as a result of a mere emotion. Yet, as she made fun of him his patience appeared to waiver and the glow of his emerald green eyes returned and shone brightly in the dark.

'Forgive me, Serena,' he said softly. As the words left his

lips the snow that had nestled on his skin evanesced and stepping towards her, he placed his hand on her chest. Like a bolt of lightning she felt his power course through her, his emotion searching within her for something. It was as if he had held a defibrillator to her bosom, her heart pounding, cracking the foundation of the walls that she had built around it.

'How dare you!' she screamed, clenching her fist and landing a powerful uppercut to his jaw. Adam tumbled through the crystal filled air as he flew away from her. But, before he hit the ground, Serena saw him change. His shoulders snapped back, his hands and feet stretched and grew. His head broadened and an elongated snout formed from his face. By the time he landed on the bed of white, his skin had turned to a cinnamon and grey fur and his green eyes were now a fathomless amber. On all fours he stood as tall as her, baring his large teeth. The power of the beast was undeniable. He stared at her, conveying a message with his eyes, asking once again for forgiveness before he let out an almighty howl and darted off into the shadows of the trees. 'Hmph!' As she turned and began to walk away, another beast appeared before her. This one had fur of black and an emotionless look in its brown eyes that felt familiar. It looked at her as it passed, acknowledging her like a brother would his sister, before it too galloped off into the dark, following Adam's footprints.

Sickened by Adams apparent frailty, Serena returned to the car furious. Her driver stood shivering by her door, covered in snow he was wet and clearly freezing. He opened the car door for her and once she was inside, he raced to the driver's door, jumped in and started the engine, cranking the heating up to full.

'Wh... wh... where to, ma'am?' he stuttered, his teeth chattering away. Serena wanted to take her anger out on something, anything. Adam had penetrated her core and she could not ignore the feeling he had stirred inside of her.

Contemplating where she could inflict the most damage, she gave the driver his heading and slumped back into the seat as he began to drive. She struggled to control her breathing, and she sat restlessly in her seat, the contents of nearby whiskey and champagne bottles began to boil. Thankfully, it wasn't far, so the journey did not take long, ensuring the rage she had within was still burning brightly. Not able to wait for her dithering driver to open her door, she climbed out and slammed it behind her, her anger evident by the lack of snow that encircled her as she stood outside the building. *Adam, you bastard! You fucking... AHH!* She walked under the glow of outside lights towards the entrance of the building. With each and every step, the snow before her melted away, vanishing from existence. She stood for a moment once inside, watching the people bustle about. She observed the chaos of those with a fraction of time to make a difference on this earth, wasting that which they had on trivial mortal affairs. She did not remember what it felt like to be frail. Age and health had not mattered for so long a time, that standing here, seeing the old, the unwell, she felt dirty somehow and yet their insignificant existence for some reason tweaked on a heart string. *ADAM!* She screamed inside, slamming her foot down in anger.

'Can I help you miss?' a shy voice asked from behind a desk. The receptionist was a petite girl with long auburn hair, tied back. She smiled at Serena which warmed her, as well as infuriating her further. Taking a deep breath, she stepped towards the desk.

'I'm here to visit a friend,' Serena said, as calmly as she could. 'Would you be able to point me in the direction of Michael Ward's room?' The receptionist smiled again and looked at her computer monitor. She gave Serena the room number and kindly pointed out the location of the elevator to reach the correct floor. It was outside of visiting hours, but the young girl seemed to take pity on Serena for making the journey in such terrible weather and simply asked her to make sure it was a quick visit. She travelled up the floors in the elevator, watching the numbers roll by until she reached his floor. She smiled as she walked along the hall, but she couldn't understand the conflict inside. She looked forward to inflicting pain, but something else stirred inside her, a gut feeling of simply wanting to see him. Angered by the confusion of her emotions she had every intention of taking the door clean off its hinges and grasping him by the throat until blood ran from his eye sockets, but as she reached the window that looked into his room, her anger subsided at the sight of him asleep in the bed. She looked away in frustration, but her gaze was soon drawn back to the glass. *Adam, what have you done to me...?* Almost sadly, she stood looking in at the mere mortal that, for some unknown reason, she couldn't bring herself to hurt now. As a woman approached, Serena hastily turned away from the window and paced across the hall. The woman entered Mike's room and took up a seat next to his bed and Serena could tell that she was the one that he protected during their time together. She was the one who held his heart, for now.

Annoyed by this newfound weakness that Adam had inflicted on her, she left the hospital and instructed her driver to take her out of the city. She fidgeted in her seat, unable to get comfortable, the fire inside burned relentlessly and once they had crossed the bridge, she screamed at her driver to stop. She felt a welling behind her eyes and a single tear squeezed itself out of her tear duct. She caught it with her finger and watched as it evaporated. The smell of burning leather filled the air as she began to sink in her seat. Her driver turned to look at her with such fear in his eyes. She was hurting, every inch of her insides felt as if they were tearing apart and she detested the feeling.

'AHHH!' she screamed as she engulphed the entire vehicle in an inferno so furious that the paint was instantly stripped away, tyres burst, windows shattered and the burnt-out husk of her driver sat unmoving in his seat.

25

Krysta Rose-Anderson

'What the hell we doing here, Krys?' Lucy asked, with her arms outstretched. She was stood on the opposite side of the vehicle, dressed in a black work suit with a white buttoned blouse. Blue latex gloves covered her hands and she wore her F.B.I. jacket and a thick woollen scarf; wrapped around her neck it covered her chin and she had to tip her head back slightly to speak. 'There's a bomb threat on Times Square tomorrow and here we are dicking about with a burnt-out car outside the city.' A distinct frustration clung to every word, but she knew why they were looking into this, perhaps she just needed reminding.

'Luce,' Krysta said, almost fed up with her colleagues whining. 'The car is highly likely to be connected to Serena - you know, the red-haired bitch that Mike says tortured him.' She had gained her friends attention with her bluntness. 'Anything connected to this shit is worth looking into,' she said, as she knelt down again to investigate the ground surrounding the car. 'So weird...' Krysta was puzzled by what she was looking at.

'What's up?' Lucy questioned, half-heartedly hearing Krysta speak her thoughts.

'The ground...' Krysta paused for a moment, assembling her next sentence in her head. 'It's un-scorched, even where the wheels meet the ground.'

'So what? Car was probably moved,' Lucy shrugged, clearly not putting much thought into the investigation.

'So... since when have you seen a car fire that's so hot to weld the frame of the vehicle to the bones of the sorry bastard in it, yet, stay contained enough to leave the entire surrounding area untouched.?' Krysta looked at Lucy with a clear, wide-eyed stare expecting an answer, yet her colleague remained uninterested. It was another remarkable, yet troubling, revelation in the investigation into the Avunaye. If this was Serena, it meant that starting fires was just the tip of the iceberg when it came to what she was capable of. The thought sent shivers down Krysta's spine. *As if it wasn't cold enough out here already.*

'All I'm saying, Krys, is Seamus sent me the message and now he's gone. Surely there's someone else that could be looking into this?' Trying to justify her current attitude, Lucy looked at Krysta with a puppy-dog expression.

'We're meeting with the NYPD and C.I.A. later, Luce,' Krysta said sharply, hoping Lucy would now focus on the job at hand. Seeming to have done the trick at first, Lucy's mind was only occupied for so long.

'How's things with Jake?' she asked timidly. Krysta could tell by her tone that she knew that it wasn't the greatest subject to bring up. Frankly, Krysta wanted to avoid speaking about her personal life. She had buried any and all feelings as deep as she could, unable to interact with her boyfriend. Since the attack, her skin had crawled at every touch. She had spent every available minute away from the apartment, burying herself in work and staying with Lucy when possible. She knew that it was unfair on Jake, after all he had had no part in it, yet how she felt at the thought of being intimate with someone took precedence over anyone else's feelings right now. She knew that it could spell the end of their relationship, if he was unwilling to wait, potentially indefinitely, but she needed to put herself first.

'Luce...' she said, emotionally depleted; the single word

conveying an abundance of excuses that only a true friend could translate. In return, Lucy smiled and rubbed her smurf-coloured hands together, knuckling down to work.

It had been decided that due to the amount of available office space, the Times Square Tower would be a suitable base of operations; so Solomon's team, the C.I.A. - namely Zane - and the chief of the NYPD were to meet there at 2pm to finalise their plan for preventing any form of attack that Markovic, Cardoza or the Avunaye had concocted. Brimming with hardware for surveillance, Krysta could see the fruit of Claire's handywork as she looked about the converted conference room. The entirety of Times Square and its surrounding blocks had been set up with cameras designed to recognise any one of their enemies. Dozens of 'techies' and officers buzzed about the room, conveying messages to teams on the outside. It was all very impressive. Yet for all its wonder, Krysta couldn't shake the feeling that their technology and manpower would not quite be enough against the supernatural threat.

She and Lucy were twenty minutes early and yet it looked as if the meeting had already started some time ago. In a separate room, surrounded by windows, stood all the senior personnel involved in this operation. Krysta instantly saw Solomon stood rigidly amongst the rest. The yellow letters F.B.I. stood out proudly on his jacket and the stern expression on his face told everyone how serious the matter was. Krysta's and Lucy's arrival caught his eye and although his expression did not change, she could feel a warmth in his eyes: he was glad to see them. Stood with him was Kit. He too had donned an F.B.I. jacket, although he looked prepared for a gun fight. Visible beneath his jacket Kyle wore a Kevlar vest and was carrying his sidearm. His face was a distinctly different picture to Solomon's, portraying a sense of concern and fear. His hair looked to have been hurriedly styled today and he carried a little more than the average five o'clock shadow. Krysta recognised Zane Brown, the deputy director of the C.I.A., looked a lot more casual than his surrounding counterparts. He stood, seemingly calm, dressed in a white ribbed turtleneck jumper and blue jeans. He smiled at Krysta and Lucy when he saw them, however, Krysta felt as if it was intended more for Lucy than herself. Completing the set was Chief Pérez of the NYPD and a couple of other suits, of which she assumed were from Homeland Security and possibly the N.S.A. The pair decided to park themselves outside of the 'intensity room' for now, taking in everything around them. Krysta also wanted to wait for the rest of her team to arrive.

'No, no, no! For Christ's sake! Three hundred and sixty degrees and you need to... I set everything up for you guys... I do all the work and you can't even... move aside.' Claire's voice was unmistakable, yet her authoritative tone was somewhat surprising. She clocked her colleagues after dealing with the problem she appeared to be having and headed straight over. 'My god, are these nitwits slow on the uptake or what?!' she said, as she came face-to-face with Krysta and Lucy. There was something about her, a confidence. Krysta thought maybe it was simply being in her element that brought it out of her. Claire laughed, a huge smile spreading across her face. 'Look at me, giving orders, shouting at people. How cool is this?! Impending attack not so good, but you get what I mean.' She was doing what she did best and was a little excited, Krysta understood.

'Claire, you okay?' Lucy asked. She didn't seem too worried, and was more likely checking on her colleague's current mental state.

'Sorry. Ha! Yeah, I'm fine, fine. By the way they've given me the go ahead for directing this technology fest, so I'll be in your ears all the way tomorrow, making sure you're safe.' She couldn't help but smile, however, the more she smiled the more the underlining anxiety seemed to show through the cracks of her excited masquerade.

'That's great Claire, you'll do great. It feels good to know you'll be watching out for us,' Krysta smiled, giving Claire an ounce of reassurance.

'Yeah, fan-bloody-tastic,' Lucy said, looking back into the room of senior officials. Lucy's words were less encouraging and justifiably received a nudge from Krysta.

'Oh! Paul's just arrived!' Claire said smiling again, pointing to an image on the tablet she held. 'No one gets in without me knowing,' she said, visibly chuffed with herself.

The three of them talked amongst themselves until Hale joined them, who suggested that they had better make their way into the meeting. *It's real now.* She crossed the threshold into the office. Up until this point it was just talk, research, investigations, rumours, leads. Now it was time for action, the threat was real. Christmas wasn't going to be the same this year. A large map of the city lay spread out on the table, a smaller map of Times Square on top of it. Dots, circles, scribbles, all detailing locations of cameras, of where undercover teams will be positioned, sniper locations. These markers were reassuring. Usually they would also mark down the potential points for ground zero, potential sites where the device might be planted, but the sad fact was, they had no idea. Every building was a possibility, every street, subway entrance, every square inch had to be covered; a near impossible undertaking.

'It's a logistical nightmare. We simply can't cover enough ground,' said Valentina Pérez. Fully suited in her uniform, she did look the part. 'You've almost got everyone at your disposal but it's still not enough.'

'That's where the tech comes in. Hey, Solomon.' Zane glanced at Claire, then locked eyes with Solomon.

'There are thousands of people out there, tomorrow will be busier. Agent Davenport assures me the cameras are currently registering eight in ten...' Solomon was cut short by a raised hand from one of the unknown suits; he clearly pulled some weight as the room quietened.

'Some big holes in those nets of yours.' Krysta could tell

Solomon wanted to say something in reply, but bit his tongue for now. The clean shaven, bald, suited man looked down at the map for a moment, the entire room waiting silently for his next words. 'Evac isn't an option, less than 9.5 is unacceptable,' He looked at Solomon, then to Zane and finally to Claire. 'Please see to it that the numbers are improved.' With the request, Claire looked to Solomon and, receiving a nod, she left the room. The man gestured to Solomon that it was OK to continue.

'That's Markus Hicks, DOJ,' Hale whispered to Krysta, catching Lucy's ear also. *That explains it. Department of Justice are getting involved now, just great.* Another agency getting involved, one that could easily rule over what Solomon ordered. Zane was the only one in the room exempt from reporting upwards, the C.I.A. practically made their own rules.

'We wait. First sign of any of the high-end targets and my team, with the assistance of the NYPD, SWAT and the C.I.A., move in discretely and disable the threat.' Solomon spoke clearly and assertively, appearing confident with the plan. That, or at least he made one hell of a poker player. The focus turned back to Hicks once again. He made sure to keep everyone waiting with bated breath.

'You get the cameras registering at least 9.5 out of 10 people out on those streets and you ensure each of these markers has a team on them...' he paused for a moment. Krysta hoped he wasn't changing his mind. 'This investigation has been bullshit from the start. People with extraordinary abilities? Mass murder? Assaults on federal buildings?' Things were turning sour. The suit had everyone's attention in the palm of his hand, and he was beginning to become irritated. 'You've made the plan. Execute the plan. I want the weapon returned, Vladimir dead or behind bars along with everyone else involved and I don't ever want to read fictional crap about fucking superpowers again.' Krysta waited for everyone else to acknowledge the order first, but it appeared it did not warrant any replies. Hicks had said his bit and he knew everyone had heard him, loud and clear. Confident with his own actions, Hicks began to leave the room when Zane chirped up.

'Good talk, Markus. Truly, inspiring...' His sarcasm almost drenched everyone close by. Hicks, however, seemed to ignore the comment and continued to leave, the other suit following him close behind. With the exit of Markus Hicks, the room came to life again with chatter as everyone went over each detail, again and again. The repetition was draining, and Krysta found her mind wandering. She caught Zane starring at Lucy, and when he realised he'd been caught, he quickly turned his focus towards her instead.

'So, Krysta. Seen Adam lately?' His question was direct but was laced with insinuations.

'No...' Krysta answered honestly. She couldn't deny that she had wondered where he was, what he was doing. In fact, since the attack on her home, Adam had been on her mind a lot. She couldn't shake him. Zane looked at her, his deep brown eyes peeling away her defences, hoping to read something different to what she replied perhaps. Yet seemingly finding nothing, he turned away and walked around the table to join Solomon and Chief Pérez.

'Chief Pérez?' Lucy called across the table interrupting everyone. The whole room looked at her. Krysta couldn't help but wonder what her friend was doing. 'Sorry...' she said hesitantly, but almost instantly regained her bullish confidence. 'Actually no, I'm not. Officer McCarthy provided us with this intel we so desperately needed, yet not one fucking word has been said about him...' Lucy was annoyed and was now feeling a little under pressure no doubt, as all of the senior players looked at her.

'Agent Rodri...' Kyle said, frowning at Lucy for her outburst, but Zane quickly placed a hand on his shoulder, reigning him back in.

'Agent Rodriguez, is it?' Chief Pérez said, her voice holding a strong womanly power. 'Officer Seamus McCarthy disregarded protective custody, sneaking out of the safe house your department provided him and his family. Yes, we are using the information he supplied you, coupled with a number of other sources. He is currently missing, presumed dead.' She stopped there and then continued her discussion with Solomon, Kyle and Zane, leaving Lucy looking slightly sheepish and crestfallen. Krysta placed her arm around her friend.

'Chin up, Luce. Tomorrow this shit ends.' She almost believed her own words.

It was Christmas Eve and her eyes were dry and sore through lack of sleep. Krysta, Lucy, Solomon and Hale sat in a black SUV, waiting. Kyle had opted to assist Claire with running the operation from the tower office block. He said that a level of authority would be good for the team, working away, analysing the data and watching the footage. Krysta knew better. He was scared. The fact was the car stank of fear, each of them had doubts of how this was going to go down, but they believed in each other and that's what was going to get them through.

'Turkey, stuffing, cranberry sauce... all in a toasted baguette.' Hale spoke of his sandwich as if he was marketing it to the masses. He was, of course, attempting to lighten the mood. Other than going over the plan or checking in, no one had said much all day. Krysta had been deep in thought, trying to work out her own issues. Her work, her personal life, both had somehow been mashed together and fed threw a grinder until nothing quite made sense in her head. If she was honest with herself, she wished that she could just shut off from the world, disappear, curl up and close her eyes until everything had righted itself.

'Hey, Krys, wake up!' Lucy yelled, snapping Krysta out of her daydream. *When did the sun go down?* Krysta returned to reality. That big motherfucker just got picked up waltzing into the Marriott,' Lucy said. 'We're en route.' Lucy was quickly checking all her gear, fastening straps and checking magazines. Solomon was pushing the accelerator to the floor, the Marquis Hotel was only a few blocks away from where they had been stationed, but every second counted. Krysta's heart began to beat faster, the ecstasy of the chase, the adrenaline, the chill of fear. Her body produced a tune within as the SUV swung around the final corner and screeched to a halt. She didn't have to think, she simply felt her body doing the work as she and the team exited the vehicle and moved quickly into the mouth of the giant brutalist block-like structure. Two dozen pairs of footsteps echoed throughout the prodigious atrium of the beast. Officers cleared out civilians, securing the area.

'Sol! This bastard has almost nineteen hundred rooms!' Krysta exclaimed, as she looked up the hollow centre that almost didn't seem to have a ceiling. There were a number of elevators, each leading to different sets of floors. She looked at Solomon and then to Hale, silently asking for direction.

'He took the elevator to floor forty-seven!' a receptionist called, whilst being ushered from the building. Brandt was not one to go unnoticed, Krysta figured that the receptionist must be speaking of him. Solomon quickly ordered the NYPD officers to secure the floors above and below forty-seven, and then, with his team and a handful of SWAT personnel along with two bomb disposal experts, they boarded the elevators. Krysta stood watching the digital numbers increase as they went from floor to floor, each climb causing her heart to pound faster.

'Ready, Krys?' Lucy asked just before they reached their destination. Her friend and colleague had a fire in her eyes, she was determined to end this here and now. Krysta took a deep breath and nodded in reply. The elevator doors opened and Hale and Lucy, weapons at the ready, looked out to the left and right to check if it was clear. Solomon checked over the comms to see if the teams of officers and the six-man SWAT unit were in position. Happy with their responses he gave the order to move out into the hall.

'Solomon,' Claire's voice sounded across the comms, a welcome sound through all the chatter. 'The only room to have its door opened on floor forty-seven is room four, seven, one, eight. No activity on that floor for over half an hour besides that.'

'Thanks, Claire,' Solomon replied, before indicating which way his team needed to proceed. Krysta's heart was relentlessly beating as she approached the corner of the hallway. You couldn't hear anything up here, not the celebrations on the street below, nor the traffic. It was silent. As the four of them moved down the hall towards room 4718, they saw the SWAT team come around the corner at the opposite end, boxing the enemy in. *Something can't be right here.* Krysta watched as they halted seven or eight feet away from the door to the room. It was still so quiet. They were crouched, weapons at the ready. Solomon gave the order for the SWAT team to move forward and breach the door. Krysta knew the leader of the team to be named James, however, at this moment, his surname eluded her. He and the rest of his team moved forward until they were adjacent to the door. Placing a small charge on the door, James looked at Solomon, yet his fearful gaze caused alarm bells to ring throughout.

'It's... hot...' he said. His eyes behind his mask widened and told a thousand words within a second, screaming for help, as if he knew in that moment what the future held. Time slowed down; the door hurtled off its hinges, knocking James out of the way, hitting the wall opposite and then proceeding to fly down the hall until it collided with Solomon and Lucy. Flames exploded out into the hall, engulfing the two nearest SWAT members and then continued to climb along the floor, the walls and the ceiling, devouring everything in its path. Krysta didn't think - she couldn't think - she turned and tried to clamber away from the heat when she was slammed into the door of the next room by Hale as he forced her out of harms way. They collided with the door with force, falling through the doorway into the room, escaping the fire.

'Lucy!' she screamed out after shaking off the blow from the fall. She tried to clamber back out into the hall, but Paul was holding her back. 'LUCY!' Krysta cried out as she tried to shrug off Hale's grasp to go and help her friend, and that was when the silence that had governed the building was completely gone. The distinctive sound of gunfire could be heard from above and below. Krysta lay on the ground with Paul pinning her down, looking through the opening to the room to the smoke ridden hallway, and as if every other sound was stripped from existence, she suddenly heard a whistle from outside the door:

Half a pound of tuppenny rice...

It rang and through the smoke she saw the mammoth figure of Brandt as he walked across the doorway, his red glowing eyes shining through the black smog. Fighting Paul's protective hold, Krysta got to her feet and charged out of the room, ignoring the path that Brandt had taken and turning to where the rest of her team had been crouched. Solomon lay on the floor, barely moving as the heavy wooden door lay on top of him. Krysta looked down the hall. The flames appeared to stop just past the opening from which they had originated in her direction, yet moving up the hallway, the orange, red and yellow animal had clambered to the end, blasting through the SWAT team, leaving a trail of squirming, writhing bodies that screamed out in agony as the fiery blaze consumed each and every one of them. Krysta quickly crouched down beside Solomon, lifting the door up off of him.

'Sol? Where's Lucy?' she asked as she cleared the debris and looked upon his face. He didn't seem too injured, more stunned than anything as he pushed himself up onto his feet. Yet as he rose up, Krysta saw an image reflected in his eyes: she had found Lucy. Spinning on her heels, Krysta frantically grasped her weapon and aimed at what she had seen. Hale was stood just behind her, he too ready to shoot at the red-headed woman that stood at the end of the passage.

'Tut tut,' she said, waving her index finger at them as they aimed their firearms towards her. 'She'd be dead long before me,' she revealed, grinning maliciously. The crimson haired beauty stood confidently, her hair flickering like the flames before her. She was barefoot, the cream linen pants she wore were soot-ridden and had several scorch marks; her red, light cotton vest barely covered her breasts as it too had been damaged by the heat. Stood side on to Krysta and the team, she had Lucy to her left, pinned in the corner, flames surrounding her, but for now she seemed unharmed. The sound of minor explosions and gunfire persisted from other floors and the fire that had decimated the SWAT team continued to rage on. Serena was in control, Krysta could feel it, her power in this moment was palpable. 'My brother is no doubt tearing your backup limb from limb,' she said, almost enviously.

'Let her go,' Hale said firmly, but cautiously, as he didn't want to invoke her wrath.

'*Let her go!*' Serena mocked. She seemed angry, yes, but also frustrated. 'Her name is LUCY!' she yelled. Her eyes flashed red then white in an instant and the flames began to encroach down the hall.

'Please...' Krysta said, hoping to appeal to any fragment of humanity the bitch might have left.

'Please?' Serena laughed, her tone almost saddened. 'What makes *her* so special?' she asked. 'Why *her*?' Krysta was confused, as was everyone else, no doubt. Serena was not making much sense, she seemed angry, yet not at them. 'Why... why did Adam do this to me?' the question seemed to be directed at them but also at herself. 'Only in grief shall humanity know peace...' she said solemnly. *What can we do?* Krysta watched her friend trapped behind a wall of flame, but her question was answered as the sound of gunfire came from close behind. Solomon's bullet flew past her and hit Serena in the right shoulder. Blood ran down her arm and trickled onto the carpet.

'AHHH!' Serena howled in anger, her scream one of rage but not pain. She outstretched her hand and fire blazed around her, bounding across the ceiling like a stampede. Krysta, Hale and Solomon were forced to drop to the floor as the wave crashed over their heads. The heat was so intense, Krysta could feel her skin boiling under her body armour. The fire only persisted for fifteen seconds or so, yet it felt as if it would never end.

'Krys!' Lucy shouted, but Krysta couldn't raise her head to see if she was okay. 'Krys!' she called again; this time Krysta felt her friend's hand touch her. Looking up, Lucy was crouched in front of her, unharmed. There was no sign of flames, as if every flicker had been extinguished in an instant. Realising that Serena was gone and that her friend was still alive Krysta rushed to get up onto her knees and grasped Lucy, embracing her tightly.

'Solomon! Markovic is here!' Claire cried out across the comms. The joy Krysta felt holding Lucy was suddenly replaced once again with fear.

Picking themselves up, the team moved as fast as they could. Fear and panic filled the air outside of the hotel as civilians ran in terror from what was happening inside. More police officers and firemen rushed inwards as Krysta and her team sprinted for their vehicle. Paul drove, if you could call it driving, Krysta had never been thrown about so much traveling a few blocks, and she had taken many taxi journeys. His desperation to get to the tower was evident. The tyres screeched as they reached their destination, yet Krysta was surprised at what she saw.

'What the fuck are you doing out here?!' she yelled, storming towards Kyle, who was in the middle of directing some officers.

'I'm...' but before he could answer, Lucy clocked him across his jaw, knocking him to the ground.

'Son of a bitch! Where the fuck is Claire?!' Lucy screamed at him. Krysta looked around, she hadn't noticed at first, but Claire was nowhere to be seen. Paul held Lucy back as she looked as though she was about to go in for seconds.

'You fucking bitch!' Kyle shouted, as he climbed to his feet and made a move towards Lucy. Solomon quickly stepped in his way.

'Johnston!' Solomon commanded. 'Report!' Like an army general, Solomon squared up to his subordinate.

'Markovic, a group of his men and some freaky looking dude stormed the floor. I managed to help half a dozen people escape before they sealed themselves off.' Kyle straightened himself up as he spoke of his own heroics.

'You mean you fucking ran!' Lucy shouted, still having to be held back by Paul. Kyle looked at her as if what she was accusing him of was unspeakable, yet Krysta could tell that he wasn't sorry for saving himself.

'Where is Davenport?' Solomon demanded, placing his hands on Kyles shoulders, ensuring he had his attention.

'Claire, Chief Pérez, and a few officers and techs are trapped on the floor. Solomon, the freaky looking guy was carrying the device.' The mention of 'the freaky looking guy' seemed to instil a level of fear in Kit that he'd rarely felt.

'Rodriguez, Hale, Anderson?' Solomon said looking around at his team. 'Good to go?' Despite what they had just been through, Krysta felt ready for anything. They all nodded and followed Solomon into the tower. They took the stairs, rushing as fast as they could. 1... 2... 3... Krysta kept count of the floors as they climbed, keeping her mind occupied, distracting herself from how scared she felt and how tired she was. They reached the floor below the conference room where they had set up their base of operations. So far there had been no resistance, it was as if they were invited. Krysta went to climb the last set of steps when there was an almighty scream. *Claire!* Krysta panicked at the sound of the woman's scream. The lights in the stairwell flickered, their radios crackled and then died. It was as if an EMP had been emitted.

'Solomon?' Hale spoke, confused. 'Was that an EMP?' Solomon had no answer, looking just as confused as Paul was. The team pushed on in the dark, moving towards Claire, hoping she was okay. Three hostiles guarded the corridor beyond the stairwell. Solomon and Lucy took point. Swiftly entering the corridor, Solomon shot the furthest target in the head whilst Lucy simultaneously disabled the other two without even taking a breath. Looking through the windows on the opposite side of the room before them, into the conference room, Krysta could see everyone. Chief Pérez, three officers and a few technicians were stood up against the far wall, hands bound in front of them. Markovic stood in the centre of the room, one hand holding a cigar, the other was resting on the device that sat on the table. Krysta only recognised the other man due to Lucy's horror story of what had happened in Los Angeles. It was Seymour. He stood looking in their direction, waiting. Dressed in a dark robe, his long purpley-grey hair fell over one of his shoulders and his mottled blue-grey eyes were fixed on Krysta, unblinkingly. Vladimir's knuckles were covered in blood, Krysta noticed, but there was no sign of Claire.

'Solomon Grey. Please, come in,' Markovic said loudly, before rolling the cigar under his nose, smelling its worth. Krysta looked to Solomon to see what he wanted to do. It was a hostage situation nothing was going to be simple. Vladimir sighed before bending down and reaching for something. When he rose back up, he had Claire in his grasp, his large bloodied hand wrapped around her neck. Claire's face was bleeding. Krysta wanted nothing more than to rush in there. 'Solomon Grey, come in,' Vladimir said once again, this time the ghostly figure of Seymour moved behind him and grabbed a technician by the arm. He looked over at Krysta again, as if there were no obstacles between them and he could see her as clearly as if she were stood right in front of him. He smiled a toothless smile and then released the technician. The fear on the man's face was incalculable. His eyes ran with tears before he suddenly charged headfirst into one of the unbroken windows. The glass smashed, and as blood ran from the man's forehead, he quickly grabbed a piece of broken glass with his bound hands and proceeded to open up his own throat. 'I had wanted to be a thousand miles away from here, but Seymour here, he assured me that I would be immune to the virus,' Markovic spoke confidently but there was an underlining anger or irritation to his words. 'I decided to stay because I wanted to see the look in your eyes as you died.' As he spoke, he lifted Claire up a little further; she was barely moving. 'Then this little...' he began to speak in Serbian, clearly angry with Claire. 'She almost ruined it.' He looked at Claire's face, before brushing some of her hair out of the way. 'She almost ruined EVERYTHING!' He screamed and then threw Claire up against the ceiling as if she weighed nothing. Solomon moved in, weapon at the ready, his team in tow.

'Step back and raise your hands!' Solomon ordered of Markovic and Seymour, only for Seymour to laugh in return.

'Officer Reeves...' he said, looking at the next hostage in line. He brushed the officers face with his fingertips before handing him his own firearm. The NYPD officer looked at Krysta. She recognised him from when he had come to her apartment. Tears began to run from his tired eyes before he took his gun and placed it under his own chin. Blood splattered up the wall and across the ceiling before his body hit the floor with a thud. Krysta knew that they couldn't just open fire with the hostages stood right behind Markovic and

Seymour. Her stomach was full of panic and her heart raced uncontrollably.

'There's no way out of this one Markovic!' Solomon said, aiming his rifle at him. His words must have panicked the large Serbian as he swiftly turned and grabbed Chief Pérez to use as a shield. Krysta aimed her rifle at Seymour, watching his every movement. *Just make a move you bastard.* She desperately fought the urge to open fire.

'Seymour, if you please,' Vladimir said with a cunning smile. 'No loose ends.' With that, Seymour vanished, disappearing into the shadows, as if becoming one of them. The team panicked whilst trying to keep an eye on Markovic, they couldn't help but frantically look about the rooms, terrified of where the deathly figure had gone.

'Krysta! Don't let him touch you!' Lucy shouted. Krysta turned to see her friends, Solomon and Paul flung in different directions, thrown by a shadow against desks, walls and equipment. The shadows moved towards her, a dark shape of a man reaching out with a black gaseous like hand. She fired at him, only to hit the wall beyond and nothing else. She could feel his presence, a chill, an unnatural cold in the air. A bead of nervous sweat fell from her forehead and caressed her cheek, and like a light inside her being switched off, she felt his icy grasp. All hope, and joy, and love had been stripped away, leaving a hollow, dark and solitary place for her heart to reside. Darkness reigned. Yet as she drifted out into a sea of despair, she saw a glow in the distance. Outside the window overlooking the street, the glow of hope, of life.

'Enough!' the voice called, smashing all the windows around them, shattering the glass. From where the glimmer of hope had shone, the wall surrounding the empty window frame crumbled at his presence as he propelled into the building, landing at Krysta's feet. He quickly grabbed her attacker and threw him back into the meeting room from whence he came. He raised a hand and touched her cheek, setting right all that had been made wrong. Then, he flashed into the meeting room to challenge Seymour. Adam grasped the bringer of despair around the throat, squeezing hard in a furious fashion. Seymour grabbed both of Adam's arms, seemingly trying to counteract whatever it was that Adam was doing to him. Krysta looked over to see her team back on their feet, watching anxiously, not sure what to do. Krysta could tell that Seymour's darkness was losing out to the purity of Adam's light. Seymour began to laugh as he released his hold in defeat.

'You're a fool, Adam' he said smiling. Then, looking at Krysta, staring deep into her eyes, he said: 'Here she comes...' before once again re-joining the darkness and vanishing from sight.

Seeing Seymour vanish startled Markovic, who quickly pounced onto the device before him and hurriedly pressed at the buttons before Adam grasped his hands.

'It's too late! You fucking... Now you get to watch them die!' He continued to speak to Adam in his native tongue. Adam turned to Krysta and her team; his face was one of sorrow and she knew in that moment that there was nothing he could do. Krysta screamed to Lucy, Hale and Solomon, begging them to run. The remaining hostages panicked and tried to flee as well. She looked to Claire, still lying on the ground next to Adam and Markovic. She had to get to her and get her out.

'Krysta! Please - run! I'll get Claire! Now go!' Adam commanded. He had released his hold on the Serbian and proceeded to pick up her colleague and friend. Krysta turned from him and moved as quickly as she could towards the stairwell, part of her knowing that it would make no difference, but the rest of her knowing that she had to try. Chief Pérez, her two remaining officers and the remainder of Claire's team made it to the ground floor. Solomon, Paul and Lucy too. Yet, as Krysta looked back up the steps, there was no sign of Adam, nor of Claire and her heart sank.

26

Adam

'Carmen!' he shouted as he shook Claire. She was unconscious but he could see the essence of his sibling all around the F.B.I. agent before him. He was confused as to how it was her, mentally clawing at his own memory like a wild animal trying to break through a barrier, trying to piece things together. 'Claire?' he said softly. He was losing hope, of all the power he harnessed could he not stop what was about happen? He shook her again and this time she opened her eyes. 'Claire?' he said once more, deciding it was time for them to run. 'We need to...'

'Brother?' she said, only it was the blonde goddess inside of her speaking, using this brunette vessel to harness her being. 'I... forgive you.' As the words left her lips the device on the table began to make a subtle hissing sound as a gas began to be dispersed into the air. Adam looked despairingly into Claire's hazel eyes; suddenly they began to flicker, blue sparks zipping across the lenses like miniature lightning strikes. The flashes sprayed out like fountain, the electricity flowing over her entire body, forcing Adam to let go of her. Yet, even though he was no longer holding her up, she did not fall to the ground. Instead, she floated, exactly where she was, the air surrounding her electrified. The gas that was slowly filling the room and heading for the exits, trying to escape into the world to infect and destroy, was also being lit up. Like a storm cloud within the room, it was as if the charge Claire was emitting was attacking the particles of the virus, zapping each and every molecule, eradicating it, until there was no more.

The event took its toll on the girl as she fell towards the ground once she was done. Adam rushed to her, catching her just before she hit the floor. Placing his hand on her chest, he attempted to heal her. She was weak, frail. Her heartbeat was but a whisper. 'Adam... you can't save us both... ' she said, but he would try. He lifted her up off the floor and held her tightly, every inch of him pulsing with life, trying to save theirs. Her heartbeat grew weaker and weaker until he could hear it no more. He brushed strands of hair from her bruised face and, as he did, the cuts and bruises on her head healed and the strands changed from brown to blonde, creating a streak. Her heart began to beat again.

'What a bitch,' a voice behind him said bluntly. He knew the voice, the one voice he could never forget. 'I go to all this effort, and it's Carmen who saves the day.' He turned to see her. 'Honestly... I could have sworn I killed that bitch centuries ago...' Evelina stood in the doorway between the two rooms, leaning against what was left of the door frame. She was wearing a pair of black over-the-knee flat boots with the flesh of her lower thighs on display, and a grey woollen jumper dress that hung off her left shoulder. Her blonde hair was tied up at the back, styled, with a side parting that left a few strands falling in front of one of her ears; her appearance was utterly prepossessing. Looking at Adam, her green eyes stared straight through him.

'Matthias...' Adam began to say as he climbed to his feet.

'Matthias? Please, Adam, don't tell me you bought into the whole, 'Matthias' devious plan' thing...? she mocked him. Her smile shone brightly in the dark of night, Adam wanted to despise her, her arrogance, her obvious ill intent, yet he was, as always, at her mercy. 'You look as if you want to ask why, my love... Isn't it obvious?' She stepped away from her leaning post and walked towards him. Adam was trembling with anger but was unable to act. Grabbing his hand, she ran it up her neck and onto her cheek seductively, letting him feel her skin, her beauty and warmth. 'Be still, my love,' she said, staring into his eyes, and by her command his anger began to subside.

'The fucking plan failed!' Markovic interrupted. He looked dumfounded by Adam's inability to react, but also perturbed by her inaction.

'Vladimir, pipe down. You're lucky I still have a use for you,' she snapped, irritated with the brute of a man. Markovic instantly did as he was ordered. 'The plan worked perfectly. We just didn't get the big finale that we were after.' The look of glee on her face turned Adam's stomach, he knew exactly what she meant, and he began to see everything much more clearly. 'You see, Adam here was the only one who could break the... Rules? Curse? Whatever you want to call it... For as long as I can remember he has resisted the temptation to act of his own free will and kill in cold blood. Yet here we are, free. As free to act as the mortal's themselves.' She bit her lip as she grinned, knowing that her words would be piercing Adam's heart like white hot needles. 'Vlad, be a dear and grab the girl. If Carmen is still in there somewhere, I'd love to torture the bitch.' Markovic proceeded to pick up Claire, but as he went to move, there was a shout from the hallway that made him stop in his tracks.

'Freeze! F.B.I.! Put Claire down, step away and put your hands up above your head!' It was Krysta. She had made her way back up the stairs and stumbled into the maw of the beast. Evelina closed her eyes and smiled at the sound of Krysta's voice. Adam's heartbeat began to betray him.

'So...' Evelina said, letting go of Adam's hand and turning to face the rifle wielding agent at the door. 'We finally meet.' She stepped towards Krysta subtly, unfazed by Krysta's aim moving from Markovic to her. 'Darling, put down the gun, it won't do you much good here,' she instructed. Yet Krysta stayed true, unblinkingly aiming at her chest, at the beating core of her. 'I can feel his anxiety, his nervousness... Oh my god, is that...?' She turned on her heels to look back at Adam in amazement. She was wearing down his defences, feeling her way through his mind, his heart, his soul. Every door in his mind was being unlocked, his secrets being laid bare.

'Stop!' he yelled, clenching his fists. Her intrusion angered him, but he was struggling to hold her back.

'Does she know?' Evelina asked, intending to spite him. He could never stop her from entering, she had always had free reign to his emotions, but he desperately wanted that to change, to end, now. 'She doesn't know...' she placed a finger on her lips and turned back to Krysta. Krysta stood unflinching in body, but her eyes told the pair of them that she was curious as to what Evelina meant.

'Get down on your knees and...' Krysta trailed off.

'Or what?' Evelina responded. Within a fraction of a second, she had quickly moved back behind Adam, using him as a shield. Still looking at Krysta, she wrapped her arm around him, running her hand over his torso and then up to his face. She turned his head to face her and kissed him, biting his lip as their mouths parted. 'If she knew... then that thing - that emotion she doesn't quite understand, that curiosity for my love - that would die...' She grabbed at Adam's hair. 'Would you like to tell her, or can I? Please, let me...' Adam wanted nothing more than to plunge his fist into Evelina's chest, wrap his fingers around her beating heart and tear it asunder, but he could barely move. 'Krysta, darling, Adam here has feelings for you.' Her words cut Adam deep; she spoke truly but the words were not hers to say. Krysta looked at him a little confused; she was afraid, afraid for Claire, afraid for herself and afraid for him. He could feel it. 'And you feel something for him... Oh, this is perfect. How is Jake, Krysta? Is he, is he okay?' Adam wanted to make her stop, his head pounded, his heart ached, every inch of him was tense. Krysta was now distracted, wanting to know what this woman was talking about. That was when Evelina made her move.

In a flash, she had moved across the room, disarmed Krysta, forced her to take a knee and knelt beside her, looking over her shoulder at Adam, still unmoving. 'I hear Jake has such a kind soul,' she whispered to Krysta. 'Almost too good to be true.' Adam could feel it inside of him. It obeyed her command and shifted to the surface but only for a second, yet a second too long. 'See Krysta... Adam has a big, dark secret...' Evelina laughed at his anguish, elongating her words so as to truly torture. He desperately looked at Krysta, tears were welling up in her eyes as the feeling of betrayal sank in. 'I can't believe he finally broke, because of you... to save *you!*' she grabbed Krysta's chin with one hand, the other clutching the back of her neck as if to snap the life from her. 'It's a shame it will never last... However, if Adam here gives up the one thing I want more than his undivided love, the thing he took from me, from my family. Then maybe you'll stand a chance. How about it, Adam? Where is it?' Adam could never give her what she wanted, but he couldn't watch her take Krysta's life either. His heart beat fiercely within his chest and he felt real fear for the first time in a long time. Like a whirlpool inside of him, his emotions span around and around, swirling, spiralling up from their once quiescent birthplace, up until there was nowhere else to go but outwards. His hands ached as his fists tightened, his jaw groaned as he bared his gritted teeth.

'Evelina... EVE!' he screamed as a rush of anger exploded inside him. His eyes were a rush with blood, with hate. A red glow possessed the world and he found that he was able to move once again. He stepped towards Evelina and Krysta. He could see the terror in both of their eyes, but the need to protect Krysta and the insatiable desire to punish his counterpart was so strong, he couldn't resist. He held his hand out and a force from within sent Krysta flying in one direction, and Evelina another, pinning her against a wall.

'Adam! Stop!' Evelina cried, for all the power she had, seemed like nothing at present. He forced his emotion once again, pushing her harder against the building's foundation, crushing her against its earthen might. He wanted to end her, every fibre in his body told him that he could do it, that she deserved it. 'Adam!' she pleaded, unable to move she tried to fight against his hold but to no avail.

Krysta scrambled across the floor and headed over to Claire, dragging her colleague away from Markovic, attempting to find somewhere relatively safe to take cover. The Serbian stood in awe of Adam's power for mere moments before the fear of being next sank in. He took advantage of all the commotion and took his leave, escaping through a broken window out onto a fire escape; he didn't even stop to look back as he fled. Adam could feel the pain of Evelina's bones crushing under the pressure he exerted onto her, and the surge of her blood that attempted to heal her injuries almost as quickly as they were inflicted. She was fighting back, striving to survive as best she could.

'Krysta...' Evelina said in a whimper, a last-ditch effort to distract him from fulfilling his desire. He tried to resist the temptation to see if Krysta was okay, it was not his intention to harm her, yet as he thought of her, the image of her hurtling across the room brought up questions in his mind. *Is she okay?* His thoughts fighting against his desire to kill. *She's fine. Evelina must pay!* His power seared behind his eyes, he could feel the pain, her pain, his pain, all of it was a blur, a red-hot blinding blur.

'Claire. Claire please wake up.' He could hear Krysta's voice; she was so afraid. She needed him. He could hear the terror in her heartbeat, her frantic breathing. He could feel her sorrow, her sadness, her fear.

'AH!!!!!!' he screamed, his howl shaking the very foundations of the building in which they resided. 'Krysta... ' he said, turning away from Evelina, releasing his hold on her and letting go of his hatred. The look in her eyes told him everything he needed to know without requiring his ability to feel as she did. The world began to return to its own colour as the red in his eyes subsided and the purity of green returned. He went to step towards Claire and Krysta, yet his movement sent a sharp fearful shot through him that he knew to be an emotion that was not his own. He said sorry with his stare as a tear fell from his eye. Krysta looked to resist looking back at him, but she jumped as she heard the gunshot. The bullet hit him in his lower back, tearing through his flesh, lodging itself inside of him. He did not break his repenting look towards Krysta, his eyes filled with love. A second shot hit him slightly higher up and he could feel his own blood begin to run. His body started to heal the wounds, but a third and fourth shot hit him and he fell to his knees. He continued to look at Krysta as she stayed still, cowering with Claire, holding her as if to protect her from him. He broke his stare to look at Evelina, only she had gone and over at the doorway was Lucy and Solomon. They were aiming at him with their weapons, it was their bullets that were tearing through him. 'Krys...I..' he said, before another bullet went cleanly through his neck. He coughed as blood filled his throat. 'Stop...' he muttered, but another bullet plummeted into his back and scraped across his heart.

'I said STOP!' he shouted, as he climbed to his feet and a wave of anger possessed him; he was trying to apologise for losing control, for scaring her, but they were preventing him from doing so. His wounds were healing but the pain behind his eyes was beginning to return as they continued to try and put him down. 'PLEASE STOP!!!' he yelled at the agents as they persisted. He wanted them to stop, he needed them to stop. He rushed over to them quicker than they could react and grabbed their guns, crushing them. Lucy stepped backwards, fearing his dominance; Solomon reached for his sidearm. 'St - ' Adam tried to repeat, but all he could muster was a gasp of breath as a sharp blade pierced his back, slicing through his core, shredding through his heart.

'Lucy, Solomon! Get Claire and Krysta out of here!' It was Nahki. Adam was confused. He dropped to his knees once more, clutching at his chest, unable to breathe as he tried to speak. Blood dripped from his lip as he felt his lungs slowly filling with the thick fluid of his life's blood. He watched as Krysta and Lucy picked Claire up and carried her out of the room, Krysta not even able to look at him as she passed in front of him. 'Solomon, go! I've got this, the C.I.A. will handle him from here,' Nahki said, and more confusingly, Solomon followed the order. Adam was struggling to stay conscious as Nahki twisted the blade. He looked out at the dark, a single star visible in the black.

He closed his eyes and then opened them again. He was standing on a bridge. It was dark and the rain fell from the sky, hitting his skin with an icy chill. There were no sounds of cars, no footsteps on the ground. The bridge lead into the city and as he stood upon it, he could see her at the other end. She stood in the cold, wet, dark of night. Unmoving. He walked across the bridge towards her and as he reached her, he could tell that she had been crying. Asking her what was wrong, she bit her lip, afraid to say what she was feeling. He brushed the golden hairs from her face and placed his palm on her cheek, looking to take away her troubles. In doing so she stepped towards him, holding herself against him. He held her tightly as the rain poured down, washing over them, but as the rain turned colder and, in its place, snow began to fall. She pulled away from him and thrust that blade into his chest. He looked down at the ornate hilt, made from bone and wood, before looking at her face as she turned away from him and descended into the darkness beyond the bridge. He opened his eyes again to see the empty room before him. They had all left him. He was alone.

'I told you... I will always be there to bring about your suffering,' Nahki said coldly, before the world slipped away.

27

Tisa and Bomani

'You'd think after 72 years, we might have bothered to learn the language,' she said, as she watched the light dwindle in the eyes of her victim. Her venom was coursing through his veins; he had lost the use of his legs and his heart sounded as if it was about to bound out of his chest. Blood ran from his mouth and nose as he struggled to mumble a few words as he died. She let go of his body, allowing it to fall to the floor and join his fallen comrades. A couple dozen of them had attacked the pair, their guns and blades proving useless. 'For four centuries of heritage, they take their sweet time to learn a lesson,' she said, looking about at the destruction. Black leather chairs were scattered and upturned, white coloured seats showed up sprays of red. Tables had been broken and during the civilian panic, once the fighting started, plates and bowls of food had been spilled and left to spoil. *So much for discipline.* She glanced at the stump of a little finger on a severed hand that lay on a nearby counter. The yakuza were supposed to do as they were told, however, her twin's recent activities had caused a rift in their relations. The siblings shared a golden-brown complexion, among many other things. Tisa, the eldest of the two by mere minutes, was a shapeshifter, gifted with the ability of therianthropy. Able to change at will into the form of any animal of her choosing, she could also bring forth certain animalistic traits whilst as a human. She wore leather sandals that laced up to the knee, a sandy coloured loincloth and a bronze shaded bodice. She had full cherry coloured lips and a comely bosom; her hair was styled in long dark corn rows that hung behind her or draped over her shoulder. Her attackers had been warned of her power, and yet still they had come to seek retribution for her brother's slight. However, it was not until the last tattoo riddled assailant had surrendered that she became aware of her newfound freedom to exact punishment as she saw fit. Something had happened in the world, a change, a shift, enabling them to act of their own accord.

'I think we can call this a lesson learned...' he said. He smiled as he pulled his hand from a crater he had made in a man's chest. The gang member had attacked him with a katana, cutting the flesh on his palms as he defended himself. Yet Bomani, brother of Tisa, possessed the ability to absorb natural elements and transform his skin to match. He had turned his arm into a steel weapon and plunged it into the man, slicing through flesh and bone with ease. He had bludgeoned two of them with concrete fists and had fun deflecting bullets with a cast iron torso. Bomani had short dark hair and a toned physique. His name meant warrior, and so he had trained himself to be as lethal as possible. He dressed more casually than his twin, aiming to blend in, wearing flip flops, blue denim jeans and a pale red oval necked t-shirt that buttoned at the top. The pair of them had lived on the islands of Japan for many years, remaining behind the scenes and out of the limelight, able to orchestrate crime, manipulate government decisions and monitor the countries growth technologically, all the while unnoticed. It had been some time since they had last seen any of the Avunaye, however, with what had recently come to light, they both believed it was time to seek out their kin.

Wiping the blood on his hands onto the shirt of one of the slain, Bomani walked over to one of the counters and leaped over it. 'Killing always makes me hungry,' he said, picking up some grilled yakitori and devouring them swiftly. Tisa walked over to the counter and leapt upon it, crouching on its surface.

'Killing always makes me...' she said, slowly lying down on the countertop. She knocked off several dishes and various condiments as she lay down before running her hands through her hair. Then, whilst staring into Bomani's eyes whilst he ate, she ran her hands down her neck and onto her chest. Her breathing hastened and she tingled with excitement as she proceeded to run her fingers down along her body until she reached her waist. She bit her lip as she brought her feet up towards her and opened her thighs. Lifting her loincloth, she caressed her clitoris, rubbing it briskly, generating a friction that caused her body to ignite. She could feel her bodies appreciation as she continued to stroke it between two fingertips, the energy, the warmth, the heat. She delved deeper, slipping her fingers inside herself, ferrying them in a reciprocating, circular motion as they grew warmer and wetter. She smiled at him as she pleasured herself, breathing heavily, her heart racing. Unable to resist his sisters display of pleasure he grabbed her arm and stopped her. She held up her fingers to his lips and he could smell her, her passion. He could taste her as he sucked on her fingertips before climbing onto the counter himself. He hurriedly unbuttoned his jeans and slid them down his thighs before taking his hardened penis and thrusting it inside her ripened vagina. They were once again joined, as they were before birth, as one. He thrust hard and fast, one hand grasping one of her thighs, the other holding onto the counter, almost crumbling it as the adrenaline flurried through him. She clawed at his back, down his neck and grasped his buttocks as she urged him to continue, harder and faster.

'Yes brother!' she cried out in ecstasy as she felt herself erupt inside. 'Now!'; she moaned, begging for his seed, and as

388

the dutiful sibling he was, he exploded within her, filling her, warming her to her very core.

'If you're quite finished...' a voice sounded, from one of the seats. Tisa and Bomani both looked over to see Nahki sitting there awaiting their attention.

'I can go again, if you're interested...' she said, pursing her lips before smiling at Nahki. Bomani withdrew himself and clambered off the counter, his manhood still on display. He buttoned up his jeans and turned a nearby chair upright before placing it near to Nahki and taking a seat. 'Spoil sport...' she said disappointedly before sitting up and turning to face them both, dangling her legs, still spread apart, off the counter. 'To what do we owe this pleasure, brother?'

'I see you've been busy...' Nahki said, looking about the room at the devastation. 'You realise you weren't meant to kill the Yakuza, you were supposed to use them.' Tisa had always found his emotionless demeanour so frustrating as she was so passionate herself. She had always believed that her emotions were what defined her, her anger, her love. Therefore, Nahki's inability to feel would always spark something within her. She saw him as a challenge, for if she could make him feel something, anything, maybe she was capable of the impossible.

'We had a... disagreement,' Tisa replied, glancing at her brother.

'Bomani?' Nahki questioned, no doubt taking note of Tisa's subtle look at her twin.

'I took one of the Kumicho's daughters. They reacted, badly.' Bomani was curious as to why Nahki was here. Normally the incident would bring about punishment, but Nahki's presence suggested that something bigger was happening. 'What are you doing here Nahki?'

'Have you watched the news recently?' he said, drawing a blank look from Bomani. He then looked to Tisa. She knew of what he spoke.

'Terror plot in New York? Or should I say, failed terror

attack...' Her smile disappeared. She had seen news of the attack and presumed the Avunaye was behind it, but Nahki's presence suggested that there was more to it.

'New York City... Manhattan,' he said, staring her in the eyes. 'Home to movie stars, celebrities... the big apple!' He had her attention, but she wished he'd get to the point. 'Also, home to Adam.' Bingo. Adam's name caught both of the twin's attention.

'Adam is living in New York?' Bomani questioned. 'Not exactly the quietest spot on the planet.'

'Serena, Brandt, Seymour, Evelina and I have also been spending some time there of late.' He continued to look straight at Tisa. Six of the Avunaye in one place, Tisa knew what that meant.

'You're attempting the ritual again?' she said, almost disappointedly. Since the initiation of Nahki, the ritual had not worked again. It had become a tiresome subject for the twins, who personally, were quite content with only having nine other siblings to be concerned with.

'Carmen is in New York also...' Nahki said, much to both of their surprise. Tisa was slightly taken back by the news.

'Carmen? How?' she said hastily. 'Evelina ended her, there is no way...' yet before she could finish, Nahki raised a finger.

'She appears to have the ability to possess another human, to live on through them,' he said, his completely expressionless face continuing to annoy Tisa somewhat.

'Oh... just like that... Isn't that nice,' she said. However, she was now wanting to know what he was doing here. Surely, he wasn't just here to update them.

'Evelina orchestrated Adam's fall from grace. I imagine you have noticed your newfound freewill?' Nahki asked looking around at the bodies once again. Tisa's expression seemed to give him the answer he was looking for. 'So, he has requested that everyone else heads towards the city, it is going to be the epicentre of what's to come. We will initiate new Avunaye, wipe out those who would stand against us and bring the world peace.'

'Ah, peace, through the spilling of blood. The ecstasy of grief? That speech?' She quipped before re-registering exactly what Nahki had said. 'He? Matthias?' she questioned.

'No. Not Matthias.' Nahki almost stuttered as he said the words, which gave Tisa a clear indication of who he meant. The thought sent a chill down her spine and, as she looked to her twin, she knew he felt the same shiver. 'We have Adam for now. We *will* get the location of the garden and the tree.'

'His memories?' Tisa questioned. There was a worry to her tone. Adam needed to be controlled, but the location of the tree would require longer-term memories that would only come with time, and blood being spilt. Time that would make him stronger and less controllable.

'We'll keep him under control. He has a weakness now.' He grinned as he spoke.

'A weakness? Adam has always been weak by his value for human life... What forced him to kill?' Tisa asked. Nahki replied with a single word.

'Love.'

Acknowledgements

I am very fortunate to have had the opportunity to share the story of Adam. Writing this first installment has been a delightful challenge. However, it could not have been possible without a life thus far filled with support and inspiration.

Therefore, thanks and appreciation go to my mother and father, Jayne and Stuart, my wife Denise, our children, Lucas and Reece and to all of my extensive family.

I also give special thanks to my siblings, Emma and Mark, for their encouragement and assistance, and Laura, for her guidance and amazing creativity. To Tara, for her hard work and contribution, and Justin, for bringing the story to life.

Lightning Source UK Ltd.
Milton Keynes UK
UKHW020632240321
380904UK00011B/716

9 781916 321663